# The Reconstruction of Wilson Ryder

3/15/13

With Best Wishes,

## Other Books by Michael French

### Adult Fiction

*Club Caribe* (1977)
*Abingdon's* (1979)
*Rhythms* (1980)
*Texas Bred* (1986)
*Family Money* (1990)

### Young Adult Fiction

*The Throwing Season* (1980)
*Pursuit* (1982)
*Lifeguards Only Beyond This Point* (1984)
*Soldier Boy* (1985)
*Us Against Them* (1987)
*Circle of Revenge* (1988)
*Split Image* (1990)

### Young Adult Adaptations

*Basher Fifty-Two,* with Scott O'Grady (1997)
*Born to Fly,* with Shane Osborn (2000)
*Flags of Our Fathers,* with James Brady (2001)
*Lang Lang: Playing With Flying Keys* (2008)
*Mountains Beyond Mountains,* with Tracy Kidder (2013)

### Children's Book Adaptations

*Flyers* (1983)
*Indiana Jones and the Temple of Doom* (1984)

### Other Books

*Speaking for Ourselves, Too* (1990)
*The Art of Frank Howell* (1997)
*Why Men Fall Out of Love* (2007)

# The Reconstruction of Wilson Ryder

*A novel by*

Michael French

Santa Fe, New Mexico

Published by Terra Nova Books, Santa Fe, New Mexico.
www.TerraNovaBooks.com

ISBN 978-1-480037-61-8

*For RDF*

Who showed me things even
when I wasn't looking

*My daddy's face is a study. Winter moves into it and presides there. His eyes become a cliff of snow threatening to avalanche, his eyebrows bend like black limbs of leafless trees. His skin takes on the pale cheerless yellow of winter sun; for a jaw he has the edges of a snowbound field dotted with stubble; his high forehead is the frozen sweep of the Erie.*

—Toni Morrison, *The Bluest Eye*

*If you see a tree as blue, then make it blue.*

—Paul Gauguin

August 13, 1982

Dear Henry:

*I received your letter last week, and this will be my only reply. To answer your question, I am never coming back to Santo Tomás. I believe one can and should live many lives, in separate universes, as it were, unconnected by guilt, remorse, hope, or any other sentiment. Emotions are a waste of time.*

*You may ask all you want, but I will not comment on the events just before my departure. I left and divorced you because I was no longer in love with you.*

*I am leaving both children in your custody. You've asked me never to contact them. I have no intention of contacting them. I have no interest in them whatsoever other than I hope they are healthy. I know you feel I've abandoned them, however I will not argue the point because it's not important to me. You also wrote that they need your nurturing. What you mean, really, is you want to protect them from me.*

*I'm now living in Texas with Willard and growing more tired of him by the day. The qualities that first draw us to a lover can become those that irritate us the most. You didn't ask, but I'm still painting. I will always be painting. I have never doubted what brings me meaning and what I was meant to do.*

Regards,
Susan

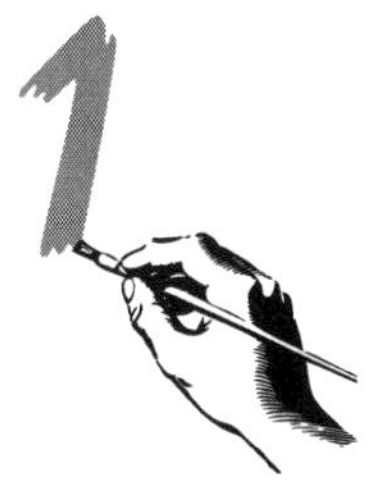

Long before I knew where my life was taking me, I was a small boy living in Santo Tomás, New Mexico. As I approached my fifth birthday, I remember that I wanted to throw myself a party—my first ever. The thought filled me with as much anxiety as excitement. I imagined I was an acrobat on a tightrope crossing a deep and endless canyon.

I wasn't in school yet, so I had no friends. Besides my father and ten-year-old sister, my only pal was Mrs. Gutierrez. She had once been Hannah's baby sitter, too, and she was as ancient as stone. Sometimes we watched television—cooking shows were her favorite—or played hearts or canasta. Much of the day, I was a prisoner to the Bible. Mrs. Gutierrez insisted I spend hours listening to her read Scripture, and that I commit to memory as many verses as possible. "It's for your own good. It's for your salvation, *hito,*" she said. I had no idea what she meant by my salvation, but when I was four and five, I memorized hundreds of passages from the Old and New Testaments. Her eyes would light up when I stood obediently, arms at my side, reciting them back to her like the Pledge of Allegiance. Even at that age, I had a magnet for a memory.

I was afraid to tell my father what Mrs. Gutierrez put me through, because in addition to not believing in God, he had asked her to read me only books he'd selected from his personal library.

But Mrs. Gutierrez told me the Bible came first, and that if we ever finished it, we would read something else.

My father believed that because I was so different from other children, I was to be granted what he called "B&P." I could watch television, play with my action figures, listen to Stevie Wonder and the Bee Gees, and eat M&Ms—no conditions imposed, except one: I had to let him nurture my mind. Benefits and Privileges had their place, but real joy, he said, as his index finger tapped his forehead twice, came from up here. Every evening, he or Hannah would open a book and read to me. Like a flashlight in a dark cave, my father promised, my imagination would lead me to discoveries that remained hidden from those whose curiosity was never kindled.

"What did Mrs. Gutierrez read to you today?" he asked one night at dinner.

"A little of this and a little of that."

"Can you be more specific?"

My shoulders shrugged.

"She makes you learn the Bible, doesn't she?" Hannah piped up.

My eyes slid away. "Maybe."

"I guess it's OK," my father said, reaching over and rubbing my head. He had probably known what was happening all along. "The Bible is great literature. There're some terrific stories in it. Lots to learn."

I still worried that at any moment, he might fire Mrs. Gutierrez for disobedience, and with Hannah in school and my father at work, I'd be all alone in the house. What if burglars broke in? Or I escaped down the street and got lost, or suddenly went blind and couldn't find my way back? Even if Mrs. Gutierrez didn't lose her job, I still wanted someone else around. The idea of throwing myself a birthday party struck like a clap of thunder, and because it was my idea, I was sure it was destined to happen. My imagination was suddenly full of new faces running around our backyard. I was going to make instant and lasting friends.

For several days, my father and Hannah discussed the wisdom of my having a party. When they finally gave the green light, I made invitations for three boys and two girls. Because I wasn't allowed out of the house, I knew my guests only by watching from a window as they played on the sidewalk or passed in their family cars. But Hannah, in her normally efficient way, produced their names and addresses for me.

On the front of each invitation, because I had watched a travelogue on Morocco with Mrs. Gutierrez, I was inspired to sketch a palm tree and a camel. Inside, as Hannah dictated the words, I wrote in block letters, as carefully as I could: Come celebrate my fifth birthday from two to four p.m., October 10, at 3657 Calle Norte. Barbecued hot dogs, hamburgers, soft drinks, and cake will be served. Please RSVP at 887-3952. Sincerely yours, Will Ryder.

It took forever to finish each invitation, but I wanted my handwriting to be as elegant as my sister's, even if it fell far short.

"What's RSVP?" I asked Hannah.

"It's French. *Répondez s'il vous plaît.* It means your guests have to tell you ahead of time if they're coming."

"Rayponday . . . sillvuplay," I repeated, making it rhyme.

Hannah thought it important that I sound as mature as possible. She said this was called "making an impression." Phrases like "RSVP" couldn't hurt. She had toyed with having me sign the invitation Mr. Will Ryder but decided that would sound too serious. As it was, by throwing a party, I was adding to the mystery I'd already established as the neighborhood shut-in. Hannah promised that no one could resist the chance to finally meet me. In private, however, I worried that somebody might not understand French. Or what if everybody answered "no"?

The first response came within a few days, from the mother of Christy Steadman, a skinny girl with freckles and bangs. Within a week, the other calls trickled in. Maybe Hannah had been right about the element of mystery. They were all coming.

I promptly began inventing characteristics, even personalities, for my friends-to-be, without regard to my lack of facts. Charlie Buchanan was a bed-wetter and afraid of the dark. Lizzie Franklin, a tomboy with scabs on her knees, collected centipedes and snails. Billy Garcia never missed a day of Sunday school, and on weekends, he and his father pasted old stamps into a thick album. Kevin Lopez played with miniature tin soldiers. He also suffered from weed allergies. Christy Steadman baked extraordinary chocolate chip cookies and was a whiz with a jump rope. None of these were kids I had even once said hello to.

"Aren't you excited, Will?" Hannah asked as we baked my cake the night before the party.

"This is the most exciting thing in the world!" I gushed. I began running circles in the kitchen, my arms out like airplane wings as I mimicked the whine of takeoff. My father, trying to give me a calmer perspective, said I'd already celebrated four birthdays. But this was different: This was my first party.

On the afternoon of the party, I made sure everything was in place. Next to the Weber grill in our backyard, the picnic table was set for six because I insisted my father and sister eat by themselves. Hannah had already hoisted a piñata filled with hard candy and taffy up into the elm. I thought it would be a fine idea if we all played T-ball, too, since I dreamed of being a major leaguer.

When my father went to answer the bell, I dashed around him and got to the bronze knob first, twisting it with both hands. In the past two years, the only one I'd opened it for was Mrs. Gutierrez.

"Hi, I'm Will," I said with a burst before the door was fully open. I had expected Christy Steadman to be first, because she'd RSVP'd first. But to my amazement, all five guests were clustered on the porch. I couldn't understand the coincidence, but my father must have, because he put a hand on my shoulder as though reassuring me that everything would be fine. No parents were in sight. Whoever had brought the group to our house had vanished like someone leaving a box of kittens. Only years later did Hannah tell me that just the opposite was true. The parents had all talked about my party ahead of time and agreed that arriving in a group was a necessary precaution; should something awkward happen, there was strength in numbers, and they could all leave together as well.

Because I thought it was the proper thing for a host, I reached out to shake hands with each of my new friends. Christy, the skinny girl with the galaxy of freckles, smiled broadly but avoided my gaze. Rather than shake my hand, she thrust a small wrapped box with a frilly ribbon into my arms. I sniffed it like a dog, wondering if it held the cookies I had imagined. The other kids quickly streamed past and stacked their presents on the entry table. Then they thundered outside like buffalo on the prairie.

"Quite the crowd," my father said as we followed them into the yard, shaking my hand because no one else had. Hannah offered everyone something to drink and explained the piñata. What was inside? Who'd get the first whack with the stick? How much candy could they keep? Then my guests scattered to explore every crevice of the yard. I thought of ants marching into new territory.

I watched and hung sheepishly by Hannah as she lit the charcoal in the barbecue.

"What do you want to do first, Will?"

"T-ball," I said, but suddenly wishing I had pin-the-tail-on-the-donkey to fall back on. Despite my big-league dreams, I'd never swung at a baseball.

Hannah organized us into two teams of three, and as the birthday boy, I got to hit first. Cocking the bat over my shoulder, I watched her put the ball belt high on its plastic holder, looming as large as the moon. But when I took my first swing, I missed. No one said a thing. As I swung again, one of my feet tripped over the other, and I fell on my butt.

"You can do it!" my father called out.

He was right! On my third try, I slammed the ball off the tee out to near his roses in the far corner of the yard. The only outfielder—the bed-wetter Charlie Buchanan—was caught off guard and ran to his left when he should have gone right. As his teammates screamed at him, I galloped around the bases, and at home plate, I stomped both feet on the plastic disc, like I'd seen players do on TV. My teammates cheered—both of them.

The party seemed like a success. Amid bursts of giggles from my guests, candies poured out of a gaping hole in the piñata, I opened my presents, and we all jammed around the picnic table to eat. Kevin Lopez insisted that at birthday parties, his parents let him have two hamburgers and two pieces of cake. But beneath the excitement that buoyed me along, I began to notice no one was really talking to me. I was a stranger, unknown to everyone except through neighborhood stories. I had imagined a richly detailed life for each of my guests, but they knew little about me. Some stared irresistibly at my face, because they had seen nothing like it. Others, like Christy, self-consciously focused on my belt buckle.

If I became a ghost, I suddenly thought—if they couldn't see my face—maybe they would like me better. As the party was ending, I rummaged through my closet and returned to the living room with a sheet over my head. The kids were all near the piano, waiting to be picked up. My father and Hannah were cleaning up in the kitchen. Sightless, I began running in a rough circle, guided only by the gyroscope of my imagination.

"Boo! Boo! Boo!" I yelled in between my riffs of out-of-control laughter. Everyone laughed with me as I ricocheted off walls and chairs. I liked being the center of attention. Suddenly, at full speed, I ran into Lizzie Franklin, knocking her to the floor. Then I tripped and landed on top of her. Her screams filled the room. I could hear voices calling for help.

For a moment, I was motionless. Then, without knowing why, I started squirming around on top of her, feeling the warmth of her body. Lizzie pounded her hands on my chest. I heard people moving toward the door. When I tried pulling off the sheet, I only got deeper in its folds.

"Lizzie? Oh, dear God!" It was her mother—seeing my contortions, her daughter's legs apart underneath me.

"Dear, dear god!" she exclaimed again, as if she'd stumbled on the crime of the century. I felt her pulling Lizzie out from under me, like someone pinned under a car wreck.

"Will Ryder!" She was breathless. "What is wrong with you!"

I struggled up, finally throwing off the sheet. My face was hot. I might be arrested, I thought, and taken to jail. Hannah wrapped me in her arms and held me as I saw the exodus to the door become a stampede behind Lizzie's mother.

Then it was over, a descent into silence that meant my party was finished. I felt the injustice. I wanted to go to court, like they did on television, so the judge could hear my side. I was the host. It was my party. I was only a pretend ghost. There was nothing to be afraid of.

I ran to my room, to cry alone. A minute later, my father knocked. "Go away!" I yelled. He came in anyway and put his arm around me as I sat on my bed.

"Some party," he said after a while as my sobs slowed down. His chiseled face and gold-blue eyes—the same color as Hannah's—floated in front of me with infinite patience. "Why don't we just say it never happened, Will?"

"What do you mean?"

"You imagined it. Or maybe it was a dream. Tomorrow you'll wake up and everything will be fine. I'm going to fix you pancakes with whipped cream and strawberries for breakfast. How does that sound?" He dabbed at my eyes with a corner of the sheet.

My father's voice was soothing, but I knew what he said wasn't true. I couldn't have imagined that party, or dreamed it. It was too horrible. I would never forget it.

I could guess what the neighbors were saying. I was an out-of-control holy terror, to be avoided like a street gang. My father and sister told me paying attention to gossip was a waste of time. But I saw from their expressions that the chatter went on for weeks, and it bothered them, too. It was a big reason I didn't want to go to kindergarten that year. My father decided I could stay home and continue learning from him and Hannah and Mrs. Gutierrez. If we delayed school for a year, he said, I'd have time to mature and gain confidence in myself, without being picked on by the village idiots.

When I was about to turn six, I began to believe I had the power to read moods. My mother's I thought was full of lightning and thunderstorms. My father's was a windswept desert, marked only by his solitary footprints. My sister's was a periscope rising from a shimmering ocean, studying everything around her, missing nothing. Her dream was to be a ballerina. In the late summer of 1984, a week before school started in Santo Tomás, I made a charcoal drawing of Hannah in pink ballet slippers and a green tutu, jumping between clouds. I rolled it up like a scroll, looped a bow of red yarn around it, and gave her my present one Saturday afternoon.

"Oh, Will, this is beautiful!" Hannah declared as she opened my creation and held it at arm's length. She studied it carefully. "This reminds me of Edgar Degas. I'm going to frame it and hang it over my bed."

"Who's Edgar Daygaw?"

"A very famous artist. He painted lots of ballerinas. One of the great ones."

"Where does he live?"

"Once upon a time, he lived in France. He's dead now. But like all great artists, his work lives on."

I blinked self-consciously, embarrassed to be not quite six and compared with a famous adult, alive or dead. But I believed Hannah's praise. My precocious sister was my trusted link to the outside world. She seemed to have endless knowledge. Twenty years ago, how else would I have heard of Edgar Degas?

"Why are you giving me a present?" Hannah suddenly asked. "It's not my birthday."

"Because you're pretty," I said.

"That's very sweet. You're a wonderful brother. And such a talented artist. Only you forgot to sign your name." She pointed to the bottom right-hand corner of my drawing. I ran to get a stick of charcoal. "Serious artists do that," her voice trailed after me. "And what do you call it? Every picture should have a title, don't you think?"

I came back and printed Will Ryder where Hannah had indicated, and because I couldn't spell ballerina, at the top, I wrote "dancir."

"Did you work on this for a long time?"

"Yes," I said, if all day was a long time to spend on a drawing. I had no idea. Maybe Degas worked for a month. Almost nothing occupied my attention for more than fifteen minutes. When I drew with my crayons or charcoals, though, time stopped. I wanted everything to be perfect. I watched as Hannah carried my drawing to her room. She came back and kissed me on the cheek.

A minute later, her backpack strapped on, she was out the door for her weekend piano lesson. I hurried to the window seat next to the front door, where I had a full view of the street. Jumping on her bicycle, Hannah bounced up and down like a piston, her blonde ponytail bobbing with each pedal stroke, her gold and blue eyes fixed determinedly ahead. When she was four and first began to play, my father was her teacher, but by age seven, he decided she needed a professional.

Mrs. Neiman, a classical pianist in her native Germany, had been teaching in Santo Tomás for a while. I felt I knew her from Hannah's description. Her honey-colored hair once had made her a beauty; now, thinned by age, it dripped over her forehead like candle wax. Her simple print dresses hid her shapeless body, letting her high heels—bold, bright colors—speak for her youth. In her living room, photos showed her dancing in a ballroom with her husband, a German infantry officer. When teaching piano, Mrs.

Neiman had a way of peering at you over her owlish glasses when you made a mistake, Hannah said. Her jowls would quiver, like an attack dog before it pounced. I wanted to do a drawing of her, too.

How a German war widow ended up in southern New Mexico intrigued me even then, though it was no more improbable than my parents' journey. The sixteenth-century conquistadores had come first, from Mexico after they defeated the Aztecs and Maya. The Anglos came three hundred fifty years later, mostly traders and farmers. A lot more, like Mrs. Neiman, drifted in after World War II. Henry and Susan Ryder, my parents, showed up in 1970.

Married and still in love, they'd left the Upper West Side in Manhattan after my mother read a travel article about the climate and sparse beauty of southern New Mexico. According to my father, most everything in the photos was pinkish or earth-brown—the desert itself, the foothills and mountains, the stucco on the houses—drab and forlorn colors that fit my mother's temperament. This was where they would be moving, she announced to the world.

My father demurred—weren't there other places to investigate?—but my mother insisted. Their friends couldn't understand why they'd leave New York for anyplace else, except maybe Paris. My mother didn't even bother to visit their future home but merely imagined them both in the magazine spread. In those days, my father claimed, abandoning common sense was proof that you weren't tied down or owned by anything.

For him, balancing my mother's risk-taking with his own Vermont skepticism, the jump into the void came with a safety net. He applied to teach English at the Santo Tomás campus of New Mexico State University, and, with a Ph.D. behind him, got the job. They rented a twenty-four-foot U-Haul and packed it with their every worldly possession, including a half-dozen of my mother's best paintings.

Though she'd taken a few art courses at Columbia, she was largely self-taught. Showing in New York galleries—fringe ones she called "off-off-off Broadway"—had brought my mother little success. After five years of rejection, there was no point sticking around, she told my father. Picking up and moving great distances was habit for her. The only child of a career Army sergeant and his unhappy wife, she'd made stops at ten different military posts before she turned eighteen. Her four years at Columbia were the most time she'd spent in one place.

My father didn't step out of Vermont until he was eighteen. He was already at his full height of six-foot-four. Thick in the shoulders and legs, he had a lean, sculpted face and overlapping thatches of chestnut hair. He was earning his doctorate in comparative literature when he met my mother at Columbia in something of an accident. My father had been set up on a blind date, and thought by mistake that my mother, who was waiting for a friend at the student union, was her. Playing along, she got a free dinner she never expected, and didn't tell my father the truth until the next day. They dated for a year, finished up with their degrees, and decided to get married. It was a self-described hippie ceremony, officiated by a justice of the peace in Central Park and attended by a couple of dozen friends, half of whom my father said were stoned start to end.

For the wedding, my father wore the Wrangler jeans, blue work shirt, and scuffed leather boots that had been his daily attire in Vermont. The wardrobe seemed highly transportable to southern New Mexico with its open frontiers and rugged mountains. He owned one suit for special occasions, which did not include church, since he respectfully stayed away from all houses of worship. In addition to ideas and books, atheism was another magnet he and my mother were drawn to. They didn't go out of their way to broadcast their belief because people would inevitably say they felt sorry for them: When Judgment Day came, they'd be screwed. But their feelings were clear and had an impact on Hannah and me. God did not exist, insisted my father, except in our minds, in our need for a deity.

It took seven days to cross the country in the U-Haul. While my father did the driving, my mother, smoking plenty of weed, talked about how many artists never found their true voices until they threw off the yoke of the safe and familiar. If you weren't willing to take risks, she said in a magazine interview I didn't find until I was in my 20s, you should take your place in the zombie queue and never leave. The zombie queue—that was the colorful way my mother sometimes talked. She seemed unfazed that they would be arriving in the dusty, mountain-ringed valley of Santo Tomás, a city of 42,000, knowing absolutely no one. For her, it was just like arriving at another Army post.

They bought a modest, three-bedroom tract home not far from the city's downtown. Friendships were formed with other university couples and the small Santo Tomás arts community. After trying our garage for a few months, my mother rented space in a warehouse and began painting on linen canvases. When she showed the results, public reception was lukewarm, but she wasn't daunted. Becoming a successful artist was her only vision for life. Hannah was born two years after the move, and I came five and a half years later. Neither of us was "planned," my father admitted when I was old enough to understand. "You both just happened, but that didn't mean you weren't loved deeply." He meant by him. We were both beautiful babies with flawless skin—I have the photos to prove it. Hannah had my father's athletic frame, though her legs were definitely more svelte, and I came with my mother's deep-set eyes, large and dark as marbles, and a smile brighter than the moon.

When Hannah returned from Mrs. Neiman that Saturday afternoon, she immediately went to work on next week's lesson. My father had bought a faded upright piano at a garage sale years earlier, and while it looked like it had been left in the rain, the insides were airtight. When he disappeared for his weekend tennis game, Hannah began playing a Mozart sonata. There were difficult passages for an eleven-year-old, but as I watched, her eyes glued themselves to the sheets of music as though someone might steal them at any moment. After two hours of playing, she was on the phone with a friend. Keeping everyone on schedule, my father returned from tennis and drove Hannah to her ballet class on the other side of town. He promised to be back in half an hour. I was almost never left alone, but if I was, I locked the door and sat at my usual seat by the window, watching neighborhood life unfurl in its lazy summer cadence.

"Everyone hungry?" my father asked that evening as he prepared a Caesar salad and spaghetti Bolognese, making the sauce from scratch. He was more than a decent cook. Each time we had spaghetti, the sauce was slightly different. Tonight he threw in diced mushrooms.

"You like mushrooms, Will," he said as if it were a fact.

"Are there onions?" I asked.

"Just a little. That's how most cooks make it, for flavor."

"Can I add sugar?"

"I don't think that would help, champ."

"Can I have my spaghetti without sauce?"

He thought about it. "OK this time, but maybe you'll have some on the side. Mushrooms are meaty and filling. Never hurts to expand your horizons."

As we ate, Timbuktu, our animal shelter cat, rubbed against my leg. She was the size of a small dog, and like most dogs, she'd rather have spaghetti with meat sauce than canned pet food. I would sneak her some under the table while my father talked about current events. Time was a void best filled with knowledge, he believed. Like a TV anchor, he had a soothing way of delivering the news, even the tragedies, which were what stuck most in my memory. The prime minister of India, a woman named Indira Gandhi who looked a little bit like Mrs. Gutierrez, was shot to death by her own bodyguards while visiting a place called Ethiopia. Michael Jackson's hair caught on fire while he was filming a Pepsi commercial. A scientist at the National Cancer Institute announced he had discovered the virus that caused AIDS. Then Hannah and my father started talking about where the AIDS virus came from. I asked them if someone who caught it felt as much pain as being shot by a bullet or having your hair catch on fire. Hannah told me that none of those things were going to happen to me, but I wasn't sure. I was afraid that any kind of pain was felt by every cell in your body.

"School starts in a week," my father announced, rolling a fork of spaghetti into a spoon like they did in Europe, he said. He was looking at Hannah. "Aren't you excited, honey? Sixth grade. Big stuff!"

"Mrs. Womack's been around forever. She's supposed to give tons of homework. But she likes taking field trips, which'll be cool. White Sands. Carlsbad Caverns."

Hannah had already checked everything out. I was going to ask what was special about White Sands and Carlsbad Caverns, but the conversation had already jumped to school supplies. A couple of three-ring notebook binders, lined paper, a three-hole punch, compass, protractor. . . . I was sure Hannah was already thinking about junior high and beyond, when life would be more challenging than buying school supplies. My father began reminiscing about his sixth-grade class in Brattleboro—Mrs. Godfrey, an older black woman with lightning-white hair, holding students hostage seven hours a day. Despite her strictness, girls flirted openly, and some of the boys, rebels in the making like my father, sneaked Chesterfields in the bathroom.

"And you, Will?" my father asked, his eyes shifting to me. "First grade beckons. Are you ready?"

"I'm not sure," I said.

"Well, if you're not certain, I understand."

"It's not against the law to stay home, is it?" Hannah had already told me it was OK so long as my father "home-schooled" me, something his flexible teaching schedule left ample time for. I was already learning some American history, like the fact that my father considered the twenty-eighth president, Woodrow Wilson, a great enough man to borrow his surname for me.

"Is that what you really want to do, stay home?" he asked. "You aren't curious about the rest of the world? You don't want to be taught by a teacher in a real classroom?"

"You said I could learn everything from books."

"Practically everything," Dad said. "But some things have to be experienced."

"Why do I have to know everything? Nobody knows everything." I was sounding much wiser than my age, because when in doubt about what to say, I imitated Hannah.

The truth was, as worried as I was about the unknown, I still wanted to explore it. Because I'd skipped kindergarten after my birthday party disaster, I was more restless than ever. Secluding myself in the house had made me question much of what I learned, even from my father and Hannah. Without confirmation from my eyes and ears, what ended up in my head was a stew of impressions and opinions. Like the current events we talked about at dinner—which ones should be important to me and which didn't matter? Viewing the world at a safe distance was like sailing on a ship that never dropped anchor.

On occasion, though, I did get to shore. I had been out of the house a couple of dozen times, hunkered down in the used Chevy wagon my father bought when he moved to Santo Tomás. No matter how many miles on the odometer, he knew enough about engines to keep it going forever. He would never buy a new car. He didn't believe in spending on luxury or status.

In addition to seeing my doctors in Albuquerque, he would take me to someplace he knew outside town where I could fly a kite or ride a bike without being seen. Sometimes I wore a Riddler or a Joker mask, declaring I was a criminal on the run so Batman or the FBI won't find me. There was a reward for my capture. I was Public Enemy No. 1. My father and Hannah made a "Wanted—Alive" poster, with a photo of me at the bottom, and stuck it on the fridge.

"If I went to first grade, I'd have to be careful of the police," I said, twining spaghetti around my fork. "Otherwise, I could end up in jail."

When I searched my father's face, he seemed beneath his smile to be no more certain than I was about the best thing to do. He took a breath, deliberated, and chose caution. "If you want to stay home, I'd be happy to teach you, Will. For as long as you want. Home-schooled kids often end up at the best colleges. Anyway, wouldn't want my boy to go to jail. I'd have to hire a couple of thugs to break him out."

Hannah and my father studied me over slices of apple pie à la mode. While I shaped my pie into a rocket ship, they debated my future. Years later, she would explain my father's dilemma. He didn't want the house to be my jail but was reluctant to push me into a world I wasn't ready for emotionally. He felt that most people, even children, knew what was best for them, given enough time to think about their situation. As I listened to them debate, I suddenly knew what I would do. It was time to leave my perch by the window. I would be as bold as my parents when they'd left New York for New Mexico.

"I'm going to first grade," I interrupted the discussion.

"You just said you wanted to stay home," my father reminded me.

"I changed my mind."

"Just like that?" said Hannah.

"Yes."

"You're sure?" she pushed.

I nodded excessively.

"You know, you can have a few days to think about this, champ."

"No, I want to go," I insisted. "Can we buy school supplies tomorrow?"

Under my bravado, I felt more than a stab or two of anxiety as I continued to sculpt my dessert, wondering if I'd made the right choice. My father had gone into the living room and turned on the stereo, as he did most evenings, settling down with a book while the house flooded with strains of *La Bohème.* Puccini was one of his favorites, and he considered *Bohème* a masterpiece. Hannah had patiently explained the story to me. It was about starving young artists and the tragedy of a love story that ended in death. I asked what a tragedy was. "When someone suffers great sorrow," she answered. I grew anxious whenever I listened to Puccini but never more than now. Would first grade be a tragedy for me? Would I fall in love first, whatever that meant? Would I have to die?

My head filled with questions. Except for my birthday party, I would be making contact with the real world—with strangers—for the first time since my accident.

"Do you know how to tie your shoes, Will?"

I stared up into the melon face of Ms. Jarowski. Her eyes fluttered like a couple of moths. My first-grade teacher was in her 20s, short and stocky, and had on a beige pants suit with a blue and green scarf around her neck. Her hands peeked out of her jacket sleeves like fluffy balls of cotton. Ms. Jarowski had wanted to be a primary school teacher ever since she grew up in Santo Tomás, Hannah had told me. She wasn't married; her first-grade class was her family. I would be in trustworthy hands.

My father had taken me early for my first day, hoping to get me oriented before the other kids arrived. My teacher liked being called "Ms.," rather than "Miss," Jarowski, he said, like a growing number of women. Her desk anchored a front corner of the room between an American flag and a blackboard. Next to the large clock above the door was a cross with the crucified Jesus, his thin body drooped in exhaustion. In Santo Tomás, there was sometimes no distinction between church and state.

I stared down at my shoes. My sister had already briefed me on the requirements for attending first grade. Know how to double-knot your laces, tell time, sing the first verse of *America the Beautiful,* and write your name, address, and phone number.

I bent down, untied my shoes, and laced them back in a perfect double knot.

"And what time is it, Will?"

"Eight eighteen and thirty-two seconds," I said, keeping track of the sweep hand on the clock. I also had my own watch in my pocket, silvery and delicate with a jeweled face with the word Bulova stamped on it. It sparkled in the light. My mother had forgotten it in her nightstand drawer.

"Very good, Will. Now, where do you live?"

"3657 Calle Norte. My phone number is 887-3952."

I was prepared to cough up the National Anthem next for extra credit, or a few passages from Deuteronomy, but Ms. Jarowski moved on, and I never had the chance. She had already talked with my father about what lay ahead and the possibility that some kids would make fun of me. The first time it happened, she said, the other pupil would be asked to apologize; anyone who committed a second offense would be sent to the principal; a third, the parents would be notified. Ms. Jarowski wanted to lay down the law for everyone upfront.

I heard her ask my father if I was overly shy or self-conscious. He assured her I was unusually bold and self-confident. I had stayed home instead of attending kindergarten last year, but it was now my choice to be here. Ms. Jarowski said she wouldn't single me out with an elaborate introduction, other than that I was Hannah's brother. Better if I worked myself into the class at my own pace. She would keep an eye out.

When he had finished his huddle with Ms. Jarowski, my father came over and reached down to hug me. "See you right at two, champ," he said. "I think you made the right choice. Learn everything you can." He tapped his forehead twice again.

I waved good-bye and went to the row of cubbies Ms. Jarowski had labeled with everyone's name. Carefully, I positioned my lunch box facing out, with "Will Ryder" as prominent on the front as the Luke Skywalker image, so no one would mistakenly take my peanut butter sandwich. Hannah had also tipped me off about the coatroom. When the weather got cooler, a nametag sewn on my jacket was not much protection against a troublemaker bent on stealing or hiding it. Once you became a scapegoat, Hannah warned, everyone would jump on the bandwagon. If I wanted respect, I had to be able to defend myself.

"What's a scapegoat?" I asked.

"Someone who gets picked on."

"Should I carry a knife?"

"No, that would make you a barbarian."

"Is it OK if I beat them up with my fists?" I had seen pictures of Muhammad Ali, and immediately assumed the pose of a boxer. Maybe I could watch some of his old fights on television and learn to box like him. I had yet to throw my first punch.

"We're a family of intellectuals. There's no need to be physical. Use your wits."

By 9 a.m., the classroom was full of small bodies in their starched fall clothes, moving in random orbits. They all knew each other from kindergarten, and almost everybody was in a giddy mood, glad to be reunited after a long summer. Voices rose and fell like a swarm of bees. I made my thumb and forefinger into a telescope and watched Lizzie Franklin and Christy Steadman through the imaginary lens, their faces inches apart, talking nonstop as if they hadn't seen each other in years. Did they talk about my birthday party anymore? The boys had their own rituals as they stomped around the room saluting each other, shaking their heads from side to side, or throwing a small orange ball at each other's butt. Ms. Jarowski clapped her hands several times, and then read off her seating chart to tell everybody where their assigned desk was. Mine was in the very back, allowing a commanding view of the room. I moved toward it with an adult seriousness to hide my nerves.

"Good morning everyone," Ms. Jarowski began, beaming at the twenty faces staring back. "I hope you all had a wonderful summer. We have an exciting year ahead. We're going to learn so much together."

A few nodded their heads, but most looked as if Ms. Jarowski were speaking Latin. I raised my hand.

"Yes, Will?" she said, pleased to see I was fitting in.

"What are we going to learn?"

"We're going to become good readers, first and foremost. We're going to add and subtract numbers, and learn a little bit about science, too. We're also going to study the geography of New Mexico. And, of course, there's music and painting and working with clay—"

"I like reading," I volunteered.

"Yes, your father told me."

"I like reading about famous people who changed the world," I added, thinking of the biographies Hannah had read to me.

Everyone turned to stare before Ms. Jarowski could formally introduce me. Some cringed when they saw my face. I wasn't sure what came over me, but I suddenly rose from my chair and walked to the blackboard. With a piece of blue chalk, I wrote "Wilson Louis Ryder" in cursive, in eight-inch letters. I turned to my classmates, waved, and returned to my seat.

"That's excellent handwriting, Will. But in the future, please raise your hand if you want to express something like this. Everyone, say hello to Will Ryder. Many of you already know his sister, Hannah."

Four or five kids said "Hi, Will" in rote voices. The rest of the class was silent. Even without my strange appearance, I was making life more difficult than it needed to be. I was the outsider who asked too many questions. I was too virtuous, too eager, too caught up with learning. A few kids turned and whispered to each other; others kept looking at me like they wished I'd disappear. Drops of sweat trickled down my neck. I raised my hand and told Ms. Jarowski my stomach was queasy, and asked if I could go to the bathroom.

"Of course, Will. Take this pass," she said, ignoring some snickering. She gave me a piece of tattered cardboard with "First Grade" stamped on it.

"You have to be back in five minutes, OK?"

"Yes, Ms. Jarowski."

When I stepped into the bathroom, I could hear the blood rushing through my ears. The overhead fluorescent lights made my eyes burn. I was afraid to move even one step closer to the bank of mirrors on the far side of the room.

To most people, it would seem impossible: I was six years old and had never looked in a mirror. When I was three and came home from eight weeks in the hospital, my father had accomplished two things. He had hired workers to quickly rebuild the parts of the house damaged by the fire, and he'd removed virtually every mirror in it. This was on the advice of Dr. Glaspell, a friend who was a professor at the university. He was afraid I was too young to accept seeing my face, not without experiencing serious trauma. My father and Hannah had small pocket mirrors in their bathrooms, but they kept them hidden.

Of course, I could have looked into some reflective surface or the rear view mirror of the Chevy, but my father's explanation won out over my bouts of curiosity. He told me my face had been burned in a fire in my bedroom, and that I looked different from everyone else. But I shouldn't be too concerned about it, he said. My body was simply a container, useful but of comparatively minor value, like a carton for the milk inside or a dust jacket for a book. What was important was the content. I had a personality, a will, an imagination, and, most important, a soul. There was also a thing called the brain, and I had a particularly nimble one, he said.

I stood alone in the bathroom, waiting for the courage to move forward. I didn't know what compelled me on my first day of school to challenge the secret I had successfully kept from myself for three years. I took a breath and marched like a soldier toward battle. My heart was rattling. As in a dream, I couldn't quite find the strength to lift my head, which seemed to belong to someone else. I waited a moment, then raised my eyes to the gleaming glass in front of me.

When I was sixteen and kissed a girl for the first time, my reaction was the same as that morning in first grade. I didn't wince or pull back in self-consciousness. I was filled with wonder as I stared in the mirror. Warmth flooded my chest. I felt like I was studying a piece of abstract sculpture: the distorted, slightly twisted lips—a collage of purple and pink; the pale, mottled nose that seemed to detach from my face and shimmer like an ornament; the misshapen cheeks, squared rather than rounded, melted almost to the bone by the flames and then left angled and sharp-edged by the surgery.

My chin looked almost normal, but the nerve damage had been extensive. I pressed my finger against the knob of flesh, but, like always, I could feel nothing there. For fun, I reached up and pulled on my ear lobes, which had somehow shrunk in the fire and were crusty with scar tissue. My best feature was my eyes, big and shiny, dark as mud, but alive.

Once I began studying my image, I couldn't stop. It was as if I had encountered myself from another lifetime, through some magical passage of time, and in this unexpected rendezvous, I waited for the face in the mirror to tell me a secret. What journey had I been on? What had I seen and learned? What would happen to me next? I reached out and touched the boy in the mirror, expecting him to smile or frown at me in our special conspiracy. Instead, he was mute and stoical, watching as if waiting for me to share my secret. I had come into the bathroom to see what everybody else saw, but my surprise was finding something nobody would ever notice, no matter how carefully they looked. I saw a boy who lived safely behind the glass, protected from the world. Would he ever come out?

"Will, are you all right?" I heard a voice from the hallway. "May I come in?" I looked at the tiny-jeweled hands on my mother's watch. I had been gone ten minutes.

I went out to the hall instead. When I joined her, Ms. Jarowski looked to see if I'd been crying, wondering if I had something to tell her. I looked back politely but distantly. What I had seen in the mirror I was not going to share with anyone.

In the classroom, twenty art easels had been set up. Everyone had a smock on, waiting for me before dabbing their brushes into old orange juice cans of egg tempera and water. My fidgety classmates were growing even more intolerant. Who was I to keep them all waiting? I put on my smock and hurried to my easel.

"Last year," Ms. Jarowski told the future generation of Picassos, "your teacher let everybody paint whatever they wanted. Most of you painted your house. This year, I'd like you to try something different. You might want to paint your church, or something you saw this summer—or in a book. You can choose whatever subject you want, just no houses, please."

Everyone plunged ahead. I was afraid somebody would paint me. Ignoring Ms. Jarowski, several boys began painting houses, either pretending no one would notice or out of fear that they couldn't do anything else. The houses all looked alike: boxes for windows divided by crosses for panes; lopsided chimneys; oversized front doors; sometimes stick figures of a family floating above a front lawn, as if gravity didn't exist. The girls were more adventurous. They painted horses, dogs and cats, flowers and trees, kids making lemonade.

I thrust my brush into a soupy green mix and smeared a sky across the top of the paper. Against the green I made my clouds yellow; an airplane came with large red wings and blue stars on its tail. Below, a garden erupted from the pink earth, shaped by every color at my disposal. Plants and trees entwined like an exotic forest in which I left no spot bare. The colors exploded first in my imagination, then on the paper, piling on top of each other like coats on a bed. Unlike my cautious, calculated drawing of Hannah in her tutu, my garden had come alive through nervous energy—and maybe a speck or two of madness. There was no stopping me as paint flew everywhere, including on my face. I thought I could make my garden grow to the sky.

I felt Ms. Jarowski's hand on my arm, gently pulling my brush down and interrupting my trance-like rapture. Half a dozen kids had clustered around me. Amid mostly murmurs of wonder, there were some skeptics.

"That's not a sky," one girl said. "Skies are blue."

"And clouds are white," her friend chimed in with certainty.

But by now, I had struck everyone as so different, so weird, that I was less a target of derision than a source of speculation. Had I come from Mars? What did I eat? Did I need sleep? My painting looked just as unreal as I did.

"Come, Will," Ms. Jarowski said, leading me to a small sink by the coatroom. I scrubbed my hands vigorously. She was gentle with the paper towel on my face, as if she feared pressing too hard would hurt me. By the time I returned to my desk, she had hung my frenzied painting on a clothesline, like a pair of wet overalls, not just to dry, she said, but also to show everyone how different and wonderful a painting could be. The golden light shining on my garden from the window made it come even more alive.

For the next hour, Ms. Jarowski read to us from Rudyard Kipling's *Kim,* then passed out our readers for the semester. I was a weak speller, but with Hannah's help, I had breezed through the reader over the summer. When my turn came, the words glided effortlessly off my lips. I read better than anyone else, but I kept my eyes down, not wanting to draw more attention.

When the bell rang for recess, I tagged behind some of the kids who'd come to my birthday party. I couldn't find Hannah in the playground. Christy and Lizzie drifted to a part of the blacktop where older girls had already gathered. The jump ropes lying in a pile looked like a den of snakes.

Christy and Lizzie seemed confident in their skill even though the third- and fourth-graders were showing off fancy tricks like Double Dutch. I realized I was the only boy around. Christy asked if I wanted to join them.

"I can't jump rope," I said, though I'd watched Hannah do it in our yard.

"It's easy. You take one end and Lizzie will take the other. I'll jump. You can do that, can't you?"

I could have declined and vanished into the general population of boys, but Christy's challenge made me want to stay. Despite the fiasco of my birthday party, I still had thoughts of us becoming friends. I took the handle and started turning my wrist around like Lizzie was doing at the other end. In seconds, the rope was whirling and humming between us. Like someone dashing to cross the street in front of a speeding car, Christy raced into the middle. Her posture was ramrod straight, her small, staccato jumps perfectly timed.

"Faster," she commanded without looking at Lizzie or me. I could feel her concentration, and demanded the same from myself.

We picked up the pace. In a blur, the jump rope skimmed an inch above the asphalt with each rotation, whining in my ear like a mosquito. The hypnotic speed struck me as magical, the rope moving so fast it might lift all three of us into space.

*"¡Mi amorcita! ¿Cómo estás? ¿Dónde están tu madre y padre?"*

The voice floated up from behind me. My head twisted around just enough to throw off my rhythm, and the rope died at Christy's feet. I was looking at two boys—identical twins, I was slow to realize—with their jeans rolled up three or four inches at the cuff, and checkerboard black-and-white flannel shirts over their white T-shirts. It was too hot for anyone to wear a flannel shirt, but what

I didn't know was that Richie and Tito wore the same clothes every day, regardless of the weather. They were in the fourth grade, gangly kids with cauliflower ears and slicked-back black hair. I knew enough Spanish from Mrs. Gutierrez to understand I was being ridiculed.

I felt Lizzie and Christy stirring behind me, wondering what I was going to do. Though the twins were at least a foot taller than me, I thought about assuming a boxing position, ready to take them on. Then I remembered Hannah's advice.

"My mother and father are not here," I answered. "But they're fine. How are your mother and father? Do they dress you like clowns every morning?"

I had no idea where my words came from. Was this what Hannah meant by using my wits? Richie curled his lip.

"Only girls jump rope! You must be a girl!" His throat made a gurgling sound, then he spit down on the tip of my sneaker.

"No, I'm not a girl." I said, "but maybe you are."

"*¿Qué paseó con tus labios? ¿Quién te dió un golpe?*" Richie replied with sarcasm. What happened to your lips? Did someone hit you? Tito stuck his hands in his pockets and grinned. I would learn that he liked to pretend he was deaf and mute.

"*¡Adiós, amigos!*" I said dramatically, remembering a line from a movie, "I will meet you in hell."

I wanted to vanish, but when I turned to run, Richie stepped in front of me. He was too close to spit again. Even though he looked at the crowd, he was still talking to me.

"Tell us the truth, *mi pequeño amigo.* Did someone put your face in a meat grinder?"

I froze. I was sure my life was in jeopardy, but I couldn't think of anything to say. Then Hannah came into the corner of my eye, her stride more purposeful than usual.

Tito reacted to the arrival of a sixth grader, even if it was a girl, by moving closer to his brother, forming a wall of solidarity. I was confident my sister's wits would bury them like a bulldozer.

Richie looked at Hannah like she was some pesky fly ready to be swatted away. "Are you a freak, too?" he asked. "Does it run in the family, *fea hermana?*"

My sister's nose twitched like she smelled something repulsive. She walked past Richie without giving him a glance and pulled the jump rope from Christy's hands. Before anyone knew what was happening, Hannah had looped the rope chest-high around an amused Richie and Tito, who refused to take her seriously. She cinched the rope with a knot, then started pulling the twins like a cowboy breaking in a horse. They began fighting back, but Hannah had too much strength and momentum. Richie yelled and he and Tito flapped their arms as they lurched about like a couple of drunks. Hannah just kept pulling. After one last effort to win the struggle, Richie and Tito ended up in a heap on the ground.

But Hannah wasn't done—I could see the fury still building in her eyes.

"Don't pick on my brother again," she warned, with her right foot pressing on Richie's chest until a tear rolled down his cheek. "If you do, my friends and I will come back and kick the shit out of you so bad you'll never walk again. *¿Comprendes?*"

Hannah turned and left before the teacher in the playground could get there to sort things out. I trailed behind like an obedient dog, pleased but confused. Had my sister turned into a barbarian? The twins freed themselves and began hurling curses at us. I might have been terrified if I hadn't believed more in my sister as a protector than Richie and Tito as my mortal enemies.

As the bell rang to end recess, everyone hurried back into the school. I took my seat in the back of the room, staring up at my dreamy, besotted garden of unholy colors. It was still drying on the clothesline. Enraptured by it, I wondered where all the beauty had come from.

As I grew older, moving with undiminished energy through Santo Tomás Elementary, I found myself at the lofty pinnacle of sixth grade. It was the year of the Gulf War, along with the crumbling of the once-invincible Soviet Union, which my father dwelled on as an important historical event. On television the year before, we had watched the Berlin Wall being torn down by East and West Germans, piece by piece. My teacher, Mrs. Newcomb, shared my interest in current events and encouraged me to contribute what I'd learned. She had ankles the size of grapefruits, and little gray-pink whiskers peeking from her facial pores. They were the same color as her hair, whose waves and texture were like cotton candy. Seriously overweight, she would budge from her chair only when absolutely necessary, like writing a homework assignment on the blackboard.

As the year progressed, Mrs. Newcomb was the target of behind-her-back jokes about flatulence, witchcraft, and being married to a blind man (because who else could love a fat lady). I never joined in. Perhaps she was aware of my loyalty, because she showered me with responsibilities. I was called on to pass out books, run messages to the principal, and carry things to her car at the end of the day. Despite the resentment I stirred, I didn't mind being the teacher's pet, and put up with playground name-calling almost proudly. I had the same reaction if anyone made fun of my face. I liked the attention, even if it was negative. Being noticed as much as possible was suddenly important to me. It would be far more painful, I thought, to be invisible.

I would have spent most of my free time doing homework, reading, or making drawings as a gift for Mrs. Newcomb, but my father had other ideas. In his mind, "well-roundedness" was part of my education. I had little interest in sports, other than watching them on television, but my father insisted that every afternoon after school, we throw a baseball or football or ride our bikes. He also liked to wrestle—rough-housing, he called it—which was more fun. He would tackle me and pin me to the ground, and I would do the same to him in the backyard. He taught me a half nelson, a double leg takedown with knee cut, and an overhook and hip throw. After an hour, winded, I closed the door to my room and began my homework.

Around nine, before I fell asleep, I would lie in the dark and play with my face. I pretended it was a lump of clay that I could knead and shape at will. I started by sweeping my fingers through my closely cropped hair, rubbing my scalp, and then drifted south, inch by inch. My forehead would bunch under my fingertips as I rippled the skin from side to side. I knew intimately the map of bumps and dips and hollows, but running my fingers over their landscape, I sometimes felt it was for the first time—that I'd found a new ridge or valley, and more discoveries were waiting for me as my face changed. I took pleasure wherever I could feel sensation, especially my lips. Despite being burned, the nerves had survived or regenerated underneath. Parts of my face, like my chin, were like patches of desert, but where it was green, I would rub and caress it endlessly, enjoying a secret pleasure.

One day after school, I rode my bike to my favorite tienda, Cuatro Caminos Super Mercado at El Camino and Walker Street, one of the busier intersections in the city. I'd promised my father I'd stick to the sidewalk as much as possible, because Santo Tomás's streets had more crazy drivers, he said, than Italy and France combined. I was also an impatient, sometimes-reckless, cyclist. If it was a pedestrian I hit instead of a car, at least I wouldn't be hurt too badly, nor, he hoped, would my victim.

I parked in front of the tienda and savored the smells drifting through its open doors: chickens dripping fat with every turn on the rotisserie; cochinillo asado; gambas al ajillo; paella; and separate pots with ladles holding beans, posole, and menudo, a spicy soup made with tripe that was known as a cure for hangovers. The tienda was open from 6 a.m. to midnight, seven days a week, and the hot foods take-out section was the most popular. Warm corn or flour tortillas were an after-school favorite; so were candy bars and cans of soda, with a dozen flavors available. Old pharmacy bottles lined the windows. Ceiling rafters were decked with colorful pennants. The narrow aisles were crowded with every meat, fish, and vegetable that could be squeezed into a jar or can.

In a dimly lit corner were over a hundred different magazines, splayed in racks whose upper rungs reached above my head. Men usually gathered around the automobile section, hunting and guns, or the dog-eared copies of *Playboy* and *Hustler*. I was left alone at the other end to leaf through the half-dozen art magazines that arrived every month. On my tiptoes, I pulled down copies of *The Artist's Magazine, American Artist,* and *American Artist Watercolor*. Together they consumed half my monthly allowance, so I could only afford to thumb through the others. The articles in *ARTnews* were too difficult for me, but the photos and captions piqued my interest. I didn't know any artists personally, what they were like, what they talked about, or what inspired them to paint. I didn't even know if I was an artist, even though my teachers praised my work every year, and I'd won several prizes in age competitions sponsored by a local bank. My father had offered me private lessons, but I kept declining.

As I thumbed through *ARTnews,* my knees suddenly grew wobbly. I was staring at the image of a woman in her early to mid-40s, with straight dark hair down to her shoulders. Her green sweatshirt proclaimed BIG APPLE. She was standing in front of an easel that held a large painting. She was expressionless, even severe looking, as if she didn't care to be the center of attention, yet beneath her hardness, I imagined something warm in her heart carefully hidden from the world. I wondered why I had stumbled upon this page in this particular magazine on this particular day. I had memorized every feature of my mother from the lone photo in our house. It didn't matter how much time had passed since she'd left. I could have picked her out in a crowded baseball stadium.

"Guess what!" I shouted when I got home, breathless from excitement. I had disobeyed my father and sped recklessly over the streets and sidewalks. Jumping curbs, I imagined I was Evel Knievel launching his motorcycle over school buses. My father was in the kitchen, grading papers fanned out on the table. His face was drawn, his eyes small and glassy. He seemed overcome with tedium. He liked to say that almost anyone could get into college these days, and the only thing worse was that almost anyone could graduate.

I opened the copy of *ARTnews* I'd bought and waved it in front of him like a winning lottery ticket. "Look! It's Mom! She's in a gallery in New York!"

He took the magazine and let his eyes drift over the photos and article. The silence that descended was one that periodically covered our house whenever my mother's name came up. It was usually raised by me, wondering where she was and why she never wrote us. Was she too busy? Did she think we'd moved?

My father and Hannah treated her like a relative who no longer was welcome to visit, as if she'd done something beyond embarrassing, and it was best that she be excluded from not just conversation but collective memory as well. I wondered what her offense could be. My father's explanation, held as true by the neighborhood, was that she'd run off with another man, deserting our family. Once, I asked why he still kept her photo in the house. No matter what she'd done, he replied, she was still my mother, and it was only right I had something to remember her by.

"Isn't that great news?" I broke the silence. "Did you have any idea she was in New York?"

"She doesn't write, Will, so no, I didn't know."

"She's never written?"

"No, she hasn't."

"Are you happy for her?" I asked

"I suppose so. Why not?"

"Go ahead, read the article," I said eagerly.

He had a lot of papers to grade, and was tired from a long day. The last thing he wanted, I imagined, was to read about the success of the woman who had abandoned him. But the miracle about my father was that he rarely rebuffed me, even when he was irritated. His endless patience came partly from feelings of guilt, Hannah said. The leaky space heater in my bedroom had blown up while I slept, and it was my father's nature to assume blame where others would dodge it. Technically, the explosion was an accident, but he could have replaced the old heater long ago. He should have known something was wrong from a slight smell the night before. I didn't fully understand the deep, sinewy tentacles of guilt, but I saw how it shaped his behavior. Raising two children alone was enough of a burden without the special one I imposed with medical bills, hyper behavior, and the gossip I provoked among neighbors. Yet he never raised his voice to me.

He settled back in his chair and began reading aloud.

"Susan Olmsted is best known for her highly abstract forms and dense, brooding colors. Creating tension not just with the menacing physicality of her objects but a metaphysical universe that strikes us as a world with constantly changing questions and answers, we end up in a state of agitation. She has been compared to the early Rauschenberg and the mature Motherwell, yet her vision of endless searching is expressed with her unique brush stroke—bold slashes that possess spontaneity and mystery. On a deeper level, rendering a sense of existence inevitably provokes a tragic expression. There is a feeling of unease if not anguish, even violence, under the surface. . . ."

"Why does she call herself Olmsted? Her name is Susan Ryder," I interrupted. He put down the magazine. There was little in the article I understood.

"Olmsted was her maiden name. Before we were married."

"Oh."

"It's not uncommon to change your name after you divorce."

My father went back to reading out loud, as if our personal discussion was over, but I was suddenly dwelling on my parents' divorce. It was illogical to me. What was the point of getting married if you were only going to end up unmarried? How could you be in love one moment and out of love the next? I imagined divorce as a jagged crack that appeared under your feet, and just as you fell into the hole, it closed around you, like a steel trap, cutting you in half.

"Do you miss her?" I interrupted his reading.

He put down *ARTnews* and peered at me over his reading glasses. Stymied, I thought, he was trying to calculate how much he should tell me. I stood there stubbornly, wanting a full confession. I was twelve and old enough, I believed, to handle any explanation.

"That's a big subject, champ." He gestured for me to sit down. "It's complicated."

"How complicated?" I was incapable of sitting. I had become a perpetual motion machine, rocking back and forth on my heels, thrusting my hands in and out of my pockets. My eyes were blinking as if sending Morse code, a desperate plea to understand my mother.

"You can miss some things about a person but not other things. You can even miss someone in every possible way but be so mad or disappointed with them about something else, something crucial, that you can't live with them any longer."

"Are you mad at her because she fell in love with another man?"

"No."

"Are you mad at me?"

"Of course not."

"Then what are you mad about?"

He looked uncertain again, as if I were pushing in a direction he didn't want to go. "You ask a lot of smart questions, and I wish I were smart enough to answer them. Now I need to ask you one: Do you miss your mother?"

My eyes kept blinking, sending out another SOS. Today was hardly the first time I had thought about her. Since I was four or five, I had tried to imagine her. I thought there were storms in her head, and that had something to do with her leaving. Yet I had no idea what I missed about her, except that she was gone. She was mostly an abstraction. All I had was the watch she'd left behind and the single photograph. A chance discovery at Cuatro Caminos had changed everything. A successful artist, my mother was alive and well in New York! I wanted to know more. I wanted to see her.

“I don’t miss her,” I lied. “Why should I? We already have our family.”

I reclaimed the *ARTnews* and retreated to my room. My father turned on the stereo, Mozart this time, and put a pot roast in the oven. I focused on the photos of my mother’s art—deep, bold slashes of color—wondering why she painted that way. Where did her moods and ideas come from? I took some art paper and sat at my desk with a set of watercolors, leaning the magazine against the wall next to me. Studying one of her canvases, I was determined to copy it exactly. I sketched the basic shapes with a pencil. Mixing and remixing colors, first I moved my brush from left to right, then right to left, to see if that made any difference. When I was finished almost an hour later, I held my work at arm’s length, then put it on the desk and retreated to the end of the room for a different perspective. I kept staring, wanting to like it, but it was nothing like my mother’s art. I tore it up and started again. The new effort was even more hopeless. Whatever was inside me was different from what was in her. I sank back in my chair, frustrated.

At dinner, I suspected that my father had already briefed Hannah about the *ARTnews.* The subject never came up, but I could guess what they were thinking. The less my mother invaded our lives, the happier the rest of us would be. I didn’t tell them about my painting efforts because my frustration would only have confirmed their theory. Hannah cast me a searching glance every few minutes, but otherwise, dinner was filled with our usual competing voices. In addition to the Soviet Union, conversations about U.S. politics were always lively. My father’s early efforts at stimulating our curiosity had borne fruit.

“I got a raise today, can you imagine?” he said suddenly, surprising Hannah and me. He rarely talked about money. “The chairman of the English Department took credit, but I should really thank the legislature, blessed with all those taxes from oil and gas. It’s always a bountiful year for exploiting the land,” he added, “so they spread a little of the wealth.”

Environmental issues were always on my father’s mind, along with persecution of dissidents in the Middle East, civil wars in Africa, and the growing gap everywhere between the haves and have-nots. He took social issues seriously, but now his voice was edged with sarcasm.

"A raise, that's great, Dad," Hannah said. "Now you can buy that Mercedes you always wanted." Her joke barely penetrated. He would as soon drive a pretentious, expensive car as invest in the stock market. He barely trusted putting his money in a savings account. "No, seriously, about time you got more money," she added.

"When was your last raise?" I asked, wanting to cheer him up, too.

His gaze rose to the ceiling, as if there was a calendar with endless pages between the light fixtures, and his mind was flipping through them one at a time. "I've been teaching at the university for twenty years," he said. "I believe this is my third modest raise which, when you allow for inflation, means I'm actually earning less, in real dollars, than when I started."

"That's a gyp," Hannah said.

"I'm going to be forty-nine in a few weeks. Maybe I get a couple of more raises before I retire. What do you think, guys?"

His sarcasm was tinged with resignation: What was the point in fighting the system if you weren't going to win. I had no idea what real dollars were, or why my father was suddenly talking about his age, but I nodded in sympathy. My father was being gypped! I wanted to come to his defense. Hannah was upset, too. After a minute, she discretely switched topics. First it was the weather, and then talk of a new Wal-Mart coming to Santo Tomás, and finally she dropped her own bomb.

"I'm thinking of leaving Santo Tomás," she said.

Dad and I looked at each other.

"I want to transfer to Albuquerque Prep—if I can get a scholarship."

Several of her teachers were encouraging the move, she said, because Prep had advanced science and math classes, and she'd be challenged in other areas, too. She'd also be able to take classes at one of the top ballet academies in the Southwest if she could pass the audition, though she'd need a scholarship for that, too.

The news pulled my father out of his trance. He smiled at Hannah and said he thought he could afford something toward her tuition. He endorsed anything that would further his children's talents. Her move wouldn't happen until the fall, but the more she talked about it, the thought of not seeing her every day suddenly hit me. A pit opened in my stomach.

"I think it's a bad idea," I said, focusing on my broccoli.

"Why?" she asked.

"Just because."

"Albuquerque is only four hours away," she pointed out. "You can visit on weekends, or I can come home."

"What if you get too busy?"

"I won't."

"But what if you do?"

"I'll never be too busy for you or Dad."

"Hmmm."

Hannah sighed. "Stop trying to make me feel guilty, please."

I was quiet through the rest of the meal. I tried to take consolation from her promise to visit, but what if she couldn't keep it? I knew how busy she kept her life. My father, after his initial happiness, seemed to be reappraising what she'd said. He would miss Hannah even more than I would. After stacking the dishes in the sink, he told us he was taking a walk. He should have been in the living room, reading a book while Chopin or Bach eased his mind. A solo after-dinner stroll happened about as often as a solar eclipse.

"What's wrong with Dad?" I asked Hannah as we tackled the dishes.

"Think about it. Three raises in twenty years? Pathetic. It's not just the money that bothers him. He's being taken advantage of by the system. Do you know how health insurance works?"

I shook my head. I didn't know what "the system" meant either.

"Besides his salary, the university pays for Dad's medical expenses, and ours, too. But it doesn't cover everything. Like elective surgery."

"What's that?"

"The insurance company paid for your first operation and when you were in the hospital, but after that, they said your surgeries were an option, not a necessity. The company wouldn't pay one dime."

"You mean I was gypped!" I said, angry like she was.

"It made Dad furious, too."

After a moment, Hannah added, "I know one thing. I'm never going to let myself be poor. Or be taken advantage of."

I was still boiling. I suddenly hated insurance companies. Finally, curious, I asked Hannah, "Do dancers make a lot of money?"

"Only if you become famous, I think."

We went back to discussing our father. Despite Hannah's concerns, I wasn't completely sure what he was going through. He wasn't always clear about his feelings. Only rarely did he act supremely happy, but he didn't walk around with his head down either. The drumbeat that accompanied his step was steady. But maybe Hannah was right. Tonight he had seen a message scrawled across the kitchen ceiling, underneath that calendar. His career had gone as far as it would go. Announcing that she wanted to leave for Albuquerque in the fall, Hannah had unintentionally made him feel worse.

"Can you keep an eye on Dad?" she asked. "Think of yourself as Sherlock Holmes. Give me a report once a week."

"What kind of report?"

"If Dad does anything different or strange. Or just what he's thinking. I'm concerned."

She said she knew what a midlife crisis was from talking to friends about their parents; she thought it was a little bit like waking up one morning in someone else's body. She told me about Franz Kafka's novella, *The Metamorphosis.* I swallowed hard at the thought of my father turning into a cockroach. She assured me Kafka's story was a fable, a metaphor for when things that used to make sense no longer did. She explained what a metaphor was, but the image of my father becoming a cockroach stayed in my mind.

When he returned from his walk, he went to his room without saying good night. I saw Hannah's frown. I crept over and put my ear to his door. It wasn't until I heard his fingers turning pages that I felt some relief.

For the next few weeks, I no longer stayed after school to help Mrs. Newcomb. I came straight home. One afternoon, I found my father hunched over his IBM Selectric, working on a new article. A serious student of James Joyce, his scholarship had been published in several literary journals. He wasn't a famous Joyce scholar, the kind who wrote books, but he hoped to be one some day. If he succeeded at his dream, I thought, maybe his midlife crisis would go away. I watched the little steel ball of letters spinning madly over the page. He once told me he could type a hundred forty words a minute. That was faster than James Joyce, I'd bet.

Taking a break, he fixed me a sandwich, and we lounged in the kitchen.

"And how are you?" I asked in my best adult voice.

"Not bad."

"You're sure?"

"Sure."

"What happened to that woman?"

"What woman?"

"The one you used to date. Mary. She worked at the bank."

"No idea, frankly," he said. "Why are you asking?"

Over the years, my father had dated several women, one at a time. Mary was a thin brunette with an efficient manner and alert eyes, and even if their relationship didn't turn into anything permanent, he had seemed much happier than when he was alone. He gave me a look that said I was silly for bringing up the matter. When he returned to his typewriter, I wandered off to start my homework.

I was making a lousy Sherlock Homes, but I reported to Hannah as instructed. My father rarely played tennis with his friends anymore. When we went to the supermarket, he was absent minded about his shopping list. He hadn't had a haircut in two months. At home, his books occupied his time more than conversations with me.

One afternoon, I found him in the well-creased red club chair that accommodated his dozing, reading, munching on leftovers, and spinning private thoughts. He was staring at the elm in the backyard, but his gaze quickly rotated to me. The day's mail was in his lap. I recognized the opened envelope on top. It was in my handwriting, addressed to the Leo Castelli Gallery on East 77th Street in New York City. "Return to Sender" was stamped across the front.

"Can you explain this?" he asked, holding up the envelope like we were in court and it was a pivotal piece of evidence.

I was angry that the gallery owner had not forwarded it. How lazy or blind could he be? I had printed Susan Olmsted in large block letters. There could be no mistaking who it was for.

Ignoring my silence, my father went on. "Why didn't you tell me you missed your mother? There was no reason not to be honest."

I had invited my mother to visit. I'd even volunteered to fly to New York if it was more convenient for her. I asked a dozen questions about her paintings and told her I wanted to be an artist, too. I said I was proud of her and couldn't wait until we met.

"Because I didn't think you wanted me to see her," I said.

"I don't. It's not the best thing for you. Maybe when you're older—that would be up to you. But not right now. You have to take my word on that."

"How much older?"

He looked as conflicted as when I'd asked him to read the article in *ARTnews.* "I don't know. Hannah's age maybe."

My sister was seventeen. I was twelve. Five years struck me as a century. "Why do I have to wait so long?"

"Because you're not old enough to understand everything."

"I understand divorce," I insisted.

"There's more to this than divorce."

"Then why don't you tell me," I said, frustrated. I felt my chest heave up, and then I began to cry. When he put his arm around me, I pushed against his chest to free myself. He pulled me even closer, fighting me, giving me a long and deep hug, until my heart began to slow.

"I can't tell you, champ."

"That's not fair."

"Will, I don't want this to come between us. You need to promise not to contact your mother again. Not for a long while."

I'd always trusted my father. Yet it took forever before I could open my mouth and the words "I promise" came out.

That night, after the light in my father's bedroom was off, I knocked on Hannah's door. I was sure she knew about our afternoon confrontation. My father hadn't forbidden me to discuss my mother with her.

"Come in," she said.

My drawing of Hannah in her tutu was framed and centered above her headboard. She was on top of the covers in her bathrobe, with two pillows propped behind her, staring into a textbook. Her face was covered with a white cream that left only the tip of her nose, eyebrows, and lips exposed. I gave her a look. Women's beauty products were a mystery to me.

"Why can't I see my mother?" I began.

"You're determined, I give you that." Hannah put down her book. "That's a good quality to have. You and I are so much alike in some ways."

"Why is everything a big fat secret around here?"

"A big fat secret? I'm not keeping anything from you. I don't know everything that Dad knows."

"What do you know?"

She pursed her lips, as though debating the wisdom of a full discussion. But she had to tell me. She felt bad for deciding to leave me behind in the fall. Telling the truth now was the least she could do.

"It's nothing to do with you, Will. Mom's not right in the head. I think Dad doesn't know how to explain mental illness to you."

"How can she be mentally ill? She's a great painter."

"Being mentally ill doesn't mean you can't be an artist. Look at Van Gogh or Munch or Gauguin. What it means is she couldn't handle what happened to you in the fire. That's what Dad told me. She flipped out. She left us. . . ."

"You're lying. What you mean is she couldn't stand to look at me," I said.

Hannah paused long enough for a seed of doubt to put down its roots in me.

"I'm going to tell you the truth. I was at sleepaway camp when the fire happened. I only found out when I got home. Dad had moved us into an apartment because the house had to be repaired. You were in the hospital. Mom had had a breakdown and was under a doctor's care. A few days later, she bolted, without a goodbye to any of us. She managed to leave a three-sentence note. It might as well have begun "to whom it may concern." She split with some pathetic loser named Willard. He didn't have a family. Maybe that was part of the attraction. Mom didn't like any of us.

"What I'm saying, Will, is she didn't leave just because of you. She left all of us. She just couldn't handle . . . events."

I didn't believe her. I was the event. I was suddenly feeling light-headed, and began swaying on my feet.

"What I want you to know," Hannah emphasized, "is that I didn't forgive her. If she was ill, why couldn't she have gotten help? She was a coward. If she really cared about us, she would have come back. She could have at least written and given an explanation."

I stared back at my sister, wanting to be brave and hear everything.

"I never want her back in my life. When I get married, I'm not going to invite her to my wedding. And if I were you," she added, sitting up to make sure she had my full attention, "I wouldn't forgive her either. She's a monster."

When my sister was sure about something, nothing could sway her to believe otherwise. She never wanted to see our mother or her art or hear stories about her. Hannah swore she would turn out nothing like her, and if somehow she did—God forbid!—she'd have to see a therapist for the rest of her life.

I wanted to tell her things were more complicated for me. I couldn't disown my mother. She was an accomplished artist, like I wanted to be one day. While Hannah and my father believed in me and wanted me to keep painting, I didn't know what my mother thought. How could I shut her out without at least knowing that?

My heart was still hammering away when I said good night. Moving toward my room felt like I was descending a series of endless steps. As they grew steeper, they became a spiral so tight I could go no farther—but I couldn't go back up either. Something was pressing on my chest. Bright riffs of color exploded in my eyes. I had no idea what was happening or where I was, other than trapped in one of my mother's fearsome paintings, captive of a woman I didn't even know.

I rode my bike to the library the next day and discovered dozens of old issues of *ARTnews.* There were three articles on my mother, mostly technical in nature but two contained early biographical information. The mental issues that Hannah had talked about weren't mentioned anywhere, and the only thing about our family was a casual reference to "an early marriage and two children." My mother was quoted about her childhood and teen-aged years as an Army brat, and the fact that she had attended Columbia but was largely self-taught as a painter. Suddenly, it seemed, she was living in New York, an upcoming abstract expressionist who'd caught the attention of serious critics. What was missing was all but the scantiest details of the ten years before her success—missing for a reason, I suspected. I wondered if my mother was ashamed of us, or we simply weren't important to her.

I waited for a Saturday when Hannah was in Albuquerque and my father had gone for an all-day hike with a friend. The first thing I did was to rummage through the garage, followed by a search of kitchen drawers, a hallway trastero, living room bookshelves, and finally under the sofa cushions and my father's red club chair. I came up empty-handed. I wanted facts—something about my mother besides a watch and a photograph—to cast light on Hannah's and my father's version of events. I trusted them more than anyone in the world, but I knew I didn't know everything.

There was only one other place to look, the most obvious but also the most forbidding. I would be trespassing. When I entered my father's bedroom, it felt strange and claustrophobic. Nothing looked familiar. As well as I knew the room's ordered simplicity—a desk in one corner, a dresser in another, a reading table and brass lamp next to the double bed—I was sure I'd never been here. I told myself to turn and leave, only to be pinned there by a terrible silence.

When I searched my father's desk and dresser, I was struck anew by the sparseness of his life. His closet left the same impression: five pairs of jeans, some khakis, a half-dozen shirts and a few ties that were older than me, one winter and one fall jacket, and four pairs of shoes. The closet also held a set of built-in drawers; several cardboard boxes were clustered on the floor and the shelf over the clothes bar. My fingers dug through everything. In one corner was a dusty accordion file loosely secured by a string. Inside was a slide show of my father's life before I had come along. Photos of him as a young man, letters home from a Boy Scout camp, what looked like a girlfriend, a car he had proudly fixed up, some friends on a fishing trip. There were no photos after age fifteen or sixteen until he was suddenly at Columbia with a mustache or a beard, a clutch of books under his arm. There were letters from people I didn't know but nothing from my mother, as if she'd been purged. I found a large envelope of Hannah's and my baby and childhood photos, snapped by his Instamatic. Me kite flying and bicycle riding (my face shimmered like a mask under a scalding wafer of a sun), Hannah at her piano recital, swimming with friends in the Santo Tomás city pool, studying at her desk at home with one finger twining her pony tail.

I began to assume that if there were any other trace of my mother in Santo Tomás, it wasn't at our house. Going for the long shot, I flipped on my back and squirmed under the bed, looking up into the box spring like a mechanic examining a car chassis.

In the grainy light, it took a moment to spot the envelope wedged deep into the frame. I teased it out of its hiding place. A letter opener had sliced through the top. Looking at the fine dust that covered it, I wondered when it had last been read, and what was so important to require this secrecy. My temples throbbed as I sat on the bed to examine the envelope—plain, legal-sized—like some ancient text of unknown value. It was addressed to Mr. Henry Ryder. My mother's name had a return address in Texas. I pulled out the letter delicately, like something that might explode in my hands.

*August 13, 1982*

*Dear Henry:*

*I received your letter last week, and this will be my only reply. To answer your question, I am never coming back to Santo Tomás. I believe one can and should live many lives, in separate universes, as it were, unconnected by guilt, remorse, hope, or any other sentiment. Emotions are a waste of time.*

*You may ask all you want, but I will not comment on the events just before my departure. I left and divorced you because I was no longer in love with you.*

My eyes scanned the letter twice to be sure of what I was reading as the bewilderment took hold of me.

*I am leaving both children in your custody. You've asked me never to contact them. I have no intention of contacting them. I have no interest in them whatsoever other than I hope they are healthy. I know you feel I've abandoned them, however I will not argue the point because it's not important to me. . . .*

I thought Hannah had exaggerated when she called my mother a monster. I was sure she'd never seen this letter; if she had, her words would have been stronger. Yet I was confused. Hannah claimed my mother left because she couldn't handle what the fire had done—she'd had a breakdown—but the letter was saying she'd fallen out of love with my father. I didn't understand. One thing was clear, however. She didn't give a shit about anyone, including me. She didn't want anything to do with us. Light headed, I put the letter in the envelope and back in its hiding place.

A tornado of thoughts and feelings swept me out of the house, down our porch steps, across the lawn. I began to run, block after block. My feelings overwhelmed me. I didn't know why or in what order my thoughts came any more than I knew where I was running, just that I had to keep moving if I wanted to get as far from my mother as possible.

When my lungs began to burn, I slowed down. But my mind kept racing. I could never tell my father I'd been snooping in his room, but I understood why he had lied when he said my mother never wrote him. He was only protecting me. She never wanted to see me again not because of my face but because I wasn't important to her. Neither Hannah nor I mattered at all. Nothing was important but her art. I had felt her selfishness in every sentence of the letter. She seemed almost angry. Maybe she thought my sister and I had delayed her from becoming a great artist. That was why the ten years were left out of her story. They were the years in which we were her burden. We had stolen her time. She didn't have to write that she wished we were never born. It was obvious.

Night had fallen when I got back home. I could smell a chicken roasting in the oven.

"Will, where've you been?" my father gently scolded. Hannah looked equally curious.

"I felt like taking a walk."

"We've been home since four. You usually leave a note," she said.

"Sorry."

"What's wrong?" Hannah asked.

"Nothing."

"You look upset."

"I'm fine."

"Good to know. Dinner in half an hour," my father said cheerfully.

I closed the door to my room. I needed to take stock of myself, to be strong, to resist my mother's words. They hurt, but I realized it wasn't as bad as a few hours ago. I had a choice. Be crushed or be strong. The pain didn't have to weaken me. If I kept my mother out of my thoughts, she didn't really exist, any more than I existed for her.

When I joined my father and Hannah for dinner, I didn't see them in my usual way. I was only twelve but I felt much older, and more independent. I listened to them talk about junior high school, the significant transition I'd be facing in the fall. My father wanted to prepare me, like a coach with his football team. Hannah had her list for me, too—as if I would always need their help.

My eyes floated between them for a moment. Then I changed the subject.

It was just after lunch, and I was late for fifth-period study hall. Much had changed between spring and fall. I was thirteen years old, and a growth spurt had left me slightly taller than most seventh graders. Over the summer, Hannah urged me to beef up my pathetically skinny frame, as if junior high is like prison and I'd need to fight for my life on a daily basis. My father bought me a rusted barbell at Goodwill with a dozen ten- and twenty-pound weights, and a padded bench. I worked out in the garage.

"Look at you, Will," Hannah said half seriously every week, squeezing my biceps, "it's actually working. You're getting a nice pair of guns." September folded into October, November into December. The large iron gates of Edward Chavez Junior High opened every morning like the jaws of a shark, swallowing a thousand of us whole.

As I glided down the hallway toward study hall, a ninth-grader approached from the other direction. Louie Freeze was hardly a stranger to me. He was built like one of the great silverback apes in the mountains of Central Africa, with a powerful, deep chest, squatty legs, dangling arms, and a small head. As he edged closer, a predatory smile lit his coffee-colored eyes. In his cupped hand was a sewing needle the size of a small hypodermic. When you weren't looking, Louie liked to sneak up behind you and poke his needle into your butt cheek. The element of surprise, coupled with the pain, was not something easily forgotten. Most seventh-graders he attacked at random, but Louie stalked me. In sixteen weeks of school, he'd stuck me four times, and I swore there wouldn't be a fifth. Though she was three hundred miles away in Albuquerque, Hannah's voice filled my head when I most needed the courage. Slam my lunch box into Louie's jagged forest of teeth, she advised, and then for good measure, kick him in the balls. Being a barbarian was OK after all. You had to teach respect before you get it back.

Louie passed me in the empty hallway, and for a second, I thought I was safe. Then I heard the pivoting squeak of his sneakers. He turned, and like the great ape he is, charged fast toward me. But I was ready. I'd packed two ten-pound weights in my lunch box, and as I faced him, I pulled it back below my hip. My trajectory swung up and gained momentum as Louie rushed me. He was slow to recognize the danger, but I was in danger, too. Swinging up, my arm felt like it detached from my shoulder. The lunch box went airborne, sailing an inch or two over Louie's head. The latch holding it together opened, and the weights flew out in parallel tracks, crashing into a nearby locker like miniature flying saucers. We stared together at the dented locker, thinking similar but different thoughts. I was thinking my enemy was lucky to be alive. Louie was thinking I was about to be dead.

"You better not come closer," I warned.

"Or what, dickless wonder?"

"You'll be sorry."

"You're a faggot artist," he declared, as if that meant a diseased specimen.

Everyone in school knew I loved to paint, which somehow made me gay. There was no defense against the demon that owned Louie Freeze's mind. I had nothing witty to say. No words could save me anyway. The great ape tackled me to the linoleum floor. In my panic, I couldn't remember a single wrestling maneuver my father had taught me. I squirmed on my back, trying to wiggle away, but Louie shoved his forearm into my neck, pinning me like an insect. I couldn't breathe, and for a moment, was convinced I would suffocate—but not without being tortured first. In his free hand, he dangled the sewing needle above my right eye, so close that my left eye couldn't determine the needle's distance. It floated in and out of focus. I squeezed my right eye shut but tears leaked out. Louie's breath came in warm, foul spurts.

"You know what your face looks like?" he said.

"Fuck you!"

"A bunch of squashed snails."

I felt the tip of his needle pressing against my eyelid. I heard Mrs. Gutierrez's voice in my head, reciting the Twenty-Third Psalm. The valley of the shadow of death flashed before me in brilliant neon, and I thought I was going to wet myself. But it was my stomach that revolted first. As my mouth sprang open, my digested ham sandwich sprayed Louie's face like a burst from a nozzle, a chunky varnish that clung to his forehead and eyes.

"Son of a bitch," he hissed. He jumped off me, afraid to touch his face. I watched him run to the bathroom. I thought I no longer was in danger, yet the ceiling tiles were spinning crazily above me, and I was tumbling down a well, unable to break my fall, into watery blackness.

The pungent smell of hydrogen peroxide woke me. My eyes fluttered open and swam around the school nurse's office. She was swabbing a cotton ball over what felt like a lump on my neck. When she finished, she told me to close my eyes and rest. Ten minutes later, my father arrived and gave me the full story he'd gotten from the principal. Louie, half-blinded by my puke, had missed my eye but jabbed the needle into my neck. A teacher had found me that way passed out in the hallway, the end of the needle dangling as if from a voodoo doll. If Louie had pushed it in a little more, he said, it might have penetrated my carotid artery.

"You're lucky to be alive," my father emphasized as he drove us home, his hands squeezing the steering wheel, his voice held in tight control. "Mr. Freeze will be expelled for a month."

Whenever he called a student "Mr.," my father meant he should be treated as an adult. In my father's eyes, being fifteen didn't entitle anyone to special dispensation, not when it came to violence. "I think the police should get involved," he said. "Carrying a concealed weapon, assault and battery. . . ."

His gaze shifted to me. "What were you doing with those weights in your lunch box? They could be considered a weapon, too."

"He started it."

"That doesn't matter. This has been going on for some time between you two, hasn't it?"

"So what?"

"Why didn't you tell someone you were being harassed? Why didn't you tell me?"

"I can fight my own battles."

"Well, sorry to say the principal suspended you, too. Two weeks. That will give you time to think."

"Two weeks?" I was furious.

What upset me most was that Dad wasn't taking my side. I was being partly blamed for something that wasn't one ounce my fault. "I wish I'd killed him," I blurted out.

His eyes blazed at me. "What's happened to your common sense, Will? You have to keep a cool head about these things."

My father's silence dovetailed with mine as the Chevy pulled into the driveway. What did he want me to think about? If Louie attacked me again, I'd bludgeon him with a fifty-pound weight. Did I have to remind him about Darwin—survival of the fittest? I worked out in the garage for an hour, then stewed in my room about how badly I'd just gotten screwed.

At dinner, we flipped between politics and history and ended up talking about Hannah. My father missed her even more than he'd expected. He looked forward to her evening calls from Albuquerque, usually twice a week, stretching them out as long as possible. To an outside observer, my sister at seventeen had blossomed into a fully liberated adult. She had accepted that she wasn't the best dancer at the academy, and that a professional ballet career was unlikely. Instead, she was fully focused on academics now, and was applying to Harvard, Princeton, and Yale even though she knew we couldn't afford it if she didn't get a scholarship. But she'd taken a run at the SATs and scored 1580 out of 1600. Her grade point average in Santo Tomás had been 4.0, and though Albuquerque Prep was more challenging, it remained the same. Academically, she was No. 1 in her class.

After we washed the dishes, we waited for her to call, my father settling in his red chair. Then I heard something in the street. I peeked through the curtain and saw a shiny red restored Ford that I didn't recognize, with two people in the front seat. It stopped under the lamp on our side of the street, announcing its presence like a celebrity at a gala. The engine cut off, but the headlights stayed on.

"Shit," I whispered, as I heard the driver's door squeak open.

"What is it?" my father asked.

He levered himself out of his chair and looked over my shoulder. The great ape was standing on the sidewalk with his goofball friend Fred, another ninth grader. He wasn't usually a troublemaker, but you had the sense that under the right circumstances, Fred could blow like Mount Vesuvius. He had brought a baseball bat, and rested it on the hood of the car.

"Dad, that's Louie and his friend."

My father and I walked out on the porch together. "Can I help you?" he asked in a calm voice.

"You must be Mr. Ryder." Louie's hands were thrust into the front pockets of his jeans, as if anchoring himself to the sidewalk.

"And you must be Mr. Freeze."

"Yeah, that's my name. Don't wear it out," Louie said.

"I'm Fred," his friend announced, not wanting to be left out.

"Is that your car?" my father asked Louie.

"You like it?"

"Aren't you too young to have a driver's license?"

"Oh really? In Santo Tomás? News flash . . . no."

"You're right," my father said. "New Mexico is different."

"She's a beaut," Louie said, studying his car before turning his gaze to my face.

"What can we do for you this evening, Mr. Freeze?"

"Nothing really. We just came to drop off some eggs."

His grin was pathetically stupid, I thought. On cue, out of their pockets poured a handful of round white missiles. Louie fired the first, which sailed over my shoulder and exploded against our door. Fred, with a windup like Sandy Koufax, hit a light fixture on the porch. Their brassy laughter rippled like something from a school bathroom.

I wanted to kill them. My father put a hand on my shoulder. "You should leave now," he said to Louie.

The great ape let loose with another heave, and this one hit my father's shoulder. The slimy yoke slid down his sleeve. Another missile struck just above his right eye. Suddenly, my father rushed toward Louie. It was like watching a war movie where one guy has had enough and decides to charge the machine gun nest.

"What are you going to do, old man?" Louie yelled, as if that would save him from the blur running toward him. "Maybe you should get snail face to help you. . . ."

Dad's punch landed on the bridge of his nose, knocking him back, but Louie didn't fall. Stunned, he came back with a roundhouse swing, but my father deflected it with an arm. Before Fred could figure out what to do, Dad grabbed his baseball bat off the hood.

"Now go," my father ordered, cocking the bat over his shoulder. The two thugs were undecided. "Get out of here," Dad told them again. They still didn't move.

He walked up to the windshield, stood there for five seconds—fair warning—and then swung the bat into the glass. Shards flew. Under the street lamp, I could see a ghastly hole, like a head had gone through the windshield. Louie's hands rose in the air, palms up, in a stunned are-you-kidding-me gesture.

"Are you leaving now?" my father asked.

"I'm not scared of you," Louie replied, but it was mostly to impress Fred.

My father sauntered over to the driver's side headlight, positioned himself, and with one blow, it went dark.

"Son of a bitch!" Louie yelled.

Taking several swings, my father hacked off the driver's side mirror.

Louie charged. My father pulled the bat back. Like a horse spotting a rattlesnake, the ape skidded to a halt inches away from him.

He did his best to stare Dad down, but there was no way he could win. My father would demolish the whole car if he had to—and Louie with it, I thought. Louie circled warily to the driver's side. Fred gave my father an even wider berth.

"I'm keeping the bat," my father told them.

He rejoined me on the porch. Louie thrust his arm out the window and up, so we could see his raised middle finger, and then we watched the tires peel away.

I looked at my father with amazement, and not just for his physical prowess. "So," I said, "what was that lecture you gave me? The one about keeping a cool head and using common sense?"

He was caught flat-footed but quickly found a way to deny his hypocrisy. "Haven't you heard? For every rule, there's an exception."

When Hannah called half an hour later, my father didn't mention the evening's excitement. He didn't know whether to be proud or ashamed of himself, or what kind of example he was setting for me. I listened to their amiable conversation about teachers, exams, and intramural sports, and then my sister mentioned something that made my father sit up in his chair.

"Come again," he said as if he hadn't heard right. Hannah talked for another minute. My father cleared his throat. "Honey, we were expecting you for Thanksgiving, Christmas, too."

I edged closer so I could hear Hannah's voice. She wasn't coming for either holiday. She had a boyfriend, a serious boyfriend, and she'd been invited to his house in Albuquerque. "Dad, I'm really sorry I can't be with you and Will."

"What's his name?" my father asked.

"David Maclean. He's a really terrific guy, Dad. We've been together almost since we met."

"Well, when do you think you'll be home?"

"I can't say for sure. Soon. I'm sorry," she apologized again.

My father sighed, concealing his real feelings. "Don't worry about it, sweetie. Santo Tomás will always be here."

The subject changed, and they talked for another twenty minutes, but I could tell Dad was digesting his disappointment. Afterward, he put on some Mozart and read from Finnegans Wake before drifting asleep in the chair. I had to wake him to say I was going to bed.

The day I returned to school after my suspension, I was sure I would be known as the coward of Edward Chavez Junior High. I was also sure Louie Freeze would launch another assault against me when his suspension was over, but he kept a wary distance, as if my father had made a lasting impression on him. Instead, I began hearing whispers about my courage. I had underestimated how much everyone disliked a bully. Almost overnight, I went from outcast to being invited to sit with new friends in the cafeteria and pal around with them after school.

I treaded carefully around my new popularity, fearing it would vanish. Every day, however, brought little surprises. Girls talked to me. Volunteering in class became easier. People found that I had a sense of humor. When my grades picked up, my pleased father bought me a new racing bike. Yet I already had my biggest reward: I had become part of a crowd. As my confidence grew, in my own strange way, I began to think of myself as a garden flower. I would make color sketches of cosmos, marigolds, and irises, and pin them over my bed to admire. I imagined I soaked up water and sun until I finally unfolded my beauty to the world. Walking down the hall or eating in the cafeteria, I wondered, beyond my defiance of Louie Freeze, what people really thought of me. What did they see behind my disfigurement? Did they see the flower? Did they realize how much I was just like them, that I craved their friendship and envied their normal looks?

One afternoon, waiting for my father to pick me up, I parked myself in the bleachers of the athletic field, huddled over a math book, pretending to do homework. The football team was scrimmaging. Closer in was the cheerleading squad, eight girls whose hourglass figures and flat bellies riveted me as they moved and jumped, their pompoms rippling in the air like chords of music, like Sirens calling out to passing ships. I fantasized about them a lot, especially their smiles. The smiles seemed to come out of nowhere, an explosion of brilliant white teeth, their lips pushing up, light tumbling out from behind their eyes.

Whenever I tried to smile, it was constricted by scar tissue and damaged muscles around my mouth. At best, the ends of my lips rose slightly—I looked like a hooked fish—but it was enough to let someone know I wanted to be friendly. Yet my mouth could never achieve what came so effortlessly to others. I remembered my early baby pictures, where my smile was wider than Hannah's. Now it took a great effort to achieve one-tenth of the result. I could never appear as happy as I sometimes felt. I wondered if people thought I didn't have all the emotions they did, just because my face refused to register them.

Glancing up from my book, I was mesmerized by the rhythm and spontaneity of eight girls I never had the courage to talk to. They were on their own pedestal, higher than my friends. Their inaccessibility was what made them most alluring. When their practice was over, they dispersed in unison toward the gym, gamboling over the grass like horses. I followed at a safe distance, heading toward a drinking fountain. I took a gulp of water, and cautiously made my way to the side of the cement bunker that was the girls' locker room. I stepped up on a bench, and stared through a partly open window. I knew how reckless and stupid it was. At any moment, someone would spot me, call a teacher, and I'd be taken to the principal's office. Expelled from school again, only this time I'd be labeled a pervert, too. I would lose the acceptance I'd gained, and I would never get it back.

Yet no amount of fear could make me turn away from what I was seeing—two cheerleaders, fully dressed, facing each other in the locker room. A blonde with an almond-shaped face had a small brush in her hand. She dabbed it into a shallow container of cakey powder. The two were giggling and fidgeting, until they suddenly turned serious. The blonde carefully spread the powder over her friend's cheeks and under her eyes. Her brushwork was delicate and instinctive. When she was done, she reached into her locker for a small vinyl bag, unzipping it to reveal a collection of foundations, creams, glosses, blushes, lipsticks—and began to work in earnest. Her hand moved with a grace as precise and intuitive as an artist's. I thought girls were already beautiful without make-up, but I saw there was no limit to transformation. There was no such thing as being too beautiful.

Without warning, more girls burst into the room, animated, talking a thousand words a minute. Startled, I jumped off the bench. No one had seen me. I skirted through the faculty parking lot to the street. I had tempted fate and gotten away with it. When my father pulled up in the Chevy, I knew better than to tell him of the jeopardy I had placed myself in. There would be no end to his lecture. What I was less sure of was whether I had learned a lesson or would be tempted to be so reckless again.

As Christmas approached, knowing Hannah wasn't coming home, my father and I were like two shipwrecked strangers on a deserted island. We were growing tired of each other's company. After a gloomy Thanksgiving weeks earlier—the highlight a telephone call from Hannah—I began to think of resuming my old duty of cheering up my father. The idea of a spectacular Christmas dinner entered my head. I had seen enough cooking shows to give me confidence, and when I mentioned it to my father, he thought it was a great suggestion and anointed me as his chief kitchen assistant.

Then he surprised me with an idea of his own. He wanted to invite a half-dozen people from the Santo Tomás homeless shelter. My father always talked about bringing the haves and have-nots of the world together. Now we were actually thinking of doing it.

"How do we know who to invite?" I asked the day before Christmas. We were in the midst of adding two card tables at the end of our dining table, and putting down place mats and settings for eight. A bed sheet was our tablecloth.

"I called the shelter director. We show up Christmas around one, pick out six folks, drive them to our house, and return them a few hours later. There are a few don'ts. No liquor, no money or gifts, no bringing everyone back after dark. . . ."

"OK," I said, wanting to be agreeable, but I still had questions. There were over two hundred people at the shelter; did my father want a few down-on-their-luck college grads he could have an intellectual conversation with, or to choose from those whom life had hit the hardest? Did hygiene, gender, and appearance have anything to do with our selections? What about drug users and the mentally unbalanced? If you picked a crazy person and things got out of control, then what?

My father suggested I was inventing problems. We were being Good Samaritans for half a day, and all we needed to be were gracious hosts. He and I talked about the menu and decided on a twenty-pound roasted turkey and a honey-and-sugar-glazed ham. For an appetizer, we would have miniature wieners on toothpicks. Then we'd roll out sliced oranges topped with cranberry slices; a salad; potatoes au gratin; string beans soaked in butter; and for dessert, a choice of pumpkin, pecan, or lemon meringue pie. No one was going to leave hungry.

Christmas Day, the sky was a glaze of pastel blues and battleship grays, pushing down on the horizon like the lid on a box. By the time we reached the shelter, a steady drizzle had begun that would last the rest of the day. The building had been a luxury hotel in the '30s, during the town's brief mining boom, but things had deteriorated. In the cavernous, poorly heated lobby, the gilded chandeliers had mostly burned-out bulbs. A "welcome desk" where hotel guests had once checked in was scarred by mysterious gashes and a dozen bullet holes. The tongue-and-groove flooring had enough missing planks to suspect that some had become smoke and ash in the mammoth fireplace. The subdued flames weren't throwing out much heat that afternoon. Almost everyone was wearing a jacket or coat. Some people hovered by a television; others read magazines. A few drifted outside to smoke a cigarette.

Three or four families were on a similar mission to ours, waiting to pick up some of the unfortunate and forgotten. A middle-aged man with a scruffy beard approached my father. He needed a hot shower, I thought, as much as a rib-sticking meal.

"What's on the menu today?" he asked pleasantly, as if ordering at a restaurant.

"Well, it's Christmas," my father said. "Turkey with stuffing, ham, potatoes, string beans, pecan and pumpkin pie. . . ."

"Will there be fried chicken?"

"No," my father said.

The man approached another family and asked the same questions. When the wife answered yes, they were serving fried chicken, he stuck with them.

We picked three men and three women, pretty much at random.

Every other family chose just a single holiday guest. Maybe the shelter was largely a home of shy or suspicious loners, because no one in our group seemed to know any of the others well. My father squeezed four people into the back seat, while the last two snuggled into the cargo bay, half lying down. To entertain everyone, I turned on the radio. I peeked continually in the rear view mirror. Sometimes I saw glances sneaked back at my face, but I didn't feel any judgment, no more than I was judging them. Just as I was making new friends at school, I imagined, under different circumstances, I could be a friend of anyone here.

"Where's everybody from?" my father asked over the squawking on the radio. Voices rang out reluctantly, like school kids answering roll call: Austin, Los Angeles, Baltimore, Denver, New Orleans, Albuquerque. With more prodding, first names followed: Laurie, Gloria, James, Frank, Michael, Amy. I could tell my father was tempted to ask how everyone had ended up in Santo Tomás, but he launched instead into his own biography. I didn't mind hearing it again: the two-thousand-mile trip from New York by U-Haul, he and my mother on their quest to find their destinies. Like an exotic vine, they had planted themselves in the arid, dusty clime of southern New Mexico, one seeking nourishment from teaching, the other from painting. He'd been genuinely happy then.

As we parked in front of our house, the guests surveyed the neighborhood's small, proud homes. My father had outlined our front door in blinking red lights. Inside, the aroma of turkey and ham wafted from the kitchen. Everyone gathered in the living room. Unlike at the shelter, we enjoyed a fireplace with a good draw, and my father had filled the hearth with dry piñon logs. When he put a match to the kindling, it ignited instantly.

As I brought out the miniature franks, my father put on Bach's Christmas Oratorio. The organ's rich bass and treble made our furniture vibrate. Thunderstruck, everyone stopped eating for a moment. I knew the composition well; we played it every Christmas. It was a lot of Bach for one sitting, six parts running over three hours. To my father, though, nothing seemed excessive at Christmas. He sat at Hannah's piano and began pounding out chords to shadow the great composer's notes. His voice trilled like he was on stage at the Met. I had never been out of New Mexico, but from my father's stories, I could visualize New York's landmarks: the Met, the Museum of Modern Art, Madison Square Garden, Central Park, the Empire State Building.

*Wie soll ich dich empfangen,*
*Und wie begegn' ich dir?*
*O allei Welt Verlangen,*
*O meiner Seelen Zier!*

My father's German was nearly flawless. But though his voice was no match for the tenor on the tape, for Santo Tomás, this was an impressive show.

*O Jesu, Jesu! setze*
*Mir selbst die Fackel bei,*
*Damit, was dich ergotze,*
*Mir kund und wissend sei.*

Our guests one by one gravitated to the piano, clustering around my father. Maybe they felt they owed their host some allegiance, or the music boosted their spirits as it did mine. Their efforts to hum along like a makeshift chorus pleased my father. In our house this Christmas, no one felt like a random stranger.

When Dad finished, it was time for me to bring out the food. Small talk peppered the air. Michael volunteered to carve the turkey. He was a small man with a deeply weathered face, and said he'd worked in restaurants when he was younger. With sure, steady strokes, he sliced the ham, too. We all filled our plates. My father, in his ebullient mood, suddenly jumped from the table and returned with two bottles of red wine.

I wanted to ask what he was doing. Had he forgotten the shelter's rules? He'd also put a $5 bill under everybody's plate, even mine. There was no stopping him. He was having too good a time, the best in years, as he filled everyone's glass with a Kendall-Jackson pinot noir. I was the only one sipping a Coke.

"A toast!" declared my father. "To the spirit of Jesus Christ and the humanity in us all!"

The irony that my father was an atheist, and had probably never toasted the Son of God before, was lost on our guests. They must have assumed they were breaking bread with a deeply religious man. Maybe they thought of him as Jesus feeding the poor. They all raised their glasses. Then everyone chimed in with his or her own speech.

Amy, thin and emaciated with tattoos scattered over her arms, became teary. "I don't care about my mother and father, to be honest. They aren't nice people. . ."

"That sucks," someone said.

". . .but I love my little sister, and I wish she was with me now."

She ran her hand through her short, punk hair, nervous what people would think of her confession.

"Where is your little sister?" my father asked, like a minister addressing his flock.

"In prison."

"Oh," he said, amid murmurs of sympathy from others.

"I hope she's out soon," he offered.

I raised my glass to Amy's sister.

Like in a gospel church, there was a chorus of amens, and several of us clapped when Amy sat down. Frank, the college student whose company my father no doubt coveted, and who had already finished one glass of wine, looked us in the eye. "You gentlemen have opened your home to us. I feel like we've always known each other. That is a wonderful thing."

There was more applause. I blushed. Did someone my age qualify as a gentleman? I didn't see why not. As we began to eat, there were more toasts to long lost friends and family, mentions of pasts torn apart by bad luck, bad timing, or bad judgment. My father put on more music, but it wasn't necessary; everyone was already in high spirits. By early evening, there was nothing left of the turkey or ham, nor the vegetables or salad, nor the pies. I counted five empty bottles of wine. My father stood one more time.

"I have a confession, too," he said.

Voices quieted. I turned down the music. My head twisted in surprise to a man who I knew preferred secrets and private musings to public announcements. Whether his courage had come from the wine or the comfort of being surrounded by grateful strangers, he was ready to get something off his chest. He stood erect, his large, sinewy hands on his hips, his eyes a little unfocused but determined.

"I once did something very foolish, very stupid," he said. "And I paid a great price for it."

Everyone was still, waiting, especially me.

"I was fifteen years old when a friend and I were overtaken by the urge to steal a car. We weren't drunk, weren't stoned, just two kids with authority issues. We spotted a Pontiac convertible in a supermarket lot, a real beauty. My friend knew how to hotwire an ignition switch. I drove the two of us out of town, speeding, with the glare of the sun bouncing off the windshield. We didn't have a care in the world. In an hour, we'd return the car and get away with our caper—that was the plan. I wasn't paying attention when a man on a bicycle shot out from a side street. I hit him square on. I knew he was dead even before I pulled over. Other cars stopped behind me. I don't know whether I would have run if there hadn't been witnesses—it's a question I can't answer to this day—but there were witnesses. . . ."

My father's eyes rested for a moment on the ebbing fire. He cleared his throat and continued.

"I was convicted of involuntary manslaughter and spent two and a half years in a juvenile correctional facility. Because I was a minor, court records were sealed. Except for people in Brattleboro, no one would ever know, I thought. I had a chance to believe my life hadn't been altered, that I could go back to being the same person I always was. But inside me, everything had changed, even if I didn't know it right away. The man whose life I had taken had a wife, two young children, and many friends."

My father took his seat as more amens and understanding nods filled the room. He had finished his confession, stunning me and raising a dozen questions in my mind. For a moment, I thought he was going to ask a jury of strangers to offer him forgiveness. But he just sat with his hands on his knees, gazing down at the table like some exhausted runner, surprised he had made it to the finish line. Letting him be, the rest of us joined to clear the table and wash dishes.

It was well after dark when my father and I squired our guests back to the beat-up hotel. Amy kissed me on the cheek and Frank shook my father's hand. Everyone waved good-bye. We had broken virtually every rule the shelter had given us and were all the happier for it, as were our guests. Every moment of the dinner had gone better than planned. There had been no surprises, except for my father's confession. That was a big exception. I suddenly couldn't think of anything else.

"You killed someone. You were locked up," I said quietly as we drove home, to be sure I had the facts. Now I understood why he'd never left Vermont until he was eighteen, and why there were no photos of him at sixteen or seventeen in his closet.

"What was it like?"

He took a few moments to answer. "I was in shock most of the first year. I thought how devastated my parents would be if I'd been the one killed. I wanted to make it up to the man's family. I wrote them letters—twenty, at least—but they didn't answer one. That bothered me almost as much as the vehicular manslaughter. When there's no forgiveness, guilt and remorse are your punishment.

"The second year, I reversed my thinking. I tried to pretend the accident never happened. I learned to box and wrestle and made friends. I finished my high school requirements with correspondence courses, and did well on my SATs. Without interviewing me, without knowing anything about my sentence, both Columbia and Princeton accepted me. If I could accomplish all that, I thought, why couldn't I make the past disappear?"

I heard a breath escape his lips. "Believe me, I tried." He looked at me. "It wasn't possible, not for me."

"You never told anyone? Not my mother or Hannah. . . ."

No, he said, just a few therapists over the years, and the six people tonight who we'd probably never see again. He wanted to keep it that way. I said I would never tell, not even Hannah. I was in shock but I believed his story. He had lied about never receiving a letter from my mother for a good reason, but there was no reason to lie about this. Killing someone would always haunt him.

"Why did you tell your story tonight?"

"Partly I drank too much. Partly everyone else was laying bare his soul. But mostly I did it for you, Will. I know you think that nothing could ever be worse than the fire. You have to feel sometimes that was the day your life ended. But your life can end more than once."

"Nothing worse is going to happen to me," I said, startled by his words.

"Just promise me you'll always be careful." He was searching over the steering wheel into a moonless night, as if for a star to wish on.

"OK. I promise."

I remembered my promise, too, not to contact my mother. I intended to keep both of them.

Despite the independence I was fighting for every day, I felt a closeness to my father that night that made us seem inseparable. I wasn't the only one who'd gotten a bad break in life. How could a father and son be any closer?

"Everybody tonight forgave you," I said. "I forgive you, too, for the fire, for everything."

He started to say something but caught himself. We were quiet the rest of the way home.

Winters in Santo Tomás rarely saw snow or frigid temperatures, but the sunless, bleached skies and cold-to-the-bone winds were spirit killing. The winds would sneak up from the Sierra Madre in Mexico, howl and moan for hours, die late in the night, then reappear with new vigor the next afternoon. A day hardly got started when it was ended by darkness. Neighbors would grow withdrawn if not outright sullen. We were all living in an Ingmar Bergman movie, my father said. He was a Bergman fan and liked to watch the Swedish director's films on our VCR. My father thought there was something to learn from family life in small, isolated hamlets—the director's metaphor, he said, for people trapped in themselves, despair and all. To me, the Swedes just didn't like each other. I wasn't fond of them either. They had a hard time with basic communication, simply getting words out, as if everyone had pebbles in his mouth.

I found it more interesting to think about my own life, which felt only slightly better than living in a forlorn Scandinavian village. After studying my image in the school bathroom in first grade, I had gone six years without deliberately glancing in another mirror, not even to comb my hair or brush my teeth. There was no point. I accepted that I was disfigured, and that people would stare at me. Until I was ten or eleven, I didn't mind the attention—I wanted to be noticed—and there was something more unusual than my face to occupy my thoughts. Not even my father or Hannah knew, but I could slip into fantasies so vivid that I couldn't fall asleep. A tree was a musical instrument, the ocean a skating rink, a skyscraper a hideout for aliens dressed as elevator operators. I laughed at my inventions, and when I put them on paper with a pencil or paint, I believed that they were created by the boy deep in the mirror, someone inside me—that was my special power.

After Louie's assault in the hallway, that power became harder to summon. My father's unexpected outburst had ended Louie's bullying, but he'd already done his damage. His sewing needle almost punctured an artery. To have told my father that nothing worse was going to happen was stupid. I was always aware of my vulnerability. The fear pushed away my confidence. I knew something was missing whenever I picked up a paintbrush. Images in my head began to strike me as forgeries; they had no energy or excitement because they didn't belong to me. Every painting that I finished I tore out of my pad and folded into quarters, eighths, sixteenths, and then into bright specks of confetti. I returned to studying myself in mirrors, beholding the creature from the Black Lagoon. It made me sick.

"I don't want to be an artist anymore," I told my father one late January evening. "I stink at it." We were sitting across from one another, my father on the couch, absorbed in a book. I was slouched in the red club chair, the one he usually occupied. He cocked his head toward me. I could hear the wind rustling trees in the yard.

"What brings this on, champ?"

My shoulders shrugged. I didn't want to mention Louie Freeze. I was ashamed that one person could have such power over me. I was ashamed of being weak, and that I couldn't control my fears. But I wasn't focused just on the problem. There was a solution. I had become convinced of the path out of my misery.

"I want another operation," I said.

Ten years ago, in the burn unit of an Albuquerque hospital, the surgeons had done their best for a three-year-old with third-degree burns over seventy percent of his face. Altogether there were five operations. The fire had not touched my body below my neck, except for small patches on my hands. Now the facial scars had matured, and reconstructive surgery was not only possible, the doctor said on my last visit, but with better grafting technology "beneficial results are probable." I wouldn't be transformed into a movie star, but anything would be an improvement.

"Things are OK at school?" my father asked, ignoring what I'd said. "Is someone picking on you? Mr. Freeze?"

"No."

"Your friends are still friends?"

"Yes."

"So what is it?"

I wondered why he couldn't accept what was obvious to me. "What is it? I don't want to go through life looking like an alien. I want to be normal!" I couldn't stop my voice from rising. I expected my father to argue that an operation would be impossible because we didn't have the money. He had borrowed from relatives for the rounds of elective surgery and only recently finished paying them back.

He asked if I'd talked to Hannah about an operation.

"Why should I? This is my decision."

"You've always valued your sister's opinion."

"I'm old enough to make up my own mind."

"Even if the doctors do their best, you're still going to look different," he pointed out.

I was ready to blow. "Then I'll have another operation—and another—until I'm perfect." All I could think of were the cheerleaders, their impeccable, faultless, magical smiles.

"You'll be disappointed, Will. The only paradise," he said, as if he knew everything, "is paradise lost."

Another literary reference, I thought—that's all the world needed! I gave him a curt "good night" and marched to my room, slamming the door for good measure. Did he think he always knew what was best for me? A dam inside me began to crumble, and a deluge of frustration swept me out to sea. After our dinner for the homeless, I had felt a closeness to my father that I was sure nothing could ever breach. I would have made any sacrifice, borne any pain, followed any instruction he gave me. But then the dam broke, and nothing was the same for a long while.

I began to have difficulty looking him in the eye, let alone carrying on a conversation. Did we really have to discuss current events every night? He was getting older, too set in his ways, and locked into the small universe of Santo Tomás. Besides wanting a productive future for Hannah and me, the dream that kept him alive was to be taken seriously as a Joyce scholar. He would spend months on an article, send it off to a literary magazine, and wait another month or two for a reply, usually a rejection. He repeated the process with infinite stubbornness. I thought it showed his vanity, and I hinted that maybe he should think about giving up.

My father took my new lack of respect in stride. We silently acknowledged that living under the same roof didn't have to be pleasant, only civil. We were like a pair astronauts on a trip to the moon, where duty required a certain amount of coordination and cooperation but nothing more. I sometimes wished I could escape and visit my grandparents. But after my mother sailed her ship from our harbor, my father told me that his communication with his in-laws, which was never good, became nonexistent. His own parents were recluses and expressed interest in Hannah and me only by sending Christmas cards. I was marooned in Santa Tomas.

In February, Hannah came down for the Presidents' Day weekend. It was her first visit in six months. Entering the front door, her boyfriend carried their suitcases and walked a step behind her. "Hi, I'm David," he said. Dad and I both shook his hand vigorously, wanting him to know he was welcome. He made eye contact without staring at my face. Then we gave Hannah big hugs. She was an inch or two taller than when she'd left in August, and her blonde hair was no longer in a ponytail but cascaded to her shoulders. Her gold-blue eyes sparkled, and her complexion was flawless, elevating her from merely cute to beautiful. As my father brought out coffee and soda for everyone, my sister told us she had just been accepted to Yale. It had been disappointing to realize that the dance career she hoped for would never happen, but she'd taken it in stride. My father beamed at her mention of Yale. He was proud of both of us, but I was convinced in my disgruntled state that he lived through my sister. She was the star. Hannah was going to achieve the professional success that had eluded him.

David was a tall, floppy-haired young man with a farm boy face and quick smile, someone whose upbeat personality would disqualify him for Swedish citizenship. Nestled together on the couch, he and Hannah seemed to stop whatever they were doing every thirty seconds to kiss. While my father suspected they were already sleeping together, something old-fashioned in him insisted David share my room. For a while, I couldn't determine what made Hannah and him an item, besides physical attraction. He was the same age as my sister but hardly more mature, and no match for her brains or ambition. When we talked about colleges, he said he planned to attend the University of Colorado at Boulder. He played soccer, along with serious bridge, but admitted to being pretty much average in everything. He was nevertheless thoughtful, sincere, and well meaning, and he owned a great laugh. Years later, I would understand his deeper connection to Hannah. He didn't want to compete with her. She was the talent, and he was the support.

"Hannah tells me you're a talented artist," David said from a sleeping bag on my floor that night. His tone was without a speck of doubt, as if every word his girlfriend breathed was true.

"You must be thinking of someone else," I answered.

"What do you mean?"

"When it comes to painting, I'm an impostor."

He smiled, ignoring my pretentious air. "Maybe you can show me some of your work in the morning." He suddenly reached from the sleeping bag to his satchel, and wrestled out a thick, heavy book with Michelangelo's Sistine Chapel ceiling on its cover. "I'm taking an art appreciation class this semester," he said. "I love it."

"Suit yourself. There are some paintings in my desk. I haven't done anything new in a while.

"How did you get to know Hannah?" I thought to ask.

"We met at a social the first week of school. Then we took a French class together. Parlez-vous français?" He laughed good-naturedly. David might have come across as a nerd if his sincerity hadn't made him so likable. He wasn't trying to be anyone but himself.

"You like living in New Mexico?" he asked.

"In Santo Tomás? I think I've outgrown it."

"Ever thought about living in the ocean?"

"I'm not a fish."

"On a boat, I mean."

"Then you mean on the ocean."

"No, in the ocean. A boat is in the ocean, and not just because its hull is partly underwater. It's in the ocean because, when you think about it, we're all in the solar system. So we're in everything. Everyone says on. It should be in."

"You have an interesting mind," I said.

"You think so?" He seemed pleased by what he took as a compliment. I had almost said "weird." If I had, I don't think it would have bothered him. I asked how he ended up at Prep.

"Mom's in Denver. Dad works for the lab in Albuquerque. He's a physicist, so here I am."

"What are you going to study in college?"

"If they'd give me a degree for it, I'd buy a boat and sail around the world."

In the world, I wanted to correct him. "Do you mind?" I asked, reaching down and picking up his art book.

I began leafing through the pictures. I'd heard of most of the artists, but some were unfamiliar. Almost all the paintings were striking: Raphael, Titian, Fra Angelica, Botticelli, Caravaggio, Goya, El Greco, Vermeer, Rembrandt, van Eyck, Da Vinci. I paused on an image from a seventeenth-century painter named Jacob Jordaens. A nearly naked man was chained upside down on a slab of rock while a giant eagle was eating what looked like his intestines.

"Who's that?" I asked, cringing.

"Prometheus. According to Greek mythology, Prometheus stole fire from Zeus and gave it to humankind. Zeus was very pissed. He had Prometheus bound to a rock and sent the eagle to pluck out his liver every day. Prometheus's liver regenerated every night, so the bird had a fresh meal in the morning. That went on for a long time."

"Zeus was an asshole," I decided. I couldn't stop staring at the picture, any more than I could stop my feelings of revulsion.

"He was cruel and tyrannical sometimes, but other times, he was exceedingly generous. That was part of his power. He kept you guessing. Was he a tormentor or liberator?"

According to one myth, David added, Prometheus ultimately broke free of his chains. "Shelley wrote a play called *Prometheus Unbound*. It was about the power of the individual to overcome any obstacle."

In addition to his sincerity and quirky humor, I liked David because he didn't talk down to me. We chatted about anything—John Wayne movies, weather patterns in Antarctica, the Westminster dog show. Like my father, he read lots of books. When I drifted off to sleep, he was still talking.

In the morning, as I opened my eyes, David was dressed and had a dozen of my pictures spread around him.

"You're only thirteen?" he asked in his perky voice. I stared at him from my bed, still groggy. "Where did you learn to paint like this?"

I had taken a night class at the community college, but otherwise, I explained, I'd just learned from art magazines and studying paintings in library books. There were no art classes in junior high, and there wouldn't be any in high school either. Santo Tomás, as Hannah knew, was not an incubator of creativity. But it hardly mattered. I told David that I'd peaked in fifth or sixth grade.

"Oh, don't say that," he advised sternly, studying my paintings again. It was as if I'd threatened to jump off a bridge to my death. "Do you know how lucky you are? To see the world through your eyes. . . ."

"All I see is a bunch of crazy shit that wouldn't interest anyone else."

"You're really wrong about that. It's how you see it that's so interesting."

"If you say so." I wasn't sure what he was talking about.

The three-day weekend whizzed by. Both athletic, Hannah and David took a three-mile run before breakfast every day, and on Sunday, she insisted that my father and I join them on Santo Tomás's only public golf course. David's graceful swing and long arms reminded me of a condor taking off. I shot eighty-six for nine holes—not bad for a first timer, everyone consoled me. I sat out the back nine and ate ice cream. My father, who had played many years ago before I was born, analyzed his every stroke as if he might turn pro one day. Hannah, emotionless whether she hit a good shot or bad, was also a beginner but played better than I did. When we got home, I announced to the world that I was retiring from the sport.

Hannah asked me to walk around the neighborhood with her. We traded stories, trying to feel close again, yet not quite getting there.

"When are you coming home again?" I asked.

"This summer."

"For how long?"

"I don't know. It depends."

I reminded her that she'd promised last fall to visit us regularly, and without fail for Thanksgiving and Christmas.

"What can I say, Will? I got involved with David. Things happen. Wait till you fall in love with someone."

I was silent. I had as much confidence in that happening as my becoming a nuclear physicist. It wasn't that I didn't want to fall in love. I just had no idea who would fall in love with me.

"I understand you want to have surgery," she went on in a casual tone. I could tell she was going to make the same point as Dad.

"So?" I said defensively. "What's wrong with that?"

"I know you've been through a lot, Will, but if I were you, I'd concentrate more on what you love to do than what you look like."

"I don't love doing anything right now. And you're not me."

She put her arm around my shoulder, but I pulled away. I doubted that my sister had experienced anything but the most minor setbacks. Maybe she hadn't succeeded at becoming a professional ballerina, but everything else had been a cakewalk. Who was she to preach?

A few hours later, Hannah and I said our good-byes. My father and David had been talking about some obscure Roman emperors, hitting it off rather well. I felt sad that Hannah was leaving but only for a moment. A voice warned me not to get too excited about when she would be home again. I couldn't count on it. I gave her a kiss on the cheek, and shook David's hand. No matter how much I loved my sister, Hannah's influence over me had been thinned by time and distance.

It was a Friday afternoon, my last week of ninth grade, when an unexpected letter arrived in our mailbox. I pulled it out of the usual batch of bills and flyers. My mother's name and return address were printed neatly in the upper left-hand corner. It was addressed to me.

My stomach churned. I hadn't tried to contact her since my letter to the Leo Castelli Gallery three years earlier. After what I found under my father's bed, I had no intention of ever seeing her. Occasionally, though, like a ghost with a will of its own, she would stray into my thoughts. I'd wonder about her career or where she was living or, despite the pain her words had caused, if she ever thought about me. The ghost came unexpectedly, but I refused to let it stay for long. I banished it into exile, where the unrepentant and unforgiven belonged.

I took the envelope to my room and studied it. My father wasn't home. Part of me wanted to rip it into small pieces, into confetti like my paintings. The other part was roiled by curiosity—why was my mother writing? I left the letter on my desk, ate an apple in the kitchen, and returned with the hope it had somehow disappeared. I'd promised not to contact my mother, but who could have anticipated that she would write me? She had promised my father she wouldn't. Her tone had been emphatic. Was there something urgent?

I opened the envelope. A color photo clipped to an article from the *New York Times* spilled out. It said my mother was extremely busy with one-woman shows in Copenhagen, Berlin, London, New York, and Los Angeles. She lived in a duplex in Soho, a Manhattan neighborhood famous for artists. Her paintings had begun to sell for serious money. In the accompanying photo, she wore a pair of jeans with a sequined top, surrounded by people in tuxedos. "From Berlin opening" was written on the back, presumably in my mother's hand. She looked tallish, wafer thin, her brunette hair in bangs. She was unsmiling and had an air of mystery. Was she bored, preoccupied, or just possibly, even for a second, thinking of the life she'd left behind in New Mexico?

A letter was folded and pressed against the inside of the envelope.

*May 23, 1993*

*Dear Will,*

*I hope this greeting finds you well. A woman named Lucy came to my opening in Manhattan last week, and in our conversation we stumbled on the fact that her son, David, is Hannah's boyfriend. She spoke of Hannah's many achievements, which of course I had no idea. My daughter seems to be a serious student with ambition. Lucy also said David had been to Santo Tomás, slept overnight in your room, and admired your paintings. What a pleasant surprise to learn that you're an artist. I want to meet you after all these years. Please bring along some of your work. I'm in Phoenix in two weeks for my new opening. Enclosed is a round trip plane ticket from Santo Tomás. You'll fly through Albuquerque. The hotel is the Four Seasons, in downtown Phoenix. Take a taxi. Tell Hannah and your father hello.*

*Your mother*

The letter seemed written by a different person than the one under my father's bed. Her tone was breezy and matter of fact, friendly, not hostile. Yet I felt a formality if not deliberate distance behind her words. We were related by blood, but our only connection seemed to be art. In addition to the plane ticket, five crisp twenty-dollar bills were in the letter, presumably for my expenses.

When my father came home, I showed him the letter. I told him it had arrived out of the blue.

"Well," he said, reading it unhappily, "I always knew this day would come."

He handed it back and dropped in his chair, like someone had pushed him down. "I know your mother. What wonderful timing," he quipped.

"What do you mean?"

"I'm not sure what I mean, only that she chose this moment for a reason. I'm sure of that. She's a master of timing." He tapped his hand on the arm of the chair, elevating his eyes to the ceiling, as if there was another message there. When his gaze shifted back to me, he said, "After she left us, I wrote to ask that she not contact you or Hannah or me ever again. She promised she wouldn't. She agreed that I would have custody of both you and Hannah. . . ."

I didn't mention that I already knew. I sensed that my mother's breaking her word was deeply upsetting to him, but not as much as what her invitation represented.

"You'd be wasting your breath if you told Hannah that she wrote you," he said.

"I know, she couldn't care less."

"And you?" he said. "You want to see her?"

"I don't know."

"You promised me you'd wait until you were older."

"I'm fifteen."

"You're still a minor."

"OK," I said sullenly, "if you're going to pull rank. . . ."

"It would be a mistake, Will. You'd be putting yourself in danger."

He sat there stewing, unable to describe what danger I might be headed for. But I felt it, too. I could never forget the harshness of her first letter, and my response to stay far away from her. Yet part of me was too curious not to consider her invitation. She wanted to see my work.

"What would it hurt to meet her? She's a famous artist."

"You said you've given up on your art."

"Even so, I've never been to an opening. Wouldn't that be cool?"

We let it go, but the subject came up again at dinner. Despite my mixed feelings, it became clear to both of us that I wanted to go. My father was quiet for a while before reluctantly giving his consent—on one condition.

"Before you pack your bag, we need to visit with Dr. Glaspell," he said.

"Why?"

"There's something you don't know about the fire."

"Then tell me. Why do we have to see Dr. Glaspell?"

"Because this isn't easy for me. It's best that someone guides our conversation."

"That makes no sense to me."

"You'll see. Otherwise, no trip to Phoenix."

Over the years, whenever adjusting to the real world became a problem, my father had whisked me off to Dr. Glaspell. In addition to teaching at the university, he had his own practice. I'd had maybe two dozen sessions in ten years. When I first started junior high, I'd become so freaked out about people staring at me that we discussed whether I should wear a simple mask every day. My father said that would only bring even more attention and speculation. People would imagine that I looked far worse than I really did. Dr. Glaspell agreed, and I gave up on the idea.

Whenever we met, Dr. Glaspell's expensive gold pen would skate over his notebook pages, recording everything I said without his once looking down. How he kept his handwriting legible was a neat trick; so was his diagnosis of my insecurities. Because of the fire, he said, I was suffering from post-traumatic stress disorder, as well as other neuropsychological symptoms, such as eye and shoulder tics that came and went. He said my fantasy life was compensation for being unable to accept what had happened to my face. I should get used to living with bouts of anxiety, he added, but he was always ready to write a prescription. My father discouraged that, though; he didn't want me dependent on medication, and hoped that with enough love and support from Hannah and himself, I would largely outgrow my trauma.

What unsettled me most about Dr. Glaspell was not his quick and certain diagnoses but a simple question he asked more than once: What do you remember about the fire, Will? He had first inquired when I was six or seven, and I'd told him the truth. I didn't remember anything. He asked again a year later, and a third time, too. He wanted to prod my memory, he explained, because if I ever had clear recall of the event, reliving everything that had happened, I might, with his guidance, be freed of my negative emotions. He promised to help me the whole way. Family support was only half the cure; therapeutic intervention was the other half. It sounded to me like he was planning an exorcism.

One night in my room, closing my eyes to fall asleep, I finally did remember the fire, sort of. The images fell into my consciousness, pressing down so hard that they hurt. I saw myself lying on my back in a small bed, approached by an army of orange and yellow flames. I wasn't sure if I was remembering or imagining, but I began to recall a crackling sound, like the floor was giving way beneath me. I also smelled candle wax. A wave of heat washed over me, like a wind coming off the desert. I was too afraid to move, paralyzed by fear. I began to cry, hoping someone would hear me. Nothing seemed to happen for the longest time. Then the smoke rose to blot out the window light, stung my eyes, and filled my throat so I could no longer cry. That was all I remembered.

My father and I were at Dr. Glaspell's office the next afternoon. Like my parents, the psychologist was one of those displaced Anglos who had landed in Santo Tomás because he didn't fit anywhere else, I guessed, except perhaps late nineteenth-century Vienna with Sigmund Freud. His thick-rimmed glasses perfectly fit a round, seamless face, and a bow tie was usually clipped to his starched shirt. Keeping in character, he'd furnished his office with expensive-looking antiques.

My father sat across from me while Dr. Glaspell began running his gold pen across his notebook, his eyes jumping between the two of us as if to ask who wanted to speak first. There were no takers.

"What we're going to talk about this afternoon, Will," Dr. Glaspell began, "requires your full attention. It's important that you understand the facts. Because other family members may try to tell you differently."

"You mean my mother."

"Correct."

My father rose to his full height and began to pace, choosing his words more carefully than usual. Maybe he'd rehearsed. I was sitting on a straight-back couch, legs dangling out. My finger plucked at a button on the couch. Blood was rushing through my ears. I realized my father was talking and I hadn't heard half his words.

"Wait. Start over," I said.

He nodded and began again. "The morning of the fire, I had left early for the university. Summers, I always taught a morning class. Susan was at home. You were in your room, asleep, and she was in the living room, more or less passed out on the couch. According to a neighbor who was walking her dog, the fire was burning in your bedroom around 10:20 a.m. Your mother had been drinking and smoking pot that morning. Blood tests confirmed it. She'd been acting depressed for over a year. We had talked about getting her help, including with Dr. Glaspell. But Susan always refused. No one could tell her what to do.

"After I left the house, before your mother passed out, she placed a dozen votive candles around your room. She made a shrine to you. You were an angel who had come to bring joy to the world. That's what she told the police afterwards."

"There were candles?" As I recalled the smell of burning wax, a pain in my stomach appeared out of nowhere. I thought of slipping out of Dr. Glaspell's office and never returning.

"One candle was placed next to the wall heater. The neighbor told the fire department she didn't hear an explosion, but suddenly, flames were climbing up the draperies, and smoke began to fill the bedroom. Your mom had a chance to rescue you but didn't. After that, the fire spread quickly. The neighbor rushed in. She pulled you out of bed, burning her hands to do it. Another minute, it would have been too late for everyone. Your mother was so stoned she barely got out herself. A quarter of the house was gone by the time the fire department finished."

I was numb as I tried to visualize the details, like the scene was a painting. What was the neighbor wearing when she rushed in? Was my mother face down or up on the couch? Did she wake herself, or did the neighbor rescue her, too? My father looked anxious when his eyes fell on me, as if reliving the event had rekindled both his anger at my mother and his own guilt.

Dr. Glaspell cleared his throat, bringing me out of my trance. "Are you all right, Will? Whatever your feelings toward your mother, whatever questions you have, this is a good time to speak up." His gold pen had stopped for the moment, waiting for me to propel it forward. I think he hoped I would tell him that I suddenly remembered everything, and it was what my father had described. Then the healing could begin.

"Hannah doesn't know any of this?" I looked at my father.

He shook his head. "I kept the truth from her, too. But I'm going to tell her now."

"What happened after the fire?"

"The district attorney wanted to bring criminal negligence charges against Susan. I hired a lawyer. The last thing I wanted was for you and Hannah, let alone the whole world, to know what your mother had done. My lawyer and I insisted that the candles were not really relevant, that gas from the old, leaky heater had ignited spontaneously. The D.A. finally dropped the case."

I knew what my father was thinking. No matter what he'd told the district attorney, he had failed to fix the heater, and he believed the accident was mostly his fault. After being locked up for manslaughter, everything was his fault. If he felt he couldn't forgive himself, why should anyone, especially me, forgive my mother for her part?

"If you want my opinion, Will, I think your mother contacted you because of the fire," my father said.

"Twelve years later?"

"Guilt is a powerful thing."

"Good, then she'll apologize to me."

Dr. Glaspell differed. "Feeling guilty doesn't always mean you're sorry. It can mean you're bent on manipulating the victim, in order to make yourself feel better."

My father nodded. Dr. Glaspell, a buffer against both the past and future, encouraged me again to ask questions. I shook my head. I didn't want an exorcism. I felt too overwhelmed, too confused, too anxious to ask anything, except for a glass of water. Then I left for home with my father.

I stayed in my room the rest of the weekend. As Dr. Glaspell had probably warned my father, my numbness would wear off like an anesthetic, and no pain reliever would be up to the job. I refused to eat anything but sweets. If there was a morphine for anxiety and disbelief, it was ice cream and chocolate sauce. But sugar wore off, too. I kept seeing my mother stoned on the living room couch, oblivious to her child in the next room, to the fire, to the slightest notion of responsibility. She had abandoned me to my death. In my mind, I wrote her one angry, hateful letter after another. After snooping under my father's bed, I had merely wanted to put a distance between us. Now I imagined my mother tripping on a curb in front of an eighteen-wheeler, or a day when everybody stopped buying her paintings, she fell into obscurity, and no newspaper carried her obituary. When my father got around to telling Hannah the complete story, she would surely agree, or imagine even worse.

Dad suggested we visit Dr. Glaspell again, but I said no. I wasn't going to talk to anybody about this. The next day, I refused to attend my junior high graduation. As much as I wanted to see my friends, I was too agitated to say good-bye.

I had never been sure of the existence of God, but suddenly, I embraced atheism with the same cold-eyed certainty of my father. No God would allow what my mother had done to me. My conviction seemed rock solid for two or three days, then the ground suddenly shifted beneath me. There was a God, I corrected myself. My mother wasn't evil; I was. God was punishing me, though I didn't know for what. We were all sinners. I remembered the Bible verses Mrs. Gutierrez had me memorize. "This is for your salvation," she had said. If I needed saving, who or what was going to do it?

My father was certain my mother had a motive for her invitation, and it wasn't to save me. She was untrustworthy, he insisted. He warned how she was going to use me and abandon me all over again. I listened, but I had my own thoughts. She had written that she wanted to see my paintings. How manipulative was that? What if she were sincere? What if she thought I had talent?

It took several more days before I convinced myself to go, though with a new uncertainty that had nothing to do with my mother. In Santo Tomás, it felt like almost everyone knew or had heard of me, certainly my face. And with the comfort of familiarity, if you could call it that, my self-consciousness had diminished over time. To think of entering a huge new city unnerved me. I imagined feeling the glare of strangers' eyes like a thousand suns, and melting into a puddle of insecurity on a Phoenix sidewalk.

The day of my departure, my father eyed my bulging duffle in the hallway. The return trip was in three days, but I had packed enough clothes for a week. Though it looked obviously homemade, I'd also constructed a portfolio from the sides of two cardboard boxes to hold what I thought were my best drawings and paintings. My raincoat sat on top of the duffle. Even if rain was unlikely in the June desert, I wanted to be prepared for anything.

I was wearing a dark suit, white shirt and a blue paisley tie. My father had bought them for me last year to attend the memorial service for a university colleague. The jacket had grown tight in the shoulders and short in the sleeves, but wearing it made me feel mature. In a sophisticated city like Phoenix, I was sure most men wore suits.

My father gave me a bear hug at the airport, as if afraid my mother would kidnap me, or some other unnamed seduction awaited, and he might never see me again. Except to visit doctors in Albuquerque, I had never been out of Santo Tomás, never been on a plane, never been in a taxi, never slept in a hotel. I was a travel virgin. On my flight, an attendant offered me a Coke and peanuts, but I didn't touch them. I couldn't stop staring out my window. Soaring through cloud banks, I saw bodies in lumpy repose—souls wrapped in gossamer on their way to heaven. I wondered if their already-dead friends and relatives knew they were coming, and how the new arrivals would be greeted. Would old grievances be forgiven? Were there parties every night? Did they have art in heaven? The plane sailed higher, into an endless arc of pale sky.

At the Phoenix airport, except for a few businessmen who hurried past me, nobody was wearing a suit or even a sport coat. People stared at me in the taxi line. One woman asked if I was with the Greater Phoenix Mormon Mission; I don't know why. The cab took me downtown to the Four Seasons Hotel. One of my mother's crisp $20 bills covered the fare. A doorman loaded my duffle and portfolio onto a luggage cart while peppering me with questions about where I was from and what I thought of the weather, as if he wanted to be my friend. I didn't know about tipping, so I shook his hand and said thank you.

The lobby was spellbinding—glistening chandeliers, expensive furniture in deep, rich colors, crystal vases of exotic flowers. For a few moments, I dropped into one of the plush chairs, studying the beauty of the vast room. I had always wanted to go to Disneyland, but this place seemed just as magical.

"Welcome to the Four Seasons, sir," a man said when I approached the reception desk. At least someone else was wearing a suit and tie, though his looked more like a uniform. He held out a tray of small glasses with a fizzy amber solution.

"Thank you, but I don't drink alcohol," I said in a serious tone.

"This is non-alcoholic, sir."

"OK, thanks then." I took a sip to be sure I liked it, then gulped down the rest. I helped myself to a second glass before turning to the woman behind the desk. "I'm looking for Susan Olmsted. I believe she's expecting me."

She scanned her computer and pulled a room key from a drawer. "You're in room 734, Mr. Ryder. Ms. Olmsted is in 738, across the hall. Your luggage will be brought up. Is there anything else we can do for you?"

The last person to ask me that question was Mr. Cyrus, my third-grade teacher, after he'd cleaned up the mess I made in his supply closet. His tone had been sarcastic.

"I have my own room?" I said out loud. I don't know why I was surprised, but it felt like a special treat I didn't deserve.

"Yes, Mr. Ryder. The elevator bank is to your right."

I looked around the lobby and spotted a gleaming silver urn next to neatly stacked white cups. My father had never specifically discouraged me from drinking coffee, but all I ever had at home was fruit juice, soda, and water. "Can I help myself?" I asked her, nodding to the urn.

"Of course. Unless you'd like a fresh pot brought to your room."

At the coffee station, I filled my cup mostly with cream, added three teaspoons of sugar, and topped it off with coffee. I liked the taste. I liked the Four Seasons. No one looked at me funny. When people thought you were wealthy or important, I concluded, appearances didn't matter so much. In my room, I found a bowl of fruit festooned with a ribbon next to a bouquet of fresh-cut flowers as exquisite as anything in the lobby. Had my mother guessed how much I loved to draw flowers? A card was taped to the vase.

> *Will, make yourself comfortable. I'm meeting with a prospective client and won't be back until six. We'll go to the gallery opening together. Dinner tonight is just you and me.*

I wondered how my mother could ignore the past. Maybe the years of drug use or her mental breakdown had wiped her memory clean. I was determined not to forget my questions: Was she sorry for leaving us? Why had she never been in touch until now? With her expensive flowers, was she softening me up for some big surprise, as my father had implied? I was ready. I wasn't going to be her patsy.

I watched TV from the bed, keeping one eye on the clock. Sweat had gathered in the hollow of my neck. My fingers and toes tingled. A little after six, someone knocked on the door. I suddenly wished I had never come. I wasn't ready for a confrontation. There was another knock, followed by a voice that caught me off guard. It was thin and unassuming.

"Will, are you in there? It's me."

"Coming," I said. I felt like a petulant five-year-old, begrudgingly getting off my bed for someone I suddenly wasn't sure I wanted to meet. When I opened the door, my first thought was that this couldn't be my mother. Like in the photo from Berlin, her hair was brunette, but now it was swept back in a pony tail, gathered in an elegant silver and turquoise barrette. She wore a shapely black dress with a narrow, shiny silver belt. Kind of movie-starish, I thought, with her dark, roving eyes. She was forty-nine but looked much younger, and as quietly self-assured as I was self-conscious. I had the impression of someone who lived at some distance from the world, from people in general, an observer not a joiner. I assumed that once upon a time, I suckled on her breast, bounced on her knee, was pushed by her in a stroller, yet I couldn't imagine her as my or anyone's mother, doing motherly things, having motherly thoughts. I couldn't feel a warm bone in her body, even when she came up and gave me a hug. Our bodies barely touched.

"You're Will," she said, stepping back. "What a handsome young man. It's very good to meet you."

Instead of looking in her eyes, I settled nervously on her neck. Her tone was civil, almost business-like, as if she were properly addressing a stranger. A stranger wouldn't dislike her, I thought. He would find her sophisticated. There was an economy about her movements, nothing wasted, nothing out of place, and she was slight enough in appearance to make me think of the word "delicate." Yet something else suggested a cool, confident reserve. A stranger would definitely have shown her respect. But I was not quite a stranger. We had a brief, horrific history that joined us in a way that could never be undone.

"You don't really find me handsome," I spoke up, startled by my outspokenness. It was my sudden anger that allowed me to look her in the eye. "Why don't you be honest?"

"I find you handsome," she repeated, unfazed by my temper. "And not just because you're my son."

"What's so handsome about my face? Are you kidding?"

"This is a discussion for another time, Will. Right now, we're running late. You're coming to the opening, I hope."

I was fuming. Handsome! I had trapped her in a lie, and she wanted to escape. Or gallery business was more important than an intimate conversation. But I couldn't have continued even if she'd been willing. In the bottleneck of my emotions, words suddenly couldn't find their way out.

"Perhaps you want to stay here and rest," she suggested. Nothing seemed to ruffle her.

I thought about it. "No. I'm ready to go."

"You're sure?" She spotted my makeshift portfolio. "Bring that along then. We can look at your work over dinner."

Minutes later, I was in a black town car with tinted windows and a driver who glided through evening traffic as if expecting a lane to open for us like Moses at the Red Sea. I dealt with my nerves by imagining what corner of the gallery I could hide in tonight, or maybe I'd walk around the block fifty times and return when everyone was gone. My mother told me her gallery was one of the oldest in the Southwest, with branches in Chicago and New York. It had helped put a young Frankenthaler, Ellsworth Kelly, and Gerhard Richter on the map of important artists. She would be showing twelve new paintings tonight, and the gallery owner and my mother's agent had invited three hundred guests. I was suddenly even more nervous. You had to be wealthy to afford one of her paintings, and I realized I had never met any wealthy people.

If my mother was excited about her opening, she didn't show it. Yet how could she not be? She had left New York more than two decades earlier because no one took her work seriously. Even in backwater New Mexico, she had struck out. Now she was at the center of the universe of critical and popular fame.

My mother had timed our entrance. It was a full house. Maybe every gallery opening was different, but tonight matched the photos I'd seen in art magazines, as if everything was a movie set that got transported from city to city. I wanted to find a corner to hide in, where I could stare at one painting wall all evening, and no one could see my face. Instead, I was standing next to my mother, her escort for the evening. She introduced me as Wilson Louis Ryder, her fifteen-year-old son, a budding artist from New Mexico. I shook a lot of hands. To my relief, as at the hotel, almost no one looked twice at my face. Maybe they wondered what had happened, but I didn't feel a spotlight on me. Everywhere the gallery was a sea of middle-aged, tanned faces, guests with champagne flutes and hors d'oeuvres in their hands maneuvering through two large rooms, admiring my mother's slashes of color and contorted shapes. I heard adjectives like "cerebral," "synergistic," and "reductionist." They chatted about artists whose work they already owned—and didn't my mother remind them a little of the heavy black lines of Franz Kline, or the bold abstractions of Hans Hofmann? Yet she was an original, many insisted, a must for their collections. My mother was modest, almost self-effacing, as if she wanted to appear the opposite of her bold art. Perhaps her persona was as calculated as her entrance. By the end of the evening, she'd sold all twelve paintings.

We had dinner at an Italian trattoria, a term I wasn't familiar with, nor had I heard of pollastri alla Marengo, a chicken dish my mother suggested for me. The food was better than any restaurant back home, I admitted. She ordered oso bucco, and bottled water to drink.

"You're not having wine?" I asked.

"I gave up drinking thirteen years ago. Recreational drugs, too, obviously," she added with a calmness that rankled me, as if getting clean was no big deal. If that were so, why hadn't she done it before I was born?

"Why did you do drugs?" I asked, seeing no reason to hold back.

"To escape depression. I was eventually diagnosed with bipolar disorder. Do you know what that is?"

"No, not really."

"Severe mood swings that often come without warning. Manias characterized by racing thoughts, rapid speech, sleeplessness, snap judgments. Then suddenly you fall off a cliff, into a bottomless valley of shadows. You're so depressed that you think about taking your life. I did. Some diseases you can't cure; you only treat them. I take Prozac for depression. For my manias, there's a lithium compound called Lithobid."

"Are you on lithium right now?" I was curious. My father hadn't told me any of this. Maybe he didn't know.

"No."

I wondered how frustrating that might be, waking up one morning eager to be in your studio working, yet because you couldn't do your best, you didn't even try. I thought of the lightning and thunderstorms I had imagined occupying my mother's brain, long before I knew of her illness. Did I make a lucky guess, or from early on, had I somehow sensed an upheaval in her?

"Those are nice excuses, but I don't forgive you for leaving us," I announced, feeling a fresh surge of righteousness.

"That would be your choice. Personally, I don't care about the past. I think accepting blame or forgiving oneself is a waste of time."

"What?" I whispered, incredulous. Now that my mother was reborn, freed from her bad habits, the destruction she'd caused was irrelevant. Someone else might as well have started the fire in my bedroom. She was innocent. "You don't feel guilty?"

"That would be another waste of time."

If she really believed that, my father's theory of why she had invited me to Phoenix was out the window. I wasn't sure what to believe. She sensed my astonishment and anger, and waited patiently for another explosion. I didn't disappoint her. "You caused the fire! Sticking a bunch of candles around my bedroom. Stoned or not, you did it! You do admit that, right?"

"I do."

"What if I told the media? What would the art world think of you then? Would people still buy your work?"

"I have no idea. If that's what you want to do, no one can stop you."

"Why won't you even apologize?" I was pushed by Hannah's voice to go for the jugular. "Look at my face. You don't feel any regret? Why weren't you in touch with us?"

I brought up my letter to the Castelli Gallery. She admitted receiving it and telling the director to send it back. She had rejected the idea of seeing me, at that time at least, because she was too busy with her own life. If she'd opened the letter, I pointed out, she would have learned of my interest in art. We could have been in touch much earlier.

"I saw the letter you sent to Dad, just after the fire," I added. "You didn't give a shit about Hannah or me. You didn't want anything to do with us."

I was prepared to hear stories of her vagabond childhood, how her emotions had been repeatedly uprooted along with the rest of her life, but she said nothing. I stared at her while she calmly ate her dinner. Whatever was the cause of her willful isolation didn't matter to her, I guessed, so why should it matter to me? Yet I wanted to know. I wanted reasons, besides her mental condition or her busy schedule, why I was pushed out of her life. I wanted at least the choice of forgiving her.

"If you want an apology," she finally said, "I don't believe in those either."

"Jesus, what do you believe in? How about therapy?"

"Another waste of time, at least for me. Your father feels differently. His pal, Dr. Glaspell, is like his personal saint. Henry made you go see him, didn't he?"

"What if he did? What's wrong with talking about your emotions?"

She continued in the same measured voice as when she'd greeted me through the door to my hotel room. "When critics say my paintings are too intellectual, I take that as a compliment. Neither my life nor my art have much to do with emotion. They're about perception and consciousness—imagination—and interpreting the world in my own voice. Who cares about my feelings? When I'm dead, do you honestly think someone is going to talk about how I felt about anything? How would anyone know how I really felt? They're only going to talk about what I did."

"What you did was destroy my face," I seethed, "and you almost killed me. I care about that. I have feelings. . . ."

"Then you should get over them. Unless you have discipline and focus, you'll never be a great artist. 'Art is the escape from personality.' Do you know who said that?"

"I haven't a clue."

"You should look it up."

I felt the blood empty from my face. If my feet weren't wrapped about the legs of the chair, I would have fallen over, or perhaps leaped across the table to strangle my mother.

"I already told you that you were handsome. It wasn't a lie. Lies are useless. Your face expresses your character. Maybe one day it will be your path to learning. You won't understand any of this right now, but perhaps you're lucky to look the way you do."

I jumped to my feet. "I'm lucky to look the way I do? The fire was the best thing that ever happened to me? I should thank you? You're fucking crazy!"

I was in a rage I couldn't control. Several people twisted their heads toward us. I ignored them and just glared at my mother. What did she mean by my path to learning? What did she know about my life? If I told her I'd been saving money for an operation on my face, she would have advised me not to waste one penny. My father and sister opposed the surgery, but at least they understood my feelings.

"Sit down, Will. Do you want to hear a story?" she asked, as if the only way to pacify an angry child was with a narrative.

"Not really."

"It's my story."

I sat down, crossing my arms, not sure I wanted to hear another word about anything. I was ready to call a taxi.

"After I left Santo Tomás, I had some tough times."

"I'm sure you deserved them."

"I was living in Austin, waiting tables and cleaning houses to get by. I broke up with the man I thought I was in love with. I also saw a doctor who put me on meds. I continued to paint—that's what kept me going. I finally convinced a small gallery to show my work. Nothing sold. A year later, I approached an art co-op and got my foot in the door but still had no sales. Another year passed before I was accepted in a group show. Not right away, but all five of my paintings were purchased eventually, for $300 each. I thought my luck had finally turned. Then the gallery went out of business. A local church was willing to hang a few of my paintings, in conjunction with a rummage sale. A gentleman bought one, and wrote a glowing piece on me. He was the *Austin American-Statesman* art critic. I was pleased, and once again optimistic. Surely, some gallery would pick me up now.

"When nothing happened, a close friend urged me to get a regular job, because I was always broke. He told me to quit painting because as careers went, it was a curse. I thought about it seriously but rejected his advice. When you hit bottom, and if you have the strength to keep going, it's the most satisfying moment of your life. You never feel more alive than when you have nothing to lose. One day, a museum curator from Dallas, a friend of the Austin critic, came to me out of the blue and bought one of my paintings. He couldn't hang it in the museum but he told friends about me. Word began to spread that I was an underground artist with talent. A month later, I became friendly with a customer at the restaurant where I waited tables. He was traveling through Austin. I took him back to my apartment to show him my work. He loved it. . . ."

"Is there a point to all this?" I interrupted.

"Yes, there is a point, which I thought by now you would have grasped. You should never label events as lucky or unlucky. Good news can lead to disappointment, and despair can be followed by the break of your life. Have you heard of Albert Reingold? That's who came to my apartment. He was the art critic for the We eventually became lovers. I moved to New York to be with him. He championed my work. A reputable New York gallery picked me up. Albert was known for his fresh point of view, winning attention for himself on the backs of a half-dozen obscure artists like me. I didn't care if he exploited us. The art business has always been symbiotic. I would have been nothing without him."

I had heard of Albert Reingold. His strong, unorthodox reviews were scattered through serious art magazines. I hoped she might add that she wasn't just Albert Reingold's lover but had also fallen in love with him, and they were living happily now in Soho. When you were most in need, it wasn't financial or career success that bailed you out, I hoped, it was love. But my mother said nothing on that subject. It wasn't the point of her story.

"We're born alone, and we die alone," she said. "The rest is just filler."

I erupted again. "Families are filler? That's wonderful! Good to know! You are really crazy." More heads in the restaurant turned. I wondered why my mother had wanted to have children. Then I remembered what my father had said—both pregnancies were accidental.

"Do you ever think about Hannah?" I asked. "Do you miss her?"

"I'm curious about her the same way I'm curious about you. I understand she's bright and motivated. That's what I heard from David's mother."

"You don't want to be in touch and find out for yourself?"

"What does she think of me?"

"She despises you."

"How do you know?"

"She told me."

"Then why would I waste my time with someone who doesn't want to be with me?"

"She's your daughter."

My mother's mouth made a contemplative smile—it was almost a frown—as if acknowledging an incidental fact, but nothing more. "I thought twice before contacting even you, Will. I think the best thing a mother can do for her children is to leave them on their own as soon as possible. Other species do it. Otherwise, all we do is coddle you, worry about you, solve your problems, and deny you a chance to make mistakes. We deny you strength. I would never have written had I not heard that you loved to paint, and had talent, in David's opinion. That interested me. So I took a chance."

I shook my head, confused. "A chance on what?" Apparently the only obligation of a species was to propagate, in my mother's view. She had passed on some of her DNA to me. Her job was done. I was left to roam the Earth at will, crashing through jungles, falling off precipices, chased by wild animals. If I survived or not, it was the same to her.

"That I might give you something to think about," she said.

She had succeeded at that. I had never met anyone like my mother. I would remember this evening forever. I knew now why she'd never been in contact with Hannah or me, if the best thing a mother could do was abandon her young. I also understood why she had left my father. They had fallen in love as a couple of introverted intellectuals, determined to map their lives as one, then discovered differences that couldn't be overcome. One of them was solitary, protective, distrusted change, and towed his guilt around like an extra body part. The other reinvented herself at will, chose freedom over tradition, and didn't mind taking risks. The more, the better. Breaking up a family and moving on was almost a mandate.

"So what if I try to be a great artist and nothing happens?" I asked. "What if I'm not you?"

"You won't be me."

I corrected myself. "What if I don't come even close to succeeding, no matter how hard I work? What if I don't catch any breaks? What if I don't have talent?"

"Taking a risk and failing is better than living the same dead-end life over and over."

I was sure she was referring to my father. In my mother's mind, he had no ambition, no nerve, and would probably be in the zombie queue until the day he died.

As we ordered dessert, I began to see my mother for what she was—an agitator if not an outright anarchist. I had come to Phoenix hoping we might be more alike than my father would ever admit, that we would grow closer, could share feelings, but that idea seemed hopeless now. I didn't think we were at all alike. I saw no point in sticking around Phoenix. I would cut short my trip and fly back to New Mexico tomorrow.

"May I have a peek?" she asked, eyeing my portfolio.

I wished I had never brought my work. I couldn't tolerate her clinical dissection. My art had nothing to do with intellect and everything with emotion.

She reached for the flimsy cardboard and untied the twine. Inside were a dozen paintings and sketches. In what passed for an eternity, my mother studied them one by one, and then submitted everything to a second review.

"You have something," she announced, looking up at last. "Your use of colors is imaginative, and your composition is sophisticated for your age."

"Do you like them?" I asked pointedly.

"You have a gift," she said, not exactly answering my question. "If you want to run away from it, it's your life. I won't be disappointed if you do. But for a second, ignore your feelings about me—where do you want to be in ten years?"

At that moment, I wanted to be back in my hotel room. There was too much to ponder besides my distant future as an artist. I wondered how much more challenging high school would be than junior high. I had never had a girlfriend. Part of me wanted to see Los Angeles and New York, or any great metropolis. And what about my operation? Despite my mother's reaction, I knew what I wanted, if I could just earn enough money.

When our driver dropped us at the hotel, I told my mother I was going home early. She didn't respond. All she said was, "Good night, Will." I slept for a few hours, watched television, and called for room service. I had no idea you could order a BLT at three in the morning. I thought the Four Seasons would not be a bad place to live your entire life. You wouldn't have to go outside and let people see you if you didn't want to. Books and movies could be delivered to your room. Downstairs was a barbershop and beauty salon, and a restaurant. If I had as much money as my mother, I thought, this is where I would live.

In the morning, instead of heading to the airport, I surprised myself by changing my mind. I called to tell my mother, and she showed up at breakfast wearing a baseball cap that read I CAN'T FIX STUPID. Did she mean me? She made no reference to last night's conversation or my outbursts. After breakfast, as we visited several galleries, she pointed out which artists she considered significant, and who was hopelessly imitative or had *cajones* made of Swiss cheese, as she said. Good art, she added, drilled past the eye and into your brain. Great art realigned your perception of yourself in the universe.

I asked where her ideas came from. The dominant shapes in each painting were pulled from her subconscious, she said, what she referred to as a hypnagogic zone, experienced between light sleep and wakefulness. It could last half an hour or half a minute, but the shapes became extremely clear to her. Getting those images on canvas was another trick, though, as was finding the right palette of colors. Making everything work together was pure pain, she added, like having a string of migraines and not being allowed an aspirin. No painting could ever be rushed. Hurrying just screwed it up.

"Wow. Sounds like fun," I said.

The difference between my first impression of my mother—polite and reserved—and my second—forthright and strong-willed—was the difference between the soldier who left his sword in his scabbard and one who used it as a weapon. In my head, I kept a journal of her habits. She liked blueberries and sunflower seeds for breakfast. She swam laps in the hotel pool. She bought half a dozen magazines, read an article or two in each, then passed them on to strangers with the comment, "Here, you might find this interesting." She could stop at a fabric or bead store and spend an hour looking at colors and patterns without buying a thing. She admitted she rarely watched television, even the news. It was just more filler.

By the end of my trip, I still couldn't call her "mother" to her face. "Susan" felt almost as uncomfortable. She had no reaction to my awkwardness. I remained filled with questions: Were she and Albert still together, and what did they do when they weren't discussing art? Were there other passions? Who were her friends? What kind of books did she read? She was a mystery on many levels, none of which I felt like broaching for fear of learning something I couldn't handle. Our first meeting had been jarring enough.

She insisted on accompanying me to the airport. "I know the dean of admissions at the Chicago School of Design and Art," she began as we sat in the back of the town car. "Have you heard of it?"

I nodded. The school was mentioned often in my art magazines.

"With your permission, I'd like to show the dean your paintings. Traditionally, SDA has been for college and grad students, but it's just started a high school program. You would learn," she said, in a voice suddenly so charged it startled me. "And you need to live in a real city. That's part of your education, too."

"Are you suggesting. . . ." I cleared my throat. "Are you suggesting I move to Chicago?"

"You would start this fall. You'll live in the heart of a great city, near one of the finest art museums in the country. You can take classes in painting, illustration, sculpture, photography—learn what you like and where you excel."

Her offer was tempting but impractical, I told her, because I couldn't afford art school, and my father was counting on me to finish my education in Santo Tomás. If I stuck around and went to New Mexico State to earn my B.A, tuition would be free as the child of a professor. Raised by my father, I was inclined toward frugality and safety nets.

"I'll pay for your tuition and living expenses at SDA, all three years," she countered, like this was a chess game. "Your father won't have to pony up a dime. The rest is up to you, Will. If you decide you want to stay at SDA for college, I'll cover that as well."

"Wait a second," I said, thinking I had caught her in another lie. "You said you believe in leaving children completely on their own."

"You will be on your own. Helping you financially gives you more choices, but it doesn't necessarily influence the choices you make."

"But why would you do any of this?"

She thought for a moment. "Because no one ever did it for me."

If she was being sincere, her generosity impressed me. But there was one condition, she said. Now she sounded like my father. I looked at her uncertainly.

"The condition is you have to stay the course. Except for emergency health reasons, you can't drop out. I don't care how discouraged you might feel, or you're tempted to move back to New Mexico, or what your father advises you to do. Once you start, you have to graduate on time, first high school and then college if you decide to stay. Will you agree to that?"

I nodded, because I intended to do exactly what she'd asked if I decided to go. Why would I ever drop out of a great school? I was hurt. I'd never given any indication I was a quitter or was inclined to jump from one passion to another. Did she think I didn't have the same determination she did?

"Are those terms acceptable?" she repeated.

I gazed out on the crisscrossing freeways. What my mother called opportunity my father would surely call manipulation. But she was giving me something without asking for much back, only my steadfastness. Maybe she had something like a heart under all her thorns after all. This was my ticket out of New Mexico. Hannah had made the same leap; wasn't it my turn?

"I'll get back to you," I said. I left her my portfolio.

At the airport, we did our A-frame hug good-bye. I thanked her for pushing me to think about my future. For every moment that soared with hope, however, I experienced a cold breeze of fear. What if my talent didn't match my ambition? What if I never came close to my mother's success? If I ended up teaching art, would I still be satisfied, or more like my frustrated father, enduring a classroom of the thankless and the uninspired.

At an airport gift shop, I used the last of my mother's money and picked out a University of Arizona T-shirt, along with a blank greeting card. I asked the sales clerk, a large woman with a vermilion scarf circling her neck, to wrap everything in tissue and put a ribbon around it.

"We don't do ribbon," she said.

"How about extra tissue? I want to make it nice."

"We don't do tissue either. Just a shopping bag. Someone special?" she asked.

"Yes. My father."

When I strutted off the plane a few hours later in Santo Tomás, my father was waiting at the gate. "What's this?" he said as I handed him my present.

"Thank you for letting me go to Phoenix."

He pulled out the T-shirt, admiring it, and smiled as he read my card. I had included a quote from Friedrich von Schiller, the eighteenth-century German poet whom my father was, no doubt, one of the few people on the planet ever to have read. He had made me read Schiller, too—one of our more obscure but indelible bonds. "It is not flesh and blood but heart which makes us fathers and sons," he read out loud. The quote was sappy, but I meant it.

Dad wanted to talk almost immediately about my mother, but as we drove home, I insisted on staring out the window, remarking on the landscape. The town seemed to have shrunk in my brief absence, as if it had been through a couple of spin cycles in the dryer. In summer, it looked browner than ever. Compared with Phoenix—or Chicago, I imagined—I could fit the whole thing in my back pocket. I waited until I was home and unpacked before I joined my father in the living room. He brought me a soda. I told him I'd learned to drink coffee in Phoenix, and it was now my beverage of choice.

"Coffee," he remarked.

"With cream and sugar."

He smiled and drifted back to the kitchen, returning a couple of minutes later with two steaming cups. "Hope instant will do. All grown up, in less than a week," he concluded. "And how was your mother?"

"She was OK."

"Just OK? What did you guys do?"

"Not much. I went to her opening and said hello to a bunch of wealthy people who bought her paintings. The next day, we went to galleries and a museum. She taught me a few things about art." My tone was casual, downplaying the whole trip. I told him the truth, which was that I was glad it was over. If I'd told him the whole truth, that I'd confronted her with my feelings, and she wasn't a tiny bit sorry for anything she'd done—not for walking out, not for never contacting us—he might have insisted I not talk to her again.

"She believes in adversity," I informed him.

"What do you mean?"

"That it makes you stronger."

"That's it? That's the punch line?"

"The punch line?"

"Your mother always has a punch line. With me, it was 'We're leaving New York and moving to Santo Tomás.' Or, 'I'm never going to talk to my parents again.' And always, 'I'm going to be an important artist one day, no matter what anyone thinks.' She lives for the grand gesture. Then she bets all her poker chips. You're so in awe of her bravado that you don't argue." He gave me a look that said: Remember this. "The fact is, you can argue, but you'll never win.

"I always found it ironic," he added, "that your mother was the one who insisted we move to New Mexico. The next thing I know, she's gone, and I've been here ever since."

I pushed my shoulders into the sofa. There was no point in holding back. "She wants me to go to art school in Chicago. She's a good friend of the dean of admissions. She'll pay for everything."

My father looked like I'd hit him over the head with a two-by-four. I saw a galaxy of stars in his eyes. "She wants you to go to art school, in Chicago?" he repeated. He hadn't expected that grand a gesture

"This fall."

"This fall?"

"That's what she said."

"Didn't I warn you?" he replied, still in shock. "She had an agenda to push."

"I thought it was a generous offer."

"I'm not saying it wasn't. But there's more to come. You don't know her."

"She's weird," I agreed. "She doesn't give compliments. She thinks pain is what makes a great artist. At one point, I wanted to kill her."

"Let's get to the point, Will. Are you tempted to go? Do you feel you have to prove something to her?"

"Not to her. Myself."

He told me my mother had a way of creating self-doubt in people, and that they went out of their way to prove her wrong. They wanted her respect and approval. It had worked with him. He wasn't ashamed to admit it. Couldn't I see that's what she was doing with me?

"Why don't you think about everything, Will?"

"You let Hannah go away to school."

"It wasn't long ago you told me you stunk as a painter. And wasn't your plan to stay in Santo Tomás, at least through high school?"

"Yes," I admitted to both.

"All right," he summed up. "Don't rush into anything. Maybe next year."

I said I wasn't sure my mother's offer would be there in a year. I told him her condition about not dropping out, ever, and that in my mind, that translated to starting school right away. For my mother, this was a business proposition. It wouldn't be on the table forever.

My stubbornness, if not my sudden loyalty to my mother, dismayed him. He knew she could cast spells—but in so short a time! He gazed down at his boots, waiting for an insight worthy of his considerable intellect. He could have been more forceful with his opinion, countering my mother in her chess game, but he'd always been reluctant to impose his views on Hannah and me. Whether it was government, religion, or family, he didn't believe in telling anyone—or being told—what to do. Still, he wasn't through fighting.

"Will, think it through. You know you're vulnerable to wild dreams."

He didn't say the last sentence like it was a bad thing—it was more his assessment of my emotions, which he knew as well as anybody. My face inclined me to endless fantasies. But in the maze of adolescence, I had no clue where the exit was—fantasies didn't get you where you wanted to go—while my mother had given me a very concrete plan. I could graduate from SDA with a bachelor of fine arts. No matter what my father thought, she had rekindled my hope that I had talent.

"Your mother doesn't give without getting something back," he emphasized. "Remember I told you to keep your guard up?"

I squirmed on the sofa, caught between my parents in their undeclared war. My father acted like my mother was the snake in the Garden of Eden. It puzzled me that I wasn't more afraid of her—either that or the anxiety I did feel had been softened by her confidence in me. Of course, that was the problem with Adam and Eve. They didn't know enough to be afraid, Mrs. Gutierrez had told me. They believed everything the serpent said.

"OK, I'll think about it. I promise," I said, and left the room.

The admissions application from the Chicago School of Design and Art arrived within the week. SDA, I learned, had been around in one form or another for a hundred years, churning out graduates who would become the famous, the nearly famous, and the obscure. The storied institution had helped populate the world with fashion designers, painters, illustrators, photographers, writers, and sculptors. I treated the application like a game, filling out the ten pages in six and a half minutes, in sloppy red ink, to give my father hope. "Whatever happens, happens," I told him, in a voice as cavalier as my writing. For the essay question, "Tell us how you see yourself twenty years from now," I answered, in the finest tradition of grand gestures, that I had an equal chance of becoming homeless or selling a painting for a million dollars. Surely the admissions committee would recognize a smart-ass, reject me, and that would be the end of my indecision.

After I sent everything off, conversations with my father became peppered with small talk: our playing golf again, trekking in the Himalayas, or improving my driving skills, since I now had my learner's permit and made my father nervous every time we approached a busy four-way intersection. Three weeks later, a packet arrived from Chicago. The cover letter began, "Congratulations. We want to welcome you to SDA's high school sophomore class." The committee had favorably reviewed my paintings and drawings. My essay was evidence of "pithy irony" and "youthful complexity." I knew what my father was thinking when I showed him the letter. Thanks to my mother, everything had been rigged. I didn't take it as an insult because I thought it might be true.

A few nights later, I announced that I had made up my mind. Rigged or not, this was an opportunity I couldn't decline. I had put the personalities and agendas of my parents aside and searched my heart. I would get on a plane and travel to a sprawling, grasping, mysterious city of strangers and dreamers, and there pound my stake into the ground.

My father could have tried one last time to argue, but his stoicism prevailed. For all I knew, he had been calculating the odds of my permanent departure from Santo Tomás since the day I was invited to Phoenix. He understood the nature of fate. My Latin teacher liked to say that the best intentions of mortals were no match for the whims of the gods. Among other traits, the Ryders were destined to be a family of deserters. My mother, then Hannah, and now me, leaving my father behind like a moth-eaten sweater. I felt enough guilt that I wanted to hide under my bed and not come out.

Hannah breezed in for a couple of weeks in July, filling my father with cheer, but departed for Yale without promising when she'd be back. I wanted my father to return to his old friends, the ones he'd once played tennis with, or date a few women. He had enough money to travel. Besides the Himalayas, he sometimes spoke of visiting Joyce's Dublin—what was left of it, he liked to quip. I told him he should go, now that there was no one else in the house.

"Maybe I will take a trip," he said the day I left in September. To demonstrate my maturity and independence, I'd insisted on taking a taxi to the airport.

"Don't worry," I promised as we stood on the porch. "I'll be home for every holiday. You can count on me."

"You know what Carl Sandburg called Chicago?" he said.

I knew, but I let him tell me anyway. When he recited poetry, my father's vocal cords resonated like organ pipes.

"Hog butcher for the world, tool maker, stacker of wheat, player with railroads and the nation's freight handler, stormy, husky, brawling, city of the big shoulders. . . ."

He went on. He knew the entire poem. Maybe he had diverted us into poetry because it helped keep his feelings under control, or made my departure more acceptable. Chicago was a masculine, robust city, perfect for a young man seeking his fortune. He told me Chicago was also called the Windy City, for the blows of winter that whipped like a scourge off Lake Michigan. I would need a heavy jacket with a hood sooner than I might think.

When the taxi pulled in front of our house, my father walked me outside. He gazed for a second over the fence, into our backyard where I had endured my first birthday party, the day I had scared everyone half to death. He turned and slipped some quarters in my pocket. "Call me. I want to know you got there safely."

As we hugged, his strength wasn't as forceful as when I'd left for Phoenix, when he had squeezed the air out of my lungs. Now, his arms felt more like a blanket over my shoulders on a cold night. Acts of tender resignation gave him a certain grace. When he released me, I walked to the taxi, glancing back on his proud, New England face. I couldn't help wondering how much I was like him, how much like the mother I was starting to get to know, and what percentage of me was genuine original.

Sixteen years in Santo Tomás did not prepare me for the deafening roar of the L, the blaze of light that gathered over Lake Michigan on late summer mornings, or the glass towers that twisted along in harmony with the curves of the Chicago River. I took a morning boat tour of the skyscrapers, whose sheets of glass were mirrors of sky and water, as whimsical as the scudding clouds and the river's eddies. Chicago was a city of optical illusions and constant motion, as well as near-misses.

Rush hour on Michigan Avenue, pedestrians hurried over sidewalks and crossed streets with a momentum that seemed unstoppable; traffic lights turned yellow, but the wave of bodies pressed forward. My second day, a businessman was struck by a taxi—I saw his briefcase soar in the air. He had crossed on a red light. I ran over and joined the bystanders. The man was still unconscious when the ambulance arrived, and a medic quickly strapped an oxygen mask over his mouth. If he lived, I wondered, would he tempt fate again? When did you make the decision that certain risks were too much, after you got too close to the sun and the wax in your wings had melted? I had feared the unknown since I was a child, and now, in a new city, everything was unknown.

I took an elevator to the viewing platform of the Sears Tower and watched the vast colony of ants heading to the thousands of restaurants, shops, department stores, apartments, condos, and offices. I kept staring out at life around me, the endless, crazy energy that was laid at my feet like an emerald road. I was an ant, too, I thought, anonymous in a colony of millions, and the idea of being as invisible as possible suddenly gave me relief. Most people were too preoccupied to notice my face. I had feared just the opposite going to Phoenix, afraid of being the center of attention, only to discover that I wasn't.

My new home was in a fifteen-story converted apartment building on North State Street, in the heart of the Loop, near an SDA class building. My mother had arranged a single room for me. I wasn't surprised that she didn't greet me at the airport, or leave a note at school wishing me good luck. There was no trace of Houdini other than at the registrar's office, where I was told my tuition, room, and board had been paid in full. I was also handed a Visa card with my name on it, for expenses for the year, I assumed. After I picked up my orientation package, I took my two duffels to my sixth-floor room, with a kitchenette (Mr. Coffee and microwave included), track lighting, and views of Lake Michigan. Each floor had a faculty proctor to make sure everyone behaved. In the lobby were a television lounge, library, and laundry room. It wasn't the Four Seasons, but it wasn't a homeless shelter either—something in between.

In Santo Tomás, there were Hispanics and Anglos and maybe five black people. My dorm housed 400 students—195 in the high school program—who included blacks, Mexicans, Chinese, Koreans, Japanese, Africans and Eastern Europeans. I was living at the United Nations. At the high school orientation that evening, everybody stood and introduced themselves. A sixteen-year-old girl who called herself T Rex got my attention. She had popped out of some crazy art movie, I thought, whose ending I couldn't possibly imagine.

"Hello," she began, clutching a string of glass beads that drooped from her neck, twisting them in a mesmerizing circle. Her blonde hair was early caveman style, heaped in a beehive with loose strands dangling like twine. She stood with one leg canted out, occasionally wiggling her ankle in further evidence of nerves. "Hello. Did I already say that? I guess I did. Well, hello again." She gave an exaggerated smile. "My name is Tabitha Penelope Rex—my friends call me T Rex—and I'm from Madison, Tennessee. I'm here to study fashion design."

I smiled on the inside. Who would name herself after a dinosaur? Her jeans were a mosaic of patches and holes, and her tie-dyed T-shirt featured a picture of Mario Savio, the '60s political radical from Berkeley. He believed that free speech included the right to use obscenities whenever you wanted, Hannah once told me. I'd bet I was the only one in the room who knew who he was, except presumably T Rex.

Finished, the girl from Madison, Tennessee, bowed to our group, more like a curtsey, as if this had been her recital or she was dropping in on the Queen of England. A hint of confidence had replaced the earlier display of nerves. Tall and willowy, she had a climbing rose of a body that I envisioned twining the pillar of a southern mansion, her pretty face tilted toward the sun.

When my turn came, I could feel everyone staring at my face. It didn't help that I was wearing my ill-fitting suit—why didn't I wear jeans and a T-shirt like everyone else? I shoved my hands in my pockets to hide my shaking as I rambled through my brief resume in a monotone. When I mentioned Santo Tomás, no one's eyes expressed much interest. If you were from Slovakia or Japan, I doubted you even knew where New Mexico was. I sat down, out of breath.

When the orientation was over, I watched T Rex as she mingled for a minute or two with her new classmates. She didn't look any more comfortable than I felt. She left the lobby in a preoccupied state.

"Hi," I said when I caught up with her on the sidewalk. She was smoking a cigarette. The evening traffic on State Street was no more forgiving than the daytime's, a blur of lit-up missiles without a target.

"Smoke?" she asked, holding out a pack of Gauloises. I'd never heard of them. "They're French. Very cool."

"No thanks. I don't smoke."

She arched her head away, and a puff of acrid smoke escaped her lips. Her lipstick was a fuchsia red, like the John Cabots my father planted in our yard. "What's your name again?" she asked.

"Will Ryder."

She smiled, as if catching me in a lie. "You said Wilson Louis Ryder at the orientation. You sounded so serious. Why are you wearing a suit and tie?"

"I'm not that serious," I insisted.

"Could have fooled me. I bet you bring a briefcase to class. This isn't Harvard, you know."

I told her I didn't own a briefcase, and even if I did, I wouldn't bring it to class. "What do you know about Mario Savio?" I changed subjects, studying her T-shirt again.

"Not much, except he was a radical and free thinker. I like outspoken people."

"It's a nice T-shirt. I wouldn't be afraid to wear it. Do you know where I could find one? Maybe I could trade my suit for it."

She squinted at me, and broke into a delayed laugh when she realized I was making a joke. Her laugh ended with an accidental burp. "That's pretty funny," she said.

I didn't know if she meant her indigestion or my humor. She studied me for a moment, as if transfixed by my face.

"Do you want to get a cup of coffee?" I asked, stoking my courage.

She hesitated, like someone who suddenly remembered an important errand to run, or was afraid of me.

"You have to be somewhere?" I said.

"I promised to call someone."

Her cigarette fell to the sidewalk, and she squished it with the heel of a neon-blue high top sneaker. Her glass beads suddenly caught a glint of the streetlight. When she leaned over to tie the sneaker, her breasts flopped against her shirt like a couple of fish on a dock. She wasn't wearing a bra.

"On second thought, a cup of java sounds OK," she changed her mind, straightening to her full height. "I can meet you back here in forty-five minutes."

"OK. Great." I watched her vanish into the dorm.

To kill time, I walked around the neighborhood, fascinated by all the things that were new: the shirt-soaking humidity, the fanciful display windows, the deep-throated engines of buses as they lumbered in and out of traffic—and always the legions of eyes-ahead walkers, carrying shopping bags or listening to music through headphones or stopping to buy a magazine from a vendor. I kept checking my watch, and got back to the dorm with five minutes to spare, standing on the spot where T Rex had said good-bye. Almost an hour passed. Just when I thought I'd been stood up, I felt a tap on my shoulder. T Rex smiled but didn't apologize. She didn't even seem aware that she was late.

We ambled down the block to an uncrowded coffee shop with Naugahyde booths and scratched up Formica tops. It was the width of a railroad car, and smelled faintly of Windex. Taking off my jacket and tie, I ordered two coffees and a large plate of fries. Determined to make a good impression, I extracted a $10 bill from my wallet and laid it on the table for the waitress. Hannah had told me that on first dates, the boy was expected to pay.

"I bet this is your first time away from New Mexico," T Rex observed. "Who puts money on the table before you get the check?"

"Oh no. I'm well traveled. I've been to Phoenix."

"That's it? Phoenix?"

"So far. But I have plans."

"What kind of plans?"

"I want to see as many countries as I can. When I was growing up, I studied a map of the world every day. Did you know there're more than 180 countries? How about you?"

"I've been around," she said with an edge of weariness in her voice, like a luckless hitchhiker who no longer put her thumb out. "My father is in sales. When I was younger, we moved around a lot. He was always switching companies. My mom never said whether he got a better offer or was fired. That probably means he was fired. For the last five years, we've lived in Tennessee. My mom stays home and takes care of my brothers. Honestly, I'm glad to finally get away from them all. I'm the only sane one in the bunch."

"Good thing," I said, watching her empty virtually the entire ketchup bottle on the plate of fries. Half of them sank completely into a sea of red. Her fingers dove after one and slid it into her mouth.

"Would you like a napkin?" I asked.

"You're too polite. I bet you carry a fork in your briefcase."

I watched her eat, slithering one fry into her mouth at a time like a bird sucking down a worm.

"Before my mother met my father," I said, "she moved around a lot, too. Army brat. Then they divorced, and she kept moving, I guess it's in her blood."

"What's your mother doing now?"

"She's an artist in New York. Her name's Susan Olmsted. Maybe you've heard of her."

"Can't say that I have, but don't take that personally. I don't know many artists. Ask me about Valentino or Versace or Jean Paul Gaultier." I watched as she licked her fingers every fifteen seconds. Napkins were only for the Establishment. "You really need to get rid of that suit," she said with a pained glance at me. "I think you would open up more."

"You're probably right." I plunged my fingers into the ketchup.

"So what happened to your face?" she asked as casually as she'd commented on my clothes.

"I was in a fire."

"No kidding. How did that happen?"

"An accident in my home."

"A fire? Wow, that must have whacked you out."

"I was only three. I don't remember anything." It was a lie, but I had decided never to tell anyone the truth. My past belonged only to me. Like both my parents, I wanted to keep the lid on as tight as possible.

"I like looking at you," she volunteered.

"Really?"

"Does that bother you?"

I was startled by her candor. "Usually."

"Well, get over it. I'd say your face is compelling. It's full of character. And your eyes are beautiful. Give me your profile," she ordered. I turned to oblige. "At first, I thought it was flat, but it's a little bit like a cube," she observed. "Very cool."

"Thank you. That's not what most people think. They're creeped out."

"Who cares? Do you know what most people think of me?"

I told T Rex what I thought. She was the most unusual girl I'd ever met.

"You mean weird."

"Not necessarily. I don't really know you. But weird is OK."

"You should see my family. Especially Lard and Candy. They're weird."

I gave her a perplexed look.

"Lard and Candy Ass. My parents."

"Ass? That's a surname?" I couldn't tell if she was kidding. Hannah had once showed me a phone book with names like Hitler, Farte, and Urne.

"Then there're the five kids," she went on. "Smart Ass, Kiss Ass, Lazy Ass—that's me—Ass Bandit and Ass Wipe. Ass Wipe just turned four. He's cute as a button."

"You're the middle child. That's pretty neat."

"What planet were you born on? Being a middle child is a total bitch. Smart and Kiss are at big universities, getting straight A's. The little guys can't do any wrong. Candy and Lard think I never try hard enough."

They actually had "Establishment" names, she revealed: Gerald and Cynthia Rex. I asked why they had named her Tabitha.

"For an aunt on the Titanic. Tabitha pushed her husband overboard to get the last seat in the lifeboat." She looked at the dismay in my eyes. "Just kidding! My parents thought Tabitha was special. I didn't get a vote, obviously. Do you like it?"

"Sure."

"I hate it. One day, I'm going to go to court and change it. You can do that when you're eighteen, did you know that?"

We ordered another round of coffee. T Rex had endless stories to tell. She called her father a sweet man with rage. He never missed church, but at last count, he had twenty-three guns in the house. Candy had gone from state fair beauty queen to botox queen. When Smart and Kiss began climbing to dizzying heights in academia, T Rex was repeating sixth grade. In seventh grade, on a friend's dare, she'd gone dumpster diving behind a McDonald's, feasting on a cold Big Mac and fries. She did it every day for a week, she said, to protest. Did I know Americans threw away $500 million worth of perfectly good food every year? It was a fact! A year later, she "borrowed" her mother's car and drove to Graceland, under the influence of marijuana, and got caught trying to steal a wax effigy of Elvis. Her last year in junior high, she'd chained herself to the flagpole as a protest on behalf of underpaid teachers. Her punishment was to be expelled for a week, but when she returned, she did it all over again. I bragged that I had been expelled from school, too—for trying to kill someone. She looked impressed.

T Rex did most of the talking. I hung on every word but not without some uncertainty. If she was making up only half the stuff about her family and childhood, she was a delightful oddball. If all her stories were true, she might be insane. I felt an instant attraction.

It was past eleven when we strolled back to the dorm. I told her I was taking a private tour of the Art Institute of Chicago tomorrow. As if I knew what I was talking about, I said it was the most comprehensive fine arts museum in the world, with over 250,000 works. I boasted that I would try to see every one before I finished school; now was a good time to start. Classes didn't begin for another two days.

"A private tour. Are you a VIP?"

"No. I meant a tour by myself. Do you want to come? The museum opens at nine."

She agreed to meet me at the Michigan Avenue entrance the moment the doors opened. I wondered if she'd keep her word. I thought of T Rex as someone who'd rather sleep in. In my room, I fixed another cup of coffee and rehashed the evening in my mind. I went to sleep thinking of fish flopping on a dock.

I was at the top of the long, wide, regal white stairs a few minutes before the museum opened. Two magnificent bronze lions guarded the entrance to the Beaux Arts building. But there was no sign of T Rex. Half the world began parading through the turnstiles. Then I heard my name called. She was impossible to miss in orange jeans, a yellow top, and the same blue sneakers. She looked like a Magic Marker. She'd told me last night she designed her own clothes since she was ten. The right to self-expression was in her personal Constitution.

T Rex's hair, however, unlike last night, now was washed to a shiny blonde luster, framing her face like a yearbook headshot. Had she cleaned up for me? Her deep blue eyes stole the show. I'd barely noticed them in the coffee shop's poor light. Now they struck me as a pair of precious stones a person only stumbled on by luck.

I'd never been in the Institute, but I'd studied a map and knew where to find de Kooning's masterpiece, *Excavation.* My mother had told me to seek out a number of paintings and spend hours with them if possible, but in her view, Excavation was the breakout painting of abstract expressionism. It put America on the international art map, she said, stealing the thunder from the European Impressionists and Surrealists, and turning the Dutch-born de Kooning, along with his friend Pollock, into icons of the American century.

*Excavation* was the largest painting de Kooning ever did on an easel. The colors in the nearly seven-by-eight-and-a-half-foot canvas seemed muted, filled with creams and grays but energized by the occasional splashes of reds and sharp yellows and haunting blues. The colors were almost secondary to the twisted, lively abstractions of figures and facial profiles all jammed together, which could be interpreted in a half-dozen ways. The painting was restrained yet full of movement and understated emotion, and lots of mystery. Something was being excavated and exposed. The new American century maybe, de Kooning's soul, our culture, or just the nature of time. How did one paint time?

The painting invited you into its world of promise and chaos and wouldn't let you out. I would come back to it a dozen times during my years in Chicago—I would revere it as much as my mother did—but there's no substitute for a first impression. I felt something pressing on my chest. De Kooning had painted what looked like a small door at the bottom of the canvas, and once you entered it, one critic wrote, you had to throw away every preconception you had about art, because you couldn't get out again, not without changing your understanding of what a painting could do. De Kooning, like Pollock and Picasso, had stripped art to its bones, beaten it, bleached it, and burned it at the stake. All great painters, I would eventually come to think, wanted to invent art from scratch.

Short of breath, I turned to T Rex. "Don't you love it?"

She was standing on her tiptoes, as if looking into the canvas from above, gazing at its endless depth.

"Outstanding."

"You mean it?"

"Do you want me to sign an oath? I do love it. It's a big museum; don't you want to keep going?"

I continued standing there, spellbound. T Rex took my hand and tried to pull me away. When I wouldn't budge, she joined ranks beside me, willing to give de Kooning a deeper interpretation. My attention, however, was no longer on the painting. No girl had ever held my hand. The touch of her flesh felt like slipping into a warm bath. When she twined her fingers between mine, giving them a squeeze, I was afraid to look at her and break the spell.

Still holding hands, I led her to another room, the one housing Degas and his charcoals and oils of ballerinas. I told her about the drawing I'd made of Hannah in her green tutu.

"You're a sweet boy," she said.

We drifted from room to room, like tourists arriving at one new city after another, taking in the different sights. What held my attention were the Picassos from his Blue Period, and several of his Cubist masterpieces; I imagined I could see my own face in the contorted shapes. T Rex pronounced Edward Hopper's famous *Nighthawks* her favorite painting. She had never seen a copy of it, as common as it was. The scene of a city cafe at night, with expressionless strangers stranded on dining stools, struck a chord with her. All the Hopper paintings, depicting small town American life and solitary, sometimes-faceless figures, seemed to absorb her.

"That's me, in another life," she said as we stared at a naked woman in a light-filled, barren bedroom. The woman was watching a rising sun from her window, like a daily ritual she was sentenced to repeat.

At the museum gift shop, T Rex bought a poster of *Nighthawks* to hang in her room.

"Want to do something cool?" she said when we got outside.

I nodded without asking what. I would have done anything she wanted. She took my hand again and led me to the nearest L station. We boarded the first train to come along, squeezed together on a seat, eyes peeled out the window. We sliced through sooty neighborhoods strung together by light and shadow, etched faces, and eroded sidewalks. Her idea was to ride Chicago's ancient elevated mass transit with no special destination. We got out at random stations, jumped to another train, and continued our adventure. T Rex liked looking down on things, I decided, remembering the way she had studied *Excavation,* as if distance and perspective gave her insights that weren't available at eye level. I loved how her mouth creased into a smile when she saw something that delighted her. What was she thinking about? How much was she thinking of me? Occasionally, her eyes swam in my direction, brushing my face. I had worked up the confidence not to turn away when she looked at me.

When she announced she was hungry—starved, she insisted—we clambered down the creaky metal stairs at a platform in the middle of nowhere. There wasn't a coffee shop anywhere on a street of small stores, half of them shuttered with accordion gates. Voices suddenly rose behind us. Two boys in baggy jeans and white T-shirts, around my age, were moving toward us urgently, as if bent on returning something we'd dropped. The Hopper poster was still under T Rex's arm. The taller boy began to whistle and called out, "Hey, babe!"

"Keep moving," T Rex said, as if she knew how to handle the situation. "They'll lose interest."

We edged ahead, keeping our pace, but I felt them closing the gap. Suddenly, their dull whispering mixed with laughter. I felt a hand on my shoulder. The tall boy tried to spin me around. I pulled away from his grip.

"Whoa, now," he said like he was talking to a horse.

"Get lost," said T Rex. We had stopped to face them. Except for an elderly couple and a woman pushing a shopping cart, the sidewalk was empty.

"Lost?" the other boy chimed in. "We ain't lost, and I don't think you live here zactly. So who's lost, bitch?"

"We don't want any trouble," I said in my best adult voice. Like a human shield, I put myself in front of T Rex. She moved away, indifferent to possible disaster.

"You come here and you don't want trouble?" said the taller boy. "She-it. You come 'cause you want trouble! Ain't that right?" he called to his friend.

"Funny face," he announced, staring at me, "go way before we kick yer ass." His eyes slid back to T Rex. "Gonna do something else with you, honey."

"Oh, blow me," she said.

The other boy began to laugh, his head lolling from side to side. "Say what?"

"And blow your friend while you're at it. Or is he your brother? Do you blow your brother?"

"What you got under your arm?" the bigger kid said, eyeing the poster.

"None of your fucking business."

When he reached for it, she slapped his hand away.

He looked surprised. "Hey. . . ."

"I said go fuck yourself."

Memories hit me—of Richie and Tito bullying me at the playground, and the Great Ape and Mount Vesuvius throwing eggs at my house. Was T Rex going to save me like Hannah and my father had? I kept staring at the boys' pockets, wondering what they might be hiding. Would we be shot or stabbed? I remembered my father's warning never to put myself in needless jeopardy. It wasn't too late to turn and run.

In the deepening silence, however, my emotions took a different path. I wasn't going to run. Two boys I'd never met, whose names I didn't know—how do they get the balls to threaten us! My head began to spin with anger. As the shorter one pulled himself to his full height, edging closer to T Rex, he puckered his lips in a mock kiss. I coiled back my fist and punched it into his face, like my father had done to Louie.

It felt like I'd hit a sponge. He staggered back as blood spurted out his nose, falling on his butt on the sidewalk like someone taking a break from the heat, or winded from a game of street ball. I had done this? First, I felt confused, then another surge of adrenaline. I began to kick him. His friend tackled me from behind around the chest. T Rex yelped. We fell back, my head skimming the sidewalk. He swung at me but missed. We began to wrestle, rolling on the sidewalk in a blur of elbows and knees. Remembering my father's wrestling lessons, I pinned him easily. He began to holler. I let up a little, and he staggered to his feet, hands on his hips, filling his lungs with air. If he had a weapon, I thought, he'd have used it already.

I rushed him at full speed, toppling him like a practice dummy. Funny face, funny face, funny face, I thought, like an incantation, and began kicking him again.

My anger kept building. I could hear and smell the fire—the crackling joists, the smoke and melting wax. I drove my foot into his ribs as if he were responsible for setting it, for my terror and helplessness, for every snicker and insult I'd ever suffered. I suddenly understood why I'd never told my father or Dr. Glaspell about my memories of the fire. There was nothing anyone could do about it. My rage was unhealable.

"Will, stop it!" T Rex yelled, grabbing my arm repeatedly until I stopped.

"Muthafucka," the boy bellowed. He held his side as he struggled up. His sidekick took off with him at a half gallop.

"What are you, the Incredible Hulk?" T Rex said.

We went quickly, almost running, back to the train station before they could find reinforcements. T Rex was shaking her head at the whole drama, as if only now was the adrenaline vaporizing and the feeling of danger sinking in. We were lucky to have escaped, she said. I had a different thought. I was lucky I didn't kill them.

We took the L back to Michigan Avenue and found a Greek restaurant that looked like it had been around for a century. Dripping slabs of lamb were turning on a spit in the fogged window. T Rex ordered a salad with olive oil, tomatoes, and feta cheese. We ate mostly in silence, still thinking about our adventure.

"You eat like a bird. I thought T Rexes were carnivores," I joked, trying to break the tension.

"I suppose I should thank you," she said.

"For what?" I was playing dumb, but I wanted to be thanked. The closest I'd ever come to being a hero was throwing a weighted lunch box at a Neanderthal. Saving a girl who had held my hand

and might have feelings for me was far more promising. It was nothing. Anyone would have done the same thing. Don't worry about it. . . . But no words came out. I tried to smile. My face muscles weren't cooperating.

"Why do you think what happened today happened?" she asked.

I shook my head

"Why were you and I at that particular spot at that particular time?"

"We took the wrong exit from the L."

"What is it with you?" she said, disappointed. "If you don't know everything, if you can't scientifically explain cause and effect, then you have to believe in fate."

The disappointment, if not hurt, in T Rex's voice stung me. I was killing the mood I desperately wanted to kindle. As we headed back to the dorm, I apologized for not knowing what I was talking about. Everything was fate, I swore. We were mere cogs in the wheels of the universe, controlled by a bunch of gods. That was what the Greeks had based their mythology on. As T Rex listened, she seemed to forgive me for my earlier ignorance. I believed in feelings of desire, too, I wanted to add. That was the fate I suddenly wanted to explore.

In my room, I locked the door, and we snuggled on my bed. The act of surviving together had brought us closer. As she circled her arms around me, I pushed away the image of my distorted, bluish lips, and dared to kiss my first kiss. A shiver went through my heart. I was afraid T Rex would recoil and turn away. She would say that her emotions had deceived her, or that physical attraction just wasn't there. Instead, she met my lips with a tenderness that made me shudder. I didn't recoil either. We made out for half an hour. I felt relief, and ecstasy, and most of all grateful that my lips, unlike much of my face, had nerves under the scar tissue. I could feel her. Every time her breath slipped into my lungs, up and away I floated, until I was looking down on T Rex, on us, the way she safely looked down on paintings at the museum, on the rest of the world. She had carried me up to her perch, and at the same time opened a chamber of her heart to me.

When she tugged on my belt, I hesitated. "You're a virgin," she marveled, with a smile. "Relax, it's OK," she whispered, slipping off my shirt first. Her anticipation was tempered by an examination of my neck, where the burn tissue folded into flesh as normal as any other boy she had slept with. The contrast absorbed her, as if she found the more normal part of me almost a disappointment. I slithered out of my jeans carefully, while she flung her clothes across the room in abandon. I was shaking. What she didn't know was that over the years, I had come to regard my body as an extension of my face. I wasn't comfortable with how any part of me looked. Even in summer, I didn't walk around without a shirt, no matter how hot the day. Taking a shower with fifty boys after gym class was a punishment worse than chewing glass. My self-consciousness extended to every cell of my body.

"Are you all right?" she asked when I finally took off my underwear. I lay there with my arms pinned at my sides, my head squared back on the pillow, like I was in a doctor's office for an examination.

"I'm uncomfortable without my clothes," I admitted.

"Well, you're going to have to get used it." She studied my erection. "I'd say you're doing fine."

She began rubbing my chest, gently, like she was coaxing a genie from a bottle. I moaned with pleasure.

"Lie on top of me," she whispered.

I knew what to do. I didn't need help. Just as I had spent endless, lonely nights wondering if this moment would ever happen, how it would happen, and what I might feel, I wondered now why it ever had to end.

Making love to T Rex transported me long after she left my room. It had been a day of firsts for me. My happiness kept deepening. Before the glow faded, I took a pad and with colored charcoal drew our bodies twined together, brilliantly colored shapes of desire, floating in a white void. I signed it and gave it to T Rex the next day. I wrote at the top, in pencil, *The Shining Light of Uncertain Infinity.* I don't know where I found those words, much less what they meant. They simply felt right, conjuring up the tumultuous, grasping hunger of my soul. T Rex beamed, holding my drawing to her chest. She promised to keep it forever.

Not long after classes started, the humidity of summer began yielding to cooler mornings and crisp evenings. One October weekend, the incessant hum of the air conditioning in our favorite coffee shop was replaced by the hissing of radiators. Getting a jump on winter, I bought a down-filled parka with a hood at an Army surplus store. On weekends, T Rex and I visited the Art Institute to bask in the sun of Matisse, Gauguin, and Cezanne. There was no serious artist whose work didn't have some appeal to me, but what I was most drawn to was hard to describe. Sometime it was technique, sometimes composition, sometimes color. I was always attracted to originality. The work of a physical, emotional painter like Rothko stopped my heart. From where in his psyche, I wondered, did those mysterious blocks of color come?

If I had my choice, I would have spent most of my time wandering through the endless labyrinth of the museum, analyzing and daydreaming. School by contrast was often frustrating. Line and perspective didn't come naturally to me. Some days, I was afraid my drawing teacher would ask me to leave school; surely he would see I was an impostor, that my mother had pulled strings, and I would have to say good-bye to T Rex, which was the most painful thought of all. I was drawn to her originality like I was to a Rothko or Pollock. Sitting with her over coffee, talking to the girl I was falling in love with—why did I even bother with classes?

But I did. I never missed a single one. I refused to get discouraged, partly because I had promised my mother not to and partly because I began to build on my instincts and skills. Using crayons, charcoal, or just a No. 1 pencil, I worked through the most basic concepts. How did two or three lines, perfectly executed, convey so much, yet six or seven, slightly misplaced, mean imbalance and confusion? How could I create the deepest impression with the most economic interpretation? In drawing realistically, emotion was subordinated to the intellect, to technique, and everything had to be slowed down in my head. I reminded myself every day to be patient. We copied a lot of William Merritt Chase and Peter Benoit, masters of the ordinary object, particularly bowls of fruit. I worked and reworked every drawing until my fingers cramped.

There was another class that gave me equal difficulty but for a different reason. The Philosophy of Art explored the universe of art since the Greeks, the ever-changing answer to what exactly art was. When the professor began dissecting abstract expressionism, my ears picked up with the hope of unraveling the secrets of my mother's work. I understood how something made me feel, but the why was more challenging. I liked my mother's art because, besides the bold colors and forms, it seemed to be about destruction and creation, though what was being destroyed and what was reconstructed was up to interpretation.

In class we talked about the destruction of cultural, political, and personal values—things I thought could apply to my mother, her life as well as her art—and how by dismantling them, you were free to put things back together any way you wanted. The more complete the destruction, the greater the possibilities of renewal. If you took a sledgehammer to the existing order, smashing it into a thousand shining pieces, you had that much more material to work with. Therein lay the challenge—what did you keep, what did you elevate in importance, and how in general did you turn confusion and frustration into purpose and personal expression?

Painting class was more appealing to me. While I liked wrestling with ideas and abstractions, playing with colors was tactile and visceral. I was like a child in the mud. I was in love with primary colors, their range of values, especially pigments of blue. Blue was associated with ice, water, sky, winter, boys, sadness, cold, calm, and magic. I imagined my soul had been dunked in a can of blue. For a while, I put something blue into almost everything I painted. In addition to choosing my colors carefully, I learned what individual brushes and brushwork could achieve. I liked imitating the impressionists—layering oils on Masonite and shaping them with a palette knife. Some nights, I was too excited to sleep.

"You need a break," T Rex announced one evening. "Let's get some beer and make a night of it."

"I'm underage."

"I was introduced to beer by Kiss Ass when I was ten."

"Kiss Ass is your perfect older sister," I noted.

"Don't blame her. I hounded her until she gave in."

T Rex showed me her ID. She was wearing a red wig and had deep circles under her eyes. The birth date made her twenty-three. She said something about alcohol being good for my circulatory system, as if that would win me over. I didn't need to be convinced. I'd become dependent on T Rex, emotionally and physically, swept up in her web of crazy ideas and passions. If we'd already had sex in my room, there was no reason we couldn't smuggle in a couple of six-packs. Our floor proctor paid more attention to polishing her nails than the student handbook.

"Here's to Chicago," T Rex toasted as we opened the first two bottles. The night sky had a milky gloss, like someone had swiped it with a paint roller. Apartment buildings were cardboard cutouts, beaming back at us with a thousand eyes.

"Hog butcher to the world!" I roared, approaching the view.

"What are you talking about? What pigs are there in Chicago?"

I explained who Carl Sandburg was, and that when he wrote his famous poem, there were lots of slaughterhouses in Chicago. T Rex called him Carol Sandburg. She didn't like overly masculine men. I had told my father, on my weekly calls home, about my new girlfriend, and when he pressed me to describe my attraction to her, I had no shortage of stories. He said he looked forward to seeing me at Christmas, and it was fine if T Rex came too. I'd already extended her an invitation, if she wanted a break from Lard and Candy. She told me yes, definitely, she would be there. I was thrilled.

Being loved by the girl from Madison, Tennessee, was matched by my fascination with her free-spirited, rule-breaking, borderline insanity. I never knew what would pop out of her mouth. I longed to know her deeper secrets, buried in some cavity of her soul, but those were harder to come by.

"You're Mr. Literature," she said, breaking into the second six-pack. "Have you heard of Richard Brautigan?"

I said I didn't know the name.

"He was popular in the '60s—and then. . . ." She put her index finger to her temple and pulled her thumb. "He wasn't even fifty."

"Why did he kill himself?"

"He must have thought it was time. Your life can't last forever. *A Confederate General From Big Sur. In Watermelon Sugar. Trout Fishing in America.* Those are his legacy. You know what he once said? 'All of us have a place in history. Mine is clouds.' "

"I like clouds," I said.

"You'd like his books," she added, and began to recite a passage from memory. "Our waving seemed to be very distant traveling from our arms like two people waving at each other in different cities, perhaps between Tacoma and Salem, and our waving was merely an echo of their waving across thousands of miles. . . ."

I saw a tear in the pocket of her eye, but she banished it with a quick smile and moved to another subject. We never ran out of things to talk about. We didn't hang with other people. We were a crowd of two.

"What are you going to do when you get tired of me?" she asked suddenly, her back propped against a pillow on the bed.

"When I get tired of you? What are you talking about? How could I ever do that?"

"When you find somebody else, you're going to forget me. Why don't you admit it?"

I didn't know what had turned her so serious. Maybe it was the beer or Brautigan, or something else. "I'll never get tired of you," I swore.

"Everybody gets tired of everybody, sooner or later."

"Not me."

"That's a lie, even if you don't know it."

"I'd do anything for you," I said.

"Bullshit."

"No. I mean it."

"You shouldn't say that."

"I'm saying it!"

"Then open the window and jump out."

"Tabitha, you're drunk."

"I think you heard me." She stared at me like someone who was aiming a gun and threatening to pull the trigger. In those cobalt blue eyes, I saw a deep disappointment over something in the past. I imagined she didn't ask just anybody to jump out a window. She had special expectations for the boy who had saved her life and whom she had made love to. I didn't want to be the one to disappoint her again.

"OK. I'll show you that you're wrong," I said. I had more than a buzz from the beer.

I stumbled to the five-foot-tall window and unlocked the slider, shoving it theatrically to one side. The air was freezing. I expected her to say "Stop," or "Don't be an idiot," but T Rex was silent. In my socks, I balanced the balls of my feet on the sill, looking down on the tiny sidewalk with its flow of midgets. We were on the sixth floor. For anyone glancing up, I must have presented an odd image gripping the sides, hunched down to fit into the window frame, balanced precariously. But no one looked up.

"So let go," she said.

"What?"

"You said if you loved me. . . ."

"I do love you."

"Then nothing will happen to you . . . if our love is meant to last forever."

I gazed down again, like some god safe in the heavens above the fray of mortal suffering and indecision. I was beginning to catch on to T Rex's thinking. Everything was about fate, and I had to trust it. I released my hand, teetering like a nervous cat on a tree limb. I would be saved by love; I would have to be.

"OK, watch me," I proclaimed. In the night shadows, the sidewalk didn't look so terribly far away, though if I thought, I'd realize it was seventy feet to the ground. A poplar tree growing straight up stopped just below my window. I could grab it after I jumped. If I missed, an awning three floors down might break my fall. I tried not to think about it. Love could do anything, I told myself.

When I glanced back, wanting to see T Rex's face before I leaped, the bed was empty. I called her name, like she was a Brautigan character in a faraway city. I searched the bathroom, the closet, under the bed. Had she stormed out, certain I wasn't going to act? Maybe she realized she was drunk and wanted to let me off the hook. I had no idea. I had jumped into the void of endless, crazy, suspicious love. I decided to leave her alone; we'd talk tomorrow. What had happened the last ten minutes meant nothing.

T Rex was missing in our English class the next morning, nor did she make our afternoon rendezvous at the coffee shop. She lived two floors above me. I banged on her door before dinner. Her roommate answered, a girl with braces and a neck like a giraffe. A strap with a gigantic Nikon dangled from her neck. Her side of the room was filled with photography equipment. She had let the world know she was going to be the next Richard Avedon.

"What do you want?" she asked.

"Where's T Rex?"

"What, is it my job to babysit?" Her laughter was like little burps of a machine gun. "If you want to know," she said, "she cleaned out her closet this morning. I'd like you to leave now, please."

"Bullshit," I said.

"Hey, smartass," she said, offended that I would doubt her, "it's true."

I barreled past her to T Rex's closet. The Magic Marker clothes were gone, books, the *Nighthawks* poster, suitcases. It was like she'd never been here.

"Asshole," the roommate muttered as I left in a panic. Where had T Rex gone, and why hadn't she told me—and was this my fault?

When I checked in the morning, the registrar informed me that Tabitha Penelope Rex had taken an indefinite leave of absence from SDA. I called information in Madison, Tennessee, and got a number for Gerald and Cynthia Rex. Gerald answered the phone. I imagined someone with an impossibly large ass.

"Who's this?" he inquired, friendly enough.

"My name's Will Ryder. I was wondering if T Rex was home from Chicago yet."

"Will Ryder?" He was drawing a blank.

"I'm a student with your daughter at SDA. Is she there, please?"

"Oh, that Will Ryder," he said, which made me feel slightly better. Suddenly, his hand covered the mouthpiece, and I endured the rise and fall of background voices that seemed unending, punctuated by a symphony of chairs moving, objects dropping, and doors slamming, as if an earthquake had suddenly jolted Madison.

"She'll have to return your call, Will," Mr. Rex said, getting back on the phone. He seemed gracious and thoughtful enough.

"When?"

"No idea on that one, son. Patience is a virtue."

"Is she all right? I don't know why she left school. She just disappeared."

"Well, that sounds like our T Rex." He chuckled, like someone enjoying a private family joke, as if the middle child was forever keeping everyone guessing. "Son, do you know what a Roman candle is?"

"As in fireworks?"

"A Roman candle shoots off with a deafening noise and blazing speed, and it's so dazzling that you think it's going all the way to the moon. But when you look up again, it's nowhere close to the moon. Instead, it's gone, just like that, and the sky's black as pitch again."

"Mr. Rex," I implored, "can you please tell me if she's OK?"

His hand covered the phone again, I assumed for another debate over my request, whether family secrets had priority over a stranger's need to know. But I was not exactly a stranger, and my need to know was deeper than her family could imagine. Why wouldn't T Rex come to the phone? Was she still upset with me for not jumping out the window? I craved hearing her voice. I wanted to tell her father I couldn't eat or sleep until I had every piece of information. I was dying a slow death in Chicago.

"She was coming home with me for Christmas," I said, hoping to be heard over the commotion in the room.

A voice came back into the receiver. "What's that?"

"We were going to New Mexico." Christmas was less than six weeks away.

"Why would she be going to New Mexico?"

"I live there. Your daughter and I are very close. I'm her boyfriend. Didn't she tell you?"

"Her boyfriend?"

"Yes, sir," I said proudly.

"She already has a boyfriend. Jeremy's here right now."

I took the news reasonably well. I didn't scream or slam the phone into the cradle. I didn't even bother to hang up. The receiver simply slid out of my hand, and I walked away. I skipped classes that afternoon. At our favorite coffee shop, I drank a gallon of black coffee, hoping it would have the same effect as hemlock. Back in my room, I cried, literally banged my head against a wall, and tried to understand. The evening T Rex and I first had coffee, was she late because she'd been talking to Jeremy? When she'd promised to come home with me for Christmas, had she sensed all along that she wouldn't make it? She meant well, I firmly believed, but her mercurial nature held her hostage. She didn't always know what she would do from one moment to the next. That's one reason I loved her. The next day, a friend told me T Rex's departure was not exactly voluntary. She had missed half her classes, and been asked to leave.

I called her house every day for two weeks. T Rex never answered the phone. At first, her mother or father gave me a polite brush-off, but eventually, their attitude changed.

"Now, listen up, son," Mr. Rex said, like someone whose patience had worn thin. "You're like a cross between a tax collector and a coon dog. You haven't gotten the hint. You are to stop calling this house, is that clear?"

"No," I said politely.

"If you try to be in touch with my daughter one more time, I'm calling not only the police but the Federal Bureau of Investigation."

"Why?"

"Because you're a Commie menace."

"If that's how you feel. . . ."

"It's not just how I feel. It's what I'm going to do," he threatened, and hung up.

That afternoon, I wrote T Rex a five-page letter begging her to name a spot where we could meet in secret, or at least a time when she could call me. I went on interminably about my feelings. I couldn't accept that she was in love with someone else and had only been taking me on a three-month joy ride. Why didn't she tell me about Jeremy? What about all our talk about fate? Our souls were welded together like a piece of sculpture, and we both knew it.

For Thanksgiving dinner, an unsmiling boy on my floor named Franklin Jones Jr. invited me to his home, a triplex near the Sears Tower. I thought he felt sorry for me for what I'd gone through with T Rex. I no longer had my suit, so I arrived in jeans and a dress shirt. Franklin, his father, and stepmother were dressed like they were going to be seated at the captain's table on the Queen Mary. I asked if I might have a scotch and soda. "Sure," Franklin said, and made himself one as well. The triplex must have cost a couple of million, but that didn't match the value of the art on the walls. Franklin paraded me by a half-dozen Frankenthalers, Motherwells, and Rauschenbergs as if he were a museum curator, which, in fact, was his ambition. When we finally sat down for dinner, two men in white jackets served us from sterling silver platters. The pinot noir, it was pointed out, hailed from an elite vineyard in southern France, and I was allowed to drink as much as I wanted. Franklin Sr. began telling me about stocks and bonds, especially a killing he had made with Proctor & Gamble. I nodded like I knew what he was talking about. Mrs. Jones, thin as a stick, looked about twenty, and as Junior's stepmom, she kept correcting his table manners. I could tell he hated her. She had a pitying smile for me, like she'd have for a war vet with missing legs. I kept thinking of T Rex. What was she doing for Thanksgiving? I finally said good night to everyone and made it to the street before throwing up.

In the four weeks before Christmas, the only thing that cheered me was the prospect of going home. With Hannah returning from Yale, and David meeting us in Santo Tomás, it would be a family reunion. I thought about all the things I'd taken for granted, the pleasures that had been left behind in my rush to get to Chicago: classical music floating through the house, the abiding aromas of the Cuatro Caminos Super Mercado, sleeping in my own bed. Every Christmas Eve, the older, traditional neighborhoods were lined with farolitos—candles in folded paper bags—and small bonfires called luminarias. Families strolled up and down the sidewalks bundled in their jackets and stopping at the fires to drink hot cider and catch up with old friends. It was a magical time.

The day before my flight home, the floor proctor slipped a note under my door. I was hoping it was a message from T Rex, but instead, my mother had sent it. She had called from New York, telling me to contact her immediately. I wondered if something was wrong.

"It's Will," I said when she answered the phone. "Is everything OK?" I still didn't feel comfortable calling her "mother."

"How's school?" Her voice, as usual, was neither distant nor friendly, a kind of phone operator neutral.

"School's all right," I reported.

"Learning a lot?"

"Drawing class is challenging. I'm making progress."

"What else?"

"Nothing, really." I didn't know whether my mother was probing for something particular or we were just lost in small talk.

"I want to invite you for a very special Christmas," she said. "I'm staying at the Paisano Hotel in Marfa. I've already put money in your account for the plane ticket. A driver will pick you up at the El Paso airport."

"What's Marfa?" I said.

"A small town in the middle of the prairies of West Texas. Donald Judd moved there in 1972, when he wanted to escape the New York art scene. He passed away a few years ago, but a foundation was established in his will, and I know a trustee on the board. I can get you into Judd's home, his studio, the armory, everywhere. It's not just Judd you'll see. There's Chamberlain, Stella, Flavin, Johns. . . ."

Marfa finally struck a chord. I'd read about Judd, the minimalist sculptor, and his volumetric shapes. It made sense that my mother would be attracted to a fellow egghead. Judd had studied philosophy in college, and, like my mother, brought an intellectual rigor to the creative process. He didn't even call his sculptures "art." He called them objects. He read voraciously, liked to drink, and had difficulty sustaining relationships with women. If he'd ever gotten to know my mother, I thought whimsically, they might have ended up lovers.

"Thanks for the offer," I said. "It's very generous. But this is kind of last minute. I'm leaving for Santo Tomás tomorrow."

"But what do you want to do?"

"What do you mean?"

"Are you just pleasing your father, or do you want to see incredible art in an intimate way? These chances don't come along every day."

"I'm not pleasing my father. I'm homesick. I miss Santo Tomás."

"What if you spent a few days in Marfa, then went home for Christmas?" she suggested. She could think on her feet much faster than me. "Call me back in an hour, Will."

"I need a little more time to think. . . ."

"Good-bye."

I felt my face warm. She was making me uncomfortable, keeping me off balance, just like she had in Phoenix. I understood what my father meant about the difficulty of winning arguments with her. When my mother got you in a choke hold, unless you had a flashy counter-move, the next thing you knew, you were on the mat. I returned to my room and finished packing. I had eleven days off. If I spent four in Marfa, I reasoned, I could still be home for the farolito walk. I hoped the Marfa invitation wasn't my mother's attempt to throw a monkey wrench into my father's plans. This was her Christmas present, and it would be wrong not to accept it. I called her back and confirmed that I'd meet her driver at the El Paso airport. That afternoon, I made a sketch of a Chicago street scene, and signed it "Merry Christmas, Will." I would give it to her as a present in Marfa.

When I called my father, I told him about the unexpected invitation and that it might be good politics to spend a few days with my mother. I made it sound like a business decision, which it partly was. She was my financial support, my patron, and I didn't want to alienate her. Without fail, I said, I'd be in Santo Tomás before

Christmas Eve. When I added that my girlfriend wouldn't be coming, he must have heard the disappointment in my voice because he said he and Hannah would cheer me up. He didn't bother to comment on my mother.

At the El Paso airport, a man in a dark suit was holding up a placard with "Wilson Louis Ryder" written in bold felt pen, like I was a VIP.

"That's me," I said, feeling important.

"Right this way, sir."

He carried my bag to a black town car. When we broke away from the freeway clutter, the stretches of road were shared mostly with pickups and eighteen-wheelers, gliding past farmland, ranches, and pockets of grazing cattle. We climbed gradually into the mountains. The sky turned an ice blue, and the temperature dropped into the thirties. I was glad I'd brought warm clothes. Marfa stood between three mountain ranges at an altitude of five thousand feet, a town so small you could wrap it in tinfoil and take it to-go, I thought when we reached our destination. The Hotel Paisano, named for one of the mountain ranges, was a picturesque, rambling, turn-of-the-century hotel in a downtown that was at most eight blocks long. The bellhop wore jeans and a cowboy hat. I would have said, "Howdy, pardner," but he told me straight away he was from Baltimore and trying to raise money to get home. I gave him ten bucks.

Christmas lights were strung across the lip of the reception desk, and in a corner of the lobby was a fifteen-foot Douglas fir decked with silver tinsel and red and white blinking bulbs. A holiday party was in full swing in an adjoining room. I heard someone say the hotel was completely booked.

"Hello, Will," a voice greeted me. The man had on a stylish suit and narrow designer tie, close-cropped black hair, and wire-rimmed glasses. He looked in his 50s. His teeth were crooked and discolored, and the soft folds of his neck hung like rubber over his shirt collar. He took my hand in a vise of a grip and wouldn't let go until I winced.

"I'm Albert Reingold," he said with a voice as firm as his handshake. "Why don't you call me Albert?"

Call me slow, I thought. It had never occurred to me that Albert Reingold was my mother's friend on the Judd Foundation board, and that they were probably still lovers. She never referred to him in our conversations. Then again, when it came to real news from my mother, anything personal, I might as well have been marooned on a South Pacific island.

"Pleasant drive?" asked Albert. "Need to freshen up?"

"I'm OK. Where's Susan?"

"We have a special tour this afternoon. Just the three of us. You're in for a treat."

Albert was pleasant enough, but he seemed all business, not unlike my mother. She joined us a minute later, looking as she had in Phoenix—her hair pulled back in a pony tail, with simple but elegant jewelry and not much makeup, just lipstick and eyeliner. She wore jeans and a green pullover, with a canary scarf to keep her neck warm. She gave me her usual A-frame hug and a minute or two of conversation before our Marfa tour began at a brisk pace.

Judd, Albert told me, invested in Marfa real estate when his work began to sell for serious money. When he died, he owned sixteen buildings and three nearby ranches, and had a whopping $462 in his checking account. Was he just a spending fool? Albert said he bought buildings to display his and his friends' art, and because he liked to renovate—architecture was another talent—he had purchased the local Safeway and made it his studio. The ranches were weekend getaways. I walked through the old Safeway. Every tool, paintbrush, and half-finished object was exactly where Judd had left it. Everything felt surreal. I thought I could smell the last ham sandwich he'd eaten there. I could feel his ghost floating between the steel rafters, checking on visitors, maybe to make sure no one stole anything. I kept my hands in my pockets to prove I could be trusted.

My mother delivered a brief speech on perfection and integrity. Judd was obsessed with his boxes, their symmetry or asymmetry, and the spaces that they trapped. Most of the waist-high cubes looked identical in shape and size, but in fact, no two were exactly alike. Some were open on the top and had five sides instead of six. I saw that others had a Plexiglas partition in the middle that made two rectangles, or a five-degree ramp at the bottom. They all were empty and looked like they were never meant to hold anything but light and air. Plywood was the only material Judd could afford when he was starting out, my mother said. Much later, when he worked with professional fabricators, the cubes were made of anodized aluminum, stainless steel, brass or copper, even concrete. I couldn't pry my eyes from them. They energized my thinking about what art could be.

"Come here," my mother called, pointing to a steel cube that was open at the top. Painted a glossy Chinese red, it sat neglected in a corner. "The fabricators made this to his specifications, but when it arrived, Judd rejected it," she said. "Can you see why?"

I searched in vain for a flaw in the paint or welding. I asked if there was a problem with the design.

Her finger traced a metal lip protruding a few centimeters along one side of the interior. It created asymmetry and made you ponder the space and its limitations. "He was happy with the design on paper," my mother said, "but this metal lip, when he saw it, nagged at him. He thought it didn't belong. He refused to sell the work, even if he could have made a million dollars. He had changed his mind. Great artists do that."

"I think there's a more philosophical explanation," Albert interrupted, raising his brow at my mother. He wanted me to know he was the real expert here. "For Judd, art was about finding the perfect marriage of mathematics to philosophy, concept to material, and that lip could not fit into an equation without upsetting some universal law. Art was part science to him. It was about the relationship between numbers—you can see that from his sketches—because that was far more certain and dependable than a relationship between people." Albert spoke the last line with some sarcasm.

Our tour took three hours: the turn-of-the-century Bank of Marfa with its gilded teller cages and Greek columns, which Judd had never finished renovating; a print shop; his architecture office; and several private homes he had fallen in love with and mercurially bought for his real estate portfolio. Albert kept competing with my mother for who had the most to say. Their approaches were different. My mother spoke of the creative process with comfort and intimacy, from a personal point of view. Albert was more abstract. He dissected concepts carefully and endlessly. I began to think of him as a windbag.

I walked back to the hotel, took a nap, and joined my mother and Albert at a fancy restaurant for Judd fans from around the world. Germans, Italians, and Japanese were particularly fond of the artist and were in evidence tonight. Albert told me that Judd had eaten regularly at another nearby restaurant, but it had gone out of business. This was the closest facsimile. Judd would consume his favorite scotch, Chivas Regal, and talk deep into the night with friends, ignoring any sycophantic fans. Albert was also no stranger to scotch. He lit a cigarette as he studied the menu. As usual, my mother refused to touch any stimulant, and she looked impatient when Albert lit a second cigarette, as if one should have been enough, or he should at least go outside.

"Well, thanks for inviting me to Marfa," I said cheerfully but feeling like an interloper.

"We're happy you're here," my mother said. I ordered the rib eye with shoestring onion rings, hoping the night would end relatively soon. I wasn't comfortable talking to an important art critic. What if he thought I was an ignoramus?

"How did you meet my mother?" I began when I found Albert looking at me.

"I was married with three kids, and Susan came along and stole me like a four-carat diamond from a Tiffany window."

"Stole you, like some great prize?" she asked.

"You can't deny it."

I wondered how you could steal anything from Tiffany's. I had read that the jewelry store had tighter security than the Secret Service.

"You wanted to be seduced," she corrected him. "You wanted out of your marriage. We fell in love."

"So a bad thing turned into a good thing," I said, remembering my mother's philosophy.

Albert didn't know what I was talking about, and he ordered another scotch. He was barely looking at me now.

Changing subjects, I asked, "Where are you guys living now, upstate or in the city?" I was never sure where my mother lived at any given time. At one point, she was in Manhattan, in Soho, but another article reported her living upstate, in Woodstock. There had also been primary residences in Maine and Massachusetts. She was all over the board. "You two live together, right?" I asked.

"Like the universe, everything's in flux," Albert said opaquely. He was suddenly acting like a diffident companion who had been coerced to dinner. Or maybe this was how he got when he drank. I could hear my mother's foot tapping.

"Did you know Judd personally?" I asked.

It turned out to be the right question. Albert blew a perfect ring from his cigarette, over his shoulder so it wouldn't hit us, but it struck a passing waiter in the face. Albert half-smiled an apology. "We became friends when he was living in Soho. Don was starting to have some luck with galleries, but as a conceptual artist, there wasn't much of a following. I was just out of college, bumming around the village and Soho, which then was a bunch of warehouses. I was selling photorealist graphics for a gallery. It was just a job. Don and I got to know each other at a bar one night. We had endless discussions about art history and theory. He was a brilliant writer and critic as well as an artist. I recognized his genius before the public did. I visited him in Marfa numerous times."

"That's very cool," I said.

"Cool," he repeated, as if the word amused him. "What do you think, Susan? Was the way I met Don cool?"

I ignored his sarcasm, but my mother had had enough.

"Albert, this is a week for Will," she said. "To teach him how artists think, how you think as a critic, and for us to learn what he's thinking."

She hadn't raised her voice, but her tone was like a fist slammed on the table. Albert came to attention, his eyes roving warily between us, as if there might be some conspiracy he didn't know about. He was a bully who liked to have the last word on everything, but at that moment, he chose silence. I excused myself before dessert and was happy to escape to the hotel.

The next morning, the sound of rapid knocking broke into my sleep. My eyes opened one at a time. It wasn't even seven. It was my mother. She said through the door that we needed to talk. Her tone was impatient if not urgent. I met her in the dining room five minutes later.

Unlike my mother, I was fond of big breakfasts, with freshly squeezed orange juice and several cups of coffee, a habit I'd picked up at the Four Seasons. I wondered what Judd ate for breakfast. He was a Renaissance man, so maybe he'd invented a couple of recipes in his exile, like eggs Marfa or sausage Paisano.

"What do you think of Albert?" she asked after we'd ordered.

I put down my fork, surprised by the question. Was someone as private and self-contained as my mother, who viewed children as half-formed beings ideally left to develop on their own, really seeking my opinion? I was an ignorant outsider; what did I possibly know?

"He seems OK," I said, wanting to stay neutral.

"He's a pompous jackass," she answered. "Can't you see that?"

All I knew was that Albert had a healthy opinion of scotch, Donald Judd, and himself. All right, I agreed, he was an asshole.

"He doesn't know it yet," she announced, "but I'm going to be leaving him. It's over."

"Your relationship? You're kidding."

"It's time to move on."

"Why are you telling me this?"

"Who else am I going to tell?"

"When are you going to tell Albert?"

"In a few days. Don't worry. It will all happen after you leave." We were scheduled to visit Judd's private compound and then the museum housed in a former military installation called Fort Marfa, and tomorrow, Judd's Chinati ranch. It could be a long two days, I thought.

"How many years have you been together?" I asked, sounding like Dr. Glaspell, ready to dig to the root of the problem.

"Eight years."

"That's a long time. What about your professional relationship?" I thought to add. "What if Albert gets vindictive and writes that you're nothing but a glorified house painter?" That was my mother's description for any artist she didn't respect.

"He always says and writes what he pleases. I can't control that. I just can't stick around him any longer. That I can control."

Her voice trailed off. No matter what she believed about grand gestures and moving on, dealing with an ego like Albert's wouldn't be easy. "Is there someone else in your life, someone close, to fall back on?"

"Absolutely no one," she said, indifferent to the prospect of being alone.

"Well, you have friends. . . ."

She was quiet. If she had any, she didn't seem to rely on them either. She believed that life was a process, and ultimately, things would change. They always did, so you rode out any storm. Fortunes rose and fell and rose again. She didn't need to be consoled about any of it.

When Albert joined us an hour later, my mother pretended nothing was amiss. She was honoring her promise that our Marfa holiday was meant for me.

The Judd compound was hidden on a side street and defined by high adobe walls all around it. My mother said he was paranoid, and even a deep admirer like Albert suggested that Judd could be difficult—petulant and standoffish. Inside the walls was a plain, practical house, except for Judd's and his friends' remarkable art, which was scattered about haphazardly. I was attracted to the midnight blues and Chinese reds of the rigid metal furniture he designed. I wondered how he'd found the time to accomplish so much. Albert said Judd was probably an insomniac. His library was eclectic, everything from travel tales and biographies to history and philosophy, endless books lined up on endless wood shelves to keep him company on long nights. He had a big kitchen and a dining table that could seat twenty. His friends came and went.

I tried to keep my attention on a man whose impact on twentieth-century art couldn't be overestimated, but in the back of my mind, I worried about my mother. The next day, as the three of us milled about through more of the Judd empire, I began to think of Albert as a prizefighter determined to come out victorious no matter what the arena of combat. After they broke up, would my mother be free from his bullying? Why should I care? She and I lived on opposite sides of the planet, connected only by the bridge of art.

Christmas Eve morning, I was packed by seven and ate breakfast alone in the hotel dining room. My driver was outside, ready to whisk me through El Paso and on to Santo Tomás. I would see my family by early afternoon. I had rehearsed a brief thank you and good-bye speech, not sure when I would see Albert again, or if I wanted to. But it was important to me to be polite. My mother was investing in my education, and I didn't see why it shouldn't include manners. Albert could be an important connection in the future, too, my personal feelings aside.

When no one had appeared by eight thirty, I scribbled a note to my mother wishing her a Merry Christmas, then put a ribbon around the Chicago street drawing, and delivered both to the man at the reception desk. A booming voice suddenly erupted in the hallway. When I turned, Alfred was in his boxers and an overly tight T-shirt, chasing after my mother, who had her suitcase in her hand. He was right behind her, then beside her, gesturing like an opera singer. His sentences were as jumbled as his voice was loud. Twice he grabbed her wrist. She threw off his hand both times.

My mother was being chased by a half-naked man, who appeared more like a lunatic than a famous art critic or a trustee on the Judd Foundation board. The next thing I knew, I was in the car and my mother was beside me in the back seat. She was trembling and out of breath, like a refugee who'd just found asylum, and suddenly fumbling through her handbag.

"Is that lithium?" I asked when she pulled out a prescription vial.

"No. Valium, for anxiety."

She swallowed the pill dry—I watched her throat bob in relief—and then she closed her eyes, as if to deny the chaos around us. Albert was suddenly beside the car, slamming his palm repeatedly against our closed window, like someone trying to break in. As the driver sped away, Albert bellowed like a large mammal in heat.

"Did he hurt you?" I said as I spotted a bruise on my mother's wrist. She was too distracted to answer. I turned and looked though the rear window. Albert's face was contorted helplessly, grotesquely, as if someone had robbed him of his last dime and he was desperate to get it back. He seemed unaware or unconcerned about the attention he was attracting. A dozen hotel guests lined the sidewalk. Maybe he liked being the center of attention, I thought. He was an art critic.

I looked at my mother in confusion. "I thought you were going to wait to split with him—until I left."

"I couldn't stand him one second longer. So I told him we were through. And then he turned into a madman." She shook her head. "I take that back. He already was a madman. He became Attila the Hun."

I had to think to figure out the next step. In El Paso, I would drop my mother at the airport. She would fly home, and I would continue on to Santo Tomás with the driver. I'd be home by two or three, well before the farolito walk. My mother sat back, arms cradled in her lap, still shaken. After being humiliated by Albert, would she ever show her face in Marfa again?

"You're lucky to be rid of him," I said.

"This reminds me of when I was a little girl. We were always leaving in a hurry."

"Was someone screaming at you, too?"

"Not exactly. But it felt like something was chasing us."

"Like what?"

"Never mind. It's a waste of time to resurrect your childhood."

"I don't mind hearing."

She gave me an "if you insist" look; digging into her memory seemed to take forever. "My mother was a sweet, lost soul who tried to hide her unhappiness. She would spend a month packing up an entire household, say good-bye to her friends, and off we drove, following the moving van to whatever new base my father had been assigned. She'd put on the radio and merrily sing along while my father drove in silence. We moved nine or ten times, and on each occasion, her soul shrank a little more at the prospect of starting over. All she wanted was to have lasting friends. My father lived in a world of duty. It wasn't his fault that he had to deny her what she wanted, yet he could have been more sympathetic.

"What was chasing me," she added, "was the fear that when I became an adult, I'd never be able to settle down in one place either."

Her fear had come true, I thought, and I wanted to know more. Like stumbling by luck on the combination to a bank vault, I had somehow gotten my mother to open up. I wanted to see everything inside. Why did she always keep moving? No one forced her. What made her so restless?

"Are you happy?" I asked suddenly.

"I don't think about happiness any more. Not since I was at Columbia. Happiness comes and goes. Why dwell on something so ephemeral? Sadness doesn't leave so quickly. But I don't think about that either."

"I get sad," I told her, my thoughts flashing to T Rex.

"You're young. You'll learn it's a waste of time."

"What if I don't learn that?"

"Then you'll never be a great artist."

"You keep saying that. How can you possibly generalize?"

I remembered what she had told me in Phoenix, that great art was about the absence of personality. Back home, I had looked in my father's Bartlett's Quotations. My mother had been quoting T.S. Eliot, so maybe she had a point. But it was irrelevant to me. I would never be that kind of painter.

We were interrupted by what sounded like an Indian war whoop from our driver. "Watch out!" he cried. He was staring in the rear-view mirror and suddenly pushed the accelerator hard. The car shot ahead. I nudged my mother, who looked as confused as I was. We turned to the rear window and saw Albert in his rental car, veering wildly and bearing down on us like a missile.

"Faster," I told the driver. As rapidly as we were moving, Albert had more horsepower. I watched his car edge closer. I could imagine his eyes widening. He leaned over the steering wheel like it could give him more momentum.

Our driver must have had the accelerator jammed down. I saw 100 on the speedometer. We were wearing our seat belts, but they didn't seem like enough. My mother was frozen in her seat, incapable of saying or doing anything. I gazed back at Albert's look of maniacal glee.

Suddenly he rammed us, like in a high-speed movie chase. Our car felt lifted in the air; then it landed with a jolt and kept moving.

Pain spiraled through my lower back. I kept my eyes on Albert. He eased back, either to assess how terrified we were or measure his need for further revenge. Did he want to kill us? My mother grabbed my hand. Albert's face was suddenly as rigid as one of Judd's cubes.

The second time, he hit us harder and sent our car skidding. The driver braked, overcorrected, and veered helplessly toward a utility pole. I was afraid we'd flip over. Instead, when we hit, the front end crumpled like paper. My mother banged her knees into the front seat. The driver was shaken but OK. My head struck the side window. The last thing I remembered before blacking out for a minute was the blare of Albert's off-key horn, as if declaring his triumph to the world.

Our driver had a cell phone. A police cruiser and an ambulance showed up within fifteen minutes. Albert stayed in his car. He never bothered to ask if anyone was hurt. The ambulance took my mother and me to a hospital in Alpine, about twenty-five miles from Marfa. My mother's knees were bruised but nothing more than that. I had a badly sprained left ankle. A doctor fitted me with a cast and said I'd be there twenty-four hours for observation because I had a possible concussion.

The next morning, my mother flew east. For our good-bye, she leaned over my bed and patted my shoulder. There was no kiss or even a hug—and no apology for anything. I told her I'd left her a Christmas gift at the Paisano. She promised she would have it sent to her. Another car and driver would take me to Santo Tomás, she said, and we would be in touch during the school year, though she didn't say when. My mother was back to her old self, moving briskly through life, propelled by her own schedule. I had lost my chance of getting to know her better when Attila the Hun chased us down.

I spent Christmas Day in the hospital, reading magazines and listening to carols on the radio. When I called home to tell everyone what happened, my father was outraged by Albert Reingold's homicidal behavior but relieved that my injuries weren't worse. He asked more than once if the doctors knew what they were doing, as if he were ready to drive to Alpine and rescue me. I assured him I was fine and said I was sorry not to be back for Christmas; I'd be home in a day or two. I didn't know whether to blame my mother or Albert or both, or to lay the whole misadventure in the lap of fate.

When I was released from the hospital, a detective was waiting in the lobby and drove me to the police station. He needed a full statement about the accident, and my mother was gone. Albert had been cited for reckless driving and then released, claiming his brakes had failed and that the accident wasn't his fault. Because failing brakes didn't explain why he'd hit the gas a second time, the police suspected there was more to the story. I told them in my statement about Albert's tirade at the Hotel Paisano because my mother had ended their relationship. I had seen his wild glare through the window just before he turned his car into a battering ram. I signed the statement and hobbled out of the station on crutches, happy to have a chance to tell the truth. The case was going to be turned over to the district attorney.

"Will, my God, are you OK?" my father said when the driver dropped me at our house. I nodded, but I was chagrined to be two days late. I struggled with my crutches up the front steps to the porch, where I turned and surveyed the neighborhood. Nothing seemed to change in Santo Tomás except the seasons. The trees had lost their leaves and looked like props in a Bergman movie. A rare blanket of snow was on the lawns. The neighbors' bicycles were scattered about in almost the exact spots as when I'd left four months earlier.

"Hi, Will!" Hannah threw her arms around me in the hallway. In jeans and a sweater, she had survived her time at Yale without noticeable wear. Her glow still lit the room. David had a golf club in his hand, and good-naturedly tapped my cast with it. "I bet there's a great story behind this," he said. "Don't leave out any details."

"Honestly, there's nothing more than what I told you on the phone," I replied. As much as possible, I wanted to keep my mother's life a secret, confining her to a separate world from the one I had in Santo Tomás. Inhabiting two different universes was less stressful when they didn't intersect.

"Sit down, take a load off," my father urged. "Tell us about school, Will. Tell us everything."

"I want to hear from Hannah first."

"We've already heard from Hannah," my father said. "It's your turn."

I wasn't sure where to start—T Rex, Chicago, the Art Institute, SDA classes?—and my ankle was beginning to throb under the cast. David brought out aspirin from the kitchen along with a platter of food and a fresh pot of coffee.

My audience was rapt as I filled in most of the blanks. I purposely skipped how I beat up two kids in the street or put my life in harm's way a second time by nearly jumping from a sixth-story window. I told stories of how competitive art school was. Egos at SDA were the size of the Sears Tower. For some kids, happiness was not only when your own work was praised but when your friends' paintings got trashed, too. By the time I brought up T Rex and the end of our relationship, my emotional pain had been buffered by all the attention I was getting.

Yale academics were intense, too, Hannah told me privately, but I knew she thrived on competition. She didn't know what her major would be. She was leaning away from both the humanities and sciences, considering options that would mean a more-secure livelihood. I remembered her vow not to be poor. She was enjoying her professors, new friends, and all that New Haven culture had to offer. She asked me more about T Rex. As I described her unorthodox life, Hannah suggested that maybe I was better off without her. T Rex was the type who, consciously or not, left a pile of boyfriends in her wake. She might be wild and fun, but she didn't understand responsibility and consequences.

"I can't move on. I'm in love," I told Hannah the next day as we worked in the yard. My father had gone for a walk with David. Hannah was raking up a pile of damp, rotted leaves. Despite my cast, I could still hold a trash bag and scoop in the compost.

"You know something about being in love. You and David are happy," I said.

"We are. But that doesn't mean I haven't dated other guys at Yale."

"You do?" I exclaimed. "Does David know?"

"He does the same thing. We want to make sure we're right for each other. I don't want to get married and a few years later start looking around. I'll never do what Mom did to Dad."

"Maybe I'm different than you. I know who's right for me."

"Will, you're sixteen. What happened with T Rex has to really hurt, but you need to take the long view. There'll be other girls."

"I don't have a long view. I'm an artist," I said evasively, unsure what I meant. I should have added that when you looked like Frankenstein, getting girls was something of a challenge. Like a watch commander on the bridge, Hannah had been peering with binoculars into the swirling mists of the unknown since she was in grade school, determined to keep everybody safe, especially me. I wanted to tell her to butt out. I could navigate my own way now.

My sister smiled tightly, wondering how to make her point more clearly. "I want to be honest, Will. I think you have a habit of connecting with people who aren't good for you. I don't mean just T Rex."

"Who could you possibly be thinking of?"

She ignored my sarcasm. "Seriously, look what happened when you let her back in your life. You end up in a hospital. That moron of an art critic almost kills you. What's next?"

"I have no idea. Maybe she'll never want to see me again."

Hannah gave me a "you should be so lucky" look. "You know, she just plays with your head."

"What's that supposed to mean?"

"Remember her Bulova watch that you used to carry around in grade school? She didn't accidentally leave it behind. She knew you'd find it, or Dad would give it to you. She wanted you to be thinking about her."

"Why is that a bad thing?"

"Because her motive was manipulation."

"You're full of it. She forgot the watch, pure and simple."

Hannah wasn't finished. "If human beings ever evolve into a species that eat their young, guess who's the prototype? And you walked right into her trap. . . ."

"What kind of trap is it," I snapped, "to have your education completely paid for? I'd call that an incredible favor."

"A favor? It's a debt she's trying to work off. She owes you for the rest of your life. If I set one of my kids on fire. . . ."

"Stop it!" I gathered the first full sack of leaves and tied the bag with a strip of plastic-coated wire. I refused to look at my sister.

Hannah had my mother all figured out, from her own point of view. From mine, things were more sticky. I blamed my mother for my disfigurement, but I also had feelings of never being quite good enough for her, that I somehow had to justify her investment in me. My father had been right about how she motivated people. I wanted her approval.

"I'm just watching your back, Will. If you want my opinion, she's your tormentor."

"My tormentor," I repeated.

"Isn't it obvious?"

"Are you finished now?"

After another round of leaf gathering, we stored the rake and trash bags in the garage. My father wasn't back from his walk. Hannah asked how I thought he was doing.

"He seems fine to me," I said, still upset with my sister.

"He missed you a lot. He told me that. He said he keeps busy. Nothing's changed at the university. If you want my opinion, he could be a lot happier."

"It's none of my business if he's happy or not. Dad can take care of himself. So can I."

I hobbled away. I hated whenever Hannah said, "If you want my opinion. . . ." She volunteered her thoughts whether I wanted them or not. Despite the joy of catching up with my father, I would blame my sister for dampening my Christmas spirit that year. Except for Albert's maniacal behavior and his car crash finale, I'd had a better time in Marfa.

I flew back to Chicago on a Sunday, focusing on the semester ahead. A large box was waiting for me in my room, with a belated Christmas note from my mother. She hoped my ankle was on the mend, she wrote, and that I would have a productive finish to my first year at SDA. She thanked me for the "competent sketch" that the Hotel Paisano had sent on to her.

I opened her box to find an IBM desktop computer. Few at SDA had their own computers. It was a generous gift, a gesture of support. If my mother was my tormentor, I thought, she administered an ambiguous kind of infliction. I began to think of her as Zeus. I didn't steal fire, but my mother had set me ablaze with it, perhaps for something I'd done in another life. I had no idea how long my punishment would last. If I were to believe Hannah, it would be indefinite, because nothing good would happen as long as I hung around my mother.

I wanted to tell Hannah she had a few blind spots of her own. What if my mother, showing me a way out of my confusion, proved to be my liberator? To some degree, though Hannah would never admit it, she was my sister's liberator as well. Hannah had a lot in common with the woman who had given us life. They were both strong-willed, independent, and didn't let anything interrupt their optimism or ambition.

I had my own goals, but they were vague, and I was often distracted from them. Nor would I call myself an unflagging optimist. I was too conscious of my limitations. As infants, my sister and I had suckled on separate teats of my mother, and the milk of life from one tasted very different from the other.

My third week back at SDA, in the middle of an Arctic-like storm and freezing temperatures that shut down O'Hare, I received a letter from Madison, Tennessee. As if the January weather wasn't drama enough, hearing from the girl who I was sure had forgotten me sent my heart into its own kind of storm. Hope collided with doubt. Did she want to get back together? Why send a letter when she could have called? She was going to Dear John me. I waited until after classes, sitting on my bed with the door locked, before I found my courage to open the letter.

> *Hi Will. How are you? I know I've been a real turd, and I don't expect you to forgive me. I don't even want you to. I'm in the I'm-Screwed-Up-and-There's-Nothing-Anyone-Can-Do-About-It club—I'm thinking of running for president, actually—so maybe it's best you forget me. The irony is I always tried to make myself unforgettable to the world—to you in particular—and I failed miserably. It sucks when you don't have a clue why you do what you do. When I called you a sweet boy, I did it both from truth and envy. I wish I were sweet. You're talented too. And patient, kind and loving. I was a lucky girl for three months.*

*For the moment I'm stuck in Gulag Tennessee at the mercy of Lard and Candy. Not only am I forbidden to call you, my other friends are also off limits, except for my boyfriend, Jeremy, because he's a quote unquote stabilizing influence. Don't worry, we don't have sex. He's just a shadow that follows me around, a puppy at the screen door. Lard and Candy are enrolling me in a "revered institution" in Massachusetts next week. It's called the Horton Anderson Preparatory School. You go out on wilderness trips where you learn self-reliance that you stick up your ass afterwards, and in between there are small classes you have to attend, and if you don't finish your homework on time, they pull out your fingernails with dental pliers. The goal is to make you tougher than a cheap steak. I'm not sure I'll ever turn into the Incredible Hulk like you, but Lard and Candy have high hopes.*

*It takes some courage to write someone that you've hurt and disappointed. I think about you every day, wondering if you're foolish enough to come and rescue me. However, my father would probably shoot you on sight with his bolt-action Remington. He thinks you're the most dangerous man in America, worse than Bill Clinton. I even write short stories about it, your rescue of me. You ride in on a black unicorn—weird, huh?—and swoop me up. Strangely, I've lost interest in designing clothes, at least for the moment, but whenever I start writing I can't stop. Sometimes I think my writing is even funny! I know you wrote me a letter but Lard burned it before I could read a word. Maybe you could write me at Horton Anderson.*

*Stay safe.*
*T Rex*

By the time I finished reading, my emotions had been scattered around like flimsy deck furniture. T Rex's confused, up-and-down letter filled me with curiosity, sadness, frustration, hope, and heart-sick longing. I wasn't going to write her back. There wasn't time if she was going to be shipped off to another school. I was going to find a black unicorn somewhere, and bring T Rex back to Chicago. If no unicorns were available, a plane and a rental car would do. The insistent need to save T Rex, to hold her in my arms again, overwhelmed me.

By morning, I had decided I could accomplish my mission in less than a week. I would be back at SDA without being missed or searched for. I would find a nearby apartment for T Rex, hidden from the world, where we would plot our future.

The storm had cleared enough for planes to start leaving on schedule. I packed a suitcase and used my Visa to withdraw $2,000, in case of emergencies, and took a taxi to O'Hare. A round trip to Nashville, which was a stone's throw from Madison, cost $600. You had to be at least twenty-five to rent a car, I learned, but I'd figure something out when I got there. My spirits rose and fell as we took off and soared into rain, and I wondered whether I knew what I was doing.

I had been in agitated states before, but at the moment, perhaps I would fail a standard sanity test. Did obsessive love make any distinction between a girl and a piece of art? Falling in love with *Excavation* wasn't much different than falling in love with T Rex—each passion was all consuming—but while one was relatively safe, the other meant desperation and recklessness. My heart had turned into a swollen, tumultuous river, disregarding reason and sweeping me into the unknown. There was no escape.

At the Nashville airport, I marched up to every rental car counter and pleaded special circumstances. "I know I'm not old enough, but this is an emergency," I declared, telling anyone who would listen about T Rex. I was politely rebuffed until I found a local agency called Nashville Wheels. The attendant only cared that I had a valid driver's license and credit card, and paid for extra insurance because of my age. "Drive carefully," he advised, as if there was something a little dangerous about a teenager in love.

Madison was northeast of Nashville, actually a suburb, a town of small, unpretentious homes not particularly well cared for, and a few strip malls. I bought a bag of snacks, a cup of coffee, and a dozen yellow roses from a street vendor. My heart began to knock when I found T Rex's street and glided toward a two-story Colonial with a manicured lawn and white picket fence.

In size and upkeep, the house was a step or two above its neighbors. A late-model station wagon was in the driveway. There were a number of cars on both sides of the street, and I chose an inconspicuous spot a hundred feet away that gave a clear view of the house. Like a TV detective, I settled back with my coffee. Part of me had always wondered about T Rex's stories, but an hour later, when Lard and Candy emerged from the front door with two small boys who had to be Ass Wipe and Ass Bandit, I gave her credit for total accuracy. Lard not only had a big ass but broad shoulders as well and forearms like two anvils. Candy was svelte, more like T Rex, with a tinted bouffant.

When the station wagon vanished down the street, I walked toward the house, praying that T Rex was inside, trying to look inconspicuous if any neighbors were watching. No one answered the doorbell. The back door into the kitchen was unlocked. I had never trespassed before, and stealing over squeaky wooden floors made me think someone could hear me, like one of T Rex's sisters perhaps. "Hello?" I called out. There was no answer. I climbed the stairs and peeked into bedrooms. Lard and Candy had Bibles on their nightstands, and above their TV was the head of a horned antelope, presumably bagged by Mr. Rex, its glass eyes following me around the room.

There was no mistaking T Rex's bedroom. Bright clothes were scattered everywhere, and the only mattress was on the floor. Her window had a private view of the street, a perch that looked down on the world. The desk was piled with magazines, gum wrappers, beauty products, a bowl of colorful rocks, binoculars, two apples, and a sculpture made from paper clips that reminded me of Giacometti. On the chair, a yellow legal pad was filled with long sentences and quirky drawings T Rex had done. One of the pictures was a sketch of a classic Greek building with Ionic columns. On the frieze were embedded the words Horton Anderson Preparatory

School, and below, Teaching leadership, responsibility and trust for over two hundred years. The facade was riddled with grapefruit-sized bazooka holes. "Do I look like leadership material to you?" T Rex had scrawled below the edifice. I couldn't visualize her in a school where tough was evaluated on a daily basis. In certain categories, T Rex was unevaluable.

I scribbled a six-sentence note, folded it in half, and stuck it in the middle of the legal pad. When T Rex discovered it, I hoped, she wouldn't be too blown away not to follow my instructions.

The Rex family wagon suddenly lurched into the driveway with a loud whooshing noise, like the power steering fluid was low. Looking down from the window, I could see the back loaded with groceries. One of the boys was crying. Candy put her finger to her lips to shush him, but it didn't help.

I took the stairs two at a time, scrambled out the kitchen door, and sank out of breath behind some azalea bushes. Candy and Lard went in through the front but spent twenty minutes in the kitchen, putting things away and intermittently staring out the window in my direction, as if they'd seen something moving. After a while, I made my break and slipped back to my car. I began to worry. What if they'd already packed T Rex off to school? What if Lard found my note? My anxiety was hitting new highs every hour. I nibbled on potato chips and watched as a lemon-colored moon sprang through the darkness.

I must have dozed, because the next thing I knew, someone was knocking on my window. I struggled up and stared into a flashlight. I couldn't see a thing. I imagined Mr. Rex, or an officious neighbor, scrutinizing me, and I would have to tell them I was a Pentecostal living in my car and selling Bibles. When the flashlight flicked off, my eyes adjusted on T Rex. It was almost midnight. A street lamp slashed its arc of soft light across her bemused face, as if asking how crazy could I possibly be to have taken her suggestion to show up. Her hair was cut short into blonde spikes of defiance, and she was bundled in a plaid jacket that didn't look warm enough. Her breath clouded the window. I was overjoyed to see a suitcase in her hand. I had asked her to bring enough clothes for a week, until we got settled back in Chicago. When I got the window down, her lips pressed hungrily against mine like we'd been apart for years.

"You smell incredible," I whispered, like the starved soul I was.

She stowed her suitcase in the trunk and clambered into the front seat. "I can't believe it," she said. "You actually came."

"Aren't you happy to see me?" I scooped up the roses from the back seat. T Rex pushed her nose into the petals, blushed, and gave me another deep kiss. My hand grazed her breast, which was the most reassuring feeling in the world.

She told me she had followed my instructions, leaving a note for Candy and Lard that she was running away. She hated the school they'd picked. It was futile to search for her. She wasn't coming home again, period.

We were both pretty brave, I thought, though my stomach was starting to clutch. I imagined that at this very second, Lard had found his daughter's note and was calling the police. Or, eyes flaring, he was peering out the window, and, spotting me, would rush out with his bolt-action Remington.

"Let's get out of here," I said.

I felt better once we were on the road. My original plan was to find a motel, but out of fear of the unknown, it felt safer to park near the airport and wait out the hours. There was an 8 a.m. to Chicago. I suddenly turned to T Rex and asked why she'd left without saying good-bye or explaining things to me. I didn't know she'd skipped half her classes. Why did she keep it a secret? We were supposed to be together for Christmas. She had promised. I asked if I had I made her life too complicated.

She threw her head against the seat, like how much more of a dumb ass could I be. "This doesn't have anything to do with you. Yeah, I keep secrets, don't you sometimes? I was embarrassed. Once I screwed up at SDA, my parents made me come home. Then it was, like, house arrest."

"You could have sneaked out and called."

"I know," she apologized. She was suddenly teary, and brushed me away when I handed her a tissue. "Do you always know why you do what you do?" she asked.

"I try to think things through," I said, which was not always true. I wasn't thinking anything through right now. Neither of us had any clear view of the future, except that we wanted to be together for the next couple of eternities.

"Do you ever feel you're stuck in quicksand, and whenever you try to free yourself, you sink deeper? I'm stuck with my stupid family. I've spent the last seven years trying to get unstuck. When I'm eighteen, I'm not just changing my name, I'm never seeing them again."

"Then what?" I asked.

"Who the fuck knows!"

"Well, don't worry about it. We're together now. You never have to see them again," I reassured her, as if I would always be her protector.

I remembered her tantrum in my room, telling me to jump out the window. Never taken seriously, regarded by her family as an endless project, she'd hoped that I was someone who finally paid attention to her. Jumping from a window was an extreme test, but I was willing to do it. I was almost as desperate as she was. I wondered if T Rex had ever felt completely loved or respected a day in her life.

We parked for the night on a quiet, dark street near a cargo depot. T Rex nestled against me, and I put my arm around her. If it weren't so cold, we would have made love right there in the car, but holding each other was enough. When the sky began to lighten, we had coffee and muffins at the airport and then found the car rental return lot.

"Oh my god!" T Rex exclaimed, slinking down in the seat.

I followed her stare. It wasn't hard to spot her father, moving resolutely from one outdoor kiosk to another: Hertz to Avis to Budget—his Popeye forearms planting themselves on each counter in a stamp of authority. He'd gotten an early start. Nashville Wheels wasn't open yet. He was seeking more information, I guessed, to support his intuition. Maybe if I were in his place, I would have suspected me, too, the most dangerous man in America.

I quietly turned the car around and drove away, imagining the worst. When Lard learned my license plate number, he would call the police, and there'd be a full-scale manhunt. Accused of kidnapping his daughter, I could end up behind bars, just like my father.

At the very least, the court would forbid me to come close to the girl I loved—ever again.

"This is so cool, isn't it?" T Rex suddenly came to life. She had a cocky smile, like the coffee had kicked in, like she thought we'd outsmarted not just her father but the whole world, too.

"It's not cool, actually. Your father looked really pissed. We need to hide somewhere."

"What are you afraid of? Lard couldn't find his ass if it was painted with a bull's eye."

"That's not the impression you gave me earlier."

She chewed her lip, deliberating. "OK, I know a place. Seriously. No one's going to find us."

Before flying to Nashville, I'd studied a map of the state. It was rugged and mountainous, with no shortage of wilderness, lowlands, flood plains, and swamplands—lots of hiding places. Not that I thought we would need one—we were supposed to be hiding in Chicago—but if we got stuck here, it wasn't hopeless. There was the famous Blue Ridge in eastern Tennessee, the Great Smoky Mountains, the Chilhowee Mountains, the Appalachian Ridge and Valley, and the Gulf Coastal Plain. T Rex began to describe the Cumberland Plateau, near the Appalachian range, where there was a remote log cabin she knew that belonged to a Nashville family named Makin, whose daughter was a close friend of Kiss Ass. T Rex had been invited there a couple of times. Nobody used it in winter, she said, but there was a fireplace, with wood nearby and plenty of cached food and supplies. She remembered where the key was hidden.

T Rex hooked her arm through mine as I drove, while her free hand twirled the radio dial. I wasn't familiar with country music, but she knew most of the songs by heart. By noon, gaining altitude, we approached a dirt and gravel county access road carved into a healthy-sized mountain. It looked wide enough for one car or truck at a time, flanked tightly on both side by deciduous trees and dusky green pines. T Rex was confident she knew the way but still asked me to stop at every fork so she could jump out into the cold and make sure. Thirty minutes later, the tongue of road curled over a plateau and into deeper forest. Out of nowhere, a clearing appeared.

We were at the end of the world. "Thar she blows, mate," T Rex said, proud to have found the solitary cabin. Our getaway included a rustic fieldstone fireplace, a wraparound porch, and windows that sparkled in the clear winter light.

I hauled our suitcases in, and we settled at a kitchen table with a gingham oilcloth. Tons of cans of food were kept under the floor, in a cellar that was "safe from bars," T Rex pronounced with her wonderful laugh. She found a flashlight to help me maneuver down the narrow stairs into the cold, creepy space, and I hauled up an armful of provisions.

We might last here undiscovered for months—or be surrounded by police cars any day, I thought. For now, I was grateful to be safe and alone with T Rex. As the days blended together, every instinct in me to move on was beaten back by the gravitational force of love. I gave up trying to hatch another plan. I took solace that T Rex was beside me, reading or writing in her notebook, and whenever we took a walk, the steady winter sun convinced me time had stopped. At night, we ate by candlelight, swapping stories. I told her everything about the fire in our house and about my mother, how she'd abandoned us and then come back into my life, sending me to SDA, without an apology for the past. T Rex found her an interesting, enigmatic character. "You never know which way the wind blows with someone like that," she said. At the end of every evening, dishes washed, we jumped into a bed of thick blankets and soft sheets, unknown to the world.

One afternoon, sprawled out on porch chairs, T Rex read me a short story she was writing. It was called *Revenge of the Tadpole.* The setting was a girls' camp in Minnesota that she'd attended one summer. Minneapolis had been one of her father's pit stops in his sales career. Except for taking a drag on her Gauloises, T Rex read without interruption.

> *There are summers you can forget, and others have a way of sticking with you forever. When Alice was nine, her parents decided it was time for her to try sleepaway camp. Her older sisters had attended Camp Lake Wanatakee in northern*

*Minnesota, and now it was Alice's turn. She told her parents she didn't want to go—she was shy and quiet and wanted just to ride her bike that summer—but her parents showed her the brochure, stabbing their fingers at the color photos. There were girls paddling canoes, swimming, sitting around a campfire, and working in the crafts shop. They wore big goofy smiles as they splashed around like fish, spitting water at each other, like this was the most fun anyone could ever have. Her parents were convinced that if she really worked at it, Alice could become an Olympic swimmer one day. On arrival, her skills were tested in the lake, and she was assigned to the Tadpoles, the beginners' group. The best swimmers were nicknamed the Sharks. If you were a fucking tadpole, Alice learned, that meant you could barely swim fifty feet in a straight line, or you sank midway and began gasping for air. With Alice, the cold water unfailingly shot up her nose until it felt like her sinuses would explode and her eyes pop out. Every day, complaining to a counselor of a headache, she climbed out of the water and played horseshoes, or worked on making a lanyard in the crafts shop.*

*"Alice, you're pathetic. Headache, my butt," a Shark named Doreen said to her one afternoon. Alice and Doreen shared a cabin with fifteen other girls. At fourteen, Doreen had been attending Wanatakee for six summers, which was as senior a camper as you could be. Her mother had been here thirty years earlier—the dining hall was named after her, because she had donated lots of money. Doreen acted like she almost owned the place.*

*"I'm doing my best," Alice told her.*

*"You're a fake. I'm going to put a firecracker*

up your ass tomorrow. Make you swim all the way to Canada."

"Firecrackers aren't allowed at camp," said Alice.

"It's a figure of speech, idiot."

Doreen was a pretty Texas girl with impressive tits and body builder shoulders. She liked to sleep in the nude. At night, she entertained the cabin by telling how much she liked going down on boys. She described herself as an anaconda swallowing a pig. Texas boys were huge, but never underestimate the mouth of an anaconda, Doreen gloated. She opened wide for her audience, and Alice and the others peered into a dark, gaping well surrounded by a white picket fence of teeth.

The next morning, Doreen made Alice jump in a canoe, and they paddled to the middle of Lake Wanatakee.

"Jump in," Doreen said, stopping the canoe.

"It's half a mile to shore."

"I'll save you if you get in trouble."

"I can't do it."

"What?" said Doreen, pretending not to hear.

"I want to go back."

"What?" She cupped her hand around her ear.

Doreen picked up Alice like a bag of groceries, leaned over the canoe, and tossed her overboard. Alice screamed and dropped like an elevator, finally clawing her way back to the surface. Water filled her nose as usual, and she ended coughing up what she didn't swallow. Doreen smiled at her, like someone enjoying an experiment, and with her muscular shoulders began paddling back to shore.

"Come on, Tadpole, you little shit, move."

Alice stayed put, treading water. "I can't

*make it. Give me a life vest, please."*

*"You haven't even tried."*

*"I can't. . . ."*

*"I'm right here. Trust me."*

*Nervously, Alice followed the canoe, thrashing one arm in front of the other. Her eyes began to sting from her suntan cream, but she kept her head in the water and pushed ahead. She could hear Doreen's paddle slapping the surface, but after a while, it sounded far away, and then there was no sound at all, except a ringing in Alice's ears. Her head felt like a bowling ball that was too heavy to hold up. It was the weirdest sensation, she thought—one minute bobbing along like a cork, the next dropping under the surface and not being able to go higher. She was a fish in an aquarium, breathing through her gills, she decided. She didn't know how long she kept swimming that way. The water turned darker, until she couldn't see or feel anything. Then everything was pitch black. She didn't remember being pulled from the lake, but suddenly she was in a rowboat, and a counselor was breathing into her mouth.*

*Doreen got a lecture for breaking all camp rules, but the director didn't send her home because her mother was an important alumnus. That night, after dinner, everyone gathered around the campfire for a special ceremony. An elder of the Chippewa tribe, a medicine man, performed a sacred dance for the Wanatakee campers, as he did every year. The Chippewa used to live and hunt and bury their dead on the land now owned by Camp Lake Wanatakee, Alice knew. Minnesota was actually a Chippewa word. A couple of centuries ago, the tribe had freely roamed the whole state.*

Most girls thought having a bumbling old Indian around was pathetic. He brought with him a dusty, beatup knapsack, and right in the middle of his dance, he reached in and pulled a snake out of it, held it over his head, and began chanting in the Chippewa language. Every thirty seconds he turned his body in a full circle, keeping his arms steady over his head. There was something a little goofy about him, Alice thought, as he droned on in words no one understood, but what fascinated her was how well-behaved the snake was. Every once in a while, it moved its head, or its pink tongue slithered out, flickering at everyone. A couple of girls shrieked when that happened. It was a big, long, thick snake, and after the ceremony was over, Alice kept her eyes on the Indian's knapsack.

She knew from science class that snakes were cold-blooded. When the other campers had left, she approached the medicine man and told him a story. He laughed as he whispered back in her ear, and then he loaned her his knapsack.

Sometime in the night, everyone in Alice's cabin was wakened by high-pitched screams. In pandemonium, five or six flashlights clicked on and crisscrossed Doreen's bunk. She was shrieking like a mad person, tossing violently in her sleeping bag. Girls were afraid to get too close to her. She finally thrashed her way out of her bag, stumbling to her feet, naked. A couple of girls began screaming and couldn't stop. Dangling from between Doreen's legs was the snake. It had pushed its head right up her snatch. It enjoyed her warmth as much as any Texas boy loved Doreen's bottomless throat, Alice thought, and with a flash camera she'd brought from home, she took the picture to prove it.

T Rex glanced up, waiting for my opinion as she put out her cigarette. She was pleased that I was laughing. I told her I liked it very much, and that she definitely had a future as a writer. She didn't look totally convinced, just like she wasn't sure about a lot of things. I doubted the last scene was autobiographical, but it didn't matter. The snake wasn't the point, except to be funny. The point, I decided, was being left to drown by someone you were supposed to trust.

We stayed hidden for six weeks. An occasional squall would interrupt our solitude. The rain fell bitterly, and the cabin seemed to shake from the cold. Then the murk of clouds vanished and the sun came back. One afternoon, I was chopping firewood when I heard the rise and fall of voices. I put down the ax. All I could see was forest. T Rex was inside, cleaning. Because the wind was stirring, it was hard to figure where the voices had come from. I hurried inside, signaling T Rex. From the window, we saw nothing but the tops of swaying trees. Our car parked in front was impossible to miss. I thought of driving it around back.

"Wait here," T Rex said.

She went outside for a better look, leaving the door open behind her. The din of voices rose again, men laughing at each other's jokes, swearing, complaining, as if they were all alone. There were three, maybe four of them, I guessed as I watched. T Rex had taken up the ax and was splitting wood. A man appeared in the clearing, a hundred yards away. He wore a red flannel jacket, a wool hat with earflaps, and high black boots. A hiking stick was in his hand.

"Hey there," he called, stopping to take in T Rex's lonely figure. His buddies were suddenly beside him, tall, angular men dressed for the raw weather.

"Can I help you?" T Rex said. She hefted the ax over her shoulder.

"This is Stu Makin's place," the man with the hiking stick said, stating a fact as if T Rex didn't know it.

"Yes, sir. We're family friends, staying for a few days. Can I help you with anything?"

"Haven't seen anyone here in winter 'fore," one of the other men said.

"First time for everything," she replied. "What are you doing here?"

"Stu gives us permission to hike around here."

"Well, he must have forgotten to tell you about us."

I went out onto the porch, to make sure everybody knew T Rex wasn't alone, which provoked the four of them into silent deliberation. They were assessing whether T Rex was telling the truth, and if there was any point in further confrontation, including dealing with me, whoever I was. Everyone took note of my face. Even at a distance, they could see something was different, a contagious disease perhaps. That helped make up their minds.

The first man finally spoke. "What's your name, honey?"

"Gabrielle Henderson. This is my friend, Robert. Please say hello to Stu and Rachel for me."

"You bet. We're going to call them when we get back to the car."

The threat lingered in the air. T Rex didn't respond. They drifted on, taking their suspicions with them. In the cabin, I began packing with a dead feeling in my belly.

"How long do you think before your Dad finds out?" I said when T Rex came in. I already had my guess. I was imagining police cars before evening.

"How the hell would I know?" She dropped in an armchair, pouting, her thin arms folded over her chest. She suddenly looked pale and alone, as forlorn as the first stab of color on a painting.

"Come on, pack," I urged.

"And just where are we going?" she asked. "Chicago?"

"That's right."

"Then what?"

"What do you mean?"

"What happens in Chicago?"

"We take our chances," I said.

"We take our chances. That's it? Is that a plan?" She rolled her eyes at my thick-headedness.

"I'll think of one. I'll take care of you." I kept throwing everything in my duffle, waiting for T Rex to move.

"You don't get it, do you?"

I ignored her.

"Sooner or later, this all ends," she said.

She was right: I didn't get it. Suddenly she was the skeptic, and I was the romantic. "You're not making sense. We're going to be together forever."

"Lard is going to find us. One place or another. You said it yourself."

"And you said he couldn't find his ass if it had a bull's eye on it."

"Well, maybe I was wrong. When he finds us, he'd just as soon beat the crap out of you as call the police."

I was dismayed. Why was she chasing me away? Maybe she was a Roman candle when it came to passion and commitment, too. I dropped beside her, on the arm of the chair, and circled my arms around her. Whatever her father would do to me couldn't be worse than if I'd jumped out that window. I was desperate to prove my love. She had the right to distrust the world, but not me. I had never let her down.

"You need to get out of here, Will. Go back to school."

"Not without you."

"You deserve someone better than me. Haven't you figured that out?"

"Fuck, will you stop it. . . ."

"Then you're a numbskull."

Her voice had dropped to a whisper. She would stay behind in the cabin, she announced, and let her father find her. She'd been a disappointment to Lard and Candy since immemorial time; six or seven weeks on the lam was nothing too dramatic. They'd let her off with yet another warning, hoping she would eventually turn into an upright citizen. She was broken, but time and good intentions, followed by good deeds, family support, church prayers, and the right school, would fix her.

There was no out-arguing T Rex. She had made up her mind, and six weeks of solitude, wrapped in a daydream of weightless longing, had left me punch drunk. When we made love for the last time, I could feel her slipping away from me. She strolled to a window, staring out at the bleached sky like the woman in the Hopper painting. We didn't talk much because neither of us could think of anything to say that would make a difference. I kissed her goodbye and drove away in the numb, bewildered state of a young man who had lost his first and deepest love. I found my way down the mountain and back to Nashville, half expecting to be arrested at the airport for one crime or another. I learned that my credit card had been charged $1,910 for the car. I didn't protest. Boarding a half-empty plane to O'Hare, I grieved the whole way.

A cab dropped me off at my dorm. It felt like I'd been gone for a year. When I dug my room key out of my bag, it wouldn't fit in the cylinder. I kept struggling with it, when the door abruptly swung open. A heavyset young man greeted me with brooding eyes.

"Can I help you?" he said, trying to be civil, but it was clear I'd interrupted something.

I looked around to make sure I was on the sixth floor. "This is my room. . . ."

"No, it isn't."

"Yes, it is," I said, but when I peeked over his shoulder, nothing inside was mine. Not the desk, the bed, the pillows—he had a full-size refrigerator and a fancy espresso machine.

"What's your name?" he asked.

"Will Ryder."

"Well, Will Ryder, you're sort of right. This used to be your room. Someone said you didn't pay your tuition. One of the janitors put your things in the basement," he added, and without ado, he closed the door.

I slept downstairs in the TV lounge, and began calling my mother in the morning. She sounded annoyed when I finally got through, as if I'd interrupted a good painting day.

"Why didn't you pay my tuition?" I demanded.

"You remember our agreement? You had to stay in school. According to the dean, you took off and didn't tell anyone. I have copies of your Visa bill. What was going on in Nashville?"

I debated whether to fall on my knees and beg for mercy or keep my private life to myself. "An emergency came up," I said.

"Fox six weeks?"

"Yes."

"Let me guess," she said. "A girl?"

"Does it matter?"

"I'm disappointed, Will. One day, you'll understand how vastly overrated romantic love is. It certainly doesn't match up with an education."

I wanted to reach through the phone and strangle my mother. After leaving behind a girl I depended on more than food and water, I felt it would have been nice to have some sympathy. But my mother thought my emotions were interfering with the development of my talent. I had my priorities mixed up.

"I want to get back in school. Please," I said, restraining myself.

"Unless you have your own funds, this semester is out. I can reconsider my support in the fall."

"That's seven months away." I wasn't sure whether I was more furious with my mother or myself.

"You're almost seventeen. Find a job, something to support yourself while you get your bearings again."

I wanted to tell her I had my bearings. I wanted to be an artist. I needed to get back to my painting and my classes, if only to distract myself from T Rex.

"What kind of job do you suggest?" I asked coolly. Other than drawing or painting, I didn't have many skills.

"It's a big city. I have no idea. Use your imagination," she advised, and wished me a good day.

When I called Santo Tomás, I was too proud to tell my father what had happened. Not only had I been booted from school but my mother also had frozen my credit card. I wasn't to miss her point that irresponsibility carried a price. Classes were going well, I lied to my father, but I was running short of money—would he send me a thousand dollars from my savings account? I added that I might be spending the summer in Chicago, as several intern positions were opening up at the Institute. My fictional plans pleased him. When he fished for me to plan an end-of-summer visit because Hannah would be home from Yale, I promised to come. By then, surely, my punishment would be behind me.

I found a studio apartment on Rush Street, far from the glitter of downtown, for $450 a month. The *Sun-Times* classifieds gave me a peek at another side of Chicago. Twenty phone calls netted six interviews and one offer: a 5 p.m.-to-midnight janitorial shift in a pre-World War II office building. I worked alongside three older men, quiet, amicable souls who drudged their way through the night without complaint, keeping their stories to themselves.

When T Rex didn't answer my letters or phone calls, I reluctantly accepted that fate had turned its back on us once again. I bought a fake ID from a street hawker, and became a regular at a Rush Street bar, drinking enough to make me forget how my happiness had been stolen. At 2 a.m., I went to sleep hoping I would feel better in the morning, because I would have the whole day to paint. But as the weeks rolled by, my creativity seemed to fade. Even trips to the Art Institute took too much energy.

My mother called at the end of August. She asked if I was ready to be a serious student. If I lost my way again, she made clear, there would be no second chance. I had already chosen seven classes I would sign up for, including some I'd missed in the spring. As I entered my junior year in high school, no one would be more motivated, I assured her. I would stay here for the next six years, until I graduated from college, drawing and painting until my fingers blistered over. The dean found me a single room on my old floor, and after a visit home to see my father and Hannah, I restarted my education.

My mother seemed to take me at my word that I would stay in school. As least as far as I knew, she wasn't checking up on some regular basis. I worked even harder than I'd promised her. She was abroad for my high school graduation but sent me a brief email of congratulations for being in the top 5 percent of my class. I also got cards for my birthdays, and I always reciprocated. Neither of us seemed to feel the need to pick up the phone and talk.

Occasionally, she sent emails with substantive news. Albert Reingold, on the strength of my statement to the police in Alpine, had almost been nailed for attempted vehicular homicide. He had escaped prosecution, my mother wrote, only because he'd hired an expensive New York lawyer. Chastened, he was now relatively well behaved. She warned me, though, to "never feel too comfortable in the presence of a simmering volcano. Sooner or later it is bound to erupt."

When I entered SDA's college program, there was an influx of new faces and talents, new professors, and new, more challenging classes to get used to. I continued to make weekend trips to the Art Institute, fulfilling my promise to try to get to know every painting there. Usually, I went alone. My social life was limited to dorm parties and sometimes into-the-night intellectual discussions with kids who were more sophisticated than me.

Toward the end of my sophomore year, I became involved with

a girl named Elaine. She was pretty, cynical, spoke excellent French, and spent her free time watching art house movies. Her idea of a square meal was bagels and ice cream, yet she had a figure like a pogo stick. She had been raised on a farm in the middle of "bumblefuck Quebec," she said, with freezing winters and summers filled with endless chores. I thought of *Little House on the Prairie.* How she'd landed in art school I had no idea because she didn't have much talent. She was frequently depressed but took solace in painting landscapes as well as abstract portraits of herself.

She was her favorite topic of conversation. I didn't mind that she was a narcissist; all that mattered was that Elaine gave me the right kind of attention. After we got to know each other, she insisted every week that I paint her naked. She would stand on one leg in a yoga pose or curl up on her bed with a pillow, imitating Marilyn Monroe. Sometimes she posed sitting on the toilet, reading a magazine. She said I captured something that she liked: maybe it was her eyes, her breasts, the curve of her hips, or something intangible—she wasn't sure. For my reward, we had sex afterward, and fell asleep in each other's arms.

I loved the sex, but just to be held by a girl was more than enough payment for my work. I had begun to accept that my face was a significant, if not permanent, obstacle to intimacy. T Rex had been a miraculous exception. I wasn't sure how long Elaine would last. Most girls were sympathetic to me, but their feelings didn't move beyond the boundaries of friendship. One girl suggested I make an appointment with a college roommate of her father's, a Chicago plastic surgeon named Dr. Ogilvy, who specialized in helping burn victims. She would do anything to help—her heart bled for me and half the world—but she didn't want to be in an intimate relationship, not in my present condition. Human beings were attracted to physical beauty, she said, and without that chemistry, everything would just be pretend.

I knew a lot about pretending. One day, I would sell a painting for lots of money. I would be able to make sense of my complicated mother. I would wake in the morning and look like Tom Cruise, just the opposite of Kafka's character who turned into a cockroach. An Italian supermodel would fall in love with me, and we would have lunch with the Pope. A person's imagination, a professor told me, could never be outrageous enough, because it was your ultimate salvation. It kept you alive, he said, and, like a fingerprint, distinguished you from every other living soul. Mine was unashamedly self-indulgent, particularly when it came to physical intimacy. Walking down the street, I would spot an attractive woman and imagine her embracing me, or letting me take her to dinner, telling me how much she needed me, and then, of course, we would make love. I had similar fantasies in the library, in museums, in my head before falling asleep. I didn't care too much if they didn't happen; they filled me with hope.

Toward the end of my senior year, after Elaine drifted out of my life, my fantasy life grew more fervid. It wasn't just desperation from loneliness. I had turned twenty-one in the fall, and now was only two months from earning my bachelor of fine arts degree. I was clueless how I would make a living. I thought of working abroad in the Peace Corps, or teaching art at some college—but first I had to apply for the job. Every time I glanced in a mirror, I worried about the interview. I could see a problem the moment I shook someone's hand.

I made an appointment with Dr. Ogilvy, hoping to kill several birds with one well-thrown stone. Once I looked normal, I thought, my future would be a relative breeze. I would not only get a meaningful job but I'd also have an adoring woman at my side, appear in art magazines as an up-and-comer, and be liberated from the chains of self-doubt. I resisted family voices telling me that unless I was fine on the inside, change on the outside was meaningless. Once I looked normal, I answered them, I would be fine on the inside.

When my name was called in the waiting room, I followed a nurse down an endless hallway. In an examination room, Dr. Ogilvy, tall and broad shouldered, pumped my hand like he'd been expecting me. I took hope from all his diplomas on the wall.

"If you elect to have surgery, it'll be a process," he said candidly after I gave him the history of my operations in Albuquerque. "Maybe it'll take three or four rounds. But you'll definitely look better."

"Completely normal?"

"Your nose and chin should be pretty close. Your cheeks, forehead, and ears will require a lot of grafting. We'll have to see."

I looked away. Seeing my disappointment, he cited numerous studies about the psychological and emotional scars of burn victims, and offered to refer me to a support group. That would be the first step, before an operation, he said. He was a clone of Dr. Glaspell, or of my family, seeking to heal me on the inside. I didn't want anything to do with a support group. I could already imagine the stories of misery, because I was more than familiar with my own. I didn't want more therapy sessions either. Focusing on what was already the most painful thing in your life was like holding a magnifying glass to the sun. You didn't heal. You burned all the way through.

"How much will the surgery cost?" I asked.

"Numbers aren't my department, but for the OR, hospital stay, meds, physical therapy, and my fee, I'd guess about two hundred and fifty thousand. Do you have any kind of insurance?"

Seven years ago, I'd been quoted a fraction of that. "Dollars? No problem," I joked. I told him I didn't have insurance but somehow would find the money. We would be in touch. To look human again, I thought, was priceless.

For the rest of the month, my magical thinking continued. I decided I had the potential to be the next de Kooning or Rothko. I already had a technical proficiency that my teachers commented on. On a lark, I spent a week copying one of Rembrandt's small religious portraits, the uncommissioned works done after his wife had died. The church had condemned him for refusing to marry a woman he'd gotten pregnant, so the Amsterdam elite shunned the great Rembrandt. No one wanted to own the work of a degenerate. He was forced to unload his evangelists, apostles, and saints at bargain prices. My evangelist would be free to the world. He had a beautifully weathered face, strained, like someone whose faith was tested daily. Late one night, I hung him in the student union over the entrance to the cafeteria, which was cheesily named "Café de Renaissance," like something contending for a Michelin star. The next morning, I watched a group of students gather around my work, recognizing it as a petulant fraud but favorably critiquing the play of light and shadows, the textured face, and the beseeching eyes. I never told anyone it was mine.

My search to discover what kind of painter I was had propelled me to not just Rembrandt but also Thomas Hart Benton, Edvard Munch, Gustav Klimt, and finally Franz Marc, the German expressionist who was killed in World War I. He painted like a Cubist, usually animals, with deep, dazzling colors. His *Tower of Blue Horses* was my favorite painting, at least that year, and I pinned a poster of it next to my bed.

Staring at it every night, I waited to be inspired with some way to raise a quarter of a million dollars, even if it was a dollar at a time. One opportunity lay right in front of me. SDA held competitions in every department for graduating seniors. Faculty members, alumni, and prominent artists made up the juries. Winners received $25,000, along with a graduate school fellowship. I cared less about graduate school than a pile of free money.

The rules stated that only works created specifically for the contest could be entered. The competition was deep. Besides the seriously talented, there were faculty pets like Steve O'Connor, who lived on my floor and looked like Andy Warhol with muscles. He had a long face with fine blond hair combed to one side, and his eyes were magnified by horn-rimmed glasses. He worked out every day in his room—you could hear the barbells clanking away at weird hours—and then he and his girlfriend would make love, thrusting and grunting on their cheap mattress in epic marathons. I disliked him immensely. He was twenty-eight, a good old boy with a southern drawl from a dirt poor county in Alabama, self-taught as an artist before he enrolled at SDA. Academics were foreign to him. He could barely read and write. I was mesmerized by Steve like some species that should have been extinct but managed to luck out in the curve of evolution. Like Sherman marching on Atlanta, no moral dilemma, anxiety-provoking thought, or self-doubt got in the way of his ambition. He believed in his future fame like a four-year-old believed in Peter Rabbit. The faculty loved him for his positive thinking.

I don't know why I made Steve my secret enemy. We never had an argument. We barely talked. But in my heart, I could find nothing to like about him and everything to be suspicious about. He painted watercolors of small town southern life—dogs in the street, people in straw hats rocking on porches, families eating from plates of chicken—rich with Norman Rockwell-like detail. His paintings were mawkish and stylized. If anyone had asked my opinion, I would have described them as reliably mediocre.

"Hey Will, ure in the comtishun, right?" Steve asked one morning. We were standing together at the elevator.

His hands were shoveled in his front pockets as he rocked back on his cowboy boots, his biceps in his tight T-shirt rippling under the fluorescent light. I wasn't about to reveal my motive for entering, especially to Steve. I told him that I was but didn't know how I felt about art contests, which was true. Everyone wanted recognition, but that seemed irrelevant to the creative process. Just to enter something, I said, a lot of people ended up producing shit.

"Ah, come on." He was suddenly busy checking his nails, which were as shiny as diamonds. "Good Lowered, ya know we all got talnt, Will."

"You think so?" I said. "All God's creatures, right?"

"Does Howdy Doody have a wooden pecka?" Steve laughed, like someone at a nightclub enjoying a stupid joke.

"What ya paintin'?"

"I have no idea," I said honestly.

"It's gittin' kinda late, don't ya think? I'm already done."

"Guess I better get busy."

The twenty-five thousand dollars aside, I wondered what my mother would have advised about an art competition. I hadn't seen her since Marfa, more than six years ago, or talked to her since I was reinstated in school. Her last email, about six months ago, told me there was a new man in her life, a wealthy philanthropist and art collector named Simon Cleary. I looked him up on a Forbes list. When I invited my mother and Simon to my graduation, her email promptly promised they would attend. My father and Hannah were coming as well, of course. I wondered if it would be a showdown at the O.K. Corral or just ships passing in the night. I calculated that they hadn't spoken to each other in about eighteen years.

I hoped for the best. Except for the showdown in front of our house with Louie Freeze, my father was hardly confrontational. In my wallet was a color photo of him in his Wrangler jeans, Timberland boots, and faded work shirt. He was stooped over the raised hood of his Chevy, where something always needed fixing. I had taken the photo when I was around ten. He was always fiercely loyal to me, yet I'd rarely shown how much I appreciated it. I began to work on a pencil sketch based on the photo, working and reworking it until I was satisfied with the composition. I moved on to acrylics. Part of me felt like I was back in first grade, splashing colors on a canvas, creating an unyielding morass of paint with a mind of its own. But now I had the sharp eye and control of my brush and palette knife that came from years of schooling and creating. I alternated short stabs of bright colors with bold, angular lines. I wasn't the only artist to feel the conflict of precision and discipline with passion and improvisation. Sometimes I was too self-conscious; other times I was out of control. To end up someplace in the middle was like wrestling with a shark. I wanted to be as close as possible to the danger of the unknown, yet finish thinking the painting had turned out exactly as I intended.

The painting was 36 by 48 inches and allowed me to show his full form but also lots of subtle details that defined his character. As I painted my father, I remembered my first impression of him as a solitary man in an endless desert, marching to wherever duty called him. My desert was a medley of beiges, subdued reds, and sea greens. Using colors in different ways was like a scientist resequencing DNA. When you experimented with combinations of colors you hadn't used before, you expressed things you hadn't felt before. My father could see his solitary image in the windshield. His back was arched slightly, his hands splayed on the fender next to an open box of tools. What should he check first: the starter, the plugs, the carburetor? A successful image was never static. Anticipation pushed the narrative forward. I detailed his Vermont Yankee hands. His fingernails were blunt and dirty, his skin chafed. Stubble dotted his chin. The blue of his shirt was faded and graying, the blue of his jeans indigo with specks of pink. The sky looked like a tarnished belt buckle, purple as grapes on its edges.

I barely met the contest deadline. I liked what I'd created, but I worried whether it had the depth to demand someone's attention for more than thirty seconds. I had some admirers at SDA, and not just among students. If I didn't win the whole shooting match, one professor told me, he'd shave off his ten-year-old beard.

I woke the morning of my graduation in a mood of self-assessment. I had managed to stay in good health for almost twenty-two years, advanced my art skills, and fallen in love once. My future was ahead of me. I was alert and sober. Some of my classmates had been on a drinking binge for twenty-four hours, if not from the first day they enrolled. To celebrate, I had splurged on a Hugo Boss suit, midnight black with narrow lapels and narrow-legged pants, with a Versace white shirt and a midnight blue tie. It was only the second suit I'd owned. I couldn't prove it, but I thought people stared at my face less when my clothes looked sharp.

Two hundred eighty seniors marched up on the dais. The auditorium overflowed with family members and friends, waving, snapping photos, and shouting out as if this were a football game. I sat in the last row of graduates, comfortably out of view. The speakers who paraded to the microphone were interchangeable with those at any other college, reminding us of the virtues of hard work, honesty, and patience. "Good luck, class of '00!" someone shouted, sincerely, from the audience. The fellow next to me knew something about '00. He had a cab sauvignon of the same year under his gown.

After a while, I tired of the speakers' cliches, and was certain that my mother had as well. She and Simon were in the front row, awarded VIP seats, I assumed, because of either my mother's status in the art world or Simon's philanthropy. She wore a dark suit complemented by a bright Gucci scarf. Simon was tall and gray, younger than my mother by a few years, with a serenity that Albert had conspicuously lacked. Hannah, in the middle of the auditorium, looked as striking as ever, but her face was beginning to change, her features growing more chiseled like my father's. She kept darting her gaze in my direction, proud of me. She had never said it, but she thought of herself as my surrogate mother, one who had no shortage of advice. I suspected she already knew what kind of mother she would be some day—superior in every way to the one who had left us behind.

David and my father sat next to her, whispering to one another. They had become good friends even before Hannah married

David, and now he was like a second son—golfing buddy, intellectual comrade, someone to help anchor my father's meandering life. For a while, I had been jealous of his new position in the family, but I couldn't help liking him. He and Hannah had settled in Manhattan. David taught at some tony Upper East Side school. My sister, fresh out of Yale with an MBA as well as a Ph.D. in economic theory, had been hired by a Wall Street investment bank. Her dreams had taken a hundred-eighty-degree turn from her days in Santo Tomás. She seemed content now to be flying a couple of times a month to destinations halfway around the world. At twenty-seven, she was already a vice president, drawing a base salary five times what my father made after a quarter-century of teaching.

The speakers droned on like Southern Baptists. I wondered what was in the Guinness Book of Records for the world's longest graduation. When I glanced down my row at the faces I knew so well, it occurred to me that none of those people would be my friend after we said good-bye today. In seven years, I had gotten along with most people without being close to anyone.

Finally, one of the senior faculty members stepped up to the lectern. I came alert. "Before we bestow diplomas on members of the class of 2000, I want to recognize this year's outstanding seniors in the fields of painting, film, graphic arts, writing. . . ."

He carried on about how talented everyone was, how choosing the winners in some categories had been virtually impossible because the debate among judges was so intense. My gut was beginning to clutch. I hadn't told anyone in my family that I'd entered the competition. If I lost, I wouldn't be able to hide my disappointment.

"This year's award for painting goes to a very special talent, a young man with extraordinary insight into his flesh-and-blood subjects. They pulsate with dreams, humor, and self-deprecation. . . ."

Oh, please, I thought, please, please let it be me. . . .

"This year's award goes to a young man from Alabama. . . ."

The professor didn't get to finish his sentence. The applause thundered down from the heavens for Steve O'Connor. They would be cheering all night in Dixie, I thought. As he approached the lectern, my secret rival had a bounce in his step, conveying equal parts confidence and humility, as if Tony Robbins were coaching him from the sidelines. He had told friends he listened to motivational tapes while lifting weights. How could you not love someone like that? I didn't feel much of anything as I watched Steve accept his prize, least of all envy. I had concluded, as I had many years ago, that I just wasn't a very good painter.

When it was my turn to receive my diploma, my despair lifted, replaced by agony. As I walked across the stage scrutinized by a thousand strangers, twelve seconds felt like twelve minutes. Had I won the competition, I thought, I would have stood out as someone exceptional. My face wouldn't have been so important. But I hadn't won.

As I shook hands with the dean, I could see my father, Hannah, and David standing and clapping exuberantly. My mother looked indifferent, as if watching a mere formality she had seen dozens of times before. When it was over, the graduating class merged into the auditorium with relatives and friends. There were high fives, more photos, and shrieks of joy. I didn't know whether to seek out my mother or father first.

"Hey, Will!" David came up and threw his arms around me, followed by hugs from my father and Hannah. He gushed, "We are so happy for you, man!" My father's and Hannah's eyes sparkled. My spirits lifted a little as they swapped stories about my growing up. My father seemed the most proud, filled with the special gratitude a parent feels when his child is finally grown and on his own. In his eyes, I was a six-foot-one, two-hundred-pound miracle. I kept waiting for my mother and Simon to come over and say hello.

"We're taking you for a steak dinner," my father announced. "Smith & Wollensky—you can eat aged beef and drink aged scotch. You've earned it. Congratulations!"

"Sounds good," I said, thinking mostly of the scotch.

"I tied one on big time at my graduation," David confided. "Right, Han?"

"You could say that. I almost had to call an ambulance."

I looked around a final time for my mother and Simon. They had vanished. Neither Hannah nor my father seemed to care much, as if they wanted me all to themselves.

After a short cab ride, the four of us walked into Smith & Wollensky with its polished wood floors and brass railings, overlooking the meandering Chicago River. I wasted no time ordering my first shot of Chivas. It went down like soda. I liked Donald Judd's beverage of choice. If I were ever to join the ranks of serious drinkers, I thought, Chivas Regal would be my passport.

"To the next Picasso!" David said, raising his glass.

"Picasso Smasso," my father said. "I'll take a Will Ryder."

I had one, just for him, I wanted to say. I wondered if he would like my painting any more than the judges had.

"Do you like Rembrandt?" I suddenly asked Hannah.

"I'd say he's OK," she deadpanned.

"Walk over to the student union tomorrow. See what's hanging over the cafeteria entrance. It's one of his saints."

"You mean a copy."

"Yeah, but not just any copy. I channeled the Dutch master."

I laughed like there was something terribly funny about it. No one knew whether to believe me, and if it was a joke, where exactly the humor was. I just needed the attention. By the time our salads arrived, I'd had my third drink.

"Will, if you drink too much, you'll kill the taste of your steak," my father said diplomatically.

"I believe you're drinking, too, sir, are you not?" I replied.

"A glass of wine, Will."

"Soon to be followed by another and another. Won't the results be the same?"

"I'm only planning on having one."

"You say that now, but the night is young. Besides, I insist you have more."

"No, thank you, son."

As usual, the peacekeeper didn't raise his voice. Hannah looked the most stressed. She kept glancing at David as if my binge were partly due to his encouragement. Maybe she was also worrying about my future. In her heart of hearts, did she think I had as much chance of becoming a successful painter as she did of being a ballerina? Maybe I'd end up working at a 7-Eleven—painting canvases when I found the time.

"We're waiting too long for our entrees. Let's try someplace else." I suggested, rising to my feet to show my resolve.

"What? That's no reason to leave," Hannah said.

"I didn't know this was your graduation, sis."

"Will, are you upset about something?"

I debated whether to come clean about the competition. Instead, I sat down and rolled back my shoulders, trying to gather my composure. But I was still agitated.

"I wonder if I should see my mother before she leaves town," I said.

My father nodded indifferently. "We saw her in the auditorium."

"Did you say hello?"

"It was pretty crowded."

"She didn't exactly come over and say hello to us." Hannah threw in.

"So you couldn't be the bigger person? Are you ever going to forgive her?"

"I don't understand. Why do you care what I feel or do? You have your relationship with her. I have my own moral compass."

"A moral compass? I'm very impressed. How do I get one of those?"

I'd had enough of Hannah for the night. Marry your high school sweetheart. Pay back your student loans. Unleash your polydextrous Ivy League brain on the financial world and see what you can accomplish. She had that moral compass as well. In my sister's master plan, there was little room for idleness, doubt, or imperfection.

"You two stop. Please," my father implored. The couple at the next table turned to us.

"Will," David broke in. "I don't know what you're feeling right now, but everything's going to be OK. You are Prometheus—never forget that. No matter how many times the eagle plucks at your liver, you live to fight another day." He had been drinking as much as me, and was being flamboyant now, but his tone was utterly sincere. "You are here in this life to make a difference. It's a lonely role but bestowed by the gods only on the most special among us. Be proud of yourself."

His hand reached across the table and wrapped over mine.

My face warmed at his praise. I remembered when we had met

in my room and talked about art, and how he'd quickly sized me up. I thought he was saying that not only did he believe in me but he also wanted to be my friend. Having zigzagged through high school and college without being close to anyone except T Rex, I wanted that, too. David and I clinked glasses.

Our entrees arrived, and—nerves settled—the evening rolled along under the best possible circumstances. When it was over, we hugged good-bye on the sidewalk and everyone drifted off. I looked forward to flying home for a week. A few boats were silhouetted on the river, their safety lights casting a chromium glow on the water. A nearly full moon looked like a scuffed penny.

My mother hadn't told me, but I could guess where she and Simon were staying. I took a taxi to the Four Seasons on Delaware Place. At the front desk, a man with silver hair and black eyebrows rang her suite. She answered promptly. She didn't seem surprised I was downstairs.

When we met in one of the hotel restaurants, she was still dressed in her stylish suit and Gucci scarf. I was grateful to slowly be sobering up. "Why did you leave the graduation so soon?" I said. "I wanted to make plans to get together. I haven't seen you in six years."

"You were busy with your family. I didn't want to interrupt, which was what Hannah and your father preferred."

"Once upon a time, it was your family, too. Maybe it still is."

"No," she insisted, "it's not. The world isn't flat, it's round, and it will never be flat again."

"Jesus," I sighed, "don't you ever miss Hannah? You didn't even come to her wedding."

"Exactly. It was her wedding. I wasn't invited."

I ordered another coffee. My mother never gave an inch. I wondered why I kept trying to break her, as if she were a secret code. She would always keep her distance, yet she'd lingered close enough to make sure I stayed in school and graduated. Hannah still thought she was going to lead me through a trap door, into utter darkness. Maybe she was right. Yet I was the only one who understood her delicate balance: craving privacy in order to read, think, and paint but socializing when necessary to promote her work with buyers and museums. Moments like this seemed far down on her list of priorities. I felt I had better hurry to get out what I wanted to say.

"You put me through high school and college, and I want to thank you," I began. "I have just one more favor to ask. It's been burning a hole in me. I did a portrait of Dad for the painting competition. Before I give it to him, I want you to tell me if it has any merit. The judges didn't think so, but I was hoping they're wrong. Could you come by the dorm tomorrow?"

"Why should my opinion matter?"

"It always does, and you know it."

"You've been well trained at SDA."

"Please. It will only take a minute."

"Honestly, I don't have time, Will," she said, folding her hands on the table. "And I don't need to."

"I'm asking a favor. . . ."

"Your painting was very strong," she interrupted me. "The colors were bold, and the lines aggressive and uncompromising. They worked together to built the subject's character. As he looked into the car engine . . . not just in his eyes but his shoulders and his hands . . . I saw patience and determination. I came away thinking how deeply you liked and respected your subject."

"What are you talking about?"

"I'm talking about your painting."

"You haven't seen it."

"I was one of the judges. I've been a member of the SDA jury for years."

"You voted on my painting?"

"I said I was a judge. You're my son. I had to recuse myself."

I was trying to make sense of everything, wondering if the scotch was still getting in the way. "You were a judge? Why didn't you tell me?"

"Names of judges are kept secret. You know that. But what difference would it have made if you did know? You made your decision to enter the competition. I think it was a wise one. Your talent shows."

"It was demoralizing to lose to someone who thinks the author of *Tender Is the Night* was Shakespeare."

"Mr. O'Connor was a consensus choice, on the third round. I have my detractors, and they weren't going to vote for you. They think that just being my son gives you an unfair advantage."

"That would be delusional."

"Do I need to remind you about jealousy in the art world?"

"So, basically, I lost because you were on the jury."

"These things happen."

I didn't expect her to apologize because I'd been a victim of politics, or to speculate that if she hadn't been on the jury, I might have won. My mother didn't do apologies, and rarely engaged in speculation. I didn't even expect an inflection of sympathy in her voice. But I wanted more than to hear that she respected my painting.

"Do you know how infuriating you can be?" I asked.

"I don't know what you want from me, Will."

"Why don't we start with this: Tell me you love me."

She gave me her famous part-smile, part-frown. "Love is one of the most dangerous words ever conceived," she said. "If not expunged from the dictionary, the definition should be greatly expanded. Love allows people to lie, cheat, and steal from each other, whether they mean to or not. It causes as much misery as it does happiness. More, actually, because it raises expectations. . . ."

"I'm your flesh and blood," I broke in.

I was suddenly furious, wondering what expectations she had for her son. All she'd ever acknowledged was that I had some talent. I might as well have been some stranger she'd helped through school with a scholarship. She hadn't ever referred to my father by name—he was the subject of my portrait. And this was the man from whose seed I had come, with whom she had fallen in love and once imagined a future together. Maybe we were all strangers in her eyes.

As if I were a little boy again, I ordered apple pie à la mode to try to block out my pain. She finally asked what I was going to do next. Maybe a teaching assistant job in the fine arts department at New Mexico State, I answered, if my father had enough pull. She gave me her petulant Zeus smile, as though the gods had their plans for me but I'd have to wait to find out what they were. We had an awkward good-bye.

When I woke late morning, a Four Seasons envelope had been shoved under my door. My mother's note was brief, as usual, wishing me well on the next leg of my journey. "Whatever that is," she wrote, "I am going to assume that painting is a part of it." She was sure we would stay in touch, but there was nothing urgent, she added, and, in fact, she doubted I would need her anymore as a parent. In that department, she declared, her job was pretty much over. She wrote down her new email address, "for emergencies only." There was no cell number. Our relationship was essentially finished, I thought.

And then I found that she hadn't quite left me dangling over the void. Inside the envelope was a personal check made out to Wilson Louis Ryder—for $100,000. On the ledger line, my mother had written, "seed money . . . make it last."

My first exultant thought was my operation. This put me well on the way to affording it. But I knew my mother's intentions. "Seed money" was her investment in me as an artist, not in my vanity. If I spent the money on my surgery, she would of course find out, and I would probably never hear from her again.

I wondered if that was a good thing or a bad one—my opinion about my mother could change daily. It was hard to judge someone who moved in private and mysterious ways, sometimes making me think she knew more about me than I knew myself. Still, I held out hope that if I were patient, all would be revealed to me one day—the Big Bang theory of why parents do what they do to their children.

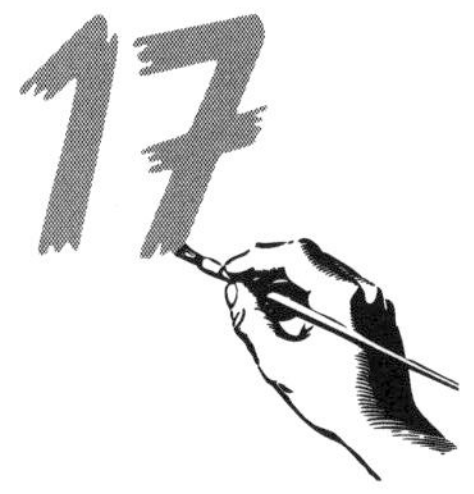


My time in Santo Tomás flew by. I told my father about my mother's unexpected check, enough money to keep me in groceries for a while, I joked, so I could paint full-time. He didn't warn me about hidden agendas and being manipulated, though I knew he still believed that. He was just happy I could do what I wanted without going into debt.

If I were to pursue painting seriously, there was only one place I wanted to live. To find herself as an artist, my mother had migrated from the East Coast to New Mexico. I would reverse directions. New York had more galleries, artists, co-ops, museums, and intellectual stimulation than any city I knew. I thought about Warhol, Basquiat, Stella, Hockney, and a dozen more who had made careers there. Striking out for Chicago seven years earlier had made my father anxious. Now, he seemed more confident of my survival skills. New York was expensive, he warned, so I had better make a budget. No doubt he'd asked Hannah and David to keep an eye on me, just in case.

My portrait of him tinkering with his Chevy had been hung above our fireplace, the centerpiece of the house, replacing a dusty map of the United States. He saw how my skills had matured. He even acknowledged my debt to my mother's gene pool. But 99 percent of the credit he gave to me. It was June 2000, a new century, my century, my father said grandiloquently.

"Give my greetings to Batman," he offered when it was time to say good-bye. I promised to call when I reached the gates of Gotham. Instead of putting a handful of quarters in my pocket, this time he handed me a cell phone. He had one, too. He had also turned in his IBM Selectric for a desktop computer, just to prove he understood the need to adapt. His job dictated that he keep up with technology, as students were now sending him their papers online. Approaching sixty, he had decided he would teach as long as possible, even if the pay and recognition were lousy. A pragmatist to the end.

Through magazine articles, and Hannah's and my father's stories, I already had a feel for the city I was about to call home. When the taxi from Newark Airport to Manhattan cost me $80, though, I choked. How could a taxi ride cost so much? On the spot, I took a vow of frugality. My mother called the $100,000 "seed money," but I had quietly put half of it away for my surgery, which meant stretching the other half for living expenses. I would come to realize that if you liked pizzerias, cafeterias, and bodegas, parts of the city could be your friend. So were the subways. Otherwise, there were so many places your pockets got picked without your even knowing it.

I stayed with Hannah and David for three days while I searched for an apartment. They had bought a cozy, two-bedroom co-op on West Fifty-Seventh, a few blocks from Central Park. The spread belonged in a newlywed magazine—rooms as cheerful and tidy as their lives, especially Hannah's, who took a 7 a.m. subway to Wall Street, returned home twelve hours later, and then usually squeezed in a run in Central Park. Often she was on a plane, sometimes flying halfway around the world for a client meeting. I wasn't envious of her hectic life, but I longed for her focus and discipline. My mind was constantly in motion, flipping through ideas and plans like a deck of cards.

When we said good-bye, Hannah made me promise to come for dinner once a week, and David insisted I think about taking up tennis. He had joined a club with indoor courts. He would teach me. I wondered if I'd be any better than I was with golf.

I put down first and last month's rent on a West Village studio with a cramped bathroom and a tiny closet. The building was pre-

World War II. The fifth-floor walkup's sole window had a view of the neighboring building twenty feet away and a smidge of gray sky. I bought a wobbly desk for my computer. The radiators were off, so I took the landlord's word that they'd come to life in winter. There was no air conditioning unless I put in a window unit, a luxury I decided I couldn't afford. My place was a dump compared with Hannah's, but it was my own. I fell asleep at night happily listening to jazz tapes.

I began every morning with a walk, as if I were an urban Lewis and Clark, covering up to a hundred blocks as I explored my new world. As in Chicago, I felt like one of a million ants sweeping along the sidewalks and artfully dodging other ants who all moved briskly with some undisclosed purpose. Most stared ahead, self-absorbed, while my gaze constantly detoured to the exotic and unfamiliar. I scribbled what I saw in a Moleskine notebook, and bought an inexpensive point-and-shoot camera to record intriguing images. New York felt like a ship squeezed into a bottle—how did it get this way, and how did it function? Compared with Chicago, there was more of everything: squadrons of taxis, crowded sidewalks, double-parked delivery trucks, high-priced clothing stores, long-legged models with their portfolios swinging off their hips, uniformed doormen, panhandlers, street vendors, cops, smells I couldn't identify, and once in a while an exploding manhole cover. It was a city rusted at its seams, leaking from its pores, but the sun came up and went down, and the next day was not much different from the last—yet I constantly found something new.

At the subway entrance closest to my apartment, I noticed a particular panhandler one morning. I was accustomed to the regulars who slept in the subways, emerging at sunrise to cadge what they could from commuters. Slipping coins in their pockets, some looked deranged, mumbling and eyeing one another with suspicion, and others seemed drugged out. After a while, they became invisible, but on this morning I looked twice. The new addition was standing apart from the others.

He was in his mid-30s, dressed in dirty jeans and an Army jacket over a T-shirt, paper thin with bent shoulders. His lumpy, misshapen face had been badly burned by a fire or an explosion. He had no eyebrows, which made his jade-colored eyes look owlish. Like me, his ears were scarred and crusty, and his lips twisted. His flesh had aged to an earth color, except for splotches of white skin on his nose and chin. He didn't make eye contact with anyone, as if afraid they'd be scared away. Most were—his open palm extended at his waist held only a small pile of coins—but not me. I pulled a bill from my pocket and laid it in his hand. When I turned and hurried on, I couldn't push his image away. I was like Scrooge, staring at the ghost of Christmas future. Would that be me in ten years? My bowels turned to ice.

I had recoiled from Dr. Ogilvy's suggestions of group therapy, but avoiding other people's stories of pain wasn't the only reason. I detested my face, and I didn't want to know anyone who looked anything like me. I would hate them, too. After that morning, I chose a different subway stop to come and go.

My daily walks grew longer, as I hoped that something would eventually inspire me. For a month, the only thing I painted were the walls of my apartment. I would stop at coffee shops with a sketchpad, drawing character faces or street scenes. Despite visits to galleries, museums, and lectures at Cooper Union, nothing stirred me to pick up a brush.

One afternoon, I saw a warehouse with a "for lease" sign in front, not far from my apartment. The top floor was 8,000 square feet, completely open, with an elevator, bathroom, kitchenette, fourteen-foot ceilings, and huge, industrial windows affording incredible east and south light. Three other artists eventually showed up before I could make up my mind. None of us knew each other, but everyone loved the space. Over coffee, we agreed to divide the loft into fourths, install our own partitions, and split the rent. We seemed to get along. One of my new loftmates told me about an inexpensive art supply house on Canal Street. I picked up an easel, tubes of oils and acrylics, drawing paper, linen canvases, some Masonite, and other necessities. If I had to pay for rent and supplies, I reasoned, I would end up painting something.

My daily routine went from aimless to relatively focused. I fixed a large breakfast, skimmed the *New York Times,* and rode a rickety freight elevator to my new workspace. The view was of what was called a transitional neighborhood—warehouses mixed with turn-of-the-century row houses, retail space, and one defunct factory that had been converted to luxury condos. I set up my easel and tried to capture the skyline. The images felt static. A narrative gave energy to a painting, but my imagination was stymied. I had no feel for New York. After one long July day, my cell phone rang as I trudged home. Though night had fallen, the air was still a blast furnace.

"Will. Will? Are you there?"

David sounded drunk or confused.

"Hey, what's up?" I said.

"I don't know how it happened. I don't. Shit, get over here, please. . . ."

"Where are you?"

He sighed, like someone too shaken to speak. "It's Hannah."

"Where are you?" I repeated.

"Lenox Hill Hospital. Lex and 77th. I'll look for you at the emergency room entrance."

He clicked off before I could ask for details. I wondered if there'd been a car accident, though Hannah and David rarely drove in the city. When a taxi dropped me off, David greeted me with a quick hug. Ambulances were coming and going. Paramedics murmured into their hand radios as they scurried around us. My friend's normally serene face had glazed over. He'd aged a couple of years.

"Hannah was running in Central Park," he began as we walked inside. "We were supposed to be going out for dinner. I called her cell four times. . . ."

His fist rose repeatedly to his chin, softly, too anxious or distracted to keep the story going. I made him look at me.

"David—what happened?"

Another sigh. "About eight o'clock, a young couple found her. She'd been beaten unconscious. They told police they saw the guy who attacked her. They scared him off. I guess thank God for that."

I absorbed the details slowly. When David arrived at the hospital, he had signed a sheaf of consent forms, then gone looking for Hannah. Doctors and staff members couldn't tell him much. We brushed past a janitor swabbing floors as we tried to get to the ICU. Stripes of different colored tape led to various destinations. Someone told us to take the yellow. There among the staff in scrub suits, a few visitors padded up and down, looking lost. Under the fluorescents, everyone's face had a greenish tint.

Hannah had been in surgery since before he got there, David said. He had talked to one of the neurosurgical nurses. X-rays and a CT scan had revealed multiple skull fractures and possibly significant nerve damage. The man had struck Hannah with something hard, maybe a rock or a club. After the hemorrhaging was stopped and her cranial cavity drained, she would be taken to the ICU.

I had the sensation of separating from my body, drifting through the hospital, looking for my sister's operating room. I imagined it was cold and sterile, like the ones I'd been in as a three-year-old. David led me into a waiting room near the ICU. An elderly Latino sat across from us, holding his rosary beads. He greeted us with a smile, as if everyone needed comfort. I smiled back.

David couldn't sit. His fists dug into his armpits as he paced, playing the "what if" game over and over. What if Hannah hadn't gone jogging, what if she'd taken a different route, what if David had picked her up at her office this evening. . . . I brought back two cups of coffee from a vending machine.

We started in on small talk, trying to cut the anxiety. She was supposed to fly to Paris tomorrow, David said. They both loved their jobs, and—more important—were thinking of starting a family. "That would make me an uncle," I said, pleased. I described the latest developments with my loft and the three other artists who shared it. I was becoming friends with them. David congratulated me, as he acknowledged that New York would never be the world's friendliest city. If you happened to look different, I thought, it was even more judgmental. I began to worry about Hannah's face—what if her attacker had smashed her mouth or nose? The thought made me sick.

The man with the rosary beads disappeared. David suddenly asked if I thought Hannah was going to make it, as if I were the operating surgeon and could predict everything.

"You know my sister, tougher than a Marine," I said.

"That's right. She's tough."

"Honestly, I don't know," I corrected myself. "I'm afraid, just like you." I watched as he put his fingertips to his eyes, trying to hold himself together. "Whatever, we're going to get through this," I said.

He nodded, straightening. "OK."

I was getting up the courage to call my father when Hannah's principal surgeon approached us in his scrubs, just out of the OR. He introduced himself as Dr. Mehra, an East Indian who nevertheless had a pure Boston accent—born in the States, I guessed. He had a middle-aged body but a still-youthful face. He talked calmly about what his team had dealt with—three fractures, two to the temporal bone, one to the occipital bone. The hemorrhaging had been stopped for now. Hannah's vitals were OK, he said, but it would be a while before anyone knew the significance of her injuries. When she'd wake up was anyone's guess. He suspected it would be a while.

Dr. Mehra assured us he would check on Hannah every few hours. She would be brought to a room in the ICU in a few minutes.

David slumped in a chair, pulling in the silence around him. I prowled the hall, peeking into open rooms where the flickering light of vital signs monitors and the rhythm of conversations filled me with envy. Steered by an orderly, a gurney softly click-clacked down a green stripe toward me. I called for David, and he hurried over. Hannah was covered with a thin white blanket, her shaved head shaped like a melon, incision marks showing where the doctors had drilled into her skull. As I'd feared, she'd been someone's punching bag. A gash on her chin had been stitched up, as well as a long jagged slice across her cheek. Her nose had been broken. Multiple contusions had turned her skin purple.

David paled and turned away, but I was unfailingly attracted to the geography of faces. From childhood, lying in my bed at night, I knew mine intimately, how the bones bent and curved and shaped the flesh, the sound I imagined eyes made when turning in their sockets, the softest whisper of a raised brow. Everything about Hannah was silent, frozen. If she lived, I wondered if her smile would ever be the same, altered if not by the physical blows then by unpredictable changes inside her. In my mind's eye, my hand floated over her cracked skull and Raggedy Ann body. I was an alchemist. I had my childhood powers back. I could raise the sick, give sight to the blind, consciousness to those who'd been left for dead. Her gurney disappeared into her room, and the door closed.

A uniformed sergeant and a plainclothes detective appeared a few minutes later. The sergeant was light-skinned, soft-spoken, and looked only a few years older than me. The barrel-chested detective was named Grunwald. His heavily lined face betrayed stress or exhaustion or both. He wrote David's and my contact information in a spiral notepad, and then showed us a Sony Walkman and a Tiffany watch found thirty feet from the crime scene. David identified both as Hannah's.

"We have a sketch, based on the couple's description," he told us as he unfolded a black-and-white rendering. "This is what he looks like." The face was egg-shaped, with a thin band of hair around his mouth. The dark eyes burned right through me. The suspect had a nose ring, and a tattoo of a Chinese symbol on his neck. Grunwald described him as about six-foot-three, two hundred eighty pounds, twenty-eight to thirty years old.

He wouldn't give us the suspect's name but said the sketch matched a police file photo, right down to the unusual tattoo. The man had been serving an eight-year sentence for a 1995 assault-and-battery on an ex-girlfriend but was released early from the Delaware County correctional facility. The police had his address, a copy of his driver's license, and names of family members and friends. They were knocking on doors right now.

"Why isn't he still in prison?" I was barely keeping it together.

The detective made a face—a blend of frustration and resignation—as if what could he do about the legal system. Sentencing guidelines and parole eligibility were a joke. "Next time we grab this guy," he promised, "it'll be different."

I wondered why. The legal system would still be full of holes.

"Was she raped?" I said. David looked upset that I'd asked. Maybe he should have been the one, but I wasn't myself.

The doctors were too busy saving Hannah's life to do a complete exam, Grunwald said. But from pelvic contusions and the suspect's history, he wouldn't be surprised. He told us he was sorry.

Despite looking tired, Grunwald had the breezy, factual tone of someone talking about the weather. The detective had found the same emotional no-man's-land as Dr. Mehra—accurate in his information but still able to buffer family members from more stress. It didn't work with me. I wanted to find the suspect and take his eyes out. Then I would borrow a gun and shoot him, slowly, one limb at a time.

Grunwald promised to be in touch as soon as he had news. I looked at David. I thought he'd gone back to what-ifing, beating himself up for not personally stopping an event that happened dozens of times a day in New York. He went from standing to sitting, sitting to standing. Finally he scooted back in his seat, as if gravity were pushing him right through the floor, like a nail into wood.

I found a quiet corner of the hallway and called my father. He answered on the second ring. I could imagine him in his club chair, reading contentedly, and then, seeing my number light up on his phone, feeling a jolt of happiness. I didn't get to say hello.

"Will! How's my favorite artist!"

"OK, thanks."

"What's new? Haven't heard from you in more than a week, son."

I apologized that I'd been busy. I had some difficult news to give, I added. It was about Hannah.

"What about Hannah?"

My father had always thought of me as the vulnerable child, and Hannah as invincible. I started slowly, trying for that safe, matter-of-fact tone of Dr. Mehra and the detective, but with every word, I knew I was throwing a rock at him, stoning him into numbness. I wouldn't have been surprised if he'd erupted in fury, as I had, or begun crying. Instead, the stoic in him prevailed. Maybe he was trying to show me he could be tough, or he knew there was no point in panicking.

"Tell me everything, again," he said when I'd finished. "Don't leave out anything."

I repeated what Grunwald had told me about the suspect—an ox of a man who'd been recently paroled from prison. The police knew where he was, and unless he'd fled the city, they expected to arrest him soon. Other than take a blunt instrument to Hannah's skull, nearly killing her, I didn't dwell on what else he'd done. Dad asked how David and I were holding up. "OK, hanging in," I answered, though I wasn't quite so sure about my friend.

My father told me to expect him no later than mid-afternoon tomorrow, then he hung up.

When I thought about my mother, I wasn't sure what to do. I didn't have her cell or house number. The pizza man had better access than I did. My only hope was email, but I wasn't sure how often she checked it. I asked at a nurse's station if I could use a computer. I felt like I was on the bridge of a sinking ship, banging on the telegraph key.

> *Hannah was badly beaten in Central Park. Her skull was crushed in three places, and she's just had hours of brain surgery at Lenox Hill Hospital. She's in a coma. Dad is flying in tomorrow. Come as soon you can. She needs all of us. Call my cell and I'll give you more details.*

When I brought another coffee to David, he was talking to someone in a plaid sport coat and mismatched tie. The young man had the blue-black skin of an African, with wiry hair and an angular, intelligent face. He introduced himself as a *New York Times* reporter who covered crime for the metro section. He'd be writing about the attack on Hannah for the morning edition. David described Hannah as well-educated, motivated, a hard-working young professional. The reporter scribbled in a notebook, then hurried away.

I convinced David we should move to some couches next to the hospital chapel; it would be more comfortable and just two minutes' walk to the ICU. I hoped I could sleep a little. David and I talked some more, anything that came into our heads, before we finally dozed. Around 6 a.m., I began strolling the hallways. I was surprised to run into Dr. Mehra. He said Hannah had experienced more cranial bleeding in the last hour. She'd go into surgery again at eight to relieve a subdural hematoma.

"This is not uncommon," he assured me when my face tightened. He asked me to tell David.

I wanted to believe Dr. Mehra. I filled up with more coffee and checked my email. Nothing from my mother. I sent her a second message about the new surgery, wondering how she could not rush here immediately if she read it. Love and compassion were fundamental to life. Yet Hannah believed that my mother was perhaps that evolved species of parent, the one who not only abandoned her children but also crushed their spirit like some mortal enemy.

Everything seemed to happen at once that morning.

The surgery took more than two hours. Dr. Mehra drained Hannah's cranial cavity with a catheter, and inserted a vertical shunt to relieve further buildup of cerebrospinal fluid. After she was back in the ICU, David and I were allowed five minutes to lightly touch her hands and feet. I whispered in her ear, and told her Dad was coming. I imagined that somehow she could hear me.

An article about a vicious attack on a young woman in Central Park was on the front page of the *Times* metro section. In addition to the couple who had rescued my sister, the piece focused on Grunwald's confidence of an imminent arrest, even if it was based on only a glimpse of the suspect under the fading summer light. The article quoted New Yorkers as being outraged, since Mayor Giuliani was on a campaign to make the city safer, and crime had become a hot issue

By eleven thirty, I had a call from Detective Grunwald that the suspect had been arrested without a struggle, and was being held at the Central Park Precinct, pending a police lineup. His name was Edward Archuleta, and he denied being anywhere near Central Park last evening. He was at the movies with his girlfriend, he said; they'd gotten into a fight, which explained the scratches on his arms. A DNA swab from Hannah's fingernails would prove or disprove his claim. For the lineup, Grunwald was trying to round up four other men with tattoos on their necks, not an easy task. He was confident the couple would identify Archuleta.

I took a nap and a shower at my apartment, and when my father called from LaGuardia, we agreed to meet at the hospital at three thirty. He'd already read the *Times* story. I told him about the morning surgery, which I called a success, judging from Dr. Mehra's tone. I also gave him news about the suspect. The arrest cheered him a little.

He was waiting with David when I got to the hospital, the *Times* tucked under his arm and a sense of purpose in his stride. He struck me as focused and together. When we got to Hannah's bed, though, it was like someone had slapped him in the face. He just stared. He said his daughter looked like a baby bird that had fallen out of its nest. He couldn't hide his shock. Someone had stolen Hannah's grace and beauty, wrapped them in a ball, and thrown it on the side of the road like a piece of trash.

It was painful reading his thoughts, because they were the same as mine. What if Hannah didn't recover? Even if she did, how lasting would the damage be? Would she be able to return to work, any kind of work? He was far more agitated than when we'd visited Dr. Glaspell to talk about the fire. While David stayed with Hannah, my father asked if I needed some air. Outside, he flagged a taxi.

"Are you coming, Will?"

"Where are you going?"

"Are . . . you . . . coming?"

I was afraid that I knew our destination. I shared his indignation, but there was a matter of common sense, too. "Hannah's going to be OK," I promised, trying to calm him.

"Would Dr. Mehra tell us that with certainty? Will, no one knows, do they?"

"No, not yet. He'd tell us we have to be patient."

"All my life I've been patient."

My father's hands were on his knees, fists clenched, as he gave the cabbie directions. He was saying that he wasn't going to be patient any longer. It was the realization that having forbearance and endurance no longer worked for his life. Studying Hannah in her bed had made him look inward. Where had patience gotten him all these years? His marriage, his career, his protection of his children—his whole life seemed to mock his attempt at virtue.

The driver turned into the park. "What's this going to prove?" I said.

"I want to see the crime scene. I want to understand everything."

The area where Hannah had been attacked was cordoned off with yellow police tape. According to the *Times,* she had been dragged behind some bushes and raped. Police speculated that Archuleta had bashed in her skull when she resisted, but maybe he'd done it without provocation. My father lingered with other spectators at the edges of the tape. Bouquets of flowers had been left near the bushes. It was impossible to ignore the comments of outrage and sympathy from strangers talking among themselves. My father didn't identify himself. He was locked into his own smoldering silence, figuring the direction Hannah had been running, her speed, when she'd last glanced at her watch, whether she couldn't hear her attacker because she was listening to her Walkman; how hard she had fought back. . . .

"Maybe we should go," I said after a minute or so. "You're tired. David gave you a key to the co-op, didn't he?"

"Why do you think this monster attacked my daughter?" he asked, refusing to move. "Was dusk the perfect time for a badass to do his thing? Was it Hannah's looks that attracted him? Did he hate women? Did he want to destroy her because she was unobtainable to him?"

"I don't know what he was thinking," I said, growing more uncomfortable. My own anger was about to erupt again.

"Does motive even matter?" he wondered. "The police have their suspect. And that's the problem, when you think about it. The only witnesses saw him for a microsecond and it was getting dark. Is that going to hold up in court? Doesn't the urgency of this whole arrest strike you as slightly political? Should we ask the mayor? I think he's going to make my daughter his poster child."

"The arrest will hold up. Wait till there's a DNA match. You'll see."

That likelihood didn't seem to satisfy my father. He still had his doubts. He continued when we got back in a cab. He had never really liked New York, he said, except for his years at Columbia.

Mayor Giuliani could blow smoke all day, but the city wasn't a safe place. A thousand arrests were made every day, a few perpetrators were convicted, but most of them walked. His own crime and sentence in Vermont had taught him remorse. That garbage who had tried to kill Hannah—what did he feel? Archuleta had been to prison, gotten out, and committed virtually the same crime again. He didn't understand remorse, penance, or moral anguish.

"Your sister has a strong sense of right and wrong," he added. "What do you think she'd want for this guy?"

"I think she'd want justice."

"And what exactly, in this very case, is that, Will? Is it another prison sentence for Mr. Archuleta?"

He was trying to teach me something, I thought, but I didn't want to hear it right now. I wanted him to cool off, as I had forced myself to do. Before we went to the co-op, he insisted on talking to Detective Grunwald. The cabbie drove us onto the Eighty-Sixth Street Transverse, where the city's oldest police precinct sat in a Victorian Gothic structure in the middle of the park.

We were pointed down the hall to a large office with beat-up furniture. His door open, Grunwald was racing his fingers across a keyboard, threw me a quick glance, and continued typing. A fly landed on his forehead, but he was too preoccupied to brush it off. I wondered if he was emailing the mayor the latest update. When was the lineup? When would the suspect be arraigned? Was the media going to make this a national story?

"Do you have a minute?" I interrupted him. "I'd like you to meet my father."

Grunwald pushed the send button on his email. "Not much more than a minute. Sorry. It's a hairy day."

My father had been right behind me, but when I turned, I couldn't find him. Seconds later, I heard a sonic boom—part-wail, part-scream, part-squall, someone half-dead inside his own grief and fury come to life. Grunwald and I rushed down the hall. Near the end, three cops were restraining my father. The object of his fury was a brooding monster in handcuffs and leg chains, the oval face brimming with disdain, his biceps shiny with tattoos. In the crazy comings and goings of fate, Archuleta and my father had ended up five feet apart, an unbridgeable abyss in my father's mind when his arms were pinned back by police. But his voice was free, and when his unearthly scream turned to words, they were a sermon to all, particularly the suspect. Red-faced, eyes bursting, my father shouted from the depths of all he had learned and known.

*"Oh, what men dare do! What men may do! What men daily do, not knowing what they do!"*

No one had to know Shakespeare to feel the torment that racked him. And I understood something else, what he had wanted to teach me in the taxi. If there was no remorse, justice could not be patient, and people could not trust the law. Another prison sentence would not suffice for this man. The suffering of the victim had to be vindicated. He was an atheist, but the Old Testament wisdom of exchanging eyes and teeth had not been lost on my father. He would have had his satisfaction but for the three policemen restraining him. He was sixty years old, and his enemy was a young thug, the size of an NFL lineman, but I had no doubt, if freed, my father would have found a way to crush Edward Archuleta's skull.

The suspect did not understand Shakespeare. I doubted he knew what empathy meant. His reaction to my father was an endless curse in Spanish, the cords of his neck bulging as his words flew in bursts. He was like a dangerous, naive adolescent declaring war on the world, convinced he would win. Two plainclothes detectives hustled him out into an unmarked car, leaving me alone with my burning father.

At home, David fixed hamburgers for everyone, but I was the only one eating. My father, distracted and exhausted, fell asleep. Around seven, I returned to the hospital. A nurse told me Hannah was stable. There'd been no new swelling in her brain, and her vitals remained strong, but she was still in a coma. Dr. Mehra had just made his rounds and would be back in the morning. I pulled my chair up to Hannah's bed. The more I gazed at her, the guiltier I felt. The last few years, I had been inexcusably cold to her, not always outwardly, but I had declared war on her easy life, on the righteousness that came when everything went your way.

I retreated to a hallway seat, cradling my head in my hands. I must have dozed, because when my neck swung up, it was after nine. Someone had brushed past, waking me like an unexpected breeze. When I checked on Hannah, nothing in her room had been disturbed. There was no evidence of a visitor. Back in the hallway, my eye caught the elevator as the door was closing, and in a split second, I glimpsed the figure that I was sure had wakened me. I rushed headlong down the stairs.

At the emergency room entrance, a black town car hugged the curb, windows closed, its engine idling. A woman was climbing into the rear, her back to me. She was thin, and her dark hair was in a bun, held by a silver and turquoise barrette. The door closed behind her. I rushed over, but it was impossible to make out anything through the tinted glass. I rapped on the window while my other hand yanked on the door handle. "Please, open the door," I shouted. Ignoring me, the driver eased the engine into first, and the car edged away, sailing into the night.

Back on Hannah's floor, I stopped one of the nurses. "Who was just here, in my sister's room?" I demanded, though I was sure I knew.

She flipped a bang from her eyes, wondering why I was so agitated. "We always check IDs if the patient is a crime victim. Her name was Susan Olmsted. The artist, right? She said she was Hannah's mother. I had no idea. She answered enough questions to pass the test. Kind of a strange woman. Where has she been all this time?"

"Why didn't someone wake me?"

"Sweetie, you were passed out cold."

"How long did she stay?"

"Ten minutes, more or less."

The nurse said she'd peeked in the room and seen my mother standing over Hannah. She had my sister's hand cupped between hers, tenderly, like someone who'd captured a ladybug from the garden, the nurse said. When she came back and checked again, my mother was still holding her hand.

She asked if I wanted to be notified if my mother came back. I said yes, but I doubted she would return. My minimalist mother, unannounced, had made the briefest visit possible, performed her sleight of hand, whatever it was, and disappeared. I felt like a kid at a magic show, lulled into complacency by the magician, and then, without warning, out from under a cape soared a dove, or an elephant became a tiger—the bigger the surprise, the more inevitable it seemed. When I looked back on my mother's history of grand gestures, perhaps this was no surprise.

The bigger surprise came the next day—when Hannah woke from her coma. David, my father, and I were there. We had to keep ourselves from shouting. I wasn't going to tell anyone about the clandestine visit, because my father would have flipped out. Surely my mother couldn't have been the cause of this miracle, he would have said. She wasn't Zeus. It was all coincidence. And how dare she show up in the middle of the night, without telling anyone—what could be more selfish?

I thought my father might have lost sight of how different they were from one another. My mother didn't particularly care about remorse, justice, or being unselfish. She didn't care that she hadn't spoken to her daughter in almost two decades. But she did care about Hannah, in spite of everything she had said about being a parent.

My sister climbed out of her coma by blinking her eyes and stirring the index finger of her right hand. Dr. Mehra watched her carefully for about twenty minutes, making sure she wasn't overstimulated. In the next few days, we witnessed additional small miracles, from wiggling her toes to sticking out her tongue, and we all began thinking about Hannah's future.

After a few days of research and consulting with doctors, my father concluded that Craig Hospital outside Denver was the top rehabilitation facility in the country for traumatic brain injury. There, Hannah would work with physical therapists, speech therapists, and psychologists, and have round-the-clock care. Her company health insurance covered everything. For brain injuries, I learned, no two paths to recovery were quite the same. Some people hit roadblocks and never got beyond them. Others made a steady and full, or nearly full, recovery. It was always wait and see. Yet from her first moments of full wakefulness, when her gaze rested on my face with the same surprise my eyes had falling on her, I believed in Hannah's rebirth.

It was difficult getting back to painting. Hannah was always on my mind. She had been flown on a special medical jet to Denver, where my father visited every weekend. David had taken a leave from teaching and rented a condo near the hospital. I wanted to be in Denver, too, but my father and David insisted Hannah was in capable hands, and she would want me to keep working; she expected great things from the artist in the family.

I made sure I got every piece of news from David. My sister's short-term memory was nonexistent, including of her attack. Unless Hannah brought up the subject, David said, he and my father had decided not to give her too many details. And a psychiatrist at Craig agreed. My sister's physical needs were more pressing. Her vision and speech were blurred, and the nerve damage also affected her hearing and sense of smell. Her motor skills were slowly improving, but there were miles to go. Because of balance problems, doctors weren't sure she'd ever walk without a cane.

I resumed my marathon trips around Lower Manhattan, exploring the unknown for fresh ideas. Unlike my father, I was no longer full of rage. I barely followed the case of Edward Archuleta, whose trial was still months away. Maybe there would never be true justice, not the kind to satisfy my father, but I never doubted he would be found guilty. What preoccupied me on my walks and in my studio was turning life into art. The feeling woke me every morning and kept me from falling asleep at night. In my notebook, I wrote: Describe having someone or something you love taken away from you, forever. Whether the loss was your fault or someone else's hardly mattered. One minute you counted on something, and the next it was gone. Hannah's life as she knew it had been taken from her, and in turn, her loss had become mine and David's and my father's. T Rex had done a vanishing act on me, turning my heart into stone. My father had been abandoned or betrayed enough times to make him reluctant to count on any steady happiness. Rothko had committed suicide in part because he thought his art never fulfilled its promise. I thought of dozens of examples. On any given day, you could lose your innocence, your friends, your confidence, your identity—as randomly as you lost your keys or wallet. I remembered what my father had told me. Your life could end at any time, and it could end more than once.

I wanted to put that concept on a canvas. At SDA, I had studied William Blake's illustrations for Milton's *Paradise Lost*—powerful, delicately limned scenes from the Book of Genesis: creation, temptation, punishment. But the story of Adam and Eve seemed epic and institutionalized. I wanted to depict loss on a human scale. Hopper had done it with his everyday vignettes of small town America. You could see the isolation not so much in his faces—he didn't do anatomic details—but in the setting, which was almost always some forlorn place. My first sketch was of Hannah in the hospital, then T Rex in the Tennessee cabin, and myself wrestling with Louie Freeze. I imagined my mother and father at different junctures of their complicated lives, and tried to draw those, too. I wondered how tragedies changed personalities, how unexpected events could turn lives upside down and sometimes keep them there. When I moved from sketching to painting, I experimented endlessly with pigment combinations. Color, I had begun to believe, was the essence of storytelling.

Two things interrupted my work that summer. On the morning of September 11, a network of foreign terrorists crashed two airplanes into the World Trade Center towers and another into the

Pentagon, and a fourth aimed at the Capitol went down in a field as passengers tried to wrestle control from the hijackers. Everyone on all four planes was killed. New York City, if not the whole country, was in pandemonium, and the aftermath of the tragedy provoked major questions about national security, Muslim extremists, and the deaths of 3,000 innocent people. On September 12, I walked to Ground Zero, getting as close as I could. There were photos on walls and placards of the dead and missing, often with flowers underneath, and messages from families seeking a brother or son or mother who might have survived. I gently put my hand on the faces, touching their eyes and foreheads as if the features were my own. It was hard to pull away. Back in my apartment, I realized that I had more stories to paint.

My second disruption was a call from my father. After making sure I was safe from the attacks, he told me Hannah was going through "a very rough period." Would I please come and visit? I was on a plane the next day. When we met at the Denver airport, my father ticked off my sister's incremental progress. She was ambulatory with a walker, could speak whole sentences lying down, sitting, or standing, and liked to play hearts with one of her nurses. But she became easily frustrated when she couldn't remember a word or event, or a therapy session didn't go well. Then she fell into tears or blew up at the world. It was hard on everyone. David, needing a break, was visiting his father in Albuquerque.

"Do you think I can really help?" I asked as we took a taxi to the hospital.

"Just be there for her, Will. It's been almost two months. Hannah thinks she's never going to get better. And the doctors won't say."

I walked into my sister's room with a box of Godiva chocolates, determined to single-handedly cheer her into full recovery. In her robe and pajamas, she was propped on the end of her bed, a book of poetry on her lap. For the first time in her life, she was wearing glasses, a pair with thin tortoise shell frames. I wasn't sure she recognized me, but after a long second, she said, slowly, "Hi Will. Don't I look gorgeous?"

"Like a movie star." I was heartened that her face had mostly healed. Unless she had plastic surgery, there would always be a scar on her cheek and the crook of a broken nose. I opened the candy for her, and she picked something soft. Chewing and swallowing were a process.

"You OK?" she asked.

"I'm great. How are you?"

She made a sideways wave of her hand, like someone who didn't want to talk about herself. Instead, Hannah wanted to know details of what had happened on 9/11: the firefighters and police who died in the collapsing towers; President Bush's visit to the site; the political repercussions in New York. I felt like an ambassador from a faraway land bringing stories not always reported in the media. Security was tight everywhere, I said, making everyone edgy. If you weren't a citizen or didn't have a green card, you could be arrested and deported. There had been demonstrations about civil liberties. Mayor Giuliani was playing the patriot card. The rubble at the site, a daily reminder of the city's wordless grief, would take months to clear away. Hannah nodded at everything I said, mesmerized by the nightmare. She had worked in a skyscraper only two blocks from Ground Zero. None of her friends or colleagues had been injured, she said, but almost everyone knew someone who had died that day.

"It's not safe," she announced, looking at me.

"What's not?"

"Maybe you can't feel safe anywhere in New York. What if there's another terrorist attack?"

"There's a lot of fear now, but things will get better," I assured her. "I feel safe."

As she pulled herself off her bed, my father hurried over, guiding her feet into a pair of slippers. Using a walker, she moved to a window with a view of the flawless green lawn and a row of fruit trees. It looked peaceful, like the Arcadian gardens the English poets had written about.

"I want to know what happened in Central Park," Hannah said.

She turned and faced my surprised father. He pursed his lips. It was the moment he had hoped would never arrive.

"What do you remember, sweetie?"

"Nothing much. Except that just now, I remember running in Central Park, and something happened. Is that true?"

Maybe it was our talk about 9/11 that finally stirred her subconscious. She was suddenly struggling to piece together her own five minutes of terror. When she'd first begun to speak, she thought she'd been in a car accident, and no one corrected her. There was never any mention of Central Park. No one had showed her the *New York Times* article, and her friends from work were told to steer clear of the facts. My father wanted to say she shouldn't care, but he wasn't going to lie to her now.

"You were attacked by a thug," he answered. "He's the one who hurt you."

"There was no car accident?"

"No."

"Who was it?"

"Just a very bad person. He's been arrested and is awaiting trial. He raped you and almost killed you. That's all I know, honey."

"I was raped?" she repeated, trying to understand. Her palm swept away a tear.

"It could have happened to anyone," he said.

"But it happened to me."

She was trying to absorb everything, to find a perspective as her feelings tumbled down around her. She was like someone in a pitch-black room feeling for a doorknob.

"You know, one day you'll be completely better," I spoke up. "You won't have missed a beat. You'll fit right in again."

"Fit in where?"

"Back in your old life."

"What if I don't want to," she said, turning back to the window. "You act as if nothing happened. Dad just said I was beaten and raped. I was nearly killed."

"Don't you miss sleeping in your own bed?" I detoured her. "Your friends, your work, your lifestyle. . . ."

"I'm not going back to New York."

My father listed his head to one side. He was probably thinking, like me, that Hannah was strong and fearless. Of course she would return, as soon as she recovered emotionally and physically, to make her mark on the world.

"There's no hurry," he said. "Maybe it takes a year or two. Who's counting?"

"Why does someone do that?" she interrupted.

"He's an animal," my father said. "He's going to prison for a long time."

"You know what it feels like?" she asked, suddenly understanding. "A stranger sneaks up on you and takes away your soul. Without warning. Without permission. Everything that I was, he took away from me. I was left with nothing. And then, if it's possible to take away nothing, he took that, too."

"No, he didn't touch your soul," my father corrected her.

"How do you know, Dad?"

"I know, honey. He couldn't. You're too strong. When your brother was burned in the fire, I nurtured him, so his soul would survive. I'll do the same for you."

"It's different now. I'm not a child," she whispered.

"No, I can help you," he insisted.

She kept shaking her head. Hannah's pain was like the shadow of a winged creature cast over the entire room, over the Earth itself. There was no shelter from it. All the psychiatrists in the world wouldn't convince her that what she felt and believed wasn't true. She knew the damage was impossible to calculate, and it would live in her forever. I understood that as well as anyone.

My father was struggling to find the right tone to console her, as he had with me in Dr. Glaspell's office. As Hannah moved to a chair, her mouth was etched with disappointment. It wasn't with my father. I could feel a shift in her mood. She was turning her humiliation and powerlessness on herself. In her whole life, she had never not taken responsibility for anything. Running alone in the park in the evening, thinking she was invulnerable, what had she expected?

"I'm not going back to New York," she repeated.

"Of course not," my father agreed. "There are other cities. You and David could live abroad. Your company has offices around the world. Someplace where you'll feel safe."

"I'll never feel safe," Hannah answered. "I'm not going anywhere. I don't care about money or a big job. I'm . . . I'm. . . ."

I watched her lips open and close. I saw the tip of her tongue. Losing a word or phrase was like dropping a diamond into a deep crevice. It was beyond frustrating not to be able to pull it out. Her eyes blazed with fury at herself.

"It's OK, we can talk about this later," I jumped in.

"No, not later. Not ever," Hannah said.

She lied down on her bed, curling up her knees, and suddenly was crying into her pillow. I could only guess what she had wanted to tell us. I'm hopeless. I'm lost. I'm a different person. Maybe there was no word or phrase to describe her emotions. Like me, my father had hoped for a small miracle, Hannah springing off the canvas after a knockdown, ready for the next round. I began to see that wasn't the miracle Hannah wanted. In her slowly healing brain, she was giving up ambition in exchange for something that would bring her peace. If she couldn't find that, I guessed, she would just as soon fade away. I had never felt so close to her as that moment. I wanted to throw my arms around her and protect her the way she used to protect me.

I stayed several days longer than I'd planned. I declined my father's offer to visit the Denver Art Museum with him. Even when her moods gyrated wildly, when she became difficult to be with, I didn't leave Hannah. No tantrum could force me out of her room. When my sister was calm, we played board games, told stories about Santo Tomás, and wondered what we'd be doing a year from now. She prayed that she'd be anywhere but in a hospital. I kidded her that she could get room service at any hour now. But living here was not like staying in a Four Seasons, she made clear. It was like floating in space for eternity, she said. The past and future were faraway galaxies.

When my visit was over, I hugged Hannah good-bye. She pressed a folded slip of paper in my hand. "You would understand this best, Will," she said. "Save it for the plane."

I was too emotional and curious to wait, and opened the paper in the taxi. It was a poem. Her once-flowing, elegant handwriting had become crabbed and determined. To dredge up a thought was one task; getting it through the pipeline to her fingers was another.

*I'm not sane*
*I'm not insane*
*I'm somewhere in between*
*I'm afraid that I'll be*
*forever*
*an engine sputtering*
*a boat half-sunken*
*I'm afraid, I'm afraid, I'm afraid*
*unless*
*one day*
*far, far away*
*I'll be happy again*
*but it won't be me.*

She was right. I did understand. Back in New York, I pinned her poem next to my kitchen table, framing Hannah in my mind whenever I read it.

I soon got lost in my work, putting in long days at the loft, determined to produce at least ten paintings with the hope some small gallery would give me a show. I was a young nobody on the New York art scene, but I thought of myself as Michelangelo finishing the ceiling of the Sistine Chapel. It was as if all the ambition my sister had desperately and deliberately thrown away had found its way to me. If color was the essence of story-telling, I relied heavily on icy blues, grays, pinks, and blacks to give my characters that special moment of recognition, when something had been stolen from them and their lives changed. I worked with acrylics on Masonite, making the faces impressionistic yet detailed and readable. My characters didn't necessarily look as distraught as Hannah. Some were wise and accepting, though there was always pain somewhere. They chopped wood, shopped in supermarkets, drove cars, talked to a friend. In every painting, I included black birds—perched on trees, on lawns, flying overhead. Black birds, according to mythology, were a repository of souls. I thought the symbolism gave a certain gravity to my work. I hoped it wouldn't be seen as pretentious.

By July 2002, almost nine months after I'd started, I had my ten paintings. Most were 36 by 36 inches, and a couple were larger. When I propped them against a wall, I was pleased to see an emotional continuity. I called the group *Birds Fall From the Sky.* I nervously asked one of my loft mates for his opinion.

Storm Baker was round and bearish, somewhere in his 40s, his face lined from chain-smoking and his balding head usually covered by a San Francisco Giants cap. He rarely smiled, but he wasn't as gruff as he appeared. Because he was cheap, he lived on hamburgers, fries, and diet Cokes, and shared an apartment with a woman he fought with loudly on the phone. He spent a couple of minutes parading up and down looking at *Birds.* "Shit," he finally murmured. "There's a whole lot of hurt here."

"I guess so," I said.

"Technically, these are all strong, Will. Amazing brushwork and colors. You should be proud. This is what you've been working on every day?"

Storm might have been cheap, but he was the most successful of the four of us by far. His collages had begun to sell for $75,000 and up. I took his opinions seriously.

"They're about the loss of something important," I explained. "I wanted to capture that moment in someone's life, or the recognition of it."

"I can feel their isolation. The birds help. But I'm not sure I see their acceptance of their loss. Isn't that the extra dimension you want?"

"Maybe they don't accept it. I don't know," I said honestly. It seemed like an awful lot of nuance to pack into a painting, maybe more than I could handle.

"I keep going back to the pain," Storm said. "That's what I see and feel the most. Your characters remind me of my parents. Whenever they got pissed off about something, they spent half the night screaming at each other. In the morning, they pretended nothing had happened. Maybe they just forgot. But the screaming matches happened over and over. Ultimately, I didn't know what was more real, when it happened or when it didn't."

What everyone took from a painting could be subjective, but I tried to convince myself that my work wasn't as ambiguous as Storm described it. The paintings conveyed a critical, objective moment in everyone's life.

"Do you like them?" was all I could think to ask.

"Your characters are haunted enough that they push you away, but then they pull you back in. That works for me. Would I hang one in my pad? If I were single, yeah, but my old lady likes happy shit."

"I'm going to hang one in mine," I said awkwardly, as if that proved something. "All I want," I added, "is a chance to see if other people respond to them the way I do."

Storm and I had talked often about the business of selling art. It seemed like every other person in the neighborhood was a painter, and there was only so much gallery space. In addition to the competition, gallery owners were tight with money. If you were an unknown, you might be asked to defray the cost of your show. No one knew what would sell, but there were endless opinions about what wouldn't.

"You want me to put the word out with some galleries?" Storm said. "Take some good photos for me."

"I'll buy you a steak at Peter Luger, too. You can get off those greasy burgers for a second."

"I like your work, Will, and I'll try to help. But honestly, you're missing the boat. You've got a world-class artist for a mother. She could get you in any gallery in New York."

"I don't want her help."

"Don't be so stuck up. If I had an advantage like that, I'd consider it criminal to not use it."

"It's not an option," I said quietly. I hadn't shared the history of my face with Storm. If I had, his response, like Hannah's, would be that my mother owed me infinite favors. My mother didn't think so. Even if she did, there were deeper reasons why I couldn't accept her help.

Storm and I dined the next week at Peter Luger, which arguably served the best steaks in the city. It was my first time there. The bill exceeded my weekly food budget, but I was happy to pay it. Storm had pitched me to four galleries, two each in Soho and Chelsea, and the directors or owners were willing to visit my studio.

"Very interesting, but honestly, too dark, and a little confusing," one told me when he came. Another said I showed promise and that we should keep in touch. Two offered me a place in their fall group shows. I could hang three or four paintings. I should have been ecstatic, but I chose to argue. All ten needed to be hung together, I insisted, or the overall effect would be diminished. The gallery owner in Soho promptly retracted her offer. The owner of Gallery Zoom in Chelsea told Storm I suffered from hubris but that he could accommodate all ten in the back room. I visited the gallery with Storm. I would be one of four artists, including a well-known biomorphic sculptor, an Agnes Martin-like minimalist, and someone who painted broad swatches of color on huge canvases. When I told him I didn't want to be buried in the back room, he smiled. The new guy always got the back room. He expected me to sell at least four or five paintings if I wanted a future show.

As we left together, Storm's eyes clouded with disbelief. "Do you know how lucky you are? You should have kissed his ass, Will. I painted for years before I got a show."

"I am grateful," I said, "but I don't think he really understood the theme."

"He had to understand something. He's giving you space. Just be happy."

"Yeah, but I have to do most of the advertising."

"Be happy," he repeated.

I called Hannah as soon as I had the opening date—October 13. "Will, that's such great news. Congratulations!" she said.

Her spirits had improved remarkably since my visit. Craig Hospital had released her in late May, after about ten months of rehab. As everyone had dared to dream, she was almost fully recovered, cognitively at least. For balance, she required a silver-handled cane she'd picked out in a Denver antique shop, and her stamina often faded late in the afternoon. But her speech, memory, and attention span were as good as before the tragedy. She and David had bought a rustic house on twenty acres outside Durango. Hannah described their new homestead as "pine-carpeted hills with enough solitude to make Thoreau envious." Her ambition, she said, was limited to planting a garden in the spring, taking walks, and reading books. David would be teaching at a public high school in the fall.

"Can you and David come?" I asked.

"You know I would. I'm so excited for you. But the thirteenth is the day we're moving into our house. It's all been scheduled."

I had wanted to invite Hannah even if I never expected her to come. Setting foot back in New York, even for a visit, was not something she looked forward to.

"No problem, I'll get you guys next time."

"Did you call Dad?"

"He has a seminar to teach."

"That's a bummer! We'll all be there in spirit."

"I know it," I said.

I began making color flyers to pin in laundromats, bookstores, on community bulletin boards. I sent out invitations, getting names from artists I'd met through Storm. I built my own website. Instead of showing my face on the home page, I used one of the paintings. After a while, I didn't mind that I was selling Gallery Zoom more than it was selling me. I wanted to prove to the owner I could make him money.

I wasn't sure what to do about my mother. I hadn't heard from her since graduation, though we'd had our phantom encounter at Lenox Hill. I had continued to track her existence through art magazines and online gossip. She and Simon had moved to Beacon, a small upstate New York town overlooking the Hudson River, not far from West Point. They were building a large spread, including a studio for my mother. Her art continued to sell at astronomical prices.

A week before the opening, I screwed up my courage and sent her an email with an attached invitation. I asked her to arrive toward the end of the night. I didn't want her presence overshadowing my modest maiden flight. We'd go to dinner somewhere, and maybe I'd have some sales to celebrate. In addition, I had another, even more important, motive for getting together. Even though she had told me her role as a parent was over, I wanted to be sure. I wanted to tell her I no longer needed her patronage in any way, that I was prepared for obstacles in my career—she had given me fair warning—but would turn them into opportunities, just as she had done. I would make it on my own.

She called back that night. Her tone was peevish. She'd try to come, she said, but why had I waited so long to send an invitation? She and Simon had a busy schedule.

I rolled my eyes. Did she think she was the only one who was busy? "It's been a crazy time. Sorry."

"I'll bring Simon."

"No. Please don't. I'm taking you to a late dinner. Just for the two of us to catch up. Can you come around eight thirty?"

I repeated the address, just in case she had deleted the invitation. The gallery was on the ground floor of an apartment building. A fashionable Bauhaus renovation, it boasted large sheets of frosted glass on the outside, a single red steel door to enter through, colored concrete floors, and high white walls. Zoom was in the heart of the new Chelsea scene, but it still felt isolated. I couldn't help think of my mother's early off-off-off Broadway days.

"Are you pleased with your work?" she asked before we hung up. It was her standard question.

"Absolutely. Plus, there're ten pieces, my lucky number. I was born the tenth day of the tenth month. I was ten years old when my first drawing won a prize. I'm not going to tell you anything about the paintings. I want you to be surprised."

I was babbling. She had to know I was nervous on many levels. She didn't comment other than to note, as usual, that she was sure I had worked hard, and she would do her best to be there. She had no prediction of success for me, no special words of encouragement. I told myself not to pay attention.

I arrived at the gallery at five, to make sure the track lighting was angled correctly and the price list was accurate. My paintings ranged from $2,500 to $4,000. I hovered in the back room, awed at seeing my work fastidiously hung on clean white walls. Ryder was unmistakable in the bottom corner of every painting. *Birds Fall From the Sky,* the wall placard announced. People streamed in exactly at six, couples, singles, small groups, most in jeans and T-shirts, but some men wore dress shirts and jackets. Storm had told me to check out everyone's watch and shoes. If they looked expensive, those were the people I needed to pay attention to. Schmooze the shoes, he said.

The other artists had sent out more invitations than I did, and by six thirty, a hundred fifty people were milling around holding plastic cups of wine and nibbling on cheese squares. Moving the paintings from my studio to a gallery had been like going from dress rehearsal to opening night. Everything stood out more. I scrutinized my work again, fussing about some of the color choices. Storm dropped in and commented that they looked subtle and powerful. A gay couple said they were contemplating buying one, maybe two. I was ecstatic when they took my card, promising to call. An elderly woman told me she had lost a niece in the South Tower on 9/11, and understood about loss and grieving. I had at least a dozen conversations with potential buyers.

Intermittently, I watched someone paste red dots next to several of the color field paintings, and even the sculptor, whose work started in the mid-five figures, sold a piece. Gulping wine, I began navigating the gallery in desperation, looking in vain for expensive shoes. My neck was sweating. Every ten minutes, I would return to the back room and search for a red dot. Around seven fifteen, a towering arrangement of flowers arrived: roses, lilies, tulips, and birds of paradise. Everyone hovered around it like a piece of art, and it was—colorful and bold yet subliminal. It had to have cost a mint. Someone brought me the attached envelope. It was my mother's stationery. Wilson Louis Ryder was in her handwriting. I opened it in private.

> *It is closing time in the gardens of the West and from now on an artist will be judged only by the resonance of his solitude or the quality of his despair.*
>
> *—Cyril Connolly.*
>
> *Will, sorry. Something urgent came up.*

I slipped the card in my pocket, hoping to keep my mother's identity private, but I heard people guessing who had sent the arrangement. Many knew who my mother was—the gallery owner hadn't kept it a secret—which made me wonder about his real motive in giving me a show. I wandered out to the sidewalk, furious. The flowers were the omnipresent shadow of a woman who had a genius for disruption and bad timing. Magically, she had turned the spotlight on herself, without even showing up. I was relieved that I wouldn't have to take her to dinner. She wouldn't care if I formally announced my independence. My feelings didn't mean anything to her. No one's did. Not once had she asked me about Hannah's recovery. I was always the one to inform her.

I reread the quote: Closing time in the gardens of the West. Connolly was a British intellectual and literary critic of the '50s and '60s. Was he predicting the eventual rise of Islamic Jihadists, or simply referring to the end of the British Empire? What did my mother mean by quoting him? Had she gone online and seen my paintings? When it came to solitude and quality of despair, she could have been referring to her own work, not just mine. Did she think we had something in common? I hated it when she deliberately cloaked herself in mystery.

I moved back inside. Twelve or fifteen strangers were suddenly gathered around my paintings, as if they'd all flocked to the back room at once. There were still no red dots, but I was excited. A man brushed my shoulder on his way out. I turned but couldn't make out his face. Something about him seemed familiar. I helped myself to more wine. By nine, only stragglers were left in the gallery, emptying the food trough, chatting about PTA meetings and a new George Clooney movie. I was left in a corner. My confidence had toppled like a tree. When I said good night to the owner, I almost apologized to him. Maybe I'd duped myself all along. It was Friday, the 13th, I realized. I consoled myself that the show had nearly a month to run; surely there would be some sales before it was over.

Five days later, I was back in my studio, moving my pencil aimlessly over a sketchpad. Storm appeared with an unlit cigarette in his mouth, and tried to hand me the latest issue of the *Village Voice.* He had the page folded to Albert Reingold's column.

"No way," I said. "Are you shitting me?"

"Are you in an OK space?" he asked.

"I don't know. Just read it to me."

Storm cleared his throat.

"A young artist, Will Ryder, showing his ten enigmatic studies of solitude at Gallery Zoom in Chelsea, manages to affront our sensibilities without really trying. Something is up with the people he paints, something important to them, but we can't figure out what.

There's a Hopperesque isolation that manages to catch our attention, but with no meaningful subtext, other than some vague dark pain. The viewer is annoyed and perplexed and finally turns away. Young artists who produce works to instantly bring meaning to their lives and ours come across as overly earnest and intellectually powerless. Ryder may have talent with his sense of color, but he is hopelessly adrift in a subject that dwarfs his comprehension. . . ."

"That's enough," I cut him off. Why didn't Albert just come over with a poleax and chop off my head?

"This is the poison you have to get used to. Reingold wants to strike fear in every artist's heart," Storm said. "I wouldn't take him too seriously."

"I don't," I said, but I couldn't deny the pain.

Storm didn't know about the car chase and my police report, and illuminating history now would only seem like an excuse. The Zoom show wasn't the only one Albert picked on in his weekly column, yet I was the painter he found worthy of crucifying. Why had my mother ever brought him into my life? Was this a bad thing that somehow was supposed to turn into a good one? Even if the review was nothing but an act of revenge, it felt like my career, barely started, had been left for dead.

I waited several months before calling my mother. I wanted to have a perspective. Zoom had closed my show on schedule, and the works of a fresh set of artists had been installed. The gallery world was a revolving door. Not even news that one of my paintings had finally sold improved my mood. Blind luck, I concluded.

When my mother picked up the phone, she didn't ask how the show had gone or explain what had been so urgent that she couldn't appear. She didn't even ask if I'd received her flowers, as if the whole event was in the distant past. Maybe it was to everyone but me. I told her I'd like to visit her. Beacon was only an hour and a half by train from Grand Central. I could be there in an instant.

"Why?" she asked.

"I have something important to tell you."

"You can't tell me on the phone?"

I shook my head. She was impossible.

"All right, what about this weekend?" she suggested. "I only have one appointment. Do you know about Dia:Beacon? It was in yesterday's *Times.*"

"No," I admitted, making me feel more than ever like an outsider.

"Dia Foundation is opening a museum here. Robert Irwin is renovating the seventy-year-old Nabisco printing plant. The Dia board wants a venue for the best contemporary art of the last fifty years. I'm meeting with them Sunday."

I could fill in the blanks. My mother's work was going to be part of the permanent collection of the Dia Foundation, which as much as any critic or other institution shaped the trends, markets, careers, reputations, and prices of contemporary art. The museum was being erected in the town where my mother and Simon had chosen to live. How cool was that? My mother lived a fabled life.

"Congratulations," I said, meaning it. "You must be thrilled. Which pieces are you giving them?"

"I haven't decided. Maybe you can help pick them out."

"Me? Choose for you?"

"You know me as well as anyone."

"I'll have to think about that."

There were times I felt I didn't know her at all. Which meant, based on her statement, that nobody understood my mother. I did have a feeling for her dark and complex art. The darkness showed up in my own paintings. Maybe that was as close as we would ever get to intimacy.

"I suppose it's a nice honor to be selected," she finally said. Her throat was scratchy, and she sounded tired. I wondered if it was the weather. October had had some bitterly cold days.

"Nice? You deserve it! You're on the A-list of collectors and museums. I just read that one of your paintings sold at Sotheby's for a million and a half dollars."

I was being 100 percent sincere. My mother was quiet. She accepted praise and compliments with as much reluctance as she gave them. I suspected she thought they were spawned by self-interest. She didn't have any right to be suspicious of me, I thought. I didn't want anything from her, except my freedom.

We agreed I would come for lunch on Saturday. She and Simon had moved into their new house, and I would be one of their first guests. The back patio overlooked the Hudson's eastern bank. It was sited among a stand of ash, oak, and sycamore—what better setting for sandwiches and iced tea, if the weather cooperated, she said.

"But you're a coffee drinker," she caught herself. "Come a little before noon, Will."

On the train, I gazed uneasily on the countryside foliage while I rehearsed my speech. It had to be smooth and economical. My mother had denied me the chance to tell her my feelings at Zoom. I didn't want to give her another excuse to turn me away. At the Beacon station, I bounded onto the platform with a sense of mission, unwilling to accept more disappointment.

Beacon was a tiny, post-industrial river town whose edges had been gentrified with gorgeous homes on large lots. A ten-minute walk from the station, my mother's home was the only contemporary in sight, a magical fabrication of glass, rock, and angular metal roofs. It was buffered by a sloping lawn on all sides, with a swimming pool on one end and her studio at the other. A gardener was methodically cutting the grass on a tractor. Another was raking leaves. Simon greeted me at the front door.

"Welcome, Will the artist!" he said. He was in khakis, a raggedy sweater, and scuffed white tennies.

"Simon, the art collector," I answered, just as comfortably, and shook hands as though we'd known each other for a while. I had spotted him at my graduation, but we never spoke. His handsome face was a shade less gray than his short hair. He was outgoing and at ease with himself, complementing my complex and introverted mother—like a clarinet to a violin, I thought. I could hear my mother's thin voice down the hall, on the phone with someone. Simon and I zigzagged through the house, stopping at his favorite paintings as he gave me a brief history of each acquisition. Every collector had his own methodology. Simon said he knew what he loved almost instantly, and with equal impulsiveness, purchased it. He had few regrets. His paintings and sculpture made my breath catch; they were even more interesting than the pieces in the Chicago triplex where I'd spent a lonely Thanksgiving.

"I should be paying you admission," I kidded. I called his house MoMA 2.

My mother appeared in a bright orange wool sweater and jeans. I kissed her on the cheek. "I'm sorry I can't join you two for lunch," Simon said diplomatically. He seemed to know the wisdom of staying out of other people's business.

My mother asked if I'd like to see her studio. It was the first thing they'd built on the property. I had never been in one of her inner sanctums, though I'd imagined her inhabiting very modest spaces in the early days of her career, even more humble than my loft. We strolled across the lawn and into a cathedral. It had a pitched ceiling with laminated trusses, and tongue-and-groove maple flooring. The sixteen-foot walls were painted a bone white. Natural light flooded through skylights and a long bank of north and east windows. My mother had a table and easel set up at one end, with all her supplies meticulously arranged. The space was climate-controlled. I remembered Judd's studio in Marfa, the converted supermarket space that evidenced his obsessive need for order. My mother, too, had a specific place for everything, down to the smallest brush and tube of paint, but unlike Judd's sanctuary, there wasn't a particle of dust or lingering food odor. The space was so sanitized and removed from the everyday world that I couldn't imagine working in it for fear of dripping paint on the floor or scuffing a wall. I would be forever cleaning up after myself, leaving no time to paint.

My mother had thirteen paintings of various sizes sitting against one wall. I had never seen any of them, but I could always recognize her magical juxtaposition of abstract shapes and urgent, slashing colors. These relationships were their own primal, silent language, like what a child might create before he or she learns to speak.

"When did you find time to do these?" I asked, astonished at her production.

"They were all completed in the last twelve months."

We were both slow painters, but she had the additional burden of forced timeouts due to her illness and her medications. "I bet you didn't spend much time traveling. Did you eat or sleep?" I joked.

When she had a clear head, untroubled by mood swings, it was hard to think of my mother ever taking a break. There was never enough time in the day. She was the inexhaustible explorer who endured great pain in the creative process, where everything had to be executed to perfection. I understood it all.

"When's your next show?" I said.

"I don't know. I'm taking a break." She saw me frown. "I haven't really taken time off in twenty years. Don't you think I deserve it?" she defended herself.

"Why did you push so hard if you weren't going to have a show?"

She dropped in a chair and asked me to study all thirteen paintings carefully. "Pick out three," she said.

I took my time. They were all exceptional. Choosing favorites was highly personal. "It's nice you have confidence in me," I said, "but you need to make the final choice for Dia."

"No. I want you to do it."

Very reluctantly, I chose three.

"I'm not you," I pointed out. "If you tell anyone I picked these, the Dia board will insist you select something else, because I didn't know shit, you were just being nice to your son. . . ."

"They'll never know," she insisted.

Of course they would. There were no secrets in the art world. Someone like Albert would find out, and I would be embarrassed anew. My mother was setting me up again, even if it was unintentional. She picked up my three paintings and walked them to a separate corner, setting them aside.

As promised, she served sandwiches on the rear patio, guarded by deciduous trees that had lost most of their foliage. She had added a wool scarf to her thick sweater, but she still looked uncomfortable. The leaves carpeted the grass around us, a thick tapestry of pigments with a distinct odor. It was earthy and robust, with an edge of bitterness, words used to describe coffee or wine, I thought, or the transition to winter. My mother brought out Jamaican Blue Mountain coffee for me. The thatch of leaves seemed to sink under her weight as she walked, as if at any moment a trap door might open and she would vanish into the earth. She pecked at her sandwich. I asked how long she'd been sick.

"A summer cold," she said dismissively.

We ate in silence before my mother brought up the Zoom show. She apologized for not being there, and asked how my first opening had gone. Was I nervous, or did I enjoy every moment of it?

I had been one huge, very frayed nerve ending, I told her, and then it got worse. Albert showed up. His *Voice* review came out a few days later. It was like an obituary. My mother said she hadn't seen it, but she didn't seem surprised that he'd wreaked havoc. Despite his recent good behavior toward her, she reminded me that Albert's life was based on throwing down gauntlets and settling scores. I reminded her that this might never have happened had she not ignored the police before leaving Alpine.

"You shouldn't think of his review as necessarily a bad thing," she said, falling back on her philosophy. "Every time Albert says black, a lot of smart people think white."

"Then why didn't anyone rush to the gallery to buy something?"

"You didn't sell one painting?"

"OK. I sold one."

"I didn't sell anything for my first show. Nor my second, actually. That just made me work harder."

"I have no idea what I'm doing in my loft every day," I confessed. "I can barely afford the rent. I produce shit. I should quit."

"Do you think you're the first artist who didn't know what he wanted to paint?"

I put down my sandwich. I had lost my appetite. That was always my mother's message. Hunker down and grind away. Ultimately, your imagination would prevail. She was the one-in-a-million long shot who somehow got into the Kentucky Derby and then swept the field. Maybe she was destined to take the Triple Crown. It happened to some lucky soul once or twice a century.

"Why couldn't you make my opening?" I asked

"Something personal. You got my flowers, didn't you?"

She was surprised when I pulled her note from my pocket. I told her I couldn't make sense of the Connolly quote. Her gift of expensive flowers was equally perplexing. I didn't need her overblown apology for not showing up. It ended up being a curse. As soon as I heard her name whispered about in the gallery, I said, everything started going downhill.

"I've always liked Connolly," she said, ignoring me again. "He understood solitude and despair, because he battled it all the time."

I asked her again what the quote referred to—her art or mine?

"What do you think?" said the connoisseur of ambiguity.

She talked a little bit about her own depression, that she regarded it no differently than any other challenge. She would keep fording rivers and slaying dragons until her last breath. In some crucial ways, I thought, I was very different from her. I didn't seek out conflict and punishment. I wanted peace. I'd finally come around to my father's and Hannah's point of view. My mother's talent approached genius, but she was hopelessly complicated, and indifferent to the chaos she created in her wake. She was my tormentor.

"The world is one big obstacle course to you," I picked a fight, "and you want it to be the same for me. That's how I'm supposed to learn. You're my teacher. Do I have it right?

"Well, you're a lousy teacher," I said before I let her answer. "You speak in riddles. You're almost impossible to get hold of. And all I learn from you is basically how to be humiliated."

I was steaming. "The way you breezed into Hannah's hospital room, too important or busy to say hello to me—what was that about? You're like a hit-and-run driver."

She raised her hand, a policeman halting the traffic of my accusations. "You don't know how wrong you are, Will. I wanted to help Hannah, just as I've helped you from time to time. But I do things my way. You do know that by now, don't you? Or do you think I'm just a crazy eccentric?"

"Crazy eccentric might be OK. Having a chunk of ice for a heart is a killer."

Her face reddened, and her torso lurched forward in her chair. I'd seen my mother hurt and scared but never angry.

"Do you think I can ever forget what happened when you were three-years-old! I made a shrine for you in your bedroom while you were sleeping. I thought of you as an angel. I loved you. . . ."

My head pulled back. She had never used that word, not in front of me.

"Oh, feelings always get me in trouble," she caught herself, suddenly rising to her feet. I couldn't be sure if I was to blame for enticing her or she'd fallen off the wagon on her own.

Arms folded over her chest, she regained her composure. "You should never come here again, Will. We don't need to be in contact anymore. Thank you for your help in the studio today."

She turned and marched into the house, as resolute as any general. I was left on the patio, my heart knocking. There had been no discussion with my mother, no dialogue. She had made an executive decision. I was not to come back into her life. Hey, I thought, I agreed. It's what I was going to tell her.

I shouldn't have been surprised that her speech had preempted mine, but it upset me. My actual good-bye would have been a little different, as I had rehearsed on the train. After declaring my emancipation, I wanted to tell her I forgave her for not saving me from the fire, because she was lost in her own pain. Her distance from the world and me was calculated and willful, because it was self-preservation for her. She had been tossed by her illness onto a sharp-edged reef in the middle of an endless ocean. It wasn't her fault that her emotions were so fragile. I wanted to tell her I understood.

I sat for a while before pulling myself out of my chair. I wanted a longer good-bye, one that she didn't control by turning her back on me. When I went in the house, I could hear a television droning from Simon's study. I saw a housekeeper drying dishes. From the other end of the hall rose the soft, jagged notes of someone crying. They rippled through the still air, like a cord to be pulled on. I had never seen my mother cry, nor even imagined it. The door to her office was open. The room lights were off, but I made out her outline, hunched over a desk, her shoulders rising and falling. Everything about her seemed shrunken. I wondered if she was crying for herself, or me, or us—for what might have been.

In a room of shadows, what was unmistakably luminous sat above her desk, under the glow of an art lamp. I studied the painting as though I'd never seen it, even if the name Ryder was in my indelible handwriting. In the context of my mother's and Simon's remarkable art, *Birds* suddenly looked powerful. It possessed the special energy I had first glimpsed in my studio but which had somehow gotten lost in the back room of a gallery. I was tempted to dismiss her purchase as another act of cunning by a great trickster. But maybe she had sensed the urgency that occupied my imagination, and wanted to honor it.

I walked up and slipped my arms around her shoulders. Her face was still pressed in her hands. "I love you, mother," I whispered. I held her until she stopped shaking, wondering if my words had surprised and unsettled her. Who else had ever spoken of loving her? Simon for sure, Albert once upon a time, and my father early in their marriage. I didn't know if there were that many others. She was someone more to admire and respect than to love. Slowly, she reached with her right hand to rest it on my arm. Then she stood and faced me, and with her fingertips traced the ridges of my face.

When she released me, I turned and found my way to the door. I walked numbly up the grassy hill to the station, and took the train back to the city.

Simon called around seven Tuesday morning, a little more than three weeks after my visit to Beacon. He apologized for waking me, and for not being in touch sooner. It was Susan's insistence that her illness be kept a secret, he said, even from me. In recent months, the cancer had metastasized from her larynx to her kidneys and pancreas. She had refused experimental treatment that might have prolonged her life. Honoring her wishes, only he and a hospice nurse were by her side last night. She had passed quietly and without pain. There would be a memorial service at the house at 4 p.m. on Saturday in two weeks. Would I call my father and Hannah?

I stirred awake, beginning to sort through my emotions. My shock slowly gave way to anger. Why hadn't she given me a hint? She had made peace with me on my visit—maybe that was enough for her. She didn't think further explanations were necessary. If I'd known she was dying, I would have pumped her with more questions about her life, her art, everything. I felt shut out. She was like a test I kept taking and failing. When my anger and frustration faded, I was drenched in sadness.

It took me a few minutes to realize my mother had given me a hint. When she'd sent flowers to my opening, her note had mystified me, but maybe the closing time in the gardens of the West was her own death. On our last visit, I might have guessed from her drawn face and hacking cough that there was something more than a common cold. But I was too caught up in my own drama.

I couldn't reach Hannah and David, but I gave my father the news. He reacted to the tremor in my voice by asking if I was all right, as if he knew I was closer to my mother than I had ever admitted to him. He promised to call Hannah for me. If possible, they would all fly into LaGuardia around noon on the day of the service, he said. He would let me know as soon as possible, and I could rent a car and drive everyone to Beacon.

When she and David stepped off the plane, Hannah had a secret she'd been saving for me. She had become a brunette, her hair cropped short, and her belly was rising like the moon. Holding David's hand, she looked content yet different in some way beyond her appearance. I couldn't figure exactly how. As I gazed at her belly, she asked me to guess.

"Boy," I threw out.

"Girl," David sang.

"You should never go to Vegas," Hannah teased me. "You had fifty-fifty odds and you blew it."

I laughed, and gave the two and a half of them a congratulatory hug. Neither the scar on Hannah's cheek nor her broken nose had healed particularly well. The scar was obvious enough to catch your eye, but being less beautiful didn't seem to bother her.

The drive to Beacon had a dream-like quality. All four of us were in good moods. My father talked about how much he was looking forward to being a grandfather. He was planning Maurice Sendak and Harry Potter read-a-thons, trips to national parks, walks in the mountains. He was ready to stand in whenever David and Hannah needed a weekend away. I glanced at Hannah in the mirror, thinking how bad the timing was. Not that the odds ever favored my mother being an attentive grandmother, but she would have had the option. My father began reminiscing about fun, crazy things they had done before they were married: make-out marathons at a New Jersey drive-in, swimming *au naturel* after dark at Jones Beach, tennis matches in which neither would quit before it was over. Before her illness took control, before the fire in my bedroom turned everything upside down, maybe she had been almost normal.

My mother's obituary had begun at the bottom of the front page of the *New York Times* and spilled inside. She was fifty-seven years old, but her considerable accomplishments, and her impact on other artists, had been largely in the last twenty years. When we arrived at the house, five or six hundred people were swarming over the broad swatch of lawn, luminaries of the art world—artists, gallery owners, curators, collectors. I knew these were people she didn't always like, but she'd kept her feelings hidden and managed to get along with most of them. Albert Reingold was in a discussion with someone, his arm slicing the air like a saber. I kept a distance. I purposefully chatted with a dozen strangers, looking for one person—perhaps a childhood friend from a military base or some casual acquaintance she had turned into a confidante—who knew my mother off-screen. I wanted to know some of her secrets, anything at all. But I couldn't find a single soul to help me. Giving up, I studied the cranes, scaffolding, and piles of brick and stone in the distance. Dia:Beacon was scheduled to open in April or May. I wondered if my mother had donated the paintings I'd selected.

As the service began, most speakers praised my mother for her innovative work, and her contribution to twentieth-century contemporary art. I was told a *catalogue raisonné* would be published in a few months. She'd never commissioned a print or any kind of multiple edition, not even a poster. Only original oils and acrylics, over two hundred in her lifetime, would be in the catalogue. I couldn't wait to see everything in one book, to study her progression as an artist.

I remembered what my mother had told me in Phoenix. When you died, no one talked about how you felt about anything, only about what you'd accomplished. Maybe she was right, but it occurred to me that people did remember how you made them feel. I had declined when Simon asked if I wanted to speak. How my mother made me feel was too personal, too convoluted, and would only alter everyone's perception of Susan Olmsted. Most saw a private, richly talented, sometimes-eccentric artist. I knew a woman who had spent most of her life internalizing conflict and unhappiness, rationalizing away love, and turning her defiance into remarkable paintings. If someone were to write a definitive biography, it would have to be me, and I would never do it.

I took Hannah aside when the service was over. "Does it feel like closure now?" I asked.

"It felt like closure a long time ago. When someone walks out on you and doesn't come back and you're eight years old, how else would it feel?"

I told her of my recent visit to Beacon, when I discovered my mother in the dark of her office. As she reached to touch my face, I thought it meant something. She had walked out on us almost twenty years earlier, disguising her guilt and regret as a need to save herself, but those feelings were still there, in some corner of her being, along with love, I said.

Hannah looked doubtful.

"When you were at Lennox Hill, she came to visit you one night. You were still in a coma. I was asleep in the hallway. She spent ten minutes with you, holding your hand. The on-duty nurse told me everything. The next day, you woke up."

Hannah's brow shot up in surprise. "Why are you telling me now?"

"I don't know. I should have told you and Dad when it happened."

"You always believed she had special powers."

"For sure in her art. I haven't made up my mind about the rest of her. Anyway, you can't say she totally disregarded you. In her own way, she did care."

I drifted off to say good-bye to Simon, letting Hannah sift through what I'd said. Maybe it would make a difference in what she told her daughter about her grandmother one day. I hoped her yearlong battle for survival had somehow made her moral compass more flexible.

On the drive back to the city, Hannah asked what I was working on. Not much, I admitted. I had artist's block. Even when things were going well, I said, I had a gestation period like an elephant.

"That's twenty-two months," my father said knowingly, with some concern. I'd admitted to him that I'd gone through my mother's first $50,000, and though I'd taken an oath never to invade the funds for my surgery, I was already spending them. He agreed with my decision to look for a part-time job.

Before I said good-bye to my father, he asked, "Will you be in

Santo Tomás for Christmas?" Hannah and David would be visiting, he said, as if that would clinch the deal. I told him I'd be there, too.

The next afternoon, after I wrote rent checks for the apartment and loft, utilities, and miscellaneous bills, I scanned the *Voice* classifieds. The Kaffee Krazee a few blocks away was hiring counter help. I knew a few things about coffee. When I got him on the phone, the manager told me to drop in after the morning rush hour.

Mr. Ruiz, athletic-looking with a tapered torso and shaved swimmer's head, greeted me at the counter, shaking my hand vigorously. After I filled out the application, we sat in two facing lounge chairs in the corner. His eyes traveled up and down my clothes and settled on my face before darting around the store. He was like a surveillance camera, keeping tabs on everything. A trendy, upscale crowd was still streaming in, and employees were moving with Swiss-watch precision.

"This is your first job? You haven't had previous experience?" he asked politely, returning to my application.

That wasn't quite true. There were my few months as a janitor, and I told him I'd had odd jobs in Santo Tomás, but I was only fourteen or fifteen and didn't think those counted. I assured him I was responsible and worked hard at whatever I did.

"What are you looking for in a job, Mr. Ryder?"

Was it a trick question? If I were interviewing for president of IBM or the Ford Foundation, I would tell him I was trying to make the world a better place. But Kaffee Krazee? It was survival money.

"I know a lot about coffee. I could put my expertise to work here."

"Most of our customers already know what they want. The menu is the menu. The skill set we're looking for is giving customers a smile and a howdy, serving their product as quickly as possible, getting it right, and repeating that process a thousand times a day. The word I think of is 'seamless.' "

"Seamless," I repeated, glancing at the cheerful souls behind the counter. I could do a howdy just fine, though most New Yorkers grunted "hi," "hey," "how's it going," or nothing at all. I could work an assembly line just fine, blending drinks, adding powders, and squirting on whipped cream. I could be part of a team.

"How are you with people?" he asked.

"Very good," I said.

His eyes flicked over my face again. They stayed a second too long. "Well, thank you for sharing your time. We'll be in touch, Mr. Ryder."

"When do you think that will be?"

"Very soon."

He shook my hand warmly. Mr. Ruiz was the politest man I'd met in New York. When I never heard from him again, I assumed he'd interviewed candidates more qualified than me. I couldn't blame him. It didn't harm sales when employees were as groomed and attractive as the customers they served.

Surely, there was a job for me in a warehouse somewhere, or an office building after dark, as in Chicago. I had Thanksgiving dinner with my artist friends, a potluck and beer fest. Some had odd jobs to support themselves, but I wouldn't say any of us specialized in making good impressions. If you painted, the impression you cared about was on a canvas.

I went to sleep ranting. I fantasized about lecturing anyone who crossed my path. When artists and writers created beauty, I told them, the raw material came from the intersection of memory and imagination. At that critical junction, you stumbled on some insight that few people paid attention to. Even if it wasn't unique to you, you saw it in a unique way. It hit you over the head, and you couldn't think of anything else. When Van Gogh started painting night skies in Saint-Rémy, he worked frantically with a palette of blues, blacks, and yellows. With textured, swirling lines, he made the heavens into an endlessly mysterious vortex. Maybe he tapped into his insanity to do it, but he created a better sky than God.

On my neighborhood walk one day, I found a volume of Keats in a used book store. Keats understood beauty. He was an expert on the subject. *Ode on a Grecian Urn* and *Ode to a Nightingale,* my father told me once, were two of the most perfect poems in the English language. Keats covered the gamut of emotions. The last lines of his *Ode to Melancholy* were ones I couldn't get out of my head.

*"His soul shall taste the sadness of her might/and be among her cloudy trophies hung."*

I had no idea what inspired Keats' melancholy, but at that special intersection of memory and imagination, I was my mother's trophy. I dangled from a jagged rock on an isolated precipice, somewhere in the frigid heavens. Paint what you feel and know, every teacher said. Whenever I went to my loft, I didn't get beyond a sketch of what resembled ominous thunderclouds colliding into one another.

In the next month, my routine began to change. I gave up looking for work. I wouldn't stir from bed until late morning. I walked to my favorite deli and ate my one meal of the day. I thought my father would be proud of my frugality. When I returned to the apartment, I read, listened to music, or fell asleep on the sofa.

One morning, the phone woke me. I let it ring a dozen times. Whoever it was hung up and tried again.

"Hello," I murmured.

"Will?"

"Hmmm."

"What's going on?" It took a moment to recognize my father's voice. He sounded worried and slightly annoyed. "Why aren't you here? Are you standing us up for Christmas again?"

"No, of course not." I rubbed the sleep out of my eyes.

"Well, tomorrow's Christmas Eve. You better get on a plane, don't you think? Hannah and David are wondering what happened to you."

I had lost track of time. Night had tumbled into day, and then it was night again. I couldn't believe it was almost Christmas. I asked how Hannah was feeling—she was due in March—and if she and David had a name for the baby. Not yet, my father said, so I was welcome to throw some suggestions in the hat. Now, when was I coming home?

"I haven't been feeling well, bad cold," I lied. "Sorry I wasn't in touch."

"Are you saying you're not coming?"

"When I think about it, it wouldn't be the smartest thing, would it? I'd get everyone sick."

"Do you need money for a plane ticket?" he asked, suspicious of my excuse.

"It's not that. I just can't make it."

"Did you get a job?"

"Kaffee Krazee hired me."

"OK, good to hear," he said, relieved. "Take some pressure off yourself. But how sick are you? Have you seen a doctor?"

"It's just the flu. I'm on antibiotics. I'll come next month, Dad."

"Will—" His tone was impatient again.

"You guys have a great Christmas, Dad."

I hung up and stared at my window like it was a trompe l'oeil painting. I had no sense of light or fresh air in the apartment. I was suffocating. My solitude had wrapped around me like a coil of rope. Sometimes I wondered if I had the same depression that afflicted my mother, or if solitude wasn't one of her tests for me, even if she was gone. I lived on the top of a mountain, in the thin, cold, breathless air of loneliness, and I knew that only I could find my way down.

In late February, I woke one morning with the real flu. Getting on my feet and dressed was an effort. After venturing out for hot tea and a bottle of NyQuil, I returned to an apartment that was colder than when I'd left. The same thing happened every day. A jacket and wool cap didn't help. The two radiators would shake and whistle for an hour, making me feel better, then refuse to turn on again until the thermostat dropped to below sixty. The landlord promised to send over a plumber. I was aware of losing weight, and being cold most of the time didn't help my energy level. Whenever my father called, asking why I wasn't coming home, the lies rolled off my tongue. When I wasn't making vanilla lattes at Kaffee Krazee, I was busy working on my art. I'd found a new gallery to represent me. He shouldn't worry. I'd get back soon.

Two days later, checking for mail in the vestibule, I found a post office notice in my box. When I retrieved the parcel, it had a Brooklyn return address I didn't recognize. The package measured about 18-by-24 inches.

I opened the wrapping carefully and spotted the edge of a picture frame. If some kind stranger had gifted me a dusty Monet found in his attic, I fantasized, I could sell it for $20 million. Then I stared. It was no Monet. The frame was new, but I would never forget the color charcoal drawing. Two lovers were entwined in a dream-like embrace. *The Shining Light of Uncertain Infinity* was penciled across the top. A note was taped to the back.

> *Hi Will! Long time no talk/see! I got your address from Gallery Zoom. I didn't hear about your show until a year after it closed, when I wandered in with a friend. It's a fact! I saw your name in a list of old Zoom shows, and when I asked, they still had a catalogue. GREAT stuff, Ryder. I hope everything sold. I've been living in Cobble Hill for almost two years now. I write a fashion column for Marie Claire—If Looks Could Kill. I had to kill about twenty people to get the job. There's enough envy and jealousy in New York to sink the good ship Lollipop. Do you like it here? Be honest. I've had your drawing hung wherever I've lived for the last six years. Long story(ies)! I can see you shaking your head. Not sure why I'm sending it to you now . . . to see if you still like it as much as I do? Wanna grab a cup of coffee? Do you know your way around Brooklyn?*
>
> *TR*

Her writing was like a glass of champagne. The bubbles flowed from every sentence, and they went right to my head. She had scribbled her phone number at the bottom. I was shaking my head. I had thought I'd never see T Rex again. I was also amazed that her personality seemed largely unchanged. But everyone changed. She was TR now. I looked at the ghost in the mirror, reduced to rubble.

My first intoxicated impulse was to grab the phone and call her immediately. I longed to know everything that had happened since Tennessee. My second reaction was to stay miles away from the girl who'd broken my heart twice. It was better to hold on to memories of deep happiness than suddenly be told I was just a friend. On the other hand, it was her idea to have coffee. I would play it safe. I would tell her my Zoom show had been a raging success, and I was busy working on new paintings for my next show. I was fulfilling my promise as an artist that she'd always believed in.

I dialed her number. The champagne voice answered after only a single ring.

"Hello."

"Hi, it's me," I said. "Your blast from the past."

"My god, Will?"

"Yep."

"Amazing to hear from you! You're alive and well!"

Her voice hadn't changed. I was thrilled to hear all the exclamation points. "Never been better," I said. I was bundled in my robe, leaning against the bedroom wall, trying not to hack into the phone.

"You live in the West Village. What's that like?" she asked.

"Just a studio for the time being. I'm looking for a two bedroom. Doorman, lobby, elevator … the works."

"So you're really doing well! I'm so happy for you.

"Oh," she paused, and her tone changed. "I read that your mother passed away. I'm so sorry. Was it sudden?"

"Actually, she was sick for a while."

"Are you OK? You two had a difficult relationship. I remember everything you told me."

"How's your wild and whacky family?" I changed the subject. I wondered if she still called them the Asses. Real or imagined, my image of Lard chasing me with a rifle was still in my mind.

"Oh, that's a long story. I have longer stories than a sailor at sea. Shall we meet and compare notes? For old times' sake?"

"Old times' sake," I echoed. I put my hand over the phone, pretending to rummage through a Day-Timer. "My calendar looks good for the weekend. How about Saturday morning?"

TR suggested we meet at her favorite coffee house, on Montague Street in Brooklyn Heights. For the next few days, I lived in a sea of anxiety, certain I would somehow disappoint her. Saturday, I put on clean clothes and hopped on the subway, my heart rising ever higher in my throat. Brooklyn Heights was only a few stops away. I was wearing two sweaters, a scarf, wool hat, and a heavy jacket, and still couldn't get warm. In all my time in the city, I'd never been to Brooklyn. I'd heard that the Heights was a trendy enclave of young professionals living in turn-of-the-century brownstones. I walked along the sidewalk, feeling like a misfit. Along with handsome couples, there were hordes of little children—in strollers, playing in the park, eating Häagen-Dazs ice cream. At the coffee house, I ordered an espresso and waited for TR. So I wouldn't get her sick, I was souped up on antibiotics. My eyes ran to the door every time it opened, searching for a woman in neon tights, blue sneakers, and a camo hunting jacket.

"Will?"

I turned, trying not to stare as I popped to my feet. TR had entered through a side door, forty minutes late. Her sinewy body was unchanged, but her face was fuller, alert, radiant. Her blonde hair was no longer in a ratty beehive but squared off below her chin. She wore jeans and fashionable high black boots, with a simple navy blue turtleneck under a double-breasted coat. If I didn't know better, I would have sworn I'd run into a New York native. The adaptation of the species had eluded me but not her.

"Tabitha Penelope Rex, look at you. You're as beautiful as ever," I said, sounding like an admiring uncle or a mushy greeting card. I couldn't find the right tone. But she was beautiful, that was indisputable. The cobalt blue eyes that had swept me off my feet years ago were doing it again.

"A fashion writer. Very nice. That is so cool. Congratulations," I babbled as she ordered a green tea with special antioxidants. She said she didn't drink coffee anymore, or alcohol except for an occasional glass of wine. I assumed she'd given up the Gauloises, too. I had bought the latest issue of *Marie Claire,* and told her I liked her column. Her fictional persona sampled a different clothing store in every issue, like a plate of hors d'oeuvres. She wrote about what she looked beautiful in and what was hopeless as she searched for the Holy Grail of an outfit that would alter her consciousness. It was what every young female professional in New York wanted, she said. People teased her that she was Carrie Bradshaw. When I asked who that was, she put her hand over her mouth.

"You're serious? You don't watch *Sex and the City*?"

I almost said, "What's that?" Instead, I complained amiably that my life was hectic enough without television.

She sighed, turning an admiring gaze on me. "You stuck it out in art school," she said, as if that were equivalent to winning a Nobel Prize. "You did what you wanted to do. You have to feel great. I'm just a dime-a-dozen writer."

"What are you talking about? You have a column in a national magazine."

She gave me a self-effacing shrug. "Tell me more about you," she said.

"No, you first."

"Are you sure? It might take all day. I can't help myself. Details are the spice, right?"

"The spicier, the better." I remembered when we'd stayed up to all hours in Chicago. The longer I could look into her eyes and not talk about myself, the happier I was.

Her stories poured out helter-skelter, like someone who had lived multiple lives and saw no reason to keep them straight. After we parted ways in Tennessee, she was in and out of five schools, finally graduating from the University of Alaska in Fairbanks. She'd gotten there by hitching from San Francisco, a two-month adventure. Her parents had divorced, and the other Asses dispersed to all corners of the world. TR had gone through a dozen boyfriends, any number of unskilled jobs, and an arrest for drug possession. After ingesting too many drugs one night, an angel appeared in her dream warning she'd be dead in a week. The scare turned her life around. She was living clean now, she said. Part of her therapy became writing funny short stories and freelancing them to magazines, including *Marie Claire.*

It was exhilarating and exhausting listening to her. No matter the hardship or challenge, I marveled, TR managed to survive. She was good at starting over; it was her specialty. I wondered if she realized how much energy she'd exerted in the last six years, enough for several lifetimes.

When she was offered a full-time job at *Marie Claire,* she was thrilled at the thought of moving to New York. Lately, however, her feelings were mixed. She couldn't put her finger on it, but something was missing for her here. She liked exploring the city, but she wasn't into wild parties, and the dating scene was crazy scary, she said. Most men were either egomaniacs, lacked imagination, or had the couth of a cow. She lived with two roomies who were constantly bringing guys back to the apartment. They came to breakfast in their underwear. How gross was that!

I smiled at everything she said. TR was still the effervescent contrarian, a spirit lighter than air. As we talked through my four coffee refills, I tried to keep my fibbing to a minimum.

"Will, this has been really great," she said suddenly. "Sorry that I have to run."

"What's so urgent?" I had wanted to take her to lunch.

"I have to meet my boyfriend. We're seeing *The Bourne Identity*. His choice." She made a face.

"A boyfriend," I remarked. I wondered how couth he was. "That's why you're not dating?"

"I've never liked being alone."

"I'm not seeing anyone," I said. "Too busy painting."

"I can't wait to see your work." She stood and slipped into her coat.

"There're four of us who share a loft. You have to come by."

I gave her the address. As we walked outside, I asked the question that had been weighing on me most.

"Why did you send the drawing back?"

She turned, cocking her head, as if disappointed that I was so clueless.

"It wasn't to see if I still liked it," I guessed. "What you wanted to know was how I felt about you."

"Brilliant. So how do you feel?"

"It was great seeing you. I've missed you."

"Me too."

My heart soared. I should have stopped right there, waved goodbye, and called her in a few days. But I was impulsive, as always, and the questions that had been swirling in my head since we talked on the phone overwhelmed me.

"I just want to be clear about some things," I said.

"Such as?"

"I want to know if you hold the past against me. I really was going to jump out that window. You shouldn't have left the room." The whole drunk, wobbly night came back to me in a rush. I wanted a do-over.

"And I still don't know what happened in Tennessee. I thought we were going to spend our lives together. What did I do wrong? Just because I didn't have a plan didn't mean we couldn't have gone away together."

She smiled tightly, absorbing everything. I felt stupid for bringing up our entire history in thirty seconds, and I couldn't think of anything witty to save me. I half expected her to turn away and never call me again.

"I was young, seventeen going on twelve," she said. "Here I am, all grown up, sort of." She paused. "I loved seeing you, Will." TR offered her drop-dead smile. I wanted to steal it and put it under my pillow.

"Hey, would you like to come over for dinner?" I blurted. "Tuesday at seven?"

"You want to cook for me? Really?"

"Yeah. I would."

"What a treat. Can I bring anything?"

I shook my head. She spun on her heels and floated down the sidewalk, finally vanishing from sight. I was thrilled until I began to consider the obstacles. I had a temperature of over a hundred. My apartment was an embarrassment. For a year, I had cooked nothing grander than a pot of spaghetti and a cheese omelet. But I was determined to pull off a romantic evening. To feel hope for the first time since my mother's death left me light-headed. No more saying inappropriate things, I admonished myself, no glitches Tuesday night.

The next morning, I settled on an ambitious menu: salad with my father's special Italian dressing, rack of lamb rubbed with herbs, red new potatoes, and asparagus cooked in lemon and olive oil, with shaved parmesan on top. On Sunday, I bought ingredients and cooked for three hours—a dress rehearsal—and brought the entire meal to my friends at the loft. My confidence steadied with their unanimous approval. On Monday, I found a classy Australian Shiraz for $30, and bought dinner ingredients for a second time. I spent the rest of the day cleaning the apartment. I covered my kitchen table with a white linen cloth and candles borrowed from Storm. *The Shining Light of Uncertain Infinity* was hung over my bed, in the simple, far-flung hope that one day life might imitate art.

I began cooking Tuesday afternoon. I broke my three-hour window into fifteen-minute increments, starting with marinating the asparagus. I was even more organized than when I'd helped my father feed the homeless. When the apartment buzzer finally rang, I dashed to the oven. The lamb should have been done. Instead, I saw that one of the two broiling coils had burned out. "Shit," I whispered. In controlled desperation, I turned the oven to six hundred.

I opened the apartment door with a flourish. TR was in jeans and a cashmere sweater, with a red beret cocked forward on her head. "Wow, you look terrific," I said, a similar intro to what I'd used at the coffee house, but I meant it. I tried to hide my anxiety. In addition to my oven problem, my newly repaired thermostat insisted on maintaining the apartment at eighty-five degrees. I took TR's coat, then propped the window open several inches. Cool air began to float in. Her eyes made a sweep of everything inside my four walls, including the drawing over the bed. It radiated enough beauty, I hoped, to eclipse any impression of poverty.

"Cheers," I said when I'd uncorked the Shiraz. I had to use water glasses because I didn't own stemware. But TR didn't seem to mind. She was still the anti-snob.

We dropped on my lumpy couch, wondering what we should toast. We'd already gone over our missing years at the coffee house. I was too nervous to suggest anything about the future.

"Are you all right, Will?" She put down her glass, tilting her face until I felt the warmth of her breath. I suddenly wanted to kiss her.

"Just fine."

"You're not very relaxed."

"Really? No, I'm fine."

"Can I help with anything?"

"Absolutely not," I said confidently.

I pushed my lips toward her just before the oven began to make popping sounds. Jumping up, I rushed over and peered through the glass . The lamb was in flames. TR grabbed a pair of oven mitts as I opened the door and helped me juggle the scorched meat to the counter. When I sliced off a rib, it had the pallor of the dead. Nothing was going right, I realized. The potatoes were too hard. The asparagus I was making in a frying pan looked like little blackened telephone poles.

"This wasn't supposed to happen," I said, staring at the food.

"Not your fault. I don't think your kitchen likes you tonight."

"It is my fault."

"Don't be so bummed."

We put everything on plates and sat at the table, TR still bubbly, but it was harder for a perfectionist to recover. I had the not-unfamiliar feeling of losing control, and whatever conspiracy had been hatched against me by my oven had unending consequences. The salad was soggy. The bread was blackened on the bottom. And I apologized for the Shiraz, too. It tasted like a $10 bottle.

"Don't worry about it," TR rallied. "It's only a glass of wine. It's not the blood of Christ."

I laughed faintly, and helped myself to another glass. The buzz I finally got was like an injection of sodium pentothal.

"I need to tell you something," I said, nibbling at the asparagus. "I'm a phony."

"What are you talking about?"

"At the coffee house, I told you a pack of lies."

"Why would you lie?"

"I sold one of ten paintings at the Zoom show, and my mother was the buyer. Albert Reingold buried me alive in his column. I'm running out of money, and I expect to be broke by summer. Kaffee Krazee wouldn't hire me because of my face. And I haven't painted anything in a long time." I pushed back in my chair. "You can leave anytime you want. I wouldn't blame you."

"You're just feeling sorry for yourself."

"Take a good look at me, and tell me why I shouldn't."

TR was confused. "Why do you make this about your looks? I knew when we were at SDA you were the best painter in the school. If I had the chance, I'm not sure I wouldn't trade places with you, face and all."

"Then you're as crazy as ever."

"Oh, that's nice to hear."

I hadn't meant to insult her, but I was getting too emotional to take it back. "How can anyone be sure of his talent?" I argued. "Even if Albert Reingold had decided my paintings were works of God, it doesn't predict the future. I could shrivel up and disappear tomorrow. One in a million were my mother's odds. You don't get two lucky horses in the same bloodline."

"Why is it," TR said, losing patience, "that you're such a chicken shit dumb ass?"

"Excuse me?"

"Or is it chicken ass dumb shit? And will you please stop talking about your mother? I'm sick of hearing it. What does she have to do with anything?" It was the old T Rex. Maybe I'd forced her out of hibernation with my constant sniveling.

"Everybody lies sometimes, to make themselves feel better," she said. "Big deal. What I don't understand is how you never look below the surface. You have no faith in yourself. You start to, get halfway to believing in your talent, and then you pull back with a bunch of excuses."

"I get it. I'm letting you down again," I said. "Actually, the last thing you just mentioned—you could be talking about yourself, too."

Her eyes narrowed, like she was ready to throw something. "There's one big difference," she said. "I may not have your talent, but I accept who I am. You always want to be something more, better, bigger. Why can't you just be yourself? Nothing is real for you but your stupid ego."

"What about the drawing over the bed? I happen to love you; that's real."

"Then prove it."

"You want me to jump out another window?"

"Dumb ass. Just get your butt to your studio and start painting."

"What's that going to prove?"

"I guess that you still love yourself."

I felt nauseous, and unable to regain my composure. How could you love yourself, I wanted to ask, when most people couldn't look at you for more than a few seconds? TR pushed away her plate, sensing the futility of the evening.

I watched as she retrieved her coat. She moved briskly out the door without a good-bye, not even a glance back, which is when I slipped into hysteria. I opened my window another foot, flung the rack of lamb into the night, and spent my frustration in piercing screams. I ripped *The Shining Light of Uncertain Infinity* off the wall and hurled it out the window, too.

"Well, that was impressive," TR might have said, had she stuck around to witness my self-massacre. Even when I dropped on my bed, acknowledging that I was a craven, wallowing piece of crap, I couldn't get her voice out of my head. She was like a muse, trying to rouse me from my self-pity, my stubborn insistence on my own inadequacy. And before I could ask her anything more, she was gone.

An eviction notice arrived the first of May. I was only a month behind, but Storm had warned me that New York landlords were as merciless as a coven of witches. He loaned me $2,000, and on his advice, I paid two months' rent in advance. Sometimes I thought about my mother's estate and all her money, but I knew she had given me whatever she wanted to in her lifetime. After taking care of the rent, I had enough for incidentals and groceries. I couldn't afford my loft space anymore, but Storm said that whenever I felt the urge to paint, I could share his studio.

"I'll take you up on that," I promised. But I had no desire to paint anything, spend an afternoon at a museum, or attend another lecture at Cooper Union. Out of embarrassment or hopelessness, I decided not to see TR again. I felt safest when I stayed in my apartment and pored over the *Times* crossword puzzle, content to be in touch with no one.

Hannah and my father, however, called regularly. I was skilled at deflecting their questions, but one Sunday in late June, my father had had enough.

"Just what are you living on?" he asked after I'd told him everything was going swimmingly.

"My job pays enough."

"You're still at the Kaffee Krazee you told me about?"

"Yeah. Why?"

"That's what I thought. I called there yesterday. I spoke to the manager, Mr. Ruiz."

"Why did you do that?" My voice had shrunk.

"He told me you applied for a job but never worked there. What's going on, Will?"

"I wanted to work, but he wouldn't hire me!"

"So you gave up looking and started lying to me."

He had every right to be angry, but instead, he let the silence sink in.

"I'm sorry I wasn't honest," I finally said. "But I'm OK. Just a couple of setbacks."

"What kind of setbacks?"

My confession tripped off my tongue, including my aborted dinner with TR and living on borrowed funds. I no longer had a studio, but I didn't need it, I said. I had lost my appetite for art because I had no idea what to paint. I never left my apartment, I told him, unless it was to buy food or a newspaper.

"You're living like a hermit. How healthy is that?" he asked with dismay.

"I'll be OK."

"You're not in a good space, Will. Maybe you should come home for a while."

"I can manage on my own."

"I'm not leaving you a choice in this matter," he said firmly.

My father rarely gave ultimatums. It was his ironclad philosophy not to impose his will on others, especially his children. In his worldview, tolerance and respect trumped meddlesome advice-givers. But I had triggered some deep alarm. After what happened to Hannah, I had exceeded his threshold of tolerance.

I quietly reminded him of my mother's philosophy—there was nothing wrong with a little hardship.

"Your mother is gone, Will. Maybe it's time to rethink her philosophy. I know she thought I coddled you, but I can tell you that's a lot better than letting someone wither in despair."

"I'm not that bad off. . . ."

"Didn't you promise me not to be reckless?" he interrupted. "Do you remember our talks about keeping your guard up?"

"I do my best," I said.

"I know. It hasn't worked out. That's all right. It's time to come home and be with your family now. Hannah and David are nearby. You're going to be an uncle soon. I can set up a meeting with Dr. Glaspell. . . ."

"Dr. Glaspell?" I shot back.

"Your mother died without telling you she was even sick. She abandoned you all over again. Can't you see that?"

I suppose I did see it, but my emotions had been on a roller coaster since her death, and my fight with TR had roiled me even more.

"You didn't understand her," I defended my mother.

"Here's what I understand. Her agenda was to live apart from the world and do her art, even if she was miserable and isolated most of the time. Which is exactly what she wanted for you. She wanted to create you in her own image."

"That's a lie!"

"Is it?"

I quietly hung up. I wondered how dire my situation really was. My father acted like the world was coming to an end. I left the apartment and began my usual desultory walk. If my mother had an agenda for me, it wasn't what my father believed. I could be lonely but never as willfully isolated as she was. That took a special talent. My mother was controlling, happily intolerant, and an enemy of intimacy. I was reckless and passionate, desperate for a girlfriend, and always wished I had more friends.

I dropped on a park bench and pulled an apple from my pocket. I hadn't eaten all day. I considered that apples had been involved with important things throughout history. Sir Isaac Newton evolved his theory of gravity. William Tell shot one off his son's head with an arrow. The apple was the forbidden fruit in the Garden of Eden. I ate mine slowly, tasting each bite as I waited for my future to illuminate itself.

Back in the apartment, I phoned my father and told him I wasn't coming home. I had decided in the park to stick it out in New York. I said I didn't want his help. He reacted like I was the Confederacy seceding from the Union, or Brutus stabbing Caesar. My decision was an immeasurable betrayal of him and my own good judgment, he said. I heard the pain and frustration in his voice, but there was nothing either of us could do about it.

When Hannah called one evening, I was startled to hear her voice. I don't know why, except that it jarred my perception I was now totally alone in the universe.

"You've been talking to Dad," I guessed after we'd chatted for a minute. "You want me to come home, too."

"I have a surprise for you. I'm not worried about you, Will, not like in the old days. It's not my job to worry about anyone."

"Are you OK?" I asked suspiciously.

"Everything's fine. The baby will be here soon. David and I are so excited." She reached to turn off a radio or television.

"Something's different," I observed.

"Can I ask you a question? This will sound silly, but it's why I'm calling. What did you think of me when we were growing up?"

"I thought you were the model of efficiency. There wasn't a mountain you couldn't climb. Why are you asking?"

"Pretty sad, huh?"

"What's wrong with being efficient and talented?"

"I hope my daughter isn't anything remotely like me. I've been thinking about this."

"I don't get it."

"I don't know if I was ever that happy. I doubt any achiever is. You're too busy for reflection. And you can never succeed enough. You had a happier childhood than I did, Will."

"You're crazy," I said, laughing. Her tragedy had altered my sister's perception of a lot of things, and now it was our childhoods. I had had some moments of real happiness, innocent moments, moments of triumph, moments of love, but waking every morning with my special face, being different in that way, was not something that had ever faded.

"What is it you want for your daughter?"

"Whatever she wants, of course. I just hope she doesn't muck it up with too much ambition. Do you know what made our family so screwed up? Dad and his Joyce articles, you and your painting, me and Wall Street—I'm not even going to mention our mother—everyone was certifiably obsessed. I hope you have a successful career, Will, because that's what you want, but more than that, I hope you're happy."

Something had definitely changed in Hannah, and the change was still going on. I had sensed it when she got off the plane at LaGuardia. I didn't think anyone would ever say being raped and almost dying was a blessing, but the consequences of a tragedy could be. I went to bed parsing our conversation, and filled with a new envy. Hannah was rebuilding her life while mine was deteriorating at warp speed. I was becoming a stubborn recluse in my apartment, or wandering the city like a vagabond. I was a nuisance to my friends. Everyone was busy with one project or another. I was afraid to stay too long at the loft for fear I wouldn't be wanted back.

Ideas came to me at strange times and in stranger places. A month after I'd defied my father, I was on a morning walk in the East Village, light-headed, living largely on caffeine and sugar. I stopped at a traffic light. The sight of the young man in a coffee shop window startled me. At first, I thought he was the panhandler from the subway I'd seen a year ago, the one I steadfastly avoided. He resembled a scarecrow. His shirt hung out, his hands dangled indifferently. I saw a perplexed expression on his face. His eyes were dead to me. The sun found the window, and for a few seconds, the image vanished in the glare. When the young man returned, I held him with my eyes, hoping he would stay long enough for me to see more than his mutilated face. When I peeled back the flap of his heart, I beheld the majesty of his turmoil. It was mine. No matter what that man in the window had told his father or sister, he was not surviving. They could not save him even if they wanted to. Everything about him was shrinking and fading.

I turned and moved on, with my usual aimlessness, when the idea overtook me. I didn't know how I had missed the obvious. Most of my life, I hadn't liked who I was, certainly not what I looked like, fleeing from it as my mother had once run from her illness. She had warned me about that inglorious moment in life when you've hit absolute bottom, and you aren't sure you have the strength to recover. But if you can recover, if you find the will, she said, it is perhaps the best moment in your life. It changes you forever. I suddenly knew what I wanted to paint. I was sure of it, without a second thought.

When a volcano erupted and you were right in front of it, there was no point in running. I was ready to confront the rage that burned inside me. It would be the second time a fire consumed me. This time, I was convinced it would save my life.

In my apartment, I grabbed my camera and rushed over to the loft. Storm was there. I had something I very badly wanted to paint, I said, but I needed his help. He had to take photos of me nearly naked. Storm laughed but said OK. He believed most artists were essentially crazy, including him, and it was in the moment when you had really lost it that you needed to be taken the most seriously. I stripped to my underwear and asked for photos of my face and torso from every angle, in full light and in shadows, close up and from ten and twenty feet away. I posted thirty high-resolution images on a large bulletin board, like mug shots in a police station, and began sketching.

When the day ended, I asked Storm if he cared if I stayed and painted all night. I was on a roll. "Knock yourself out, Will." He was curious to see what the urgency was all about.

Setting up my easel, I began to make a foundation of white gesso on a large linen canvas, and over it painted broad, seamless swatches of red. The photos Storm took were invaluable, but I didn't rely on them totally for shape and color. Those came from inside me. I didn't have to dig very far. My sense of who I was dictated short, violent stabs of the brush. My flesh tones became a sea of ochre, burnt umber, tinted brown, and black. With a palette knife, I shaped and bled the colors into one another. The image that came to life was disjointed and grotesque. The face was half in profile, half frontal, and twisted to its right side, like someone alerted to a danger that was closing in. The nose was disproportionately large, and the eyes sunken. The forehead was pushed back, shooting over the dark hairline. The chin stuck to the face like an appendage. I could feel the painting's primitive agitation and upheaval. It wasn't easy to distinguish between line and color. The self-portrait had come off my brush in a series of lightning storms. I looked like a savage under a boiling red sky.

When your emotions are an undammed river, it's hard to stop them or do anything else. In a ten-hour binge, I completed a painting I didn't want to make a single change to. In the morning, Storm couldn't stop studying it.

He told me I had given expression to a personal pain that any sane person would have fled from, never looking back. I had stared into the sun.

"Keep going," he said.

I told Storm I was completely broke. He wrote me a check for $5,000.

The following week, I painted my full torso, tubular and twisted like melted plastic. My hands and legs were in a state of disintegration. The face was hidden behind shadows, barely visible against a midnight blue that seemed to freeze the whole tableau. There was no motion this time. My body had already been pulled apart. I dug deeper for the next painting, creating a ten-year-old boy sitting alone on a corner of a lawn, with a fence around him. I concentrated less on his face than an atmosphere of isolation. My lines were more delicate than in the first two paintings. I thought of my brush as a scalpel. Pain wasn't always an explosion. It could be a series of moments gathered over time, layered on top of each other like nerve endings, until the pain was so intense that the weight was unbearable. It was as if you were a house, and the roof suddenly caved in.

I went on to paint a slightly older boy, running in a playground. In preliminary sketches, I conveyed his identity in silhouettes—

three of them, in motion—yet when I began to add color, the torsos became three dimensional. They were realistically drawn except for their disproportionately large heads. In one figure, the boy's hands were raised above his head, covering it, and in another, he was looking behind him, chased by something. In the third, he was slumped over at the waist, exhausted and out of breath.

Every night, I would fall into bed, too tired to pick up a book or newspaper. Occasionally, I sent my father an email that I was OK—honestly, I said, but I didn't elaborate. I didn't want to lose my energy to distraction. In the morning, rested, I began painting again with no clear idea where I wanted to go. An image emerged from a ground of inert colors. In the right combination, the colors shaped themselves into wild, startling emotions. The magic of reconstruction, I thought, was the magic of the impossible. I remembered my sessions with Dr. Glaspell, how his gold pen would stop in the middle of a page, waiting for me to confess the depth of my misery. I was never able to do it. Years later, in a drafty loft in New York, I had found my own exorcism and liberation. When painting, you were essentially talking to yourself, and suddenly I had a lot to say.

Every portrait was different, yet they all had mystery and premonition. I worked through the summer and fall on ten portraits, returning to two of them where I felt something was still incomplete. One was a diptych: two faces staring at each other, stretched and twisted, mirror images—to a point. In one face, I wanted to show unfocused anger, and in the other, longing. Another picture was a twelve-year-old boy; he was picking at his face with two bony fingers, as if at a scab. I reworked the fingers with blues and reds until they matched his compulsive eyes.

I had seen the faces Francis Bacon had painted. They expressed horror at World War II and its aftermath of guilt and duplicity. Mine were about personal anxiety, confusion, and self-loathing. My colors were more extreme, my shapes more jagged. When I had stared into the bathroom mirror in first grade, the innocent boy I saw had seemed beyond the reach of harm. But no soul lives undisturbed in paradise, not for long. It ends up black and blue, scarred, mutilated, mangled, and pulverized. If you were lucky, you found a key to the door that had been in front of you the whole time, and you walked through it into your new life. You were rebuilt by your imagination, by your art, and there was no power on Earth that could stop you.

One afternoon, I was alone in the loft, eating a sandwich. I didn't hear footsteps. I only felt a tap on my shoulder.

"You don't have to stare; I'm not a ghost," TR said when I spun around. She wore a pumpkin-colored fall sweater and a black pleated skirt, right out of the pages of *Marie Claire.* Her handbag was half her size. I understood and liked fashion, but I couldn't afford it. When you shopped at discount stores and thrift shops, you lived forever in the '80s. TR gave me her special smile, the one that zapped me on impact.

"Not a ghost? Are you sure?" I said.

"You invited me to see your work."

"That was months ago."

"Really?" she said, as if keeping times straight would never be a priority. I wondered how she managed deadlines at *Marie Claire.* I gave her an edited version of my recent months' highlights: painting ten to twelve hours a day, hanging out with friends on weekends, reading when I had the energy. My sister had given birth to a nine-pound girl with thick, chocolate-colored hair named Christine, whom I had yet to visit, locked in as I was by my obsession to finish what I'd started. Obsession was better than apathy, TR said. When she turned to my new work, lined up against the wall, her eyes narrowed with interest. She picked up the portrait I'd completed in my first whirlwind night.

"This is really good."

"You mean that?"

"No, I'm bullshitting you. Do you have a gallery?"

"I'm working on that with Storm."

"You painted ten. Just like at Zoom." She let her eyes travel over the paintings again.

"Ten's my lucky number."

"Maybe you should change it," she declared, like some supreme ruler of the universe. "Try eleven. What are you going to call your show?"

I told her I hadn't got that far.

She rummaged through her handbag for a scrap of paper. "Don't think I'm being meddlesome," she said. I wasn't sure whether she was addressing herself or me. She scribbled something on the paper and tucked it in my shirt pocket.

I didn't look. I was still startled TR had shown up, out of the mists. Was our fight forgotten?

"Want to grab some coffee?" I said, hopeful.

"Another time. I love your work, Will. I really do."

She kissed me on the cheek, and then the wraith was gone, though not entirely. Like her special smile, her voice had snaked into my consciousness. She could hypnotize me without trying. That was the consequence of being in love with every part of her being. Whenever I replayed her words, they made me into a different person, demanding I think in fresh ways.

I began work on an eleventh painting. Unlike the first ten, I made this canvas much larger, sixty-six by forty-eight inches. It took only a week to complete: a vision of a grown man in his 20s, sitting on a porch, hands splayed on his knees, his face twisting skyward. Something about him seemed hopeful, though just what was open to interpretation. His lumpy, disproportionate features were a swirl of reds and blacks, and his mouth was open, his teeth a brilliant white. There was something calm and reassured about him, like someone pulled from a blue-black ocean and dried under a magenta sun. When I showed it to Storm, he lingered for a long time.

Finally, his fist punched my shoulder. "That's your *pièce de résistance,* dude."

I walked home, passing my old subway stop. I glanced toward the steps. Amid the commuter rush, I saw the bent figure in his same ratty Army jacket and T-shirt, as if he never changed clothes. His hand self-consciously extended from his waist, holding the usual clutch of coins. The disfigured face had taken sanctuary in the late afternoon shadows, but it was still hard to miss. When his eyes lifted to me, I didn't turn away. I wanted to peer as deeply into his soul as I could, to compare notes with a life I knew nothing about but which had to be similar to mine. How had his face happened? Where did he come from? What kept him going? I pulled out the only bill in my wallet—a twenty, my food budget for the next three days—and handed it to him.

"Thank you," he whispered. He let his eyes drop like a curtain, our encounter over. I might have asked his name, or how long he thought he could survive like this, but I knew to move on.

I knew about the difficulty of living under the unrelenting sun of judgment. In some societies, you were considered cursed for being born with a cleft palate, shunned from birth. Lepers were dirty, untrustworthy, and a health threat to society. In the Byzantine Empire, the emperor was regarded as God's regent on Earth, and his beauty reflected the perfection of Heaven. If a sword cut his face, he was in danger of losing power. Deposed emperors were blinded and had their noses cut off by their successors; once disfigured, you could never reclaim the throne.

The mighty river of vanity churned with fear and longing, dividing the fortunate from the fallen.

When Storm appeared at the loft a few days later, he had already approached several Manhattan galleries with photos of my eleven portraits. Zanger-Forsythe, on Eighty-Fourth near Lex, was the most interested, though one of the owners had reservations about my inexperience. My record at Zoom didn't improve my chances. Storm convinced Teddy Zanger, the other principal, that my work wasn't some cliche of existential agony but a real person turned inside out. Teddy promised to visit the loft to meet me and judge for himself.

"You really think they're that strong?" I asked Storm, studying them for the hundredth time as we waited for Teddy one afternoon. I was never totally convinced about the merit of anything I did until I heard from others.

"Lose the doubt," he said. "The last one, the big one, if it doesn't sell right away, I'll buy it from you."

I wouldn't have minded trading it for the $8,000 I owed him, but Storm thought a good gallery could do much better for me. He thought it was a $20,000 painting.

Teddy Zanger was a lanky, pale German, as quiet as a banker, and relatively new on the Manhattan art scene. He told me he was searching for artists who weren't retreads. He spent half an hour examining my portraits, insisting on being alone in the studio. I went out for coffee, certain he was going to find fault, but when I ventured back, he offered me my own show. I was stunned, even more so when he insisted on aggressive pricing. He would ask between $12,000 and $18,000 per painting. I kept telling him "thank you." I'd just turned twenty-five, mature enough, I hoped, to weather the Albert Reingolds of the world. I was asked what I wanted to call my show. I'd finally read what TR scribbled on her scrap of paper.

"Prometheus Unbound," I said.

Teddy didn't care about my age, my Zoom disappointment, or my famous and overshadowing mother—he insisted that the portraits stood on their own. When he studied *Birds Falling From the Sky,* he liked their power, too, but it was the integrity and energy of the portraits that riveted him.

We talked about a January opening. I signed a standard contract, which gave half of my sales to the gallery, after a 20 percent discount to special clients. A week later, Teddy told me the artist slated for his early fall show had unexpectedly canceled. If the first three weeks of November worked, he could move me up. The timing was perfect. I'd promised everyone I'd be in Santo Tomás for Thanksgiving, a month from now. My father and I had patched things up, and I wasn't going to disappoint him again.

Storm helped me with a mailing list, generously throwing in names of his own clients. He urged me to be romantic on my invitation to TR. I was pedestrian instead, afraid of sounding too enthusiastic. "Hope you can make my opening," I scribbled across the top. "Show runs for three weeks. I'm flying home for Thanksgiving. Love to see you before then." Based on our history of mutual disappointment, I considered TR a long shot.

Yet every night, crawling into bed, I remembered her wisecracks, imagined her smile, reread her latest column in *Marie Claire,* and puzzled over the nature of fate. Why had I thrown *The Shining Light of Uncertain Infinity* out my window? Had the evening been that insane? The morning after my tantrum, I discovered its carcass in the street, run over by twenty cars.

As the opening approached and I hadn't heard from TR, I left messages on her cell and at work. There was no reply.

Opening night, Storm's friends and clients mingled with over a hundred guests that Teddy had invited, along with lots of walk-ins. There were the usual cheese and fruit wedges, and plastic cups of wine, but I noted more expensive shoes than at Zoom. Strolling through the gallery was like being in a hall of mirrors. My face was everywhere. But I didn't feel self-consciousness or discomfort. The face I'd always wanted to run from now seemed magical, even handsome, as my mother had said. The light behind the darkness was like a fire kept alive in a forgotten cave. That I had captured a feeling of transcendence with paints and a brush was the mystery of creativity. When people approached me with questions, being the center of attention felt so novel that I was sure Albert Reingold would appear at any second and ruin the party. He never showed.

Within an hour, four paintings had picked up red dots, and three more sold by the end of the evening, including the eleventh portrait, for the full price of $18,000. The buyer was a Manhattan attorney and art collector. How often did an unknown artist sell virtually everything in one night, Teddy whispered to me. He was pleased out of his mind. I went back to searching for TR.

When the gallery closed, I waited outside, bundled in an overcoat against the November winds. Friday night foot traffic came in spurts as I looked in vain for a climbing rose of a woman. The show's success kept my spirits buoyed. I couldn't wait to share my euphoria with TR.

After two hours, I gave up and took the A train home. What did you expect, I thought. People didn't change, no matter how much you wanted them to. In my dream that night, I could fly, and I chased TR through forests, over spans of water, into an endless maze of gold and red roses— never quite catching her. I woke with a feeling of frustration and deep yearning.

The last four paintings sold in the next few days, and coincided with several positive reviews, one in a neighborhood paper, another online, and the third in the *Village Voice.* Albert didn't write it. Storm told me with some satisfaction that he'd made too many enemies in the art world, and had been let go. His replacement was a young academic who liked my technical skills in addition to the paintings' emotional range. I was pleased that the reviews were different from what someone would ever write about my mother's work.

Teddy took me to dinner and presented a check for $79,400. I paid back Storm and sent the IRS its share, which left me more than enough to stake the year ahead. Teddy urged me to paint more portraits. I was exhausted from doing eleven, I told him honestly. When you were mining your soul, it wasn't like flicking a switch.

"I'm having a group show in the spring," he went on. "I'd like to include three or four of the *Birds.* Now that you're getting a name, sales will be better this time."

The next morning, at the loft, I tried to reach TR with all the good news, but no one at *Marie Claire* had seen her for over a week, nor had her roommates. Where are you? I miss you and think about you all the time. When can I see you? I gushed in an email. My heart was open like a floodgate, but in the back of my mind was the old fear that she'd done another disappearing act, without a good-bye to anyone.

I had the wild idea that someone at the Montague Street coffee house might know something, and I set out before lunch. Halfway to the subway entrance, I heard footsteps behind me. I turned to confront a man in a pinstriped suit with thick, black-framed glasses.

"Mr. Ryder, excuse me. Do you have a minute, sir?"

He gave me his business card. He was an attorney.

"My firm represents the estate of Susan Olmsted," he said. "You're a hard man to reach, Mr. Ryder. You don't open your mail apparently, or play your answering machine."

It was largely true. I had been wrapped up in my work. I asked, "Is this something urgent?"

He seemed to contemplate the word "urgent," as if the answer depended on a point of view. "There's been lots of back-and-forth with the IRS," he said, "as well as various foundations and museums, all claiming a piece of your mother's estate. Frankly, everyone is at each other's throat. Your mother's will had enough holes and contradictions to keep us very busy. Apparently, she wrote it herself, without much guidance."

I wasn't surprised. How else could she have created the maximum amount of chaos?

"One thing Ms. Olmsted was extremely clear about, however. Her instructions regarding you."

I didn't want to know, I thought.

"She asked that you visit her studio."

"I've already done that."

"She meant after her death."

"I don't see why."

The lawyer wasn't going to let me worm out. At least one part of the estate had to be resolved. "If it's convenient for you, Simon is there this Saturday. He's been trying to reach you as well."

My mother had never talked to me about her estate, other than making a casual statement that her legacy should be part of the public domain. She was indifferent to specifics. She seemed resigned, even comfortable, to let the art world judge her as it would. The paintings and money that she left to Dia:Beacon or other museums, however, would affect her reputation, as well as the marketplace for private collectors. She was too smart or vain to have been totally indifferent.

I took the subway to Brooklyn Heights. The coffee house staff knew TR as well as any other regular, but she hadn't been around in a while. On the manager's suggestion, I inquired at the dry cleaners and a bookstore around the corner. Nobody had seen her. Short of hiring a private detective, or blindly scurrying about the city, I had to live with my roller coaster fantasy: TR would arrive at my apartment and declare she was not moving anywhere, except in with me. She had a new job as an editor for a major book publisher. I kept doing paintings for Teddy, as the world opened its doors for me.

I called Simon that evening, apologizing for not being in touch. He promised to meet me at the train station Saturday afternoon, and we would walk to Dia:Beacon. He wanted me to see my mother's work hanging next to Robert Ryman, Louise Bourgeois, and dozens of other artists we both admired.

The train left Grand Central around one thirty, stopping at small, quaint stations in the Hudson River Valley that conjured up Sleepy Hollow. Couples with trail bikes and hiking poles piled on and off. The fortress walls of West Point, on the west side of the river, rose into view before fading just as quickly. By the time I reached Beacon, the cold, bright sky reminded me of my last visit. The only difference was that my mother was gone.

Simon gave me an embrace, and we made the short walk to the museum along with fifty or sixty other art lovers from the train. I hadn't paid attention to the media hoopla, but I'd been eager to see so much talent under one roof. The renovated Nabisco plant, an amalgam of brick, steel, concrete, and glass, was a model of early twentieth-century industrial architecture. Now it was surrounded by modernist landscaping, brick pathways, and a small bookstore with a coffee bar.

Inside the museum, the volumetric spaces held Richard Serra's massive, curved, steel sculptures with their rusted patina, Gerhard Richter's *Six Gray Mirrors,* and the mathematical calculations of Sol LeWitt, sprawled meticulously across white walls like a late night musing on how to pin down eternity. As we wandered through rooms, Donald Judd and his Marfa pals—Dan Flavin and John Chamberlain—jumped out at me. I loved Chamberlain's shiny strips of car wreckage, and Flavin's experiments with color and fluorescent lights. Joseph Beuys, Blinky Palermo, and Robert Smithson were also part of what I had come to regard as a hallucinogenic collection. It made me dizzy. We finally reached the space holding my mother's three canvases. Rather than austere, they suddenly seemed lush and bold, with their distinctive, floating shapes hovering delicately between harmony and chaos. I admired them for several minutes.

My mother, or maybe the Dia acquisition committee, had ignored the three paintings I'd selected. The slight wasn't altogether unexpected, but I couldn't decide if I should feel disappointed or relieved. To separate myself from my mother as an artist was an ongoing process, and this actually helped. On the walk to the house, Simon told me he was thinking of selling the property. It seemed impossibly empty without my mother. When we entered her studio, the cavernous, vaulted space, the light-washed walls, felt haunted. There was no color anywhere, except in the middle of one wall.

"Recognize those?" Simon asked.

The three canvases I'd chosen for Dia seemed to be floating in space. They were untethered to anything but the memory of my last visit.

"Orphans," I commented.

"Not anymore. Susan left them to you. She was very specific."

"They're mine?" I looked at the paintings and back at Simon.

"You would have had them much earlier, but the will was such a mess that everything got held up."

I was too much in shock to know how I felt about such a gift. Surely my mother had put strings on it.

"You can do whatever you like with them," Simon said, reading my mind. "Congratulations might seem a bizarre word, but since her death, the best of Susan's work has almost doubled in value." I walked closer to scrutinize the three, as if they might be forgeries, or suddenly would disappear on me. My mother, knowing I had pressing financial needs, had paid to insure them, Simon added.

"Doesn't that mean she doesn't want me to sell them?" I asked.

"No. That choice is totally up to you."

"Why did she do this?"

"I think that's for you to figure out."

Like most everything else my mother had done with her life, particularly with me, it challenged everyone to interpret the ambiguous. You found yourself rethinking and second-guessing. She wanted you to dig deep. There was more than one right answer.

The only thing I was suddenly certain of, no matter what I might have preferred, was that I was never going to be able to totally separate myself from my mother.

"What happened to my *Birds* painting, the one she hung in her office?"

"She wanted me to have it, for my collection. I hope that's all right with you. I like it very much."

I was still reeling when I left. I shook Simon's hand, wishing him well, whatever he decided to do with the house and the rest of his life. I thought it unlikely that our paths would cross again, but I wouldn't have minded if they did. I was a painter; he was a collector.

I took one of the last trains to the city. I hadn't expected anything from my mother. I thought she had taught and given me what she wanted during her lifetime. Maybe the paintings were confirmation of her belief in me, that one day, with enough setbacks, I could be as strong an artist as she was. If there was a hidden agenda, as my father always insisted, I hoped that was it. I felt happy, and free. What hadn't been lifted from my shoulders the last time I'd visited her had been displaced now. My gaze followed a small log as it bounced and quavered down the Hudson, hypnotically threading its way to the vast waters of the Atlantic.

A lengthy message from TR was on my answering machine when I got home. She had been traveling in New England for the last two weeks, thinking over her life. She had decided to leave *Marie Claire,* bid her roommates au revoir, and pack her bags. New York was too expensive, with too many crazy people. I shouldn't worry about how she'd survive, she added, or where she was moving, because she always ended up on her feet. She was thrilled with the reviews of my show, and before she left New York, she wanted to celebrate with me. "I know you love steak, so I'm taking you to Peter Luger, your favorite. My treat, OK?" Then the voice concluded, "One last dinner, for old times' sake."

Old times' sake. I had come to dislike the phrase intensely. It was as if the only thing that connected us was history. Her voice had been less than its perky self. There was a resignation that didn't want to be argued with. The only thing that made me happy was she had paid attention to my show.

When I called back, paraphrasing what she'd once said to me, I told her to think twice about quitting a job others would kill for.

"You're not going to try to stop me, are you?" she said.

"Could I?"

"No."

"Can I still try?"

"You never give up!"

"Did you get my email?"

"It was sweet what you wrote."

"It's all true. I've really missed you."

I waited for her to say that she had missed me, but her mind was somewhere else, and I was forcing things. She told me we could talk at dinner. She had been lucky to get reservations tomorrow night, Sunday—did seven thirty work for me? I wondered how she could afford the most expensive steak house in New York, before remembering that money was no more important to her than a prestigious writing job. I also could have told her that, thanks to my mother, things had changed for me financially, and I could help her. But that would have left her cold. Anyone who prized her independence more than TR was in a very select club.

I was at Peter Luger on time, weaving past a crowded bar amid a noise level like the Super Bowl. I expected TR to be late, as usual, but she was standing quietly in a corner, in an elegant black cocktail dress with a string of pearls. Men were staring at her. I waved and weaved through an obstacle course of bodies. I wanted to think that her being punctual meant she was eager to see me.

"You look gorgeous," I said.

"Thanks. You too, Ryder. Nice suit."

"I bought it for the Zanger opening." I gave her a hug and didn't want to let go.

"You sold all your paintings—how great does that have to feel!" she said when we were seated. We ordered drinks. TR had her one glass of wine. I was ready to order a fifth of Chivas but settled for a double.

"I was sorry you couldn't make the opening."

"I wanted to. You know how slow a writer I can be, and those stupid deadlines. I never met one that I liked."

She could always make me laugh, and for a moment, I forgot my anxiety. We reminisced about Chicago and SDA, and my desperate trip to Tennessee, breaking into her parents' house like a criminal. I was lucky not to have been caught, she said. She'd loved my recklessness all the same. It was one of our bonds.

"I did get to Zanger, four days late," TR said. "It was crowded. People around me said they wished they'd bought one of your paintings, including me, if I could have afforded it."

I ordered another drink, silently pondering the subject of bad timing, which both TR and I were masters of.

"I particularly loved the larger one. I could feel your soul in it."

"I owe part of the show to you."

"You mean the title? That's what you are. Prometheus."

"I mean you inspired me in general. And now you're leaving, just walking out—you're like the wake of a ship, disappearing into the ocean."

"What are you saying, Will?"

"I don't want you to go."

Her brow rose willfully, as if nothing, including my emotions, could stop her. I felt myself shrinking back in my chair. Whenever I got too close, she vaporized. I told her I felt like a long-distance swimmer who finally reached the finish line, ready to collect his medal, and then a tsunami came in.

"Do you know how badly I miss you, even when we're together? I've been in love with you since I was sixteen. My biggest fear is I'm always going to be in love with you, and you won't be around to know it."

She was touched, and touched her lips with steepled fingers. "You always wear your heart on your sleeve."

"I know you love me, too," I persisted.

"Please stop it, Will."

"Are you leaving town with your boyfriend?"

"Not exactly. We broke up two months ago."

"Why exactly are you going?"

"You know me better than anyone. I pick up and move on. That's just what I do." She said it like it was the most logical thing in the world. "Do I need a reason?"

We ordered a medium-rare porterhouse for two, and lots of sides—creamed spinach, French fries, onion rings. It was a feast that after a while began to feel like a wake. TR barely touched her wine. She looked as uncomfortable as I felt.

"When I came back from Tennessee," I said, determined to make my point, "my mother made sure I was kicked out of school. I was being taught a lesson. She told me that romantic love was essentially nonsense. Crazy feelings like that were a distraction from my work, and in the end, she implied, they would only let me down. She didn't know what the hell she was talking about."

"What makes me so special?"

"Except for my family, you were the first person to look at me and see more than my face."

I had been wanting to say that for a long time. My heart rose to my throat, and I was choking on it. I tried to stay in control, but I felt a couple of quiet drops from my eye. I knew TR wasn't like my mother. She believed in love on the grandest scale. She may have loved me even more than I loved her. But while love was a volcano inside me, hers was encased in protective wrapping. She could give back only so much.

We diverted ourselves with talk about my trip home in a week, and where TR might go next. Washington, D.C., was a possibility, and so was Paris or London, she said. She was particularly keen on London. She was a citizen of the world, owned by no one, and she had never been to Europe. The evening was over before I could appreciate that I might never see her again, though she promised we'd definitely keep in touch.

The next day was spent recovering from my hangover, without a word from TR. I sank into one of those deep ocean silences, waiting for something to pull me to the surface.

My mother's three paintings arrived Tuesday morning on a FedEx truck. After I shed the crating and carefully hung them in my apartment, I felt the irony of expensive art hidden away in a shabby fifth-floor walkup. I understood my mother better through her art than her life, how each slash of color might crystallize an idea or reveal a fragile stability in the universe or the powerful cyclone that was her psyche. I wanted to keep her paintings forever. Then a more-practical thought nagged at me. If I sold just one of them, I could afford my surgery. I could start my own gallery. Or I could own a luxury condo with a doorman who would call me "Mr. Ryder." At the very least, I was told when I visited a bank the next day, I could secure a healthy line of credit if I put up one of the paintings as collateral.

My mother had always believed in giving me choices. I took down one of the paintings, resecured it in its bubble wrap and crating, and called back FedEx.

Hannah phoned me a few days later, not at all happy. "What were you thinking, Will?" I could imagine her forehead wrinkling and her mouth in a pout.

"I wasn't thinking anything. It's a gift. You can't refuse it."

"Yes, I can."

"Sorry, no."

"When did she give you this?"

"It was my inheritance. I got three. You deserve one."

"You deserve them all for putting up with her," she corrected me. "I don't want anything from her."

"It's a gift from me," I clarified. "And it's bad luck to turn down a gift from someone who loves you."

She said I was extorting her. We had several more discussions. I hoped Hannah would come to the realization that there was another side to our mother. No pure monster could produce art of lasting significance and beauty. If Hannah ever wanted to sell it, I added, she could put the money to a hundred good uses, including her daughter's education. In the end, she agreed. I gave her a kiss through the phone.

I had one more thing to do before flying home for Thanksgiving. I considered it urgent. I called Teddy and said I needed to reach the collector who'd bought the eleventh painting. The matter was private. Why, he asked, slightly suspicious. I promised that I didn't want to cut him out of a future commission if the man bought any more of my works. Teddy gave me his name and number. George Yakofsky agreed to see me after work. I strolled into the St. Regis bar looking disheveled and probably intent. He was in his 40s, tan and athletic looking. After small talk, I pulled out my checkbook and asked if he'd accept $20,000 for my painting.

He was surprised. "Why do you want it back?"

"Sentimental reasons. That's a $2,000 profit for you."

"I don't think I can do it. I like your work, Mr. Ryder. It's hanging in my law office."

"How about $25,000?"

He sucked on his lower lip. "Sorry."

"Thirty thousand. Last and best offer."

He picked up the bar tab but turned me down flat. He loved the painting, he repeated, and on our way out, he said he thought I had a future as a serious artist. I went home with the stupid, reckless thought of breaking into his office and stealing it. Instead, I came back the next morning with my checkbook. I had to wait two hours because I didn't have an appointment. Mr. Yakofsky walked out to the reception area and studied me over his glasses like I was an apparition.

"You don't give up, do you?"

"I have my good days and my bad days."

"What are you going to offer me now, a hundred thousand?"

"I don't have a hundred thousand, but whatever it takes."

Our eyes locked. He wasn't looking at my face. He was assessing my determination, as if that was a quality he liked.

"Why do I have the feeling you're going to keep coming back? OK," he compromised, "give me what I paid for it. Plus I'd like a first right of refusal on your next work."

"No problem. We'll go through Teddy." I quickly wrote a check for $18,000 before he changed his mind. Two secretaries brought out my painting, and even secured it in bubble wrap for me. Storm had access to a delivery truck.

I was lucky to catch TR on her cell. She was still in New York, in a somewhat-chaotic state, she admitted, giving away nonessentials to friends, from beauty products to desk supplies, before flying to London. The first rule of starting over was to travel light.

"I need to see you right now," I declared

"Things are pretty hectic, Will."

"I have a present for you."

"That's sweet of you, but not necessary."

"Yes, it is."

She agreed to meet at the Montague Street coffee house. She could give me fifteen minutes. I promised I wouldn't take that long. When I arrived, she was already at a corner table, looking preoccupied as she sipped her green tea. I had an eight-by-ten-inch color photo of the painting I'd just bought back from George Yakofsky. I'd wrapped it in tissue in a box and cinched it with a blue ribbon, and now I laid it in front of her.

"The real thing is in my studio, waiting for you," I said as she slid off the ribbon and opened the box.

Her face lit up. "Oh, my God. Will, I don't deserve this." Her eyes flashed to me. "I thought you said you'd sold everything."

I nodded. "I bought this one back. *The Shining Light of Uncertain Infinity—Part Two.* This has nothing to do with deserving. It's a thank you. It was your idea I paint it."

"No, I can't."

"Something to remember me by in London."

Her preoccupied gaze flitted over me, like someone lost in a world of incompleteness. She thought she never deserved anything, except to dabble and graze and keep moving to another destination, hardly thinking something special would happen to her. She just did what she did. I remembered a bird my father once told me about. The Arctic Tern, all of twelve inches and two pounds, made the longest migration of any animal on the planet. Stubborn and determined, it flew from the South Pole to the North Pole and back again, every year, no doubt looking down on the world in the way I had sometimes watched TR do, enjoying the view. It was a feat of stamina and courage. The bird didn't expect anything for its extraordinary labor—it didn't know how special it was—but I did.

I kissed TR on the lips and walked away.

The day before I left for New Mexico, I purchased a hand mirror. I laid it by my bed. When I returned, I thought, I would keep on looking at it every morning. Before I definitely decided to have surgery, I wanted to be sure it was the right thing, because not just my skin and bones would be altered. Everyone's face was his biography, and maybe mine reflected more conflict and turmoil than most. My face was also the center of my universe. It determined not just the way people looked at me but also how I felt about myself, and my place in the firmament of the unknown. Where did I ultimately belong? A face so different that my imagination saw endless possibilities of expression, of places to be, was a gift. My face and imagination were deeply, impossibly entwined, and without that connection, I thought, I had no identity.

I packed lightly, planning to return within a week. As much as I wanted to see my family in Santo Tomás, my home was here, and I was eager to get back to my studio. I had new ideas and energy.

At LaGuardia, jostling with other holiday travelers, I reached the airline counter and checked my suitcase. I was out of breath, and my cheeks were flushed from the cold. I rummaged through my pockets for my ticket, and told the attendant that I'd like a window seat. Someone stirred behind me.

"You really screwed things up, you know that, right?"

I knew the voice, the perfume, the cadence of her breathing.

When I turned, TR was in a navy pea coat and jeans. I'd seen the forecast for Western Europe—an early winter had announced itself with freezing temperatures.

"What are you doing here?" I said. "International flights are out of Kennedy."

"You should never have given me the painting," she said, studying me carefully. "You knew what you were doing."

My head shook, denying I was manipulating her, which of course she would hate, but maybe I was. When you can't stand the thought of losing someone, you have more than one motive for what you do.

"You're not giving me the painting back, I hope," I said.

"I had someone pick it up and put it in storage. It's waiting for a wall to hang on."

"Maybe that's London."

"Maybe, who knows? Right now I thought I'd try New Mexico for the holidays."

She flicked her hair from her face, squinting at me, the stranger to attachment balancing on a knife edge.

"What was it, eight years ago when I invited you for Christmas?"

Her lips made the sound of air escaping from a tire. "You know me and schedules." There were four open seats on the Albuquerque flight. TR produced her credit card and charmed the agent until she'd wrangled one next to me.

The plane lifted off and knifed through lumps of clouds, its thrumming engines reminding me of warriors beating on drums. For a while, my mind stayed empty. Doubts that once stole my energy and focus had fallen away. I suddenly caught my reflection in the make-up mirror of the woman in front of us. All my life, I had either fled from or gravitated to mirrors. What I usually saw in them was the blow of remembered pain. The face I was looking at now was unchanged yet new to me, like the one in my hand mirror. I didn't need to change who I was, so long as my soul was breathing. I remembered that I had made it by myself down from the mountain's thin air of loneliness.

TR pulled out a Richard Brautigan novel and rested her head on my shoulder, at peace, at least for the moment. I had no idea what would happen, whether time would pull us closer or take us to different worlds, but the uncertainty didn't seem as important as the view in front of me. I peered out the window, imagining a distant wheel of stars.

# About the Author

Friends of Michael French describe him as a "hyperactive omnivore," (a charge he admits to) feeding on politics, art, capitalism, religion, history, travel, and popular culture.

The late night Stanford University bull sessions of decades ago have been replaced by long dinners at ethnic restaurants where conversations are kept at reasonable decibels. But the subjects remain pretty much the same. (OK, throw in technology.)

Travel hooked him early, when he went from Hollywood High School to Switzerland as a foreign exchange student. As Mark Twain wrote, travel is fatal to bigotry and prejudice, and French's first trip abroad opened his mind to "the diverse history, art, literature, and cultures of people that don't always like being next to each other—but then no one had told me about India."

After receiving an English degree from Stanford and a master's in journalism from Northwestern University, he was drafted into the Army and became editor of the post newspaper—"a two-year, tuition-free education about bureaucracy and humanity." His first "real job" after that—meaning making more than $1 an hour—was with a public relations firm in New York City, writing annual reports for Fortune 500 companies, "which was not as dull as it sounds. I learned about capitalism," French says, "the good and the bad."

He and his wife, Patricia, moved to Santa Fe in 1978, and started a real estate company and a family. Squeezing in writing time whenever he could, he published his first best-seller, *Abingdon's*, with Doubleday in 1979. "My father always said one needed a work ethic to be successful," French recalls. "But I didn't know that would mean having three jobs—the real estate company, raising children, and writing—for the next two decades."

He and Patricia still found time to take their two children to Australia, Africa, Indonesia, and Europe. At some point, children become teenagers and want nothing to do with parents or travel, but Michael and Pat persisted on their course and have now visited seventy-two countries.

For French, ideas for books come at unexpected times—visiting a hill village in Myanmar, a seventeen-hour plane haul on which sleep-deprived hallucinations can briefly turn you into a genius, or sometimes just a bite on a blueberry muffin (Proust's madeleine!). Ideas also come from listening to a friend describe his disintegrating marriage, a visit to a DeKooning exhibit at MoMA, or a late night screening of Fellini's *Juliette of the Spirits.*

The best writing ideas are never forced, French believes, and need to be strong enough to keep you going for long stretches of time. Shaping characters and plot into a meaningful read is often dark, clandestine toil, "like working for the CIA. Best not to tell anyone what you're writing—in many instances, they wouldn't get it anyway."

Sometimes, French admits, he doesn't understand why anyone is drawn to the craft as a career. "Think of a blackboard covered with a twenty-line mathematical equation, the kind Matt Damon solves in what feels like three seconds in *Good Will Hunting* but utterly mystifies and demoralizes the rest of us—'solving' the many problems that come with completing a book is not so different. Many books are finished on a near-empty tank and with a flourish of masochism before there's a sense of triumph. Then you give your book to a literary-minded friend and ask for his opinion—really, don't do that. Stick it in a drawer for a while and have a rewrite or two, then show it to someone who can be honest while appreciating how much effort you've put into this."

French's work, which includes several best-sellers, has been warmly reviewed in the *New York Times* and been honored with a number of literary prizes.

Made in the USA
San Bernardino, CA
10 February 2013